Timegate

Timegate

W L Hesse

Writer's Showcase
San Jose　New York　Lincoln　Shanghai

Timegate

All Rights Reserved © 2002 by Walter Hesse and Liz Osborne

No part of this book may be reproduced or transmitted in any form or by any means, graphic, electronic, or mechanical, including photocopying, recording, taping, or by any information storage retrieval system, without the permission in writing from the publisher.

Writer's Showcase
an imprint of iUniverse, Inc.

For information address:
iUniverse, Inc.
5220 S. 16th St., Suite 200
Lincoln, NE 68512
www.iuniverse.com

ISBN: 0-595-21264-6

Printed in the United States of America

PROLOGUE

In the spring of 1944, the world was locked in combat. The Allies and the Axis raced to develop the first atomic bomb. Germany's intelligence agency gave their scientists what they needed to build two bombs.

American military strength was concentrated in the Asian Pacific and in Europe, leaving the homeland vulnerable. German submarines successfully torpedoed tankers and freighters off the eastern seaboard, shaking American confidence.

German high command chose its targets carefully for the new bomb: Boston, home of the American Revolution, and Los Angeles, manufacturer of fighter aircraft and propaganda films. The American people were paralyzed from the shock of finding the war on their shores.

On the heels of the bombers, German military leaders took control of the major American cities with a small invading force. As in Paris, local collaborators were most helpful in identifying troublesome leaders. Congress was adjourned immediately. President Truman signed the peace treaty and retired.

Once radio communications and wire services were under German control, Americans received the "truth" about the Third Reich's goals, not the distortions fed to them earlier.

With America on her knees, England's defeat quickly followed. Only Russia continued with its pathetic resistance.

Hitler solidified his control of America by establishing a new government entity, the German Occupation Authority.

CHAPTER 1

SOUTHWEST REGIONAL PRISON
Late Afternoon, March 24, 2044

Scott Hanover sagged against the warm concrete prison wall. He closed his eyes, felt the hard floor and walls around him, and reminded himself he was safe. Not in the cage, but in his own cell. Not chained in subterranean darkness, only confined with other prisoners.

And that was safe? He grimaced at the thought, throwing his arm across his face to block out the piercing overhead light. How safe was someone awaiting execution?

For the last two years he'd dreaded death. But after the cage. . ..

He hated the German Occupation Authority. It had taken his family, his freedom, and any time now it would take his life. He wondered how others could continue to ignore what had happened to their country during the last hundred years. Most sustained a tunnel vision that kept the world at bay, choosing to ignore the loss of justice as long as it did not affect them directly.

No one cared.

It was as simple as that.

For as long as Hanover could remember, he'd conducted a one-person campaign to be a thorn in the GOA's side. He'd focused on thwarting and disrupting government activities whenever possible. Not enough to get in real trouble, but enough to annoy and harass.

Until two years ago. Now it was too late to rethink his spontaneous outbursts, his unplanned crusade.

"Alert! Alert! Prisoner Hanover, Scott, Number 907264. Alert!" The digitized voice of the prison computer echoed along the concrete halls.

Hanover stiffened. Adrenaline pumped through his body. Fists clenched, he forced himself to remain calm. Was this it? Death at last? Hell, he'd only been back in his cell a few hours. Why even bother to let him shower and change?

His cell door glided open with the faint sucking sound of hydraulics. "Prisoner Hanover, Scott, Number 907264. Proceed to east stairwell."

In his early days, before the finality of his sentence had sunk in, he'd openly jeered the computer's inability to call prisoners by anything other than this roster-style identification.

But that was before the others were summoned for their executions. Now, he was the only one left. When the last one had been dragged from his cell a month ago, screaming for mercy, Hanover broke. He'd started a riot, then demanded they haul him before the firing squad, too. Instead, they'd thrown him in the cage.

What was the point? Why didn't they just do it and get it over with? Or was this part of their torture?

With the cage, they might have stripped the outward fight from him, but they hadn't even dented his hatred of the German Occupation Authority. If possible, he hated them even more.

"Prisoner Hanover, Scott, Number 907264. Proceed to east stairwell."

"Coming," he said to the wall speaker as he pushed himself up from the metal frame cot. He glanced at the mirror over his sink. His piercing blue eyes held sparks of defiance and he forced himself to smother that—and any other emotion—so that his gaze was flat, lifeless. His dirty blond hair had grown out since they'd shaved it before throwing him into the cage. Now it lay slicked down, except for a few spikes where he'd been leaning against the wall. He ran a hand over his chin, relieved to be rid of the scratchy growth that had accumulated.

Bushy brows bracketed his eyes, and his already prominent cheekbones were thrown into even greater relief by the limited rations while in the cage. He was leaner than before, too. But during his confinement, he'd run through repetition after repetition of isometric routines to stay in shape. No, that wasn't it. He'd done them to keep from losing his mind, to concentrate on something—anything—to avoid thinking about where he was, and the execution he still faced. He studied the grim man who stared back at him. Despite the cage, he was still a fine specimen for target practice.

He exited the cell, and his footsteps echoed in the cavernous space as he walked unescorted down the long concrete corridor. Behind him, the cell door rolled on well-oiled tracks and clanged shut, the noise jarring in the deathly quiet. From their cells, other inmates eyed him warily as he passed. Some raised a hand; most silently expressed grim relief that they weren't the ones summoned to die.

Hanover acknowledged no one. Even after two years he had no friends. Nobody here did. Everyone shut their emotions down, stopped caring about anyone or anybody but themselves. It didn't pay to get close. Never knew when they'd disappear. Or if they were GOA plants sniffing for bad attitudes. In the beginning, he'd proudly demonstrated he had the worst of the bad attitudes, an unwavering resistance to an irrational sentence, and he'd learned how relentless the authorities were about changing a man's perspective. The weekly executions had taught him that.

He reached the east stairwell and hesitated. They should be watching, prepared to give the next order but nothing happened. Maybe it was shift change, although without windows he couldn't accurately judge the time. He waited, suppressing the dread. He whistled tunelessly while he shifted from one foot to the other.

"Prisoner Hanover, Scott, Number 907264. Descend to lower level. Proceed to administration. Go to second level. You will be met."

What the hell—? The admin building? Why was he being summoned there? His stomach churned and he swallowed hard against the bile that rose in his throat. Shit. *Don't let the bastards get to you,* he told himself. The cage had knocked the rough edges off his attitude, but he wasn't going to bend over for anyone. Anger shoved the last of his apprehension aside and he took the steel mesh steps two at a time and burst into the yard.

The watery midday sun stopped him. The constant darkness in the damn cage had nearly blinded him; he shaded his eyes until they adjusted. He couldn't see any guards, but he knew scanners tracked his every movement and robot sentries stationed strategically around the perimeter were programmed to fire laser guns if he crossed an invisible line. He spotted the infra-red detector that followed him across the yard and he started his customary mock salute to the robot, then stopped. No point drawing more attention to himself. Death would end the torment, but he instinctively shied away from its finality.

The hint of sage in the dry desert air smelled clean after the cell block's fetid odor of hopelessness and the cage's dank despair. He had survived his last ordeal. Hanover breathed deeply, girding himself for his next confrontation. Who knew when he'd smell fresh air again? If ever.

He slowed his pace and gazed at the bleak high desert landscape surrounding the prison. The GOA really knew how to deal with troublemakers, building hell-holes like this for American "criminals," while prisons for German nationals looked more like country clubs. Fifty kilometers to the south lay Albuquerque, a city large enough for a lone man to melt into the crowds. To the northeast was Santa Fe, his home until his smart mouth landed him in a courtroom.

Hanover paused, longing for the beckoning freedom, then continued walking toward the administration building. No walls or fences restrained him. They weren't needed. Not even the threat of his pending execution prompted him to break out. The individually coded Sonic Amplification Device imbedded behind his ear stopped him.

He hadn't understood the meaning of the S.A.D. when it was first implanted. He quickly learned. His first week, two new prisoners made a run for it. Three meters beyond the perimeter, their heads exploded. In disbelief, he started toward them but another prisoner grabbed his arm and restrained him. Horrified, he'd watched the guards haul away what was left of the bodies.

As he walked across the prison yard, Hanover considered his chances and rejected running for the thousandth time. He didn't want to die today.

A blast of warm air hit him as he entered the administration building. The door slammed shut behind him. He stood still, swallowing hard while his eyes adjusted to the dim light before climbing the stairs. On the landing, one of the few human guards in the complex waited for him. The name tag read: Bowie, Philip. Computer couldn't get the guards' names straight either, Hanover thought grimly. He eyed the guard with suspicion but said nothing.

The guard snapped his rifle into a ready position. "The warden wants to see you."

"Why?" Hanover blurted the question before he could stop himself. The cage had softened him more than he'd realized. Normally he maintained an air of silent antagonism.

Ignoring the question, the guard motioned for Hanover to walk in front of him down the hall.

Never let them know what you really think; never let them know what's really important to you. Hanover repeated the prisoners' mantra in cadence with each step he took down the hallway.

"Stop."

Hanover watched the guard knock on the door. At a muffled response, the door swung open and Hanover entered. The warden stood at the window, his back to Hanover.

"Door close."

Hanover heard the door shut behind him. He knew about security systems keyed to one person's voice, but had never seen one work before.

As he strode across the large room, Hanover glanced around. Monitors covered one gray wall, each monochrome image focused on a different section of the prison. Pewter gray metal blinds dotted with rust shut out the natural light, while fluorescent tubes cast a flickering pallor over the room. A gray computer terminal hummed from its perch on a cluttered, drab green metal desk. The blend of lousy taste with high tech surprised him. He looked for something personal but found nothing, no pictures or photographs, no mementos or memorials.

Hanover stopped in front of the desk and stared at the warden's back. He'd seen Willard Dawes, "Old Stoneface," once, when he first arrived at Southwest Regional. Since then, he'd dealt only with assistants and other underlings. Hanover waited, his confidence ebbing away, anxiety seeping in to fill the void.

At last, Dawes turned, his square jaw jutting pugnaciously, his dark eyes somber. In his younger days, his height and thick hair must have been imposing. Now his stooped-shouldered posture and shock of gray hair marked life's erosion. He wearily sat in an old chair, the leather as split as the deep lines etched in his face.

Hanover held himself stiff, his expression stoic. Dawes looked him up and down, then signaled for him to sit. The gesture, a major breach in prison etiquette, surprised Hanover. He hesitated until Dawes gave him a withering look, then slid into the metal chair.

Warden Dawes leaned forward, his elbows resting on the desk, his fingers laced together. "Hanover. . ." His deep voice echoed with authority in the large office. "You will escape tomorrow."

The words caught Hanover off guard. "What the—? I haven't got any plans to escape. Whoever told you that is lying." He struggled to keep his voice normal, to hide the dread threatening to break him. He wouldn't go back to the cage—he'd never come out alive.

The warden brushed aside his comments with an abrupt wave. "Tomorrow morning, Mr. Bowie will take you and two others for a road cleanup detail. Work yourself into a location where you can get away fast. Watch Bowie. He'll be carrying a shoulder bag. When he drops it, you take off. If he fires his weapon, it won't be at you."

Dawes paused. "Do you understand what I'm saying?"

The words filtered into Hanover's mind. He nodded, too stunned to speak. A trick. This had to be a trick. But why such an elaborate ruse? They could execute him any time they wanted. No one had protested his sentence; no one cared. "Why?"

Dawes ignored his question. "You'll find clothes in the bag. After you change, go to Neustadt. Do you know it?"

Still not believing what he was hearing, Hanover nodded again. About forty years before, the Germans had built the now-abandoned development north of Albuquerque to house laborers for the nearby mines. "I know where it is, but I've never been there. It's restricted."

"You've never given a damn about government restrictions," Dawes snapped. "Someone out there wants you, and I'm briefing you only once, so pay attention."

The intensity of Dawes instructions started to sink in. Curiosity nudged caution. "What do I do when I get there?"

"You'll be met. Within twenty-four hours of your escape you'll be listed as a fugitive with a bounty on your head. Dead or alive. Everyone will be looking for you. That's all you need to know for now." Dawes pulled himself to a standing position. The iciness in his gaze chilled Hanover. "One more thing. Don't screw up—or you'll be executed immediately."

The threat ignited Hanover. "Why don't you just shoot me now and be done with it? How do I know you won't trigger the S.A.D.? Who the hell wants me? And for what?"

Dawes glared at him. Hanover fell silent; his forehead beaded with sweat. Under ordinary circumstances, an outburst like that resulted in immediate punishment. But this wasn't an ordinary circumstance, and he was weary of being politic and polite.

"Look, Hanover, I didn't agree with your selection for this project. They need someone aggressive, physically fit and quick on his feet. That's you. But you're also a troublemaker, and we don't need that. You have two choices."

The warden raised his hand and extended his index finger. "One, you go along with this and do as your told." He extended his middle finger. "Or, two, you wait for your appointment with the firing squad, and the wait won't be pleasant." He folded his index finger to his palm, and Hanover winced at the implication.

Still he wavered. He wanted freedom. He desperately wanted freedom. But he didn't want to fall into one of their traps. He didn't want to jump into this unknown abyss. He repeated his question cautiously. "Who are 'they' and what do they want with me?"

"You don't need to know that now. When your assignment is completed, you'll be granted clemency. Just agree to follow orders and you're out of here."

That last part sounded good. A thought skittered through his mind about his chances to escape the S.A.D.'s range or even get the thing removed. Once he was out of here, he didn't have to go to Neustadt. He'd head for Canada or Mexico.

"Don't get original, Hanover. You'll have only eight hours to make your contact in Neustadt. If you don't make the contact—just remember, we can find you. Anywhere." His words hung in the air. At last he said, "Follow orders and you'll be free. Otherwise, you die when and where we want."

Hanover looked at Dawes and saw the veracity of his threat. Hanover rose from his chair and paced the room. Finally he stopped, hands on his hips, and stared at the tiled floor. Then he looked unwaveringly at the warden. "Okay. I'll do it."

Back in his cell, Hanover stretched out on his cot, his head cradled in his hands. What was the catch? The question rolled around his mind. He searched for the trick, for the flaw, but he couldn't find any reason why they should let him escape. If it wasn't a trick, could he take advantage of the opportunity and escape—even if the warden had warned of the consequences of deviating from the plan? Was the S.A.D. deterrent enough to keep him from taking a chance? They planned to kill him anyway.

One thing was certain: if the offer to escape was genuine, he'd pay a high price for his freedom. No one in government did anything out of the goodness of their hearts. They had no hearts. Government officials made offers only when they wanted something. And they must desperately want whatever it was to risk letting him go.

He still found it impossible to reconcile the death sentence for his crimes-against-the-state, that catch-all catalogue of offenses created by the GOA after the war. Any action by Americans could be twisted into a punishable grievance, an expeditious way to control malcontents and others opposed to Hitler's New Order.

The big question now was if his so-called escape was simply another trick to entrap him. But why? He wasn't important and had no real enemies. Sure, he was a troublemaker, but he had been since childhood. He rebelled against the system, any idiotic or tyrannical system he came in contact with.

He'd barely made it through high school without expulsion. After college, the state gave him a low level position in the Bureau of Controls, Permits and Documentation. He'd wondered at the assignment as it wasn't usual for a rabble-rouser like him to get a government desk job. Maybe they'd figured that keeping him in a back room with no windows and no contact with others would keep him out of trouble, he thought wryly.

But a job was what you made it. He'd accepted the dull assignment of typing permits, passes and travel papers, and then had taken perverse delight in providing documents to those who wanted to avoid official scrutiny when they traveled. He rationalized that his department's function was to provide these services to all citizens. Besides, an indifferent, ponderous bureaucracy could scarcely be expected to follow his sleight-of-hand performances. And it hadn't until a bootlicking subordinate spotted an unapproved pass and reported it to the supervisor, E.P. Grimes.

"Slimy" Grimes was one of those pompous little men, a real lightweight when it came to mental acuity. If it wasn't in the rule book, Grimes didn't know how to respond. Hanover knew Grimes didn't like him because he was better educated. It didn't help that Hanover was tall and good-looking and all the girls flirted with him. Worse yet, Grimes had friends in the GOA and owed them his position.

But in the office, Grimes avoided confrontations that might reflect badly on his managerial competence by pretending they were all one big family that worked together and got along. In retrospect, Hanover realized he should have kept his head down and his mouth shut. Instead, he responded to his supervisor's summons prepared to battle, telling Grimes his "happy family" spiel was a crock. By the time the discussion ended, Hanover had questioned Grimes' sexual preference and the legitimacy of his birth, and Grimes had called security.

An intensive investigation revealed the depth of Hanover's creative civil service and yielded a long list of names for the GOA's "people of interest" monitoring activities. He'd expected a short imprisonment. But while awaiting sentencing, another prisoner went berserk in the courtroom and killed a guard. The furious GOA judge ordered all the prisoners to be executed, as an example, he'd said. The death sentence had slashed like a knife in Hanover's gut.

The weekly executions had a chilling effect on everyone at the prison, even those who weren't on the list. No one knew who would be next. Lashing out at the injustice, Hanover challenged the prison system, doing everything from adding red dye to the prison laundry to instigating a riot—which is what triggered his trip to the cage.

So what did they have planned for him now? This wasn't release with an official pardon. They were allowing him to escape. In his mind, he replayed the warden's briefing. What was it he'd said? Someone out there wants you.

Intrigue and trouble. Those were his middle names, he thought with a sigh. The tumult of unanswered questions rolled around his brain, until he finally turned to his side and willed himself to sleep.

* * *

SOUTHWEST REGIONAL PRISON
Morning, March 25, 2044

Dank mustiness filled his nostrils. His eyes struggled for a glimmer of light and his ears strained for a sound, any sound. But there was nothing, nothing but him. The terror rose inside him, tore at his innards and he screamed—

An alarm blared through the cell block at sunrise. Hanover leaped to his feet, swinging around to get his bearings. Safe. He was safe in his cell. He bent over, hand on his knees, his panicked panting slowed as he gasped to catch his breath. He slumped on the thin polyester pad that passed for a mattress on the iron frame bed.

Today he was supposed to escape. He still thought it was a trick, but if the escape really happened, who knew when he'd eat again. Prison slop at least filled his belly.

He entered the dining hall and silently picked up a gray plastic tray. Going down the line, he glanced around. No one dared look at him—no one joined him at a corner table. Probably figured he'd been broken by the cage and now reported everything to the assistant warden.

When he finished eating, he scanned the room. He spotted Bowie, who signaled for him to follow. Others saw the signal, too, and Hanover felt contempt shimmer like a heat wave from prisoners he brushed past as he made his way across the room. It couldn't be helped.

He stepped outside. Two other prisoners already stood beside the prison's electrovan. Bowie chained the three men's ankles together, then motioned them into the back of the van.

Hanover held back. "I didn't have time to make my bed this morning. Don't want any demerits for sloppy housekeeping."

Bowie scowled and said in a low voice, "The warden said I was to get you out of here fast. Shut up and get in." He locked the door behind Hanover, then went around to the driver's seat.

Hanover hunched over to peer through the van's gun slit. They drove through the gate, the only gap in the magnetic field surrounding the prison. Two guards armed with laser guns and a guard looking down from the tower deterred other prisoners from taking advantage of the momentary opening. That and the S.A.D.

Holding his breath, Hanover touched the bump behind his ear, as if he could control it through sheer will. When it didn't explode as they left the compound, when he realized it wasn't going to explode, he relaxed a little.

He gazed at the other two prisoners leaning against the side of the van, indifferent to anything around them. When he recognized one of them, Hanover studied him with heightened interest. The grapevine said he was a plant, a GOA spy who ratted on everyone, even assistant wardens. What the hell he was doing here?

Suspicious again, Hanover smelled a set-up. Smart warden to get rid of three problems at once. Puts a prisoner awaiting execution—Hanover—with an outside spy, and shoots them for attempted escape. The third guy's probably a nobody, which makes it look even better. Who's the wiser?

He swallowed hard, dashing the glimmer of hope that maybe he really was getting out. He'd known it was too good to be true. At least he knew what he faced and could accept that. It was the unknown he didn't want to deal with anymore.

And yet. . .Why the elaborate charade when they could kill him anytime. He'd been sentenced to death two years ago. No one outside the prison waited for him or watched out for his benefit. No one out there cared.

So why go to all this trouble? Unless. . .

He knew. It hit him like a poleax, hard enough to take his breath away. He knew what they intended. The FedPos needed simulated exercises to train new agents. What better way to teach tracking and recovery than by using a real prisoner? He would be hunted down and killed, unless he made it to the contact point in Neustadt by the designated time. And then? The warden had promised him freedom, clemency, but since when did the authorities follow through with promises other than threats? He slumped into the same brooding position as his companions to rethink his options.

An hour later, the van slowed and turned onto a dirt side road. Out of sight from the main highway, the van stopped.

Bowie swung the back door open. "You know the drill. Get out and assume the position."

Hanover climbed out first, his anxiety rising when he saw the laser gun, not a shoulder bag slung over Bowie's arm. The guard didn't look at him. The other two prisoners joined Hanover. They faced the van, leaned against it with their arms and legs spread. Bowie unlocked Hanover's chain first.

He bent down to rub his ankle and quickly surveyed his surroundings. He scanned the sky, but saw no sunlight glinting off helicopters or small planes. Maybe they were hiding behind the low hills that bordered both sides of the road. A ravine ran parallel to the road, with a ridge banking the other side of the dried wash. That was his best chance of escape. He'd give those FedPo kids a real run for their money. If he could reach that huge boulder about fifty meters down the ravine and keep it between him and Bowie, if he could scramble up the sandy side of the escarpment and roll to the other side, if. . .if. . .if—

"Hanover!"

His attention snapped back to Bowie. "What?"

"Get a brush hook and go up that wash. We're going to clear out the sage and tumbleweed. Bureau of Roads says it's why the road floods. Keep in sight. I want you between me and that rock."

"I'll go to the rock and work my way back to you." Hanover held his breath. Would it work?

"Yeah. You do that."

Hanover grabbed the brush hook and slipped and slid into the ravine before Bowie changed his mind. The fine sand and pebbles would make it almost impossible to climb up the ridge. Assuming he really escaped. He reached the boulder and started whacking at the brush, feeling Bowie's laser aimed between his shoulder blades. Nice isolated place for an ambush. Or an escape.

He glanced at Bowie and inhaled sharply. Bowie still carried his weapon, but a bright yellow shoulder bag was slung across his back. Working quietly, Hanover edged closer to the boulder. So far everything was as Dawes described it, but a good frame had to be convincing up until the last moment. When it was too late to do anything about it.

Hanover watched as Bowie turned his back on him and dropped the yellow bag. The signal. Hanover froze. Then he bolted for the boulder and scrambled over the crest to the ping of laser gun fire.

CHAPTER 2

FEDERAL POLICE HEADQUARTERS
ALBUQUERQUE, NEW MEXICO
Morning, March 25, 2044

The German Occupation Authority knew what it wanted in a Federal Police officer. One parent—preferably the father—must be a German national in order to maintain loyalty to the Reich. The man must be intelligent, but not creative; following instructions maintained order while new ideas led to chaos and rebellion. The man must want to be an officer more than anything else, and be willing to do whatever it took to succeed. The FedPo branch of the GOA thought that in Willie Kant it had found the perfect officer.

Kant pulled himself to his full height, threw back his shoulders and sucked in his stomach. He stood in the tiny dressing room adjoining his office, admiring his reflection in the full-length mirror he'd installed after his transfer to this branch of the southwest regional FedPos.

A tailor fussed with the fit of Kant's coat while mumbling to himself through a mouthful of pins. Kant's stocky frame barely met FedPos' minimum height requirement, but with expert tailoring, his new uniform fit to perfection, making him appear taller, thinner. His face was deceptively soft and surprisingly smooth, given his thick black hair. His eyes were an unusual shade of blue.

As he gazed at his reflection, the new silver epaulets of a major caught his eye. He pivoted for a better view, ignoring the tailor's cry of dismay.

Major Willie Kant. It had a nice ring to it. A slow smile spread across his face. He'd been promoted quickly during his twelve years in the FedPos, and now at thirty he was the youngest major in the southwest region. He'd heard the murmurs, he'd seen the sidelong glances, the skepticism as to the real reasons for his promotions. The fact that others might overlook his efforts and very real achievements rankled, but did not diminish his satisfaction.

So far, his quick promotions had been the result of serious study of military and political history. He'd learned the lessons of the past well, and used that knowledge to make astute assessments and decisions. While his counterparts touted the modern German army and the GOA as being the only relevant systems to analyze, Kant quietly, ruthlessly, undermined and brought down those in his way.

Having a father who was Commandant of the Southwest Regional FedPos had neither helped nor hampered his career. He at times questioned how much longer his father, General Kurt Kraft, could continue his neutrality. And which direction he would swing when forced to make a decision that influenced Kant's career.

Although pleased that he'd achieved his status on his own, Kant resented the distance Kraft maintained between them, resented that a German foster family had been paid to raise him and give him their name.

"You're moving, sir. Please stand straight."

The tailor's words snapped Kant back to attention. He had the uniform of a major, and soon he would prove to any doubters that he was eminently capable of fulfilling the responsibilities of that position. Or destroy them as he had others.

The videophone on his desk buzzed. He crossed the room to his desk and activated the monitor and speaker. "Yes?"

"Captain Kant?"

He didn't recognize the man on the screen. "This is **Major** Willie Kant."

"Excuse me, Major. Didn't hear the news. Donald Hathaway here, secretary to the Commandant. The Commandant wishes to speak with you."

Kant steadied himself, anticipating the commandant's congratulations for his promotion.

"Kant?" His father's brusque tone rekindled Kant's resentments.

"Yes, sir," Kant responded impersonally.

"We've picked up rumors of a planned breakout at Southwestern Regional Prison. I want you to stop it and to arrest the perpetrators. I won't allow that kind of lawlessness to gain a foothold in my region."

"Yes, sir. I understand north central's had problems lately."

"That's what happens when you're too lenient with the native population. Letting them get away with small demands simply agitates them for more. Last I heard, Colonel Schwartz received a demand for a summit meeting to discuss grievances." General Kraft snorted. "Damn fools. Take them out and shoot them; that'd put an end to their demands."

"I agree, sir." Kant's usual reserve around his father slipped. The commandant was at last talking to him as a fellow officer, sharing his views and strategies. "I think we need to remain vigilant with these Americans so they—"

"I called to give you an assignment, Major, not discuss the weather." Kraft paused for a moment. "Normally, I'd map out the tactics I think will work best. But I heard speculation about your promotion. It makes me furious that people think I'd interfere and act on sentiment rather than what's best for the GOA. So I've decided that you might as well run with this from the beginning. If it goes well, you take the credit. If you blow it. . . .. Think you can handle it?"

"Yes, sir." Kant bite back the bitter edge in his voice. God forbid his father should even consider doing something to help him, let alone acknowledge his achievements. Kant took a deep breath to relieve the agitation churning inside. "Am I to take charge of the prison, sir?"

"No, Warden Dawes will continue to handle the prison. You conduct the investigation."

"I'll say this is a routine inspection so they don't grow suspicious."

"Good idea. Remember, Dawes is an American. I've always said it's wrong to appoint those people to positions of authority. Just can't trust them. I'll notify him that you're coming and leave it vague. You take whatever measures you deem appropriate."

"I'll have it resolved by the end of the week and a report on your desk by Monday morning."

"I don't care about any damn report. I just want those responsible detained." The video screen faded.

"Yes, sir. I understand, sir." Kant stared at the darkened screen. He plucked at his lower lip and sighed bitterly.

"May I finish my measurements, Major?"

Kant started at the tailor's words. "Yes. In a moment." He waved the man off.

An assignment directly from Commandant Kraft surprised Kant, especially coming so soon after his promotion. At least this time the commandant, as Kant had come to call his father, hadn't compared him to that Scott Hanover.

Kant remembered the countless times while he was growing up when the commandant challenged him to be as good as his schoolmate, Scott Hanover, to excel like Scott Hanover, to be a leader like Scott Hanover. Kraft continued to use him as an example, even though Kant pointed out that Hanover was in constant trouble with school authorities for infractions ranging from dropping anti-government leaflets from the third floor window to setting all the animals loose in the biology lab.

But perhaps this new assignment would dispel the commandant's fixation with Hanover once and for all. Despite the rumors, the commandant must be satisfied with Kant's performance, otherwise he would not entrust Kant with such an important mission. He would show the commandant *again* that he was superior to anyone in the FedPos. He pushed a button on his videophone.

A serious-looking young man with glasses appeared on the screen. "Motorpool."

"This is Major Kant. Get me Corporal Prinski."

"Yes, sir. One moment, sir." The screen went dark.

"Prinski here, sir." The screen lit up with the driver's face.

"Is my car available?"

"Yes, sir. Polished and fully charged."

Kant breathed easier. At least he didn't have to worry about that. At first, Kant had objected to his chauffeur's Slavic lineage, but Prinski had proved invaluable. Not only was he good with the car, he served as a second set of eyes and ears. "Fine. Pick me up in one hour."

"Can I ask where we're going, sir?"

It wasn't idle curiosity that prompted the question. Drivers were required to sign out the cars and indicate destination, passengers, purpose of the trip and so on. Kant suspected the commandant didn't want the prison break rumor spread. "We're going on a routine inspection of Southwestern Regional."

"I'll be in front in one hour, sir."

Kant anticipated a successful mission. The suppression of a prison break and the arrest of the ringleaders would earn him a commendation at least. Maybe even a transfer to a cushy assignment at FedPos regional headquarters in Santa Fe. Then he'd be in constant contact with the commandant and they could become better acquainted. The commandant would see that Kant was far more intelligent, far more shrewd than those fawning junior officers who currently surrounded him.

Determined not to be denied the splendid future he envisioned for himself, Kant returned to his dressing room for a final fitting with his tailor.

         *   *   *

Two hours later, Kant was sitting in the back seat of his car, wondering which was more monotonous, the low level whine of the electromotor or the surrounding desert landscape. He tried to focus on his upcoming interview with the warden. He needed to remain calm, in control, to avoid any behavior that was 'unbecoming', a term often used by the commandant to disparage his subordinates.

Unbecoming for an officer—and 'common', an adjective used by German nationals to describe the Americans whom they considered a mongrel race. Even those with some German ancestry were considered tainted by the purists. Kant sometimes wondered about that. The commandant was from Germany; his foster parents, too.

He could still remember vividly his foster mother's face, contorted with rage as she screeched at him, spilling the secret no one was supposed to know. That his real mother was not dead. That his real mother was an American. He learned her name and where she lived, and when he was ten, he gathered the courage to cross town and find her.

That's when he discovered he had an older brother, a half-brother, Scott Hanover. Kant hated the other boy, envied him the warmth of his home with their mother compared to the stern regimentation of his own life with uncaring foster parents. On the few occasions he saw the commandant, he'd forgotten to ask about his mother, so happy was he to leave the grim house he was growing up in and happy to see this aloof man who sired him. Finally it didn't matter anymore. He worked to excel in his studies, to be an outstanding FedPo officer. And still he hated Hanover.

"Southwestern Regional up ahead, sir."

Kant saw the angular concrete building that rose from the barren landscape. He hated these places. He hated the savage men who were sentenced to be here and the brutish men who chose to work here. He'd have to steel himself from revulsion at their physical crudity, stay alert to the slightest clue, watch for the subtlest shift in their churlish eyes.

Torture had its place. But manipulating someone who thought themselves smart, tightening the noose psychologically, until they hung themselves—sometimes literally—now that was what he enjoyed.

The car turned off the highway to a hard-packed gravel side road. In the distance, the prison loomed in isolation, farther from the highway than had first appeared. In a few minutes, they reached the main entrance, and Prinski slowed the car to a stop.

Two guards stood with laser guns in the ready position. One held back while the other approached the car. He glanced through the driver's window to the back seat and saluted Kant. The salute was sloppy, an insolent act, but this was not the time to make an example.

"What're you here for?" the guard asked in a tone that indicated he could care less.

"Major Kant," Prinski said with a quick nod toward the back seat. He held out authorization papers. "To see the warden."

The guard looked at the papers, then back at Prinski. "I'll check." He turned and walked away.

"Arrogant bastard," Prinski mumbled under his breath.

"For now," Kant said. "Before we're finished, we'll find something to charge him with."

Prinski's eyes, reflected in the rearview mirror, brightened considerably. "I'll see what I can find, sir."

The guard returned. "You're expected, Major. On my signal, drive through the gate. You'll have five seconds before the magnetic field is reactivated. Park by that building over there. Another guard will escort you to Warden Dawes' office." He stepped into his gatehouse and gave the signal.

"Hope to hell you don't stall this thing," Kant said.

"Yeah, me, too." Prinski chuckled. "I don't much like the idea of being fried." The car lurched through the entrance and then moved sedately across the hard-packed dirt yard. Prinski parked in the designated space, then opened Kant's door for him.

Stepping from the car, Kant studied the yard, as barren as the desert surrounding the prison. No one moved in the cold late afternoon sunlight.

"Stay here and keep an eye on things while I'm inside. I want to know who talks to who, the movements of the sentries, who passes through the entrance."

"Yes, sir. I won't miss nothing."

Kant scanned the interior yard once more, then entered the administration building.

"Major Kant?"

As Kant's eyes adjusted to the dimness, he saw a guard standing in the doorway. How long had he been there? Kant wondered irritably. "Yes."

"Come this way, sir. The warden is expecting you."

Kant followed the guard down the hall and was shown into the warden's office.

"Major Kant." A tall stooped-shouldered man standing behind the desk glowered at Kant, his hands clasped behind his back. No proffered handshake, no salute; just a steely gaze from dark eyes that had seen too much.

"I'm Kant. And you are—?"

"Warden Dawes." His tone was laced with sarcasm that there could be any doubt as to his identity.

Kant assessed the warden's stance and lack of greeting. Coming across authoritatively would be as effective as hitting his head against a brick wall; he decided to try the conciliatory approach instead. "I haven't had an opportunity to tour your facility before, and I'm sure I'll have nothing but good things to say in my report."

Dawes raised one eyebrow; otherwise, he moved not at all. "What report?"

"I'm here for a routine inspection. Didn't the message say that?"

Dawes' gaze never wavered, almost as if he was willing Kant to not look around, but Kant spotted the slight tremor in Dawes' hand as it rested on the desk. "I don't pay much attention to notices. They seldom say what they really mean. I just wait and make up my own mind. Now this little inspection of yours. . .The timing is curious for a routine Federal Police inspection."

"Why is that?"

"We had a breakout this morning."

The words hit Kant like ice water. "Wh—you—" he sputtered. "Prisoners escaped?"

"Three tried, but only one got away. Guard shot the other two."

"Why wasn't headquarters notified before I came?"

Dawes shrugged. "We haven't reported it yet."

"You haven't—. The prisoner who escaped, did you detonate his S.A.D.?"

Dawes snorted. "Do you have any idea how much paperwork that would generate? The GOA is so obsessed with documentation, it would take me three weeks to fill out all the reports. I figured we could handle it ourselves. No need to make a big fuss over one escaped prisoner. He's not dangerous, just a troublemaker. A crimes-against-the-state prisoner."

Furious, Kant turned away from Dawes. Damn. He'd wanted to abort the prison break and arrest those involved. Now two escapees were dead, and one was God-knew where. He still had a chance to do this right. He could order the warden to detonate the S.A.D. Kant hesitated. Wouldn't the commandant be more impressed if Kant recaptured the escapee?

He turned to face Dawes and caught the wariness that crossed the man's face. "Escapes are to be reported immediately."

"We're handling the situation," Dawes said. Kant saw the defiant fire in the warden's eyes. "Why're you federal people always sticking your nose into local business?"

"I didn't come here to stick my nose in your business," Kant lied. "You violated regulations by not immediately reporting this escape. And your failure to explode the S.A.D. indicates poor judgement. You've left me with no choice but to assume command of the facility. I want a total lock-down and every prisoner kept on restricted rations until all my questions are answered."

The two men stared at each other, neither yielding.

Finally, the warden looked away. "I have the three prisoners' files in the computer. You'll probably want to look at the escaped prisoner's first." He turned to the computer and pushed a button next to the monitor. "Bring up file 907264, Hanover, Scott."

Kant gasped. "Scott Hanover?"

The warden looked at him sharply. "You know him?"

Kant buried his shock. "From school."

"Friends?"

Kant's short laugh reverberated in the room. He swallowed the truth as it threatened to burst through. "Hardly. He was the kind who stirred up trouble wherever he went. I have always understood the importance of discipline."

"Of course."

Kant ignored the warden's derisive sneer. "The other two prisoners were shot during the attempt?"

"That is correct."

"Where's the guard?"

"Outside the door."

"Not *your* guard," Kant snapped. "The guard involved in the escape."

"He is outside the door," the warden repeated calmly.

"He hasn't been relieved of duty until the escape has been fully investigated?"

Dawes shrugged. "I saw no reason to."

Kant's eyes narrowed in suspicion. There was something very wrong here. An escape not reported. The S.A.D. not discharged. The guard not relieved of duty. A warden lax in following the most basic protocols. For a moment, Kant considered what else such a warden might be capable of doing. "Prepare the interrogation room. I'll question the guard first."

"Who else would you question? The other two prisoners are dead."

Kant recognized the attempt to undermine his confidence. Good; the warden underestimated him. That should prove useful. "It depends on what I learn—or don't learn—from your guard." He saw the brief flutter of uncertainty cross the warden's face.

"As you wish." The warden activated his phone and ordered the interrogation room readied.

The warden surprised Kant further by directing the guard to escort Kant to the interrogation room. Keeping a hand on his small laser holster, Kant followed the guard through a catacomb of windowless hallways and into a concrete block room.

"Leave your weapons outside," Kant said.

"I'm an employee of the prison, sir. I'm required by regulation to be armed at all times."

"You are also mandated by regulation to prevent prisoners from escaping. Yet one did. Now put your weapons outside."

The guard hesitated, then complied with the command. At Kant's signal, he sat on the stark wooden chair in the middle of the room and nervously rolled the brim of his hat through his fingers.

Kant paced the room, sometimes in front of the guard, sometimes behind, letting the sound of his footsteps echo in the bare room until he could almost smell the other man's fear, fear that had to be from knowing more than he should. Kant stopped; he stood in the room's shadows while the guard sat in the overhead lamp's glare.

"Your name," Kant snapped.

"Bowie, sir. Philip Bowie."

"How long have you been a guard at Southwestern Regional?"

"Five years."

"Sir."

"Sir."

"That's quite a while. Since you've been here, Mr. Bowie, how many times have prisoners tried to escape?"

Bowie hesitated. "I don't know, sir."

"Was it one or two? Or ten or fifty?"

"Maybe. . .five times, I guess."

"Si—"

"Sir."

"And how many prisoners tried to escape?"

"Two or three each time, sir."

"And of those five escape attempts, how many succeeded?"

"None, sir."

"None?" Kant let sarcasm slip into his voice. "None? So you're telling me that out of the ten to fifteen prisoners who have attempted to escape, none have succeeded?"

"Yes, sir."

"Until today."

"Yes, sir."

"Bowie, why was today different? Why did Scott Hanover escape when no one else has?"

Bowie looked down at his hands still holding his hat. "He was working farther away from me than the other two. He climbed out of the ravine and disappeared before I could stop him." His voice was quiet, small. Kant could almost see the man shrink physically, as well.

"I see." Kant stepped into the light. "When did this alleged escape occur?"

Bowie's face reddened. "There was nothing alleged. Sir. The prisoner escaped. Like I said, there was three of them and they all took off at the same time."

"They were from separate cell blocks, weren't they?"

"Yes, sir."

"So when did they plan it?"

Bowie shrugged. "Must've done it in the van on the way out there."

Kant didn't think three prisoners, essentially strangers, could develop the necessary trust and come up with a viable plan in the short time available.

"Perhaps your memory will improve if we continue this discussion where the escape occurred," Kant said.

CHAPTER 3

Kant sat in the back seat of his electrocar, silently observing Bowie seated in front of him. The guard's hair was longish, with greasy wisps sticking out from under a sweat-stained hat. His dark blue uniform looked as if it had never been pressed. Kant looked away in disgust. Much of what he'd seen this afternoon was out of compliance with GOA standards. Another reason why the entire prison system should be under FedPo control. He'd include the suggestion in his report to the commandant.

Deep inside he worried that the assignment was jinxed before he'd even had a chance. He was supposed to investigate the possibility of an escape, not an escape that had already occurred. Regulation required he report the break-in, yet he was ignoring the rules just as Dawes had, and for much the same reason. Once he reported the escape, others would quickly push him aside in their own attempts to be recognized. But this was his assignment. The commandant chose to send *him* to the prison. He would be the one to bring Hanover back. He would show them he deserved his new rank.

He gazed at the bleak landscape and hoped he wasn't wasting his time. He was counting on the warden to follow orders not to notify headquarters until Kant returned to the prison.

Except for Bowie's murmured directions to the driver, Prinski, no one had spoken since they left the prison. Kant wanted Bowie to worry, to fester in the silence. Kant glanced toward Bowie and saw the way the man kept running his finger nervously under his tight collar as if his nerves were taut enough to pluck.

Bowie pointed to a wide place in the gravel side road. "There's where I parked the electrovan."

Prinski stopped the car. Kant climbed out and approached the spot where tire tracks ended in the soft sand. He pivoted, searching the desolate terrain. The high plateau was flat, the sand littered with rounded rocks, unchanged in the last million years except by the ravages of nature. He could see a wide gully, carved from the earth by the flash floods that struck after every heavy rain.

For a moment he imagined torrents of water gushing through the ravine in a violent wave, spilling over the sides, sweeping away anything in its path.

He frowned. This region was so uncivilized, even after several hundred years of American settlement. People like the warden, who were born and raised here, still reflected a bit of the land's savagery. He hated working with them. The local leaders were an intransigent lot, and, despite a relatively peaceful occupation during the last fifty years, he had read the reports that said the undercurrents of rebellion and insurrection were growing stronger again. In his mind, that justified the iron fisted control the commandant retained over the region.

Kant's eyes narrowed as he scanned the horizon. He'd do whatever necessary to bring Hanover back. The last thing the GOA and FedPos needed was the citizenry's glorification of criminals like Hanover.

Kant turned his attention to Bowie. Standing near the electrocar, the guard looked nervously about, his hands trembled slightly.

"Mr. Bowie!" Kant was pleased to see the man's eyes widen with fear as he snapped to attention and the faint sheen of sweat on his cheeks despite the cold wind blowing across the desert. Kant tugged his own jacket collar higher around his neck.

"Yes, sir."

"Tell me exactly what happened."

"We stopped here to clear some brush, and—"

"Why would you clear in the middle of nowhere?"

"The Bureau of Roads said that gully floods the highway because of the brush backing up. We was to get rid of what's here."

Kant glanced at Prinski and raised an eyebrow. The driver nodded subtly, then slipped into the car; Kant was confident that Bowie's story would be confirmed—or denied—by the time they returned to the prison. "Where were the prisoners?" he asked.

"Two prisoners was here," Bowie said, pointing to an area close to the van where brush had been cut and stacked. "Hanover was over there. In the ravine."

"I see." Hands clasped behind his back, Kant studied the ground as he approached Bowie. Then he stood beside the guard and looked around. "If the flooding was from debris in the ravine, why were two prisoners cutting brush here?" Kant turned to look squarely at Bowie, and saw the confusion in the guard's eyes.

Bowie looked away, and after a moment said, "That's what I was told to do, sir."

"I see. You're a good soldier. You follow orders without questioning their logic."

"Well, I mean—"

"That's all right, Mr. Bowie. I respect a man who doesn't challenge his superiors' every decision." Kant fell silent again, letting Bowie stew in uncertainty for a few minutes. "Doesn't it seem odd to you?"

"What, sir?"

"An order for two prisoners to work someplace that wasn't related to fixing the problem you were supposed to be solving?"

Bowie hesitated. "I didn't give it much thought, sir."

"Even you can see it doesn't make sense, Mr. Bowie." Kant shook his head. "Now, tell me how they escaped."

"They was all working, then they started running."

"What signal did they use?"

Bowie frowned and his mouth opened, then closed. "There wasn't no signal," he said hesitantly, as though this was a schoolroom quiz and he hoped he was giving the right answer.

It was a quiz, and Kant had already decided to give Bowie a failing grade. "Then how did three men know to drop their tools and run at the same moment?"

"I don't know. They just did." His voice held more than a trace of frustration.

"Tsk, tsk, Mr. Bowie. I'm disappointed in you. I thought we understood each other."

"What do you mean, sir?"

"Surely you don't think I'm stupid enough to believe three prisoners who've had no previous contact with each other could somehow attempt an escape without a signal."

"Well. . .maybe one of them said something."

"But you're not sure."

"No, sir."

"If that's the case, how did Hanover know it was time to run? You were standing right here and didn't even hear the signal." Kant saw the desperation in Bowie's eyes and knew he had him. "Mr. Prinski, cuff Mr. Bowie."

"But I haven't done nothing," Bowie cried out in protest. He backed away from them. "I shot the two closest to me. It wasn't my fault the third one got away. He moved too fast for me."

Kant shook his head sadly. "You haven't been honest with me. I gave you a chance, but. . ." He let the words trail off.

"No, no, please. You've got it all wrong. I didn't know nothing." He bumped into the van and froze in wide-eyed panic.

"Perhaps you'll think differently by the time we return to the prison. Mr. Prinski, would you help him rethink his position?" Kant nodded for his driver to take the guard into custody. He turned away and heard the sounds of Prinski's iron fist meeting the guard's soft flesh.

Kant slid into the ravine and followed the trail of beheaded sagebrush to the boulder. He glanced over his shoulder and saw the electrocar still in plain sight. Bowie had told the truth when he said he was watching all three prisoners. But it wouldn't have taken Hanover more than a few steps to dodge behind this boulder. Kant walked around the mammoth stone, running his hand over the coarse granite surface.

Then he saw the fresh marks left by hands and feet scrambling up the other side of the ridge, the little rivulets of disturbed sand each time Hanover had broken through the thin crust.

Kant started to follow the same path. He swore as he struggled up the embankment, angry at Hanover for his easy agility, frustrated by his own physical limitations. His legs were shorter than Hanover's, his arms not as long, his body not as lean. He heard echoes of his father's comparisons, and that compelled him to scale the bank, drove him to repeat what Hanover had done. Kant slid halfway back for each step he took, and by the time he clambered over the top, his breathing was labored.

He sat for a moment, looking around as he caught his breath, then stood to examine the tracks in the sand. The footprints went a few yards away from the ravine before turning back. That was odd. Wouldn't Hanover have taken off and run as far as he could, as fast as he could?

Still, the overlaid footprints seemed to say that Hanover was confused at first, that he had no plan, wasn't running to escape the armed guard. But Bowie said he shot the other two prisoners before chasing Hanover. Kant already knew Bowie was lying, or at least not telling all he knew—yet.

Kant frowned. What would draw Hanover to the van and an armed guard? Unless. . ..

No, it was too fantastical to even imagine that Bowie would shoot the other two prisoners and simply leave Hanover behind. Unless. . ..

Unless Bowie didn't pursue Hanover because he figured a prisoner with no rations or water wouldn't last long in the desert.

Kant started walking in ever-widening circles, searching the area on either side of the ravine for a sign. He stopped; the electrocar was a good two hundred yards away and he'd found nothing. No tracks, no sign that Hanover had passed this way.

It burned deep inside that Hanover had slipped away so easily. It churned in Kant's gut that he'd have to report a failure to the commandant. Once again Hanover would be extolled as an example; even if he was a prisoner, he'd shown the intelligence and the guts to escape.

The anticipated verbal blistering he'd take from Commandant Kraft was enough for Kant to resume the search. He reached a slight rise in the otherwise flat terrain, enough elevation to give him a better view.

Then he saw it. A flash of yellow amidst a clump of sagebrush.

* * *

NEUSTADT
Late Afternoon, March 25, 2044

Hanover stumbled against the crumbling adobe hut at the outskirts of Neustadt. His legs shook, rubbery after his flight across thirty kilometers of rugged desert terrain. He tried to swallow, but had no saliva left to moisten his parched throat. A wave of fatigue dizzied him. Hands on his knees, he bent over to breath deeply, rhythmically.

Without a watch he could only guess at the time, but the lengthening shadows told him he had maybe an hour, two at the most, to reach his contact. If he didn't—.

He wouldn't think about that. Since his "escape" earlier in the day, he had run most of the way, and though running kept his confused thoughts from consuming him, it didn't make them go away.

Bowie had shot the other two prisoners, and while Hanover had hidden only a short distance away, Bowie hadn't even attempted to find him. And after, Bowie climbed into the van and drove away, leaving Hanover to wonder what it all meant. Was it a trick as he suspected, or had the warden's words been the truth?

For a few minutes Hanover had sat there, frozen by the shock. Finally he'd scanned the horizon for the shimmer of metal in the sunlight, for the tell-tale dust cloud of his trackers, the FedPo trainees he knew deep inside would come searching for him.

But nothing happened.

No one came.

His first thought had been to escape, really escape. He'd taken only a few steps when the warden's threats came back to him. It grated that he couldn't ignore the warden, couldn't seize control of his life, but if he wanted to live, he had no choice but to do what he'd been told.

Reluctantly, he'd turned toward where the electrovan had been parked. When he saw Bowie's bright yellow bag lying on the ground, Hanover hurried to it and flipped it open. Inside he found only ordinary clothes, a well-worn and nondescript khaki jacket, a wool shirt and a pair of denim pants to replace the unmistakable orange jumpsuit that was standard prison issue.

After changing quickly, Hanover buried the uniform and the yellow bag far from the scene before starting for Neustadt in the opposite direction. For now, he had to concentrate on survival.

It had taken him hours, but he was finally here, and now he couldn't dispel the strong sense of foreboding. Leaning against the aged adobe hut, he swallowed, his dry throat sticking so that he had to swallow again. Standing in the open left him vulnerable; he had to find shelter while he figured out how to locate his contact.

He rounded the corner of the hovel and stared at the sterile, characterless monotony of row upon row of empty gray tenements, all that was left of the workers' compound called Neustadt. The place had been abandoned before Hanover was born, marked off-limits to the curious. Picking his way carefully over the shards of glass and the broken masonry that crunched underfoot, he approached the nearest cinder block building. Weeds easily forced their way through crevices in the fractured pavement.

It didn't surprise him that the GOA voluntary resettlement plan had failed. Who would choose to live in a place like this, even if the placer gold mines hadn't played out? The wind moaned through the vacant streets, raising an uneasy prickle on the back of Hanover's neck. Wary, he glanced around. Except for nomadic scavengers and occasional FedPo patrols, the town was supposed to be deserted.

He eased past the carcass of a rusting stove stuck fast in the shadowed doorway, abandoned like everything else in this town. He reached out to touch it. Even in its neglected state, it was the first thing he'd seen in over four years that reflected an ordinary existence.

Checking to see the area was still clear, Hanover slipped into the next recess. The late afternoon sun lay low on the horizon now, sending a long shadow of the building across the pavement. The wind whistled again, a signal to the traffic of dust and tumbleweeds along the one-way street. Hanover shivered, feeling the temperature drop as he stood there, reminding him time was running out. Hypothermia would be a moot point if he didn't find his contact soon.

His muscles ached with fatigue, but he couldn't give in to the need for rest. Not yet. He peered cautiously around the corner, squinting to detect movements in the growing darkness and empty, staring windows of forsaken buildings that went on for blocks. How would his contact find him in this place?

Weary, he leaned against the wall and closed his eyes. A faint scratching noise caught his attention. From his position, he spied a wraith-like figure move through the shadows. The man was tall and thin to the point of emaciation. A scarecrow.

Hanover eyed him with suspicion, unsure whether to greet him or ignore him. He looked to be a scavenger, with his long greasy hair tied back with a string. A ragged coat flapped around his knees, making a scritching sound as he walked. One sleeve was torn, he had no shirt, and his pants were ripped at the knees.

The man stopped ten meters from Hanover and made a grimacing attempt to smile, revealing a mouth devoid of teeth. Even from this distance, Hanover could smell the stench of unwashed flesh.

"You got any tobaccy, friend?" the scarecrow said in a nasal whine.

Hanover glanced over his shoulder, checking that no one was creeping up behind him from inside the doorless building before he stepped into the open. He listened with all his senses for any sign.

"You got somethin' to eat?" The voice grated on Hanover's nerves.

"Sorry." He was convinced this man was not his contact.

Hanover watched him intently. The man's eyes flicked upward, directly over Hanover's head. A signal. Forewarned, Hanover stepped back, barely out of arm's reach as another man dropped from the window above, brandishing a knife.

As the man crouched, ready to spring, Hanover lashed out with his foot and clipped the man under his chin, flinging him to the ground. Hanover brought his heel down hard on the attacker's throat, felt the crunch of his wind pipe.

The man made a gurgling sound and arched his back. His heels kicked the ground and his head rolled from side to side as his hands clawed his throat in a vain attempt to breathe.

Scarecrow rushed for the knife lying beside his confederate. His hand folded over the handle. Hanover stomped on scarecrow's hand, grinding it into the pavement, then he stepped back and grabbed the knife. Yowling, Scarecrow clutched his hand, fingers bloody and twisted out of shape. Whimpering in pain, he fled down the street and disappeared into an abandoned building on the next block.

Hanover watched him go, then turned to the man lying on the ground. He was dead, his jaw slack, his unseeing eyes staring off in the distance. Hanover swallowed hard and inched away, clutching the building next to him, the concrete rasping his fingers raw.

Stumbling around the corner, he leaned against the wall. He'd never thought he would ever take someone's life. In prison, a few aikido moves and a don't-mess-with-me attitude were all he'd needed to protect himself. He'd had no choice today, he told himself, reacting instinctively. He hadn't planned to kill, only disable. But the rationalization didn't make him feel any better.

Hanover wiped his face with his sleeve and took one long, slow breath. He returned to the body, only to find it already stripped of clothing.

"Damn," he whispered as he glanced around quickly.

He saw no one; the scavengers had already faded into the growing darkness. The wind picked up, buffeting the naked body with dust and debris. Hanover felt the temperature drop again. This was not the time to worry about some stranger who would just as soon have carved out his liver.

Hanover darted across the street, past a block of empty buildings before ducking into another darkened doorway. There were no street lights, but the moon rose high and full, bringing an almost daylight brightness to the exposed street.

He hunkered down to consider his next move. He still had no inkling as to why the warden ordered him to Neustadt. All he knew was what the warden told him. Someone wanted him.

But who? And why? The questions reverberated in his mind.

A shrill whistle startled him. He cautiously peered down the street, before pulling away from the light. He rubbed his hand across his face in frustration. Two FedPo troopers and a dog were standing by the scavenger's body. Shit. Why now, of all times, would a random patrol be in Neustadt?

He ventured another look. The mutt was one of those big breeds, big nose, big mouth. Big teeth. Bad disposition. Tail erect, it aggressively sniffed the ground around the body, then paused and snorted. It looked up, and Hanover was sure it could see him standing in the shadows.

The two troopers talked and gestured excitedly, like raw recruits with their first assignment. Hanover groaned silently. Just what he needed, eager rookies determined to find the perpetrator of this heinous crime, the murder of a fine upstanding citizen passing through Neustadt, he thought sarcastically.

Suddenly the dog straightened and howled. Its voice echoed ominously off the deserted buildings. The trooper standing next to it jumped and the leash went slack. The animal lunged, jerking the leash from the trooper's hand, and lumbered down the moon-lit street, looking for all the world like a hound from hell.

Hanover hesitated only a moment. He backed into the building and scrambled over the debris littering the floor. Moonlight filtered through the broken windows, guiding him toward stairs at the rear of the building.

Eluding the troopers and their hound was not on the agenda. And Hanover's time was running out. Where the hell was his contact? Damn, he hadn't made it one block into town before running into trouble with the two groups that weren't even supposed to be around. Cursing his timing, he scurried up the stairs, hoping to avoid the dog's attention.

He paused on the second floor, but the sound of baying at the building's entrance sent him up another flight of stairs. He could hear the dog howl intermittently, and imagined its overdeveloped nose sucking up scents like a tornado.

Hanover reached the third floor and looked for a way out. A long hallway separated the once spartan apartments. He ran to the end of the hall and found a rusted fire escape ladder leading to the roof. That should stymie the beast's pursuit. He clambered out the window and prayed the rungs would hold.

The first two did, but the third snapped under his weight. He grabbed for the roof, his feet swinging free. Then he found a toe hold in the concrete wall. He hoisted himself over the side and rolled away from the edge.

Lying still, he listened, picking up the troopers' shouts of encouragement, one inside, the other from in front of the building. The dog was on the floor below, barking in high pitched frustration. Hanover heard the inside trooper call the animal, and he breathed a sigh of relief. He was safe.

The sound of metal-against-metal screeched at the other end of the roof. A hatch opened, and the dog's head emerged. Hanover looked around frantically. His only choice was to reach the next rooftop, a two meter gap, he realized with growing dismay. He looked down, the space between a dark, yawning chasm. But he had no alternative. The hound was lumbering across the roof, baying at the top of its lungs.

Hanover gave himself some running room, then charged forward, willing himself to fly through the air.

CHAPTER 4

Hanover landed hard, then tucked and rolled before he scrambled to his feet. Glancing over his shoulder as he crossed the roof, he saw the dog hesitate at the roof's edge.

The trooper emerged from the hatch. Hanover heard a shouted order. The dog bared its teeth and sprang through the air.

Hanover raced across the rooftop. The dog barreled toward him with teeth that gleamed large and sharp in the moonlight. The troopers yelled at each other, one behind and one below him. He didn't care about them; it was the beast who would catch him. He could hear its breathing now, steady and even, not at all labored, while he panted and gulped for air.

The roof ended, and Hanover jumped again, stumbling when he landed on the next building. His foot brushed against a board. He grabbed for it and swung the long, thick beam as the dog touched down, hitting it with a dull thud. The animal uttered a high-pitched yelp, then fell over. It tried to pull itself up, but couldn't. It sagged back down.

Hanover had the extra time he needed. He scrambled to his feet and ran. He needed more time to descend from the roof. He'd worry about the troopers when he reached the ground. He found the stairway door and tugged with both hands until the rusted hinges gave way. Holding his aching side, he clambered down the stairs. From the top of the stairwell, Hanover heard a long, low-pitched bark, a sound of fierce determination. He redoubled his efforts.

To his dismay, none of the landings had doors left in the jambs, nothing to shut him off from his pursuer. Hanover reached the main floor and ran down the long hallway to the opposite end of the building. He hoped to hell the troopers weren't waiting for him with raised guns.

"Hanover! Over here," a man whispered loudly.

Hanover skidded to a stop. No one was supposed to know his name. In the darkness he barely detected a man beckoning for him to exit through a rear door. The dog sounded closer now. So did the troopers who urged it on. Hanover clenched his teeth. He didn't have time to decide if this was a trap.

"I'm your contact," the man said. Hanover followed him from the building. "Is the dog still after you?"

In response, barking reverberated from within the vacant building. The man liberally sprinkled a white powder across the doorway, then tapped Hanover's arm. "That'll slow him down. Come on."

Hanover needed no further invitation. High clouds drifted across the moon, cutting off the light, enhancing the eeriness of the empty streets. He followed the man through a maze of buildings and alleys. The guy traveled as if he knew where he was going. His hooded black cape swirled below his knees, and he ambled along with a discernable limp. Using a stout staff to off-set his limp, he crossed the uneven street rapidly.

They rounded a corner and stopped. The man pushed back the hood. He was fair-haired and appeared to be in his mid-twenties. He checked behind them for signs they were not being followed. "Good. I think we've lost them for now."

Hanover collapsed against the building with relief, then stiffened as someone stepped from a doorless building. He raised his fists, prepared to fight, when he realized it was a woman, the first woman he had seen in two years. But even in the diminished light he could tell she was not someone to spark his interest. Her eyes glinted with steel, and she wore her hair like a ragged mop. Her chin jutted at a challenging angle.

Cautiously he asked, "Who are you two?"

"Travis. Joel Travis." The fair-haired man glanced over his shoulder at Hanover and extended his hand before peering back around the building. He nodded toward the woman. "She's Alicia Juarez."

"Scott Hanover."

"Yeah, we know." Alicia's voice was hard, raspy.

"Shit." Travis jerked away from the corner. "Here they come. Let's go." He led Hanover and Alicia down a narrow alley and through several abandoned warehouses before darting across a clearing.

Travis ducked into a dingy, squat structure at the outskirts of town. It was smaller, shaped differently from the other buildings, more fortress-like in appearance, and Hanover guessed it was Neustadt's original administration building.

Hanover looked over his shoulder as he urged Alicia to go after Travis. He didn't see anything, but that didn't mean the troopers weren't around the next corner. He followed his companions inside and shut the door.

They stood in an inky dark passageway. Hanover reached out to touch the wall and brushed against Alicia's hand. He had the fleeting sensation that her palms were callused before she jerked her hand from his grasp.

"Watch your step," she said. Her voice was somewhere in front of him, moving away.

He felt his way along the wall. Despite her warning, Hanover tripped on the uneven concrete floor, but caught himself before he fell. The silence, total except for the shuffling of feet, disturbed him. It was too close to the deprivation he'd experienced in the cage, too much like a coffin.

The wall opened to a room, and he followed the shuffling steps inside. Travis closed the door behind them and the lights flickered on automatically. The bright light startled Hanover, momentarily blinding him. From reflex, he stepped to the rear; his back met the wall and he shaded his eyes while his body tensed for an assault.

"It's all right," Travis said. "It's a blackout switch."

Hanover's eyes finally adjusted. He lowered his arm to see they were standing in a large, dingy room. The light came from a single ceiling fixture and cast weird shadows on the walls. Hanover felt the faint throbbing beneath his feet that told him a diesel generator lay below them. A table sat in one corner of the room with two chairs tucked into it. More chairs stood haphazardly around the perimeter, giving it the appearance of a meeting room.

A stove squatted in the corner with a propane tank propped next to it, and a jumble of cooking and eating utensils littered the shelves. The room stank of old cooking smells. Hanover's stomach growled noisily. "Got anything to eat or drink?"

Travis tossed his cloak over the back of a chair and grinned. "Sure. Alicia will fix you something."

Hanover saw her scowl at Travis, but she moved toward the make-shift kitchen without a word while he joined Travis at the table. "Nice stick you've got there."

Travis stroked the walking stick reverently with long, slender fingers. "It comes in handy. With the right moves, it can make even the most virile guy sing soprano."

Alicia slammed a tin plate on the table in front of Hanover. "There's only tea to drink. You'll have to wait for the water to heat." Hanover eyed her cautiously. If she was trying out for the surly waitress award she would win easily.

"That's fine," Hanover said. He wanted to ask for plain water but it probably needed to be boiled first anyway. Besides, he didn't want to try Alicia's generous nature by asking for anything special.

He bit into the cold sausage sandwich, expecting the bread to be stale. But the puissant, earthy taste of mold that permeated the sausage surprised him, and he had to force himself to swallow the first mouthful. Even prison food tasted better than this, but gnawing hunger won out and he finished the sandwich quickly.

Alicia brought him a cup of weak tea, sloshing it over the sides of the cup. Hanover thanked her anyway. Travis said nothing, but as she turned, he swatted her bottom.

She pivoted on her heel, her eyes flashing. "Pig," she spat, then struck his face with a blow that nearly knocked him from his chair. She stalked across the room, her shoulders squared in anger, and slammed the metal tea pot on the stove.

Ignoring the byplay, Hanover took a sip, then leaned back in his chair. He inhaled deeply, his guard slipping for the first time since leaving the prison early that morning. His hands absorbed warmth from the mug.

Some of his former determination seeped into him, filling him with a confidence he hadn't felt since before the cage. He eyed Travis. "Okay, Travis, who are you and what's going on?"

Travis glanced at Alicia, whose face masked any emotion. He turned back to Hanover. "Who we are isn't important. Besides, I can't tell you much because I don't know a damn thing myself. All I was told was to meet you and keep you here overnight. Tomorrow we're supposed to take you to Trumanville. You'll be told what to do next when you get there."

"Who told you to meet me? The warden?"

Travis looked confused. "What warden?"

Hanover realized he probably shouldn't share any information unless it was absolutely necessary. Hanover repeated, "Who told you to meet me?"

"I don't know. Let it go."

Hanover didn't want to let it go, but from the set of Travis' mouth, he wasn't going to be forthcoming. After a few minutes of silence, punctuated by Alicia banging dishes in a fit of pique, he asked, "How come the FedPos aren't beating down the doors to get in here? And what about the scavengers?"

Travis didn't answer directly. Instead, he brushed his thumb back and forth across the pads of his fingers. Hanover nodded in understanding. Everyone had their price; it was simply a matter of figuring out how high it was. Travis shifted in his chair and rubbed his leg.

"Does it hurt?" Hanover nodded toward the leg.

"Sometimes. When I was seven, my dad worked outside Albuquerque. There were some riots, and the FedPos picked up my dad for questioning. He didn't know anything, but they didn't believe him. They brought me to the interrogation place and told him they'd break my leg if he didn't tell them what he knew." Travis shrugged while he continued to massage his leg. "The leg was set poorly."

"I remember hearing about the riots, but I never knew what caused them," Hanover said. "The newspapers only print propaganda. What really started them?"

"It was winter, and power outages lasted for days. Some people froze to death. Food wasn't delivered to stores because the roads were piled high with snow and there was no gasoline for the plows." Travis thoughtfully fingered his walking stick. With a sigh, he pushed himself from the chair and walked across the room. "Would you like more tea?"

Hanover looked around and realized Alicia had slipped away. For a moment his body tensed, then he forced himself to relax. Travis obviously wasn't worried, and if he and Alicia weren't here to help him, they would have left him for the FedPos to catch.

Unless he was wrong.

How in the hell was he supposed to know if they were only pretending to protect him? Doubts spun through his head, leaving a dull ache. To be on the safe side, he'd ask all the questions and answer none. And stay vigilant.

He nodded to Travis and brought his cup over. The hot tea felt good. Even though it was weak, it washed away the dirty taste of the sandwich. "Then what happened?"

"The police refused to respond to calls, and so youth gangs started marauding the town, robbing and beating up people. I guess the last straw was when a twelve year old girl was gang raped in front of her house. Her father organized some vigilantes. They tracked the kids to an abandoned warehouse and hauled them to the roof, put ropes around their necks and gave them a shove. The kids jerked to a stop about one floor shy of the ground."

Hanover shrugged. "Sounds like they got what they deserved."

"That's what most everyone thought, except the father of one of the boys. He worked for the government, and made a big stink about it. Before anyone knew it, the vigilantes were convicted of murder and sent to prison. That touched off the burning and looting."

"What happened to your dad?"

Travis gave Hanover a hard look, then gulped the last of his tea. His cup slamming against the counter was all the answer Hanover needed. An awkward sense of connection with someone else who had lost a parent so unnecessarily filtered through him.

Hanover took a deep breath. "By the way, what was that powder you scattered when you found me?"

Travis relaxed with a bemused grin. "It's a mix of dried blood and cocaine that we started using when the FedPos brought in the dogs. One sniff and the dog can't smell its own ass."

Hanover chuckled. It sounded foreign to his ears. "One last question—what's the deal with Alicia?"

"She loves me."

Hanover leaned against the counter and crossed his arms. "You could've fooled me," he said dryly. "But besides not being enamored by your chivalry, why's she so hostile?"

Travis shrugged and looked away. "She was the twelve year old girl. She's been wary of men ever since, but for some reason she feels safe with me. Come on, I'll show you where you're sleeping."

Hanover followed Travis down a narrow corridor and stepped into a small cell-like room.

"The FedPos used to use this for interrogations," Travis said.

"Great. If I have any nightmares, I'll be in the right place," Hanover quipped to cover the uneasiness that drifted over him.

"You can wash up two doors down. The lights go off automatically in ten minutes. See you in the morning." Travis started to leave, then paused. "One more thing, Hanover. Hands off Alicia."

He started to give one of his usual flippant responses, but swallowed it when he saw the intense seriousness in Travis' eyes. Hanover raised his hands. "No problem, friend. Women are the last thing on my mind. Thanks."

Travis nodded and left Hanover alone with his thoughts. After washing up, he returned to the tiny room, fluffed the lumpy pillow and sank onto the cot as the lights flicked off.

He took a deep breath and exhaled hard. It suddenly hit him that he'd escaped almost eight hours ago, and the S.A.D. had not been detonated. Did Warden Dawes know he'd arrived and met up with Travis? Was Travis really his contact? Hanover sat quietly, hearing the blood pound in his head as his anxiety rose. Every heartbeat could be his last. Every breath. Every blink of his eyes. Every. . ..

Damn them. Damn them all for doing this to him. Was this some new torture they'd devised, an entertaining way to drive him insane bit by bit? He wouldn't let them win, wouldn't let them break him as they had so many others.

He hit the wall with his fist. He still didn't know what this was all about, or who was involved. But for the time being, he was free. He'd settle for that small victory.

As he tried to take comfort in that thought, the darkness lay heavily on him. If it weren't for the springs poking through the thin mattress, he'd think he was lost, floating in an abyss.

Just like in the cage.

The GOA had found the remnants of the cramped underground room when they built over a hundred year old prison. With built in shackles, a narrow air shaft, and walls that shed a fine caliche dust, the GOA had no need to create their own torture chamber.

Hanover swallowed hard, but the fear clawed up his throat, threatening to choke him. He couldn't let them win. Fighting the suffocation, Hanover sprang to his feet and stumbled to the door, groping for the elusive knob. By the time he jerked the door open and flung himself into the hallway, his body was dripping with sweat. He gasped for air.

This isn't the cage, this isn't the cage, this isn't the cage. Slumped against the wall, he repeated the words until his heart stopped pounding and his breathing slowed to a more normal rate.

A faint glow drew him toward the kitchen. It wasn't much, but the stove's pilot light pushed away the demons, the terror that lurked in the absolute darkness. Hanover sat in the corner opposite the door, his back flush against the wall, and felt in control again. Exhausted, his eyes fluttered closed. A muffled scratching jerked him awake. When he spotted a mouse skittering across the floor, he relaxed. How long before he didn't dread the dark? he wondered as he drifted into an uneasy sleep.

*   *   *

Sunrise
March 26, 2044

Hanover and his two companions rose long before dawn and now they were trudging across the plateau in the chilled thin light. The wind whipped through Hanover's jacket, and he tried to burrow his face in the upturned collar, his hands in the shallow pockets. What paved road remained was cracked and potholed.

Hanover concentrated on the uneven ground, figuring a twisted ankle was the last thing he needed. Besides, it was better than meeting the hostility in Alicia's gaze.

Now that he knew her story, he recognized the haunted look in her eyes, the way she avoided coming too close. Last night she'd jerked her hand away rather than help him in the dark, and he understood why. She was a survivor, and he respected her for that.

He glanced up and saw the bright morning sun bathe the semi-arid landscape in a golden light. Scattered clumps of scrub brush and stunted piñons came into vivid detail. Distant mountains etched a jagged line against the clear blue sky and the scent of desert sage spiced the crisp air.

Travis glanced back at him, and Hanover saw his reddish hair and blue eyes sparkle as if this were a pleasurable field trip, despite the fact that he leaned more heavily on his walking stick. He hoped Travis wouldn't pay too heavy a price for this journey. Although still aloof and wary, Alicia's spirits were better today. She purposely shadowed Travis, and her hand bumped his, occasionally entwining for a few steps before pulling away again.

Hanover watched the easiness between them, and loneliness emptied him. How long had he been on his own, how long since he felt as if he belonged to anything outside himself?

He never knew his father, who'd been conscripted by the Germans to fight in the ongoing war against the Russians and killed somewhere in the Ural Mountains when Hanover was only two. Except for a few vague early childhood memories of a man who played with him, he and his mother were alone until he was thirteen and she died. But even during those ten years, he sensed he'd already lost her to a depression that he attributed to his father's unnecessary death.

After that, he bounced from government residence to government residence, stirring up trouble wherever he went, yet never expelled from school nor sent to the juvenile detention camps. He'd sometimes wondered about that, especially when he was accepted by a college on a soccer scholarship; he hadn't applied to college.

Yet, even then, he'd isolated himself from close relationships, angry at the government for destroying his family. Now he watched Alicia and Travis, and felt the twinge of regret that no one cared about him. Whatever was going on now was because somebody wanted something from him, not because they cared about him. He kicked a stone out of his way and forced himself to look anywhere but at the two people in front of him, anywhere but at the reminder of how alone he really was.

An hour later, they entered a narrow valley and the wind gusted through the canyon, carrying the stench of garbage and open sewers. Hanover gagged and covered his mouth, trying to filter out the odor. But it overwhelmed his efforts. "What is that?" he gasped.

Alicia turned to him and wrinkled her nose. "Trumanville. You'll get used to it."

"I don't think so." He pulled his jacket up to cover his nose and mouth, ignoring the gap it left at his waist for the cold to seep in.

They topped a rise in the road. The squalor that was called Trumanville lay before them. The site appalled Hanover. He'd heard about places like this, shanty towns that had sprung up around the country, all named for the president everyone blamed for losing the war. But the reality far exceeded any description he'd heard.

The town appeared as an ugly stain sprawling over the side of the slope, one shack stacked against another, as if a single push would topple it all like so many dominos. Not even the GOA would care about a place like this.

"When'd this place start?" Hanover asked as they made their way toward the town.

"When the mines were closing down, people stole materials from Neustadt and the nearby mines," Travis said. "They took pipe and fittings and tapped into the reservoirs that supplied the mines so they at least had water."

They reached the outskirts and the stench worsened. Hanover looked around. "Don't they have any sewers?"

"No," Travis said. He pointed to the hydrants spaced about a hundred meters apart. The hydrants leaked, creating slimy mud holes. "They get an occasional cloudburst out here and that washes everything clean for a couple of days."

Travis raised his arm. They stopped while he scanned the buildings along the perimeter of the town. "Let's go around. Maybe we can make it without any trouble."

Hanover stiffened at Travis' words. Adrenaline pumped through him as he studied the dwellings before him. "Trouble? What kind of trouble?" The place still appalled him, sending shivers up his spine.

"There's a gang that runs this end of town. The leader is part German, and he's a real sweetheart. Pay his toll or get the crap beaten out of you." Travis' furrowed brow belied the evenness of his tone.

"Screw him," Hanover said in disgust. "Damned if I'm going to pay to walk along this lousy road. As if I had something to give."

"They know Alicia and I don't have anything, either, but that doesn't mean a damn thing." Travis shrugged. "If we go through town, we're guaranteed to run into them. If we go around and they're busy harassing someone else, we may get lucky and slip by. Then again, we may not."

At this point, Hanover didn't want to argue. He only wanted to reach their destination. "Fine. We'll go around."

They moved ahead cautiously, picking their way along the debris-strewn road that skirted the town. Hanover watched thin, ragged children play on the refuse heaps and in the alleys. The waifs ignored them, but the few visible adults stared as they passed, wariness in their eyes. Hanover felt their hostility; their suspicion bored into his back. But he didn't feel threatened.

They neared a more substantial shack. It stood straight, looking less fragile than the other structures. Four men emerged and spread themselves across the road, waiting for Hanover and his companions to approach. They halted a short distance from the four men.

"What now?" Hanover muttered under his breath.
"It looks like we pay or fight," Travis said.

CHAPTER 5

FEDPO HEADQUARTERS
ALBUQUERQUE
Mid-Day, March 26, 2044

Willie Kant stared out his office window. Spring color burgeoned through the grays and browns of the drab city sprawled below him. Any other day, he'd enjoy spending his lunch hour at the firing range or in the officers' dining room, gathering information he could use to his advantage.

But today, he'd sequestered himself in his office. He couldn't even gloat over the view window that symbolized his new rank. The way he figured it, he had 72 hours to submit a report to the commandant, 72 hours to prove to the doubters that he deserved to be a major in the Federal Police. One day had already passed, and he had discovered nothing about the prison escape. His lack of progress weighed oppressively on his shoulders. He felt a sheen of perspiration on his brow, his collar tightening around his neck. The commandant wasn't known for his patience; he wouldn't wait until the end of the week for Kant's report. But more than anything, Kant hated to lose, hated to fail.

He paced to his desk and sank into the chair. Leaning on one elbow, he plucked at his lower lip. Hanover was like a rock in his shoe that he couldn't shake out. Would he never be free of this man who haunted his every step, this half-brother who took everything that was rightfully his, everything from a father's respect to recognition for his abilities?

Kant slammed his fist on the top of his desk. Damn Scott Hanover, damn him.

Further interrogation of Bowie, the prison guard, had been futile. Kant authorized limited use of torture; too much would make the guard confess something—anything —if only to stop the pain. Kant couldn't afford delays caused by coerced lies.

Bowie either knew nothing or was amazingly loyal to an unlikely cause. He denied any knowledge of the partially buried yellow bag stamped with the prison's initials, S.R.P., saying it must belong to Hanover, but had no idea how the prisoner smuggled it onto the van. Bowie repeatedly claimed ignorance of any plot or conspiracy against the government.

Dawes also disavowed any involvement with the escape or awareness of any larger scheme, although Kant doubted that was true, either. No warden in his right mind allowed a prisoner like Hanover outside the prison walls for any reason. The temptation to run was ridiculously high for a death sentence prisoner, despite the threat of the S.A.D.

As soon as he'd left the prison, Kant ordered a tap on the warden's phone and on-line transmissions, and someone to monitor his activities away from the prison. Someone had to have helped Hanover. Rumor was someone outside the prison organized the escape. The questions kept coming back: who wanted Hanover to escape, and why?

Kant picked up a pencil and began doodling on a pad of paper. He hated Hanover; God, he hated him. Kant knew he could destroy Hanover at any time by simply triggering the S.A.D., one simple push of the button, but that was too easy. It didn't take a major, or any other rank of officer, to do that.

No, a highly skilled officer tracked his quarry and returned him for questioning and punishment. And Kant wanted Hanover alive, or, if that failed, he at least needed a body to prove he'd accomplished his mission. Besides, if Hanover was a member of an extensive underground or part of a conspiracy, Kant figured the additional names would mean even more recognition.

Despite his lack of progress, Kant had filed a preliminary report with the commandant the night before, although he'd wished someone else the pleasure of reporting the escape had already occurred. He'd been fortunate enough to call when Commandant Kraft was in a meeting, and so he left a confident, upbeat message on the videophone, purposely neglecting to include the escapee's name.

Kant counted himself even luckier to be out of the office when the commandant left an angry response that Kant's account was vague and disturbingly lacking in detail, a shortcoming the commandant expected to be corrected in the next report.

What really angered him was that the commandant had caught him unprepared. Kant hadn't read the report Dawes' gave him about Hanover, the report that said Hanover was awaiting execution. He should have read that report. He had no excuse, only a brief reprieve from a face-to-face dressing down by the commandant.

Something was wrong at the prison. No warden in his right mind sent a prisoner scheduled to die outside the compound. Kant could bring Bowie, or even Dawes, to headquarters for further interrogation. But if he did that, others would try to push their way into the investigation and usurp Kant's role. For now, only he and the commandant knew about the escape, and that's the way he wanted to keep it for as long as possible.

The lead on his pencil snapped and Kant realized his fingers were white from clenching it, the tips of his fingers numb from lack of circulation. He threw the pencil down and sighed heavily. Sitting in his office wasn't getting him anywhere, and if he wasn't careful, he feared speculation would grow as to his abilities. Ambitious, newly-promoted majors weren't supposed to spend their days confined to their offices.

The videophone beeped, and he glared at it, ambivalent about whether he wanted to answer it. "Major Willie Kant," he said finally.

"Prinski here, sir. I picked up something you might find interesting."

Kant breathed a sigh of relief. Prinski had an uncanny knack of blending into the woodwork so that he heard things he shouldn't be privy to, one of the reasons why Kant had requested the driver accompany him with each promotion. "Where are you?"

"In the lobby, sir."

"Don't move. I'll be right down." Kant punched the off button, anticipation replacing his earlier frustration. Smiling now, Kant reached for the door, then stepped back when he heard a soft knock at the door.

"Come in," he called. To his surprise, Lieutenant Colonel Heinz entered the room. "Sir," Kant said, snapping to attention and saluting.

"At ease, Kant. I just came by to congratulate you on your promotion and welcome you to headquarters." Heinz's uniform hung limply on his gaunt frame and his sparse hair was combed back, accentuating his angular face.

Kant saw past the welcoming smile to the coldness in Heinz's eyes. This wasn't a welcome, this was something else. Kant knew the rumors that Heinz's career had been side-tracked after some errors in judgement; his methods for strictly controlling the local people were too fanatical even for the GOA. Now he prowled the administration building in search of activities he could take over from younger officers.

Kant didn't report to Heinz. Technically he wasn't required to talk to him, although refusing could prove awkward. Kant wondered how to get rid of Heinz without arousing the senior officer's suspicions. Heinz was known to tag along with junior officers, and Kant didn't want him anywhere around when Prinski gave his report.

Masking his suspicions, Kant said, "Thank you, sir. I feel honored to be here. I hope I can make a contribution."

Uninvited, Heinz settled into a chair as if he intended to stay. "You must be busy. I came by yesterday afternoon and you were out."

Kant sank into a nearby chair. "I went to Southwestern Regional. For a routine inspection."

"Really? I didn't know it was due for one."

Kant shrugged. "It wasn't. I just wanted to acquaint myself with the facility."

"I heard something about an escape plot." Heinz's eyes narrowed like a snake preparing to strike, and a prickle of wariness slithered up Kant's spine. He wished it had remained a rumor.

"Interesting. I hadn't heard that," Kant lied. Enough of being polite. He rose from his chair and waited for Heinz to do the same.

Heinz sized him up. "You eager to go somewhere?"

"Not really. My driver's waiting downstairs. I thought I'd tour another facility this afternoon."

"Perhaps I should go with you, introduce you to the people you need to know." Heinz stood and crossed the room. He waited for Kant to open the door for him, then stepped into the hallway. "Where are you going?"

Kant didn't like the Lieutenant Colonel's increasingly intense scrutiny. He quickly considered places Heinz wouldn't possibly want to go. "I thought—"

"Colonel Heinz!"

Kant and Heinz turned to see a brigadier general striding toward them. They stood at attention and saluted as the general stopped in front of them. He nodded at Kant before turning his full attention to Heinz. "Major General Brinkerhoff is waiting for your report."

"Ah, yes. I'm working on it now."

"Perhaps you'd like to take this opportunity to finish it?" Still standing at attention, Kant heard the disapproving undercurrent in the brigadier's voice and felt a surge of relief.

"Of course," Heinz replied through gritted teeth. "We'll have to wait until another time, Major."

"I understand, sir." Kant maintained a bland expression. He saw the seething frustration in Heinz's eyes, and knew he wasn't completely free of this man. He'd have to keep his guard up, avoid being cornered again.

He hurried to the lift and took it to the first floor. Stepping into the lobby, Kant spotted his driver immediately.

Prinski saluted, a protocol they usually dispensed with, but in the crowded foyer, they observed all formalities. "Your car is ready, sir."

"Thank you, Prinski." Kant followed and slid into the back seat.

Prinski quickly pulled the car into traffic and began without preamble. "I was in the garage this morning, servicing the car, when I heard these two troopers come in. They're new, haven't seen them before, but they work with a dog out at Neustadt."

Kant nodded. "I worked there my first assignment. Real shit duty. Boring, too. I couldn't wait to transfer."

"From the way these two talked, it wasn't boring last night. They found a dead body, some scavenger with his throat caved in. Then their dog picked up a scent and they chased a man across the rooftops until they lost him."

Kant now listened intently. "What'd he look like?"

"They never got close enough to tell." His eyes never straying from the road, Prinski wove through the traffic as he circled the block. "But they did find another scavenger, this one with mangled fingers. He told the troopers a stranger stomped on his hand after killing his friend. Said he was tall with short, sandy hair."

"Hanover," Kant whispered. He gripped the seat back in front of him. "Where's the scavenger?"

"The troopers brought him to the clinic last night, so he's probably back at Neustadt by now."

"Did you talk to the troopers?"

"No. I heard them tell the details to the dispatcher when they turned their truck in before going off shift. They didn't see me." Prinski pulled the car to a stop in front of the GOA administration building.

"Good. Excellent work, Prinski. Go back to motorpool and wait. I'll order the car and a squad of troopers to come with us. Meet me in front in ten minutes. Oh, and Prinski? Get a pint of whiskey. The cheapest you can find."

"Yes, sir." Prinski hopped from the car and came around to open Kant's door.

Kant scrambled from the vehicle and hurried inside the building. He submitted an urgent request to the commandant's office for authorization to use back-up troops, and waited for the bureaucratic wheels to turn.

* * *

Three hours later, Prinski drove Kant's electrocar into Neustadt, a squad of troops in the vehicle behind them. As they slowly cruised the streets, Kant searched for a sign of life. The abandoned city hadn't changed at all since his tour of duty; if anything, it was more bleak.

They rounded a corner and Kant saw three scavengers sitting against a building in the cold sun. He whistled and pointed at them. "Get them," he called to the troops.

The scavengers fled, but were no match for the healthy, fit infantrymen. One scavenger tripped on his ragged coat and stumbled to the ground. A soldier hauled him to his feet, slammed him against the building and frisked him. Kant watched with anticipation, then disappointment when he saw the man's hand was not bandaged.

In a few minutes, the FedPos rounded up the remaining two scavengers and brought them to Kant. One of them jerked from the grip of a FedPo and cradled his bandaged arm. He studied the ground in front of him, with occasional wary glances at the troopers and then at Kant.

As they approached, Kant removed the pint bottle from his pocket and unscrewed the cap. He tipped the bottle and let some of the amber liquid trickle to the ground, watching the scavenger.

As if hypnotized, the man licked his lips. "You got no need to waste it like that," he said. His whine grated on Kant's ears.

"It's Major Kant to you."

"Yes, sir, your honor, Major, whatever you say, your lordship."

The feigned submissiveness repulsed Kant. "I say you're going to tell me all about the man who did that to you." He pointed to the scavenger's bandaged hand.

The old man's eyes momentarily glazed over, then he raised his injured hand and squinted at it. "Yes, sir. Comfortable shoes, clean pair of pants and. . .and a jacket, a nice khaki jacket. Would've fit me real good, they would." He licked his lips again and nodded toward the bottle. "I'm thinking a sip of that would be a powerful help to my memory, Major, sir."

Kant ignored the request. "What did he look like?"

The old man shrugged. "I told you already."

"You told me what he wore. Was he tall or short? Lean or heavy? Blond or dark-haired?"

The old man closed his eyes and screwed up his face. "I didn't see real clear. It was getting dark."

Kant poured more whiskey on the ground.

"Wait, wait." The scavenger raised his hands in supplication. "He was taller than you. Thinner, too. Don't know about his hair, but it was short."

"Where did he go?"

"I don't know, Major, sir. I swear. I ran away when he killed Elmo and smashed my hand."

Kant silently stared at him. Finally the man squirmed. "Okay, okay. I didn't see nothing myself. But I heard him and two others left for Trumanville before light."

Kant digested the man's words for a moment then signaled for the FedPos to return to their vehicle. When they were loaded, he turned back to the scavenger.

"You've been a big help." He tossed the bottle at the scavenger's feet where it smashed on the broken pavement. As they drove off, Kant watched the derelict. He was on his hands and knees, sobbing as he cupped his hands to stem the runoff and frantically lapped the wet pavement.

*   *   *

TRUMANVILLE
Mid-Day, March 26, 2044

Hanover didn't find Travis' pay-or-fight assessment of the situation encouraging as he sized up the four men squaring off in front of him.

"Watch out for the big one," Travis murmured. "He's the leader. Real mean. The other's aren't much without him. I'll do the talking."

Travis raised his walking stick in greeting. "What's the problem, Perkins?" he called in a loud voice.

"That you, Travis? What're you doing in my territory? Who's the stiff?" The man's voice was deep, a bearish growl. Dark, untidy hair hung down to his shoulders. Small squinting eyes, set close together, supported by a huge nose from which hairs hung like icicles. His mouth was thin-lipped and small. His thick neck rested on a body of bear-like proportions. He was the ugliest man Hanover had ever seen.

"A friend of mine, Perkins. We're just passing by."

"Can't let you do that 'less you pay. Got to maintain the roads, you know."

Hanover snorted and spat on the road. He crossed his arms, staring silently at Perkins.

Perkins raised his fist. "Mind your manners, asshole. You're already on the books for trespassing. Don't make me add more charges."

"You know what you can do with your friggin' charges," Hanover said with deliberate contempt.

Perkins's face turned apoplectic with rage. "You got a smart mouth. Hernandez, teach him some manners."

Hernandez approached Hanover cautiously. Hanover braced himself, sizing up the thug while keeping an eye on the others. Hernandez came within arm's reach and swung. Hanover retreated, but not quickly enough; Hernandez's fist clipped his shoulder. Hanover breathed hard from the adrenaline rushing through his body.

Another man stepped forward. "I'll get the girl," the man said to Perkins. He grabbed Alicia by the arm and hauled her toward the building. "How about you and me getting friendly, baby doll?"

Her response was to close in and ruthlessly knee him in the groin. "How's that for 'friendly,' you little worm?"

He doubled over, squealing. Travis swung his staff against the man's head, bringing an abrupt end to the noise.

Hernandez closed in on Hanover again, more quickly this time. Hanover stood his ground. He grabbed the lapels of Hernandez's tattered jacket and vigorously kicked the inside of the man's knee. Hernandez staggered under the vicious blow. Hanover jerked him forward, then pounded on his back. With a moan, Hernandez slumped to the ground at Hanover's feet.

The third man rushed Travis, who swung the other end of his staff up to stab his assailant in the pit of the stomach, temporarily paralyzing him.

"I'm gonna make *schmeerkasse* out of you, you sonnavabitch," Perkins bellowed. He reached out to grab Hanover.

Hanover caught Perkins' outstretched wrist in both hands, stepped under Perkins' arm and twisted. Perkins flipped over and landed on his back in the dirt. He reached out and caught Hanover's ankle and jerked hard, bringing Hanover to his knees, then threw himself on top of Hanover. He pummeled Hanover's side. Hanover winced under the battering, and shoved Perkin's chin with the heel of his hand. Perkin's head snapped back. Hanover thrust Perkins off him and staggered to his feet. He kicked Perkins in the side of the head. Perkins' unconscious body sagged.

Hanover looked around and saw people coming from the nearby buildings. "Let's get the hell out of here," he said.

With Travis in the lead, Hanover took the rear-guard as they double-timed down the road. Bystanders made no effort to interfere with their escape; a few even dared to cheer them on.

Ten minutes later, they reached the opposite side of Trumanville, coming to a halt in the shade of an empty building.

"How much further?" Hanover asked as he slid down against the wall.

"About ten more minutes," Travis said. He pointed ahead. "Around that bend."

Hanover nodded, more than ready to meet whoever it was Travis was bringing him to, more than ready to find out what in the hell this was all about. And why they wanted him specifically. Impatience brought him to his feet. "Come on, let's go."

Travis and Alicia struggled to join him. Travis' limp was more pronounced; Alicia had thrown his arm around her shoulders for extra support, but Hanover did not slow his pace for them. In a few minutes, they spotted buildings clustered in a small valley. Heaps of tailings in the surrounding hills gave evidence of past mining activity.

Travis pointed in that direction. "That's it over there."

Hanover saw several people moving around the dilapidated buildings. One of the men looked in their direction, then ducked inside. A late model electrovan was parked next to the largest structure. From an angle, it appeared to have a logo on the side. He couldn't make it out, but uneasiness slowed his pace. He fell behind Travis and Alicia.

Travis turned, his brows wrinkled with questions. "Come on," he said with a trace of impatience.

"I'm coming," Hanover said. He fanned out for a more direct look at the van.

Travis stopped, then looked in the same direction as Hanover. "What's the problem?"

"There's no prob—" Hanover identified the logo. German Occupation Authority. It was a trick. "Shit!"

He turned and ran. Travis threw his stick low. It tangled in Hanover's legs and he fell hard.

Travis seized the stick. "Stop. It's not what you think."

"Yeah, right," Hanover mumbled as he scrambled to his feet. Travis thwacked him across the shoulders and Hanover collapsed to the ground. Two men ran up and grabbed for Hanover's arms. He rolled and twisted, grabbing for the stick.

"Stop," Travis said again. He aimed the weapon at Hanover's belly and leaned into it.

Pain shot through Hanover. He reached for the stick, but Travis only pushed harder. The two men caught Hanover's arms and hauled him to his feet.

"Bring him inside," Travis said. He gazed steadily at Hanover. "I'm sorry." He opened his mouth to say more, then stopped.

"Yeah, sure." Hanover spat on the ground. In his mind, Travis was one of the worst, one of the ones who pretended to be a friend, an ally.

As the men half-dragged him toward the building, Hanover felt like the century's biggest sucker. He'd believed, he'd really believed these people wanted him to escape. Now it seemed it had all been a trick. But why? Why would the GOA let him escape, only to have him delivered back to them? It made no sense at all.

But then, none of it had made sense from the very beginning.

CHAPTER 6

Hanover stumbled as the two men hauled him toward the compound. He looked up to see an older man emerge from the building and wait, watching, his eyes shaded from the bright sun. As they neared, Hanover saw the sixtyish man was tall and ascetic with a fringe of white hair.

The man's blue eyes narrowed and his mouth turned down. "Bring him inside." He turned and entered the building.

Hanover jerked free from the loosened grip of his captors. He glanced over his shoulder and saw others close in behind them. There'd be no escape. At least not now.

The older man looked back at him. "Follow me, Scott." His tone was matter-of-fact rather than demanding.

Again Hanover felt confusion; nothing was as it should be, nothing was as he'd presumed it would be under the circumstances. He trailed behind the man as they made their way down a long concrete block hall. The man stopped in front of a door and pushed it open. Hanover hesitated.

"Please, Scott." The man's voice remained calm but determined.

Hanover shrugged and stepped inside. He wasn't surprised when the door closed behind him and he heard the lock click. Except for a small desk and two chairs, the room was empty. He wiped his hand across his face.

Now what?

*   *   *

Hanover paced the small, windowless office for what seemed like hours. Barely more than twenty-four hours had passed since his escape. After what he'd been through, he wasn't sure if he wanted to run a marathon or collapse.

The satisfying meal of beef stew and fresh bread he finished an hour ago left his body sated, but sluggish. At least the food, delivered by a silent guard, was a significant improvement over Alicia's offerings.

Yet despite the easing of his physical needs, his ragged thoughts remained frayed with uncertainty. Yesterday he'd stretched his endurance to the maximum, traveled without food or water, fended off attackers, and spent a restless night in fear that each minute was his last, that Dawes would detonate the S.A.D. Today he'd traveled again, surviving on the promise that his questions would be answered.

So far, none of his questions had been answered. The continued waiting sharpened Hanover's already razor-edged nerves. At this point, he no longer cared what they expected of him, just so long as he knew what they wanted.

The door's soft click caught his attention and he whirled around to see the man who'd left him here enter the room.

"Sorry to keep you waiting, Scott. Technical question came up that I had to answer. Have a seat." He pointed to the chairs as he shuffled across the room. He unlocked a cupboard, revealing a tiny sink, a burner, and some small appliances, so old, they qualified as antiques. "You enjoyed your meal?"

"Who are you?" Hanover blurted.

"Of course. Introductions." The man extended his hand. "I'm Dr. Beecker."

The name meant nothing to Hanover. He eyed the man warily. "Look, I—"

"Would you like some coffee?"

The question stopped Hanover cold. "Real coffee?" he asked, his voice hushed. The last time he'd had coffee, not the grain substitute that passed for coffee, was years ago, a thank-you gift for supplying permits for two people who wanted to travel without surveillance.

Dr. Beecker's gaze remained distant. "Yes, real coffee," he said, as if it was a most ordinary question.

Hanover sighed. What kind of trick was this? Did they want to drug him? His mouth watered with anticipation, but he shook his head. "I think I'd rather talk."

Dr. Beecker eyed him, then nodded once. He moved to the empty chair and sank into it. "Yes, I suspect you have a number of questions."

"That's putting it mildly," Hanover mumbled under his breath. Something vaguely familiar about the man stirred Hanover's memory. "Are you the Dr. Beecker from the University?"

Beecker looked surprised. "No, that's my brother, Andrew. He taught literature until he retired several years ago. I'm a physicist at Los Alamos."

The admission startled Hanover like a splash of icy water. "For the GOA?"

"Unfortunately, one must keep body and soul together." Beecker grimaced. "It also provides me with the space and equipment I need to put my theories into practice."

Hanover frowned as another memory surfaced. "Beecker. The Beecker Time Displacement Principle. I heard the lecture in college. Are you *that* Beecker?"

"The same," replied the old man somberly.

"How come the Germans haven't stolen your ideas?"

Beecker shrugged. "I told them it was only a fantasy, that in the real world, it would never work. And they believed me."

"But you gave that lecture a long time ago."

"I've been working on the theory for twenty-five years." Beecker paused, his lips pursed. "It's only recently that I've been secretly putting the idea to more practical use."

Hanover watched him intently, suddenly wary again. "Does it have anything to do with why I'm here?"

"I knew you were the right one for this." Dr. Beecker smiled stiffly. "What I'm about to tell you is known by only a few people, and we want to keep it that way. Therefore, before I go any further, I must have your assurance that what we discuss will not leave this room."

Hanover gave Beecker a hard stare. "Give me one good reason why. You work for the GOA, and I've never made any secret of how I feel about it."

Dr. Beecker leaned forward in his chair, and Hanover saw the gleam in his eye, the glow of a zealot. Now he was really worried. What in the hell was he involved with?

"We chose you because you want the same things we do," Dr. Beecker said. "We've checked your background quite thoroughly. Your college record and your attitude while working for the Bureau of Travel Permits reveal an antipathy for authority in general, and the GOA in particular. You may resist our proposal for other very valid reasons, but we're confident you won't object to it on the basis of your principles."

Great, he thought as he watched Beecker finger a paperweight and stare unflinchingly at Hanover. A fanatical fringe group. Just what he needed. So much for clemency from the GOA when he finished with these people.

The knowledge that someone had investigated him specifically left Hanover feeling dissected, and he didn't like that feeling. The bigger question, though, was what was so important to warrant these people risking discovery?

"I must insist on your assurance of silence before we continue," Dr. Beecker said.

His patience exhausted, Hanover gripped the arms of his chair to keep from exploding. "What the hell are you talking about?" he asked, his jaw clenched to hide his turmoil. "Haven't I already risked my life by going along with that so-called escape? I'm probably listed as a fugitive by now, with FedPos looking for me everywhere. Warden Dawes could detonate the S.A.D. at any minute. It seems to me I've got no choice but to be committed to whatever you've got in mind."

Dr. Beecker looked startled by Hanover's outburst. "Yes. . .well. . .you do have a point, I suppose. You see, if everything works as planned and you succeed. . .it's just that everything will be different. Everything," he whispered fervently. His eyes glowed with an inner fire. He reached for Hanover's arm and clutched it tightly. "There'll be no more GOA repression, no more shortages. Your hopes and dreams will be limited only by your ability and your willingness to work."

Hanover eased his arm free from the professor's grasp and eyed him cynically. "Sounds too good to be true. You're describing utopia, Doc, and it ain't gonna happen in my lifetime, that's for damn sure."

"But it can, Scott. It can."

The zealot-like conviction in Beecker's unblinking gaze did little to assuage Hanover's misgivings. "Are you the one who arranged my escape from Southwestern Regional?" he asked.

Beecker nodded. "Our group planned it."

"Is the warden part of this?" Beecker nodded again.

"Okay," Hanover said cautiously. "What the hell. It looks like I haven't got anything else to lose. I'll go along with your vow of silence."

"Excellent! I knew you were the right choice." Dr. Beecker leaned back in his chair, his face filled with confidence. "We hoped you would agree to join our project."

"Exactly who are 'we'?" Hanover asked.

"A group of people dissatisfied with the political and economic conditions in our country. Some of us have worked for a long time to bring about change, a major change, and we think we've found the way."

"What's that?" Hanover asked.

Beecker smiled. "We want you to return to 1944."

*   *   *

TRUMANVILLE
Mid-Afternoon, March 26, 2044

"Come on. Move it, Prinski. I can't lose him," Kant goaded his driver. He clutched the dashboard with one hand, as if by leaning forward he could hurry them toward the ghetto hamlet.

"I'm going as fast as I can, sir," Prinski said through clenched teeth. He gripped the steering wheel as he guided the electrocar around potholes and crevices in the pavement. The vehicle skirted the edges of one fissure, bouncing the two men so hard they strained against their restraint belts.

"It's not fast enough." Kant glanced over his shoulder and saw the troop transport following close behind. He faced forward again as they rounded a corner and Trumanville came into view. He pointed toward a building on the left. "Stop over there."

The vehicle skidded to a stop in front of the squat building. "Get that informer—what's his name?—Perkins?" Kant told Prinski.

The driver left the car pounded on the door until it opened. Perkins stepped out, his fists raised. He yelled at

Prinski until he saw Kant standing beside the electrocar and the vehicle full of FedPo troops. "Hey, Kant," he said with a smarmy smile as he strode toward the car. "Well, look at you, a major now. The little man's coming up in the world."

Kant bit back the urge to bring Perkins to his knees, to teach him some respect. But that would be a waste of time on a neanderthal like Perkins. Besides, Kant wanted information, and it would come much more quickly from a cooperative witness than from a resentful one.

"Tell me about the people who came through here a couple hours ago," Kant said.

Perkins shrugged. "Lots of people come here. Anyone in particular?"

Kant saw the avaricious glint in Perkins' eyes, and he nodded to Prinski who handed Perkins a thin envelope. "I'm especially interested in a man. Tall. Sandy hair."

Perkins' head jerked up and he glowered at Kant. "If I ever set eyes on that sonnavabitch again, I'll kill him."

So Hanover had been here. Kant stepped forward. "What'd he do?"

"We had this disagreement, see. He got me when my back was turned."

The petty answer annoyed Kant. "What did he do when he left here? Where'd he go?"

"That way, toward Albuquerque." Perkins waved his hand toward the south.

"Anyone with him?"

"Yeah, another guy, calls himself Travis, and his woman."

"When'd they come through here?"

Perkins shrugged again. "Must've been three, maybe four hours ago."

"Move out," Kant called to the troop carrier as he swung into the electrocar. He pointed down a narrow street through the town. "This way. Hurry."

Prinski drove rapidly through the town. Dirty children and scruffy dogs scrambled out of their path. The vehicles stirred the dusty streets, leaving a cloud to settle on the tattered laundry strung between upper level windows. In a few minutes, Kant's company emerged at the other end.

"Look over there, sir." Prinski pointed toward the left. "That old mine site. There's an official GOA electrovan in front of the building."

"That's strange. I wonder what they're doing here. Maybe they heard about the escape." That was all he needed. Help from GOA officials. Or their criticism.

"I shouldn't think so, sir. You did say the commandant wanted it kept quiet."

"That's true. But every organization has its security leaks. And the one we're after isn't a petty thief. Turn in, Prinski. Let's have a look."

Prinski swung wide into the mine compound and parked behind the electrovan. Kant climbed from their vehicle. "You men spread out and stand by. Don't let anyone leave," he ordered the troops.

*   *   *

TRUMANVILLE
Mid-Afternoon, March 26, 2044

Hanover's harsh laugh echoed in the small room. "You want me to do what?" He had expected an unusual mission, but this was ridiculous. The man was crazy!

Beecker smiled haughtily and nodded. "We want you to return to 1944," he repeated.

"If this is some kind of joke, it's not funny, Doc," Hanover said gravely.

"It's no joke, Scott. We're extremely serious. We have the means. Now we need the person, someone with certain qualifications. Quite stringent qualifications, I might add. Which you have. Will you do it?"

Hanover couldn't believe he was having this conversation. The man sitting across from him talked about time travel as calmly as if they were discussing the weather forecast. "This is insane. You can't send me back to 1944. And even if you could, why on earth would you want to?"

"Good question. Let me start with why we chose you."

Hanover rolled his eyes at the man's dogged determination.

"As I mentioned before, the mission we have in mind is quite dangerous. Not that we think you will be killed," Beecker added confidently. "While I suppose that is a remote possibility, we're more concerned that you might be trapped in 1944 and not be able to return to the present. We need someone with no close family ties or attachments."

Beecker took a deep breath and glanced at Hanover. "We need someone we can be reasonably certain would be here despite the Occupation. In other words, someone who would have been born even if the Germans had not won the war. As far as we can determine, you fit that. There is, of course, some degree of uncertainty here. We don't ah. . .want you to ah. . .disappear into limbo, shall we say, if you're successful."

"What do you mean, 'disappear'?" Hanover asked suspiciously.

Dr. Beecker raised his hands and shrugged. "Not disappear, exactly. It's more like you would simply never have existed."

"I what?"

"Don't worry. We've figured that part out."

Hanover wiped his hand across his face. "Yeah. Right."

"Now, as I was saying," Dr. Beecker continued, "we need someone resourceful. Someone who's a survivor. Someone independent who can go it alone."

Hanover rose from his seat and paced the tiny room. Beecker had that right. He was a survivor. He was independent. And he was alone. His future, if he had one, stretched bleakly ahead of him. If the FedPos recaptured him, they wouldn't waste any time before executing him. If he managed to evade the FedPos, what kind of life did he have to look forward to?

Beecker's group wanted him to go to 1944. He had nothing to lose. Nothing except his life, and it wasn't worth much, especially with the S.A.D. primed to detonate any time. What other choice did he have, except to go along with Dr. Beecker's bizarre plan?

"I think I'll have that cup of coffee now," he said with a grim smile.

Dr. Beecker nodded. "I couldn't agree more." He rose from his seat and crossed the room to open the tiny cupboard.

Hanover watched the older man carefully measure the beans into an ancient electric grinder. A high-pitched whirring filled the air, along with the aroma of fresh ground coffee. Hanover breathed deeply, his mouth watering in anticipation. Dr. Beecker filled a dented aluminum pot with water, added coffee to the filter basket, then set it on a burner to perk. The preciseness of his movements seemed almost ritualistic, and Hanover found it had a spellbinding affect as he waited for the ceremony to conclude.

"I apologize for not offering you milk or sugar," Dr. Beecker said flatly as he carried a steaming cup across the room.

"That's fine." Hanover cautiously sipped some of the brew, appreciating its mellow richness before setting the cup on the desk next to him. "All right. You've explained why me. Now explain why?"

"The why is simple. History hinges on small events, one piled on top of another. Change one, you change them all the way up the line. We want you to change one incident that we think will alter the outcome of the war in 1944."

"You want me to what?"

"We want you to stop, by any means necessary, the two German spies who stole the trigger mechanism plans for the atomic bomb from Los Alamos."

Hanover gasped in astonishment. "You want me to stop some spies?"

"Precisely. Fischer and Helmke."

Hanover sank against his chair and tried to remember his history. At the end of the war, the Third Reich had acclaimed Erwin Fischer and Herman Helmke as heros for stealing the trigger mechanism plans. The Germans made their atomic bomb operational before the Americans finished theirs, and won the war. The two spies had been decorated by the Fuhrer himself, and their bronze statues stood in front of the government buildings in Santa Fe.

"Let me explain," Dr. Beecker said in a professorial way.

"Go right ahead," Hanover said with a vague wave of his hand, stunned by Beecker's proposal.

"The history you were taught doesn't coincide with the facts. Most history is propaganda, you know. The actual events have been altered to extol the virtues of the Third Reich and its leaders. Hitler is proclaimed a genius in war and peace, a leader of men and nations. Since his death, he's been elevated to an almost god-like position in Germany. The Third Reich is described as the epitome of a national organization." Beecker's voice had risen steadily, anger coming through with increased vehemence.

"It's all rubbish, you know," he snapped. "None of it's true. Hitler was a paranoid madman. The things done in his name were unspeakable atrocities. The rest of Germany's wartime leadership was as bumbling and stupid as any group you'd name in history. They were strutting, brainless peacocks. It was a case of the inmates running the asylum."

Dr. Beecker slumped back in his chair and took several deep breaths. "We had such promise. We simply gave up too quickly. If we'd known the Nazis only had the two bombs, we could have held firm."

"You mean we could've won the war?" None of his history books had suggested that.

"We *were* winning, Scott. We were winning. Records of the actual events are very difficult to find. So much was destroyed, and the Germans have rewritten all the books. But the fact remains, we were about to win the war."

Hanover let the novel idea sink in as the ramifications swirled around in his mind. It was as Beecker said earlier. If the United States had won, everything would be different. Everything. He wiped his hand across his face, then looked back at Beecker. "Go on."

"We know when Fischer and Helmke arrived in Mexico and when they left Santa Fe. We know what route they followed and we've put together bits and pieces of their itinerary. We can give you photographs to help you identify them. How you stop them is completely up to you."

The words settled heavily on Hanover. He rose from his chair and paced the room, hands jammed in his pockets as he turned the plan over in his mind. Finally, he said, "I'm not an assassin."

Beecker gave him an icy cold stare. "They are dedicated, ruthless men who will stop at nothing to accomplish their mission. You must be just as dedicated. We aren't asking you to commit murder. Any scheme you devise to stop them is fine with us. Just so long as they are stopped. Your advantage is that you know who they are while they have no idea about you."

"What about the FedPos? Will they cooperate?"

Dr. Beecker snorted. "You won't have any problem there. The FedPos are a GOA invention. Law enforcement was much different in those days. I see we must include that in your orientation to 1944."

The door suddenly swung open and Beecker's assistant, Tim Brody charged into the room. "We've got trouble, Dr. Beecker. Two FedPo vehicles just pulled up out front. One of them's filled with troops."

Beecker sprang to his feet. "Quick. Move." He shoved their chairs aside and pushed back a dirty floor mat to reveal a trap door. He triggered the latch then stepped away.

Hanover peered into the dark hole. There were no steps, only the hole that looked to be six or seven feet deep.

Beecker jerked open a cupboard drawer and pulled out an old-fashioned flashlight. "Jump down, then follow the tunnel," he ordered. "It takes you to the mine. About thirty meters past the mine, you'll come to a wooden bridge over a wide pit. Cross the bridge, then find the winch and crank the bridge up. That'll seal off the tunnel. Wait there until we come for you. Now hurry."

Hanover hesitated. He didn't want to climb into a dark hole, didn't want to crawl underground. Dread slithered up his spine, and he took a step back.

"Go, Scott. Now." Beecker shoved Hanover hard enough that he had no choice but to jump down.

Hanover landed heavily, then shivered. He hated the fear that gnawed at him, hated the men who had made him feel this way. "What about access from the mine side?" he called.

"Not a problem," Beecker said. "The roof collapsed years ago, set off a cave-in. You'll be safe. Just go. Hurry."

Beecker and Brody shoved the trap-door into place, engulfing Hanover in total blackness. He quickly snapped the light on and flashed the distressingly dim beam around the unlit tunnel. It stood about two meters high and was slightly wider than his outstretched arms. He wouldn't suffocate from claustrophobia. At least not immediately.

He entered the tunnel and hoped the old supporting timbers would hold. He hurried along the uneven floor, careful not to stumble over any loose rocks. The tunnel sloped gently, then leveled off and gradually veered to the right.

He estimated he'd gone about fifty meters when the tunnel abruptly opened into a large cavern. This must be the mine itself. He crossed the underground chamber and found the suspension bridge. He wanted to flash the light inside the chasm to see how far he could fall, but decided it was better not to know. Holding the railing, he stepped onto the bridge, then took another step.

The board cracked beneath his weight, and he pulled back before he fell through. His heart pounded and he gulped for air as he clung to the railing. He took another step, this time standing to the side of the deck rather than the center, hoping to put less strain on the slats. Ever so slowly, he inched his way across, testing each board before transferring his full weight to it.

Finally he crossed the ten meter span. Safe on the other side, he found the winch stiff but still workable. The grating of metal-against-metal screeched in his ears as he raised the bridge. He hoped he was far enough underground that the sound wouldn't carry. With the bridge up, the chasm served as a moat, protecting him from anyone coming in the same direction he had come.

He took a few minutes to explore the rest of the tunnel, only another twenty-five meters before he reached the cave-in. He returned to the bridge and sat down to wait. His light flickered, and he reluctantly turned it off.

The darkness and the silence were complete. As complete as in the cage. He forced himself to breath normally. To think about other things. Things like stopping the Germans from winning the war.

CHAPTER 7

Kant stood outside the building's main entrance and scrutinized the two men before him. "Names," he snapped.

The older man stepped forward. "I'm Dr. Beecker. Joseph Beecker." He gestured to the man next to him. "This is my assistant, Tim Brody. And you are?"

"Your papers, please."

"And you are?" Beecker returned Kant's steely gaze.

The man's arrogance infuriated Kant. "Major Willie Kant. FedPo. Now give me your papers."

Beecker handed him the passbook. Kant riffled through the pages. "What do you do at Los Alamos?"

"I'm a physicist."

"What are you working on?"

"It's much too complicated to explain to a layman."

Kant's eyes narrowed. Most scientists knew better than to act condescending to a FedPo officer. "Perhaps you'd explain why you're here rather than at Los Alamos."

"I have authorization to use these facilities for my experiments."

Beecker's purposeful lack of elaboration stimulated Kant's curiosity even more. "What kind of experiments?"

"I'm measuring differences in the radiation penetration of rock."

Kant had no idea what Beecker was talking about. "My report will note your activities here."

He paused to see if his words had any effect; Beecker's ingenious expression disappointed him. "I'm pursuing an escaped convict. He's dangerous, possibly armed. We know he's killed at least one man. He came through Trumanville. Have you seen any strangers?"

Beecker furrowed his brow and looked at his assistant. "Did anyone come by here this morning?"

"Withholding information is punishable by imprisonment," Kant added.

"I'm aware of the penalties." Beecker stared at Kant, as if weighing in his mind what to reveal.

"A man did stop for water," Brody said to Beecker.

"That's right." Beecker sounded as if he had just remembered. "It was when we were unloading the—"

"Where is he?" Kant demanded.

Beecker shrugged. "We gave him water and he left. I have no idea what happened to him, Major. I was too busy with my equipment to pay much attention. Do you remember anything, Tim?"

"Not really. I—"

"What about the two with him?" Beecker's eyes widened almost imperceptibly, then returned to their shuttered position. Yes, Kant thought, the scientist did know more. "Well?"

Beecker's mouth tightened to a grim line before answering. "That would be a student of mine, Joel Travis, and his friend, Alicia Juarez," he said, his voice resigned. "They met a stranger on the road. It's a good thing they did because he helped them when hoodlums attacked them on the other side of town. You people should spend your time cleaning up trash like that instead of harassing other government workers," he said, his voice rising.

"Right." Kant found Beecker's attempt to put him on the defensive amusing. "I want to talk to them."

"Bring Joel here," Beecker said to Brody. "Tell him—"

"You don't need to tell him anything. Go with him, Prinski." Kant watched the two men enter the building. He waited silently, observing Beecker for any sign of nervousness. But there was none. That surprised Kant. Even people who had nothing to feel guilty about usually displayed some anxiety over being questioned by FedPos.

Brody returned with a man and a woman. Kant caught the haunted look in the woman's eyes.

"Ah, Joel, the major—"

"I can speak for myself, Dr. Beecker." Kant turned to Joel. "What do you know about the man you met last night in Neustadt?"

Silently, Joel eyed Kant. "Nothing," he said at last.

"Nothing? What do you mean, nothing? You helped him escape a FedPo patrol last night, brought him here, and you know nothing?"

Joel shrugged. "These days, you don't ask questions."

"So you didn't know he was a dangerous escaped criminal?"

"Really? I'm surprised. He seemed quite normal."

"What happened after you came here?"

"We shared something to drink, and then said goodbye."

"Did he say where he was going?"

"I think he mentioned something about Albuquerque."

"Albuquerque." Kant looked from Joel to Beecker. Damnedest bunch he'd ever seen. Not a sideways glance between them. They were either two of the best liars he'd come across. . .or they were telling the truth. "Where in Albuquerque?"

Joel shrugged again. "He didn't say."

"I know, and these days you don't ask questions." Sarcasm flowed through Kant's words.

He glanced at Alicia. Her stony expression told him she would say nothing to contradict the scientist or the young man. It didn't matter. "Take them in," Kant ordered.

After the couple was cuffed and hauled into the back of the carrier, Kant turned on his heel and stalked toward his vehicle, waving for his men to reassemble in theirs.

With Prinski driving the lead car, they swung out of the compound and roared down the road toward Albuquerque.

*   *   *

—this isn't the cage. This isn't the cage. I can leave when I want—

Hanover leaped to his feet at the sound of voices, voices that overrode the chant he'd repeated in his mind until he thought he'd go crazy.

"Scott? Are you there?" Dr. Beecker's words echoed in the cavernous mine.

Hanover couldn't stifle his irritation. "Of course I'm here. Where'd you think I'd go?"

"It's safe to come out now."

"It's about time." Hanover winced at the grating shriek of the bridge as he lowered it across the chasm.

"You're right, we haven't much time." Beecker said distractedly. He turned and strode into the tunnel. "Quickly, now. We have much to do."

Hanover hurried after him. Brody hoisted them through the trap door and they wordlessly left the building.

"Are you going to tell me what happened?" Hanover asked as they stepped outside.

"FedPo troopers looking for you. Charles, don't forget the boxes in the store room," Beecker called to a man walking by juggling a collection of glass and metal tubes.

"Right, Dr. Beecker." The man didn't break his stride.

Hanover looked around. People scurried from the building, loading boxes and equipment into trucks, then returned empty-handed to the building. "What's going on?"

Dr. Beecker glanced at him, his mouth set in a grim line. "I think the old military term is bugging-out."

"What?"

"We're bugging-out. Leaving. Retreating from the enemy. But taking everything with us, of course."

"Of course," Hanover repeated. "Can I help?"

"No, not now." Beecker drew Hanover aside. "They arrested Travis and Alicia. I don't know how long it will take for them to break, so we have to get you away from here. We're going to another site where I'll brief you on your. . .ah. . .journey."

Hanover grabbed the man's arm. "You mean I'm not leaving from here?" He couldn't hide his confusion. "Why not?"

"Well, for the simple reason that the timegate isn't here."

"Where the hell is it then?"

"It's in. . .No. If you don't know, you can't reveal it. Just in case they do catch up with us. It's safer that way."

"But what if something happens to you? What am I supposed to do then?"

Beecker sighed. "I suppose you're right. It's just that—"

"We're ready, Dr. Beecker," Tim said.

"Good. We can't leave anything behind. Come with me, Scott."

Shaking his head, Hanover followed. This whole thing was surreal. It seemed incredible that he'd been helped to escape from prison, that he'd been chosen to travel back in time to another era.

Once again he found himself wondering why. Why him? Why had he been the one chosen? And what if he was wrong?. . .What if this was all just the ramblings of some crazy scientist. . ..

But suppose it wasn't? Just suppose their plan worked? He wondered about conditions in 1944 without the Occupation. The GOA version of history painted a bleak picture of prewar America, one of poverty, despair, and lawlessness. Beecker claimed that version was a lie. Hanover wanted to believe the more optimistic view; otherwise, all the risks were pointless.

He still worried about the "we" Beecker referred to. Were they a few friends, a group of scientists working together?

Or was it part of something much larger, perhaps a part of the "Association," that nebulous entity rumored about for years. No physical evidence of sabotage had ever been attributed to it, nor had Hanover ever met anyone claiming membership. Even in prison only the vaguest of references were made about it. He'd always had doubts that the Association even existed, but now. . ..

Whatever was behind this insanity, Hanover had no doubt that Beecker's schemes would cause the GOA considerable aggravation. He had no choice but to follow along.

*   *   *

Tugging his coat tighter around his neck, Kant slumped in the passenger seat. Prinski had parked after rounding the bend in the road, just out of sight from Beecker and his people. Now they waited.

Daylight faded to a sapphire blue, not yet dark enough for stars. The clouds blowing in held the taste of a late season snow fall. That was all he needed. How Hanover could travel so quickly without interception annoyed the hell out of Kant. What kind of incompetents managed these rural sectors?

His report to the commandant would be filled with suggestions for improvement. He probably should tread softly, not appear too critical of those above him. Hell, he didn't even care if the commandant took credit for the ideas—as long as the proper credit was given to Kant for the capture of escaped prisoner, Scott Hanover, and the identification of a radical subversive group.

Kant rested his elbow on the windowless door. Other FedPo officers would treat him with greater respect after this. No one else could claim an achievement this successful, not since '25 at least, when that survivalist group was finally routed out of their encampment in the Northwest. But that had been a fluke, an accidental discovery; no one could have imagined a group holding out for eighty years after the war's end.

No, what he was doing was even more important because he knew what he was after; stalking his quarry, not tripping over it.

He glanced at his watch; they'd wait a few more minutes. How stupid did the scientist think he was? Hanover couldn't possible be headed for Albuquerque. A GOA pass was required for travel between cities; checkpoints tracked everyone who entered and left. Escaped prisoners did not have passes. Nor would Hanover have food coupons. He wasn't going to Albuquerque; he wasn't going anywhere. He was hiding at the mine. He had to be. Those people would pay, Kant thought. They'd pay for trying to make a fool out of him.

A vehicle drove past, then another, headed toward the main highway. Squinting, Kant looked over his shoulder. He was betting Hanover wasn't in one of those trucks. He couldn't afford any mistakes. Lieutenant Colonel Heinz hovered like a specter in Kant's mind, waiting to pounce on his errors, poised to snatch his rewards.

"That's long enough. Let's go."

Prinski signalled to the carrier, and they headed down the road with their lights off. As they reached the compound, snow drifted across the lights perched high on the mine's outbuildings.

Kant didn't see any sentries. Only one vehicle remained, the GOA electrovan. Kant clenched his fist. He could taste victory.

"Pull over here." He pointed to a spot that would block the electrovan.

Kant climbed from the vehicle and watched troops tumble from the open-air carrier and stomp the ground to warm up. "We're taking the compound by surprise. No shooting, no injuries. Move out."

He led the soldiers to the compound. They slipped silently into the yard. How stupid not to post guards, Kant thought. This was almost too easy. . .too easy if he'd guessed right and Hanover was still here. He crept to one of the windows, took a quick look, then drew back, rewarded by what he'd seen. Wordlessly he directed most of the troops to surround the building; two others and Prinski he kept with him.

He watched the soldiers disperse, then led his small band to the door. On his signal, the two soldiers kicked the door with explosive force. They rushed through the opening, paralyzing the occupants with the threat of readied laser guns.

Kant entered behind them and stood for a moment with his thumbs hooked in his belt and his feet spread. This was a coup of major proportions. Major proportions. The pun pleased him.

"You are all under arrest," he announced to the half dozen occupants of the room. He signaled for the two soldiers to search the rest of the building.

As he waved his laser gun around the cavernous room, Kant recognized three people: the scientist, his assistant and, standing apart from the others, Hanover. Scott Hanover.

The others faded from Kant's sight as he stared at his nemesis. A red film hazed his vision. Blood roared in his ears as years of suppressed hatred surged to the surface. The man who had caused so much trouble would trouble Kant no more. Hanover was no longer Kant's nemesis. He was Kant's ticket to recognition and further promotion.

Kant smiled.

Hanover didn't see anything friendly or amused in that smile. He watched, tense, while out of the corner of his eye he sought an escape route. But there was none. Troopers blocked all the exits. Who could have guessed this officer would figure out he'd been tricked and would return this quickly?

Of course the officer's attention focused directly on Hanover. After all, his picture was probably plastered on every government screen. But there was something in this officer's eyes that was different. This wasn't detached interest, this was personal. Very personal. Hanover motioned for Beecker and Tim to stay where they were.

The officer approached and stopped in front of Hanover. Without warning, he kicked Hanover's leg; when Hanover bent over, the officer clipped his jaw, smashing Hanover's head against the wall.

What the hell? Hanover reeled from the unwarranted assault. He shook his head to clear it, then looked at the officer, careful to mask his rage, to tamp down the urge to retaliate. Any move meant instant execution.

"You're not so big now, are you?" the officer said in a low voice that only Hanover could hear.

"I don't under—"

"Who's the clever one, now, Hanover? Who's going to protect you now?" The words were almost a hiss.

The barrage made no sense. Had this officer lost his mind?

"No more being second best to you, Hanover. Do you hear me? No more." The officer back-handed Hanover across the face.

"Who the hell are you?" Hanover gasped. He patted his mouth and felt the sticky moisture.

"Who am I? Who am I?" The question enraged the officer. He drove his fist into Hanover's stomach, then kicked his other leg. "I'm Major Willie Kant."

Hanover wanted to lash out, wanted to retaliate, but didn't want to die that bad. Yet. The major pummeled him again. Hanover struggled to remain conscious. Willie Kant. . .Willie Kant. . .Who was he? "What did I ever do to you?"

"You don't remember me?" Kant hissed. "You don't— you will once I'm done with you, after I've skinned you alive, strip by strip until you ooze from every pore, until you scream for mercy."

Through a wave of pain, Hanover looked at him in confusion. What had he ever done to warrant this viciousness? Why did this officer hate him?

Kant stepped back and looked around the room, as if surprised to see the others still there and staring at him with wide-eyed disbelief. If they knew what was best for them, they'd keep their mouths shut about what they'd seen.

"We'll take these two in the personnel carrier to FedPo headquarters in Santa Fe," he said to Prinski, pointing at Hanover and Beecker. "Have the soldiers take these others in the electrovan and our car to Albuquerque."

Soldiers poured into the room from outside, and several swept through the building to round up anyone remaining. All except Beecker and Hanover were hustled into the GOA van and Kant's car, and driven away. Kant stayed with Prinski and two soldiers to escort the remaining two prisoners.

Beecker stumbled and Hanover caught his arm as the soldiers shoved them into the back of the personnel carrier. At Kant's direction, a soldier attached wrist cuffs first to Beecker, then to Hanover, and ran a light chain along the upright stanchion between the roll bars. The soldiers huddled next to the bulkhead, out of the wind and driving snow, while Kant and Prinski hopped into the cab.

Unprotected from the elements, the icy wet cold quickly penetrated Hanover's clothing, adding to his misery. He was glad Beecker had surreptitiously grabbed a coat, but he could see the older man was having trouble balancing in the moving vehicle.

The road climbed out of the valley as the snow swirled and fell harder. Hanover tried to protect his face by tucking his head, but his upright arms hampered his efforts. He moved his fingers, flexed his knees, kept moving despite the pain from his abused body.

He couldn't believe he was still alive; surprised that Kant hadn't ordered him shot on the spot and been done with it. He couldn't imagine what he'd done to provoke the major. He burned with fury. If he weren't chained to this truck, if he had another chance, he'd fight back.

Snow settled on the truck bed. Beecker slipped on it, and Hanover winced when he saw the older man's arms wrenched when his shackles broke his fall.

God, he hoped they didn't have far to go. If this major was serious about reaching Santa Fe tonight, he'd have two frozen prisoners. But given what the major indicated he wanted to do with Hanover, perhaps freezing to death was the best option. At the rate they were going, it wouldn't be long.

Beecker sagged against his restraints, and Hanover knew the old man wouldn't last much longer. He glanced at the two soldiers huddled against the cab, now snow-covered mounds with the collars of their full-length coats pulled high and their fur hats tugged low. They didn't move; only the thin misty vapor of their breath revealed they were even alive.

Hanover fought to stay alert, but the piercing cold permeated his body and his mind. He didn't want to die. Not this way. Yet, was wasting away in prison any better? Or being destroyed by the S.A.D.?

Or going through a timegate and fading to nothingness because he didn't exist any more?

The thoughts were too much for him. Shifting, he maneuvered himself around the stanchion and let the steel support some of his weight.

He sank into oblivion, only to snap awake as the carrier turned sharply, too sharply, and slid. The driver jerked the steering wheel from side to side, trying to regain control. Fool, Hanover thought, turn into the slide. The carrier stopped sliding. It slowed for a moment, then speeded up again.

Beecker slumped limply, his full weight hanging on his wrists. Hanover nudged the scientist with his foot. When Beecker did not respond, Hanover grimaced, then kicked him. The man raised his head.

"Wrap your leg around the pole," Hanover said barely loud enough for Beecker to hear him. He wished he had a free hand to support Beecker, but he didn't. "If we crash, hold onto the roll bar." The old man nodded and shuffled into a different position.

The truck slid again. It tipped right, and Hanover saw the ditch rise up to meet them, its deepness deceptively softened by the fallen snow. The driver corrected, and the truck lurched left to the road. Hanover saw the embankment loom next to them. He didn't like that option any better, and held his breath until the truck straightened.

The sound of raised voices filtered from the cab. The two soldiers lifted their heads and reached out to hold a bar for support.

The snow obscured the road, concealed the separation between shoulder and ditch. The carrier moved too far to the right; the right front wheel slipped off the shoulder. Hanover held his breath, willing the vehicle back onto the road, but it teetered on the edge of the ditch, then slowly toppled and rolled down the embankment.

Hanover clung to the stanchion with his legs and hoped Beecker was doing the same. The truck tumbled over. He followed it, sliding back and forth along the pole. His wrists twisted against their restraints and he cried out in pain. One soldier was thrown from the truck and fell in its path; the other flew through the air and landed on an outcrop of rocks. The truck stopped at the bottom of the hill. The cab was crushed against a huge boulder, caving in the roof, coming within inches of crushing Hanover and Beecker's hands and wrists.

Hanging upside down, Hanover slowly released his legs and swung himself around. He didn't think he'd broken anything, but his wrists bled profusely. He rubbed some snow against the wounds, figuring he couldn't be much colder. Then he touched Beecker; the man was breathing, but unconscious. Hanover tugged at his handcuffs. Still secure.

He sat back on his haunches and listened for a minute. Only the sound of the wind pelting him with icy snow broke the total silence.

What the hell was he supposed to do now?

CHAPTER 8

Beecker moaned softly.

"Dr. Beecker, are you okay?" Hanover scrambled to the older man's side and shook him gently. "Come on, doc. We've got to get the hell out of here."

Beecker rewarded him with another groan and fluttering eyelids. The old man struggled to sit up, then looked around. "Where are we?"

Hanover shook his head. "I'm not sure. Near as I can tell, we're close to the Santa Fe-Albuquerque highway."

"Good." Beecker flexed his arms and legs. "Doesn't look like I broke anything."

"We have to get out of here before we freeze to death."

Beecker held up his chained wrists. "Any ideas?"

Hanover examined the chain holding the wrist iron to the overhead rail. It was made of heavy gauge wire links. He pulled the chain taut against the steel pole, braced his feet firmly against the stanchion, and twisted, trying to stretch a link open enough to break the chain.

But it only lacerated his already chafed and bloodied wrists.

He looked around and spotted the guard lying lifeless near the truck. He slid the chain along the roll bar, then nudged the guard with his foot. No response.

Hanover grasped the guard's leg with his own legs and tugged. He tried to block out the pain in his chest and his gut as he tightened his muscles; he held his breath to keep from groaning in agony. When stars danced and a black haze settled before his eyes, the body finally moved.

Clinging to consciousness, Hanover pulled the guard closer, sliding him across the snow. Beecker reached out with his leg to help, until at last they had the guard between them.

"Now what?"

"We search him."

"But our hands are cuffed."

Hanover smiled grimly. "We keep moving him around until we've checked all his pockets. I hope to hell he has the keys to these things."

They searched the guard's pockets, a laborious task with cuffed and frozen hands. Euphoria surged through Hanover when he grasped a key ring, only to be frustrated when none of the keys fit.

"There has to be something we can use. There has to be," he muttered. The wind picked up. The driving snow stabbed his face like a thousand small lances. He shielded his eyes as best he could and continued his search.

His hands closed around a stubby knife tucked in the soldier's boot. Carefully, he withdrew it and placed the sharp edge of the short thick blade into the gap. He stomped on it with his foot. Gradually the gap widened until it was spread the full thickness of the blade. He applied the same technique to the adjacent link, again widening the gap as far as possible. He turned the two links until the gaps matched, and slipped them apart. He was free.

"Excellent, Scott!"

Hanover made quick work of freeing Beecker from the chains. "Yeah, but we've still got to get rid of these wrist cuffs. I'll check the cab and see if the key's in there."

The snow had slackened and was now mixed with rain. Hanover shivered, cold seeping into his bones. He pulled off the dead soldier's coat and tossed it to Beecker. "Put this on."

He quickly checked the other soldier, confirming that he, too, was dead. Hanover tugged the heavy coat from the body and ignored the stain of frozen blood as he slipped it on. At least it cut the wind.

Slipping in the snow, he made his way to the front of the truck, lying upside down with the roof caved in by a boulder. He approached cautiously, listening for any sounds from Major Kant or the driver. But he heard nothing. He eased toward the window and looked in.

The two men hung upside down, restrained by their safety belts. The driver was jammed between the cab top and the steering wheel. Blood dripped from his nose and mouth. Nothing could be done for him. On the passenger side, the major hung free, upside down.

Hanover smashed the window next to the major with a rock and reached in to search the major's pockets for the keys. Kant's eyes were closed, fresh blood glistened on his scalp. His coat was bunched around his nose and mouth.

Hanover couldn't tell if he was breathing. He remembered Kant's vitriolic outburst at the mine. God only knew what had inspired such hatred; he sure as hell didn't.

He reached out to see if Kant was still alive. Then Hanover saw the blinking light on the dashboard, the beacon that signaled an accident. Panic returned. Frantically, he searched Kant's pockets until, finally, he found the keys. He returned to Beecker, and in moments they were both free of the cuffs.

Hanover helped Beecker rise painfully to his feet. "Come on. We have to get out of here. A patrol could show up at any time."

"What about the two inside?" Beecker asked.

"The driver's dead. From the way the major's hanging, his neck must be broken. Come on. We have to get out of here before anyone comes."

Hanover helped the older man scale the incline to the road above.

Looking back over his shoulder, Beecker said, "I wish there was something we could do."

"Look, Doc, if I'm successful with this timegate thing, all this will be academic, won't it? I mean, everything will be different."

Beecker looked at Hanover. "You're right, Scott. *If* you're successful."

"Let's think positive." He felt anything but. Hands on his hips, he stood in the middle of the road and looked in both directions. The snow-covered road rose and fell with the terrain. "Any suggestions?"

"There's a town down the road a bit. I know someone there who might help." Beecker turned to Hanover. "We can hide out tonight. Tomorrow I'll brief you on your mission and send you off."

The finality of Beecker's words slammed into Hanover. "As simple as that?"

"As simple as that."

Hanover raised an eyebrow. Nothing was ever easy once you scratched the surface. Why would anyone pretend it could be?

Gripping Beecker's arm, Hanover supported him as they walked through the slush. The rain turned to drizzle and the wind died down, making the cold less penetrating. Hanover figured he couldn't be more miserable than he was now with sodden clothes. At least the cold had numbed his bruised body.

He hoped Beecker had a plan, a real plan, for this scheme of his. So far, his "escape" from prison was the only thing that had worked as arranged. It struck him that it had been thirty-six hours since his escape. That was all. He drew a deep breath. He hoped to God he wouldn't be attacked, ambushed or arrested in the next thirty-six. Was that too much to ask?

*   *   *

Willie Kant opened his eyes. A shattering headache was his first sensation. Blinding pain. Nausea when he tried to move. He shut his eyes again and didn't move, barely breathing because even that hurt too much.

He waited a moment, trying to get his bearings. He opened his eyes enough to see his legs and feet hanging above him. That was crazy; he must be more disoriented than he'd thought. He touched his face, found the bump on the left side of his forehead, the trickle of blood that had dried and matted his hair.

Another wave of pain washed over him. So much for trying to think. It hurt too much to will the pain away, too much to even pretend it didn't hurt. But the only thing he could think was: Hanover. Where was Hanover?

It was then that Kant saw Prinski. He felt a slight pang of regret. The driver had served him well. But he didn't have time to mourn the loss. He had to find out if Hanover survived the crash.

Kant released his security belt and crawled through the open window. Broken glass lacerated his hands, leaving a trail of fresh blood in the melting snow. He grabbed a pair of gloves from the cab and pulled them on. Pain and nausea overcame him and he sat back, breathing rhythmically, deeply, until the waves subsided.

Slowly he made his way around to the back of the troop carrier. The rain had stopped, the clouds passed, leaving a sky lit with moonlight. The first thing that registered was the coatless body of a soldier; next was the empty wrist cuffs lying in the snow.

"Son of a bitch!" Pain seared through his head. He clung to the stanchion and forced himself to breath again.

Hanover escaped. Hanover escaped. The words throbbed to the beat of the pounding in his head. He saw the links pried open, the wrist cuffs next to the key ring. His key ring. It didn't take a genius to figure out what had happened.

He looked around and saw the other soldier's body, crushed and covered with blood, part way up the embankment. Kant alone had survived. Except for Hanover and the scientist. Kant returned to the cab and saw the beacon. Depending on the weather, and whether the signal was picked up from this location, help could arrive tonight—or three days from now. He couldn't count on being found.

After a brief search, Kant spotted his portaphone lying on an outcrop of rocks. Smashed. Useless. He threw it across the remaining snow, then winced at the hammering that coursed through his head.

He made his way slowly up the embankment. Rain had melted much of the snow, making it easier to reach the road. But the rain had also obliterated any sign of Hanover's route.

Earlier visions of praise and recognition from the commandant and other GOA officials faded, replaced by the scorn and criticism he would receive for losing two prisoners, three soldiers, and an expensive vehicle. The image of a future like Heinz's loomed before him and brought a shiver of revulsion, along with bitterness that Hanover had bested him again.

Kant remembered passing a small town a few kilometers back. He'd go there and organize a search party; Hanover and the scientist were his immediate concern. Then he'd send someone to pick up the bodies.

Kant realized that once he reached the town, Hanover's escape would no longer be a secret between him and the commandant. Every vulture in the FedPo's and GOA would descend to garner their share. Frustration brought on a fresh assault of pain. Kant staggered a few steps, waiting for it to subside.

It couldn't be helped. He'd lost control of the mission the minute Prinski wrecked the carrier. Now all he could hope was that he recovered his prisoners—and his reputation. Quickly.

At least the other people at the mine, including that Travis fellow and the girl, had been taken to Albuquerque. If he didn't find Hanover in the next twelve hours, he'd interrogate them. He found it curious that Hanover was with a scientist.

Kant wasn't familiar with Beecker's work, but he knew those at Los Alamos were considered brilliant in their field. What would a scientist like Beecker have in common with a criminal like Hanover? Such an odd alliance.

He reached the outskirts of town about midnight, and easily found the FedPo station. The door was unlocked. Stepping inside, Kant felt the welcoming gust of warmth.

The outer waiting area was sparse, rustic, with bare wood walls, simple wood chairs, a bench with faded cushions. The counter was scarred, the varnish worn to the point that splinters were a hazard. Kant raised an eyebrow at the room; hardly FedPo standards. Perhaps that was why the locals were so out of control and traveled without hindrance. Another comment for his final report; at least he'd have something worthwhile in it.

"Anybody here?" He heard the scrape of a chair from the other room, as if someone had been sleeping with his feet up on the desk.

His impression was confirmed by the sergeant-in-charge's appearance. Coatless, sparse hair rumpled, the man didn't even hide the broad yawn. The lack of discipline brought Kant's headache pounding back.

"What do you want?" the man asked churlishly.

"I'm Major Willie Kant, Santa Fe. We were transporting two prisoners when our vehicle overturned. They may have come this way. Seal off the town and organize a search party."

The sergeant looked less than thrilled at the orders. "I'll need some more information before I can do that, sir. Name of the escaped prisoners?"

Kant pounded his fist on the counter. "Don't give me your backwoods stall tactics. I can bust your ass to sentry duty in Nome. Now get that perimeter guard up. I don't want anything getting in or out of this town, not even a mouse, without one of your people giving it clearance. You got that?"

The sergeant nodded, his eyes wide with fear. "Certainly, sir. I'll get right on it."

Kant listened as the sergeant contacted his men. Only a secondary highway passed through the area. The other few streets dead-ended into the desert. At this early hour there was little traffic, and Kant felt certain his quarry was hiding nearby. Where else could they go with no food, water, or passes?

Once the perimeter was secure, he'd order a house-to-house search. If that produced nothing, he'd have no recourse but request helicopters for a wider search. He hoped it wouldn't come to that. Explaining the need for helicopters would be embarrassing. His stellar career in the FedPos dimmed before his eyes. He'd be another Heinz.

Not if he could help it, he vowed. Not if it took his last breath to recapture Hanover.

The sergeant stepped from his office. "My troops are moving into position, sir."

"Good. How many are there?"

"Ten are stationed here."

Kant stifled a groan. He needed ten times that number to search the area. "Have there been any reports of vagrants entering town on foot?"

"No, sir. Roving patrols have been making their usual rounds. Per regulations," the sergeant added smugly.

Kant saw the challenge in the sergeant's eyes, but wasn't interested in pennyante games with a hick who wasn't going anywhere. "Notify me immediately of any incoming reports. I need to use your phone."

The sergeant escorted Kant into the office. Kant was dismayed to see the antique phone. "Don't you have a videophone?"

The sergeant shrugged. "Don't have much need for it."

"I suppose you don't have automatic conferencing capabilities, either."

"Sorry, sir." The sergeant's tone indicated he didn't regret the lack in the least. "Will you be charging the calls to your account, sir?"

Glaring at him, Kant picked up the phone and waited until the sergeant got the hint and left the room.

Kant quickly contacted the watch commander in Albuquerque. "This is Major Kant. I'm pursuing a prisoner who escaped from Southwestern Regional Prison, Scott Hanover, thirty-one, tall, medium build, sandy blond hair and light blue eyes. He's with an accomplice, Joseph Beecker, sixtyish, tall, very thin, fringe of white hair. Works at Los Alamos. Look for chafing on their wrists. They may be heading toward Albuquerque. I want road blocks set up to intercept them. Call me at this number immediately if your men see anything suspicious."

Kant hung up before the watch commander could ask any embarrassing questions, such as when did the escape occur. He repeated the call to the Santa Fe watch commander. When he finished, he acknowledged that his head was still pounding.

He stepped into the waiting room and pointed at the sergeant. "Get me a medic. I need something for this headache."

*   *   *

Beecker led the way up a dark side street. They'd circumvented the main thoroughfare to avoid roving patrols and clung to the shadows until they reached a small house set well back from the road. Tall shrubs covered their approach to the front porch.

Hanover kept watch while Beecker knocked softly on the door. "Get down," he hissed. The two men flattened themselves between the house and a bush as two soldiers strode down the street.

"They look pretty casual. I don't think they know about us yet," Hanover said.

"I hope you're right." Beecker knocked again, louder this time.

Hanover saw a light come on from deep inside the house, then the curtain parted, only to be dropped into place. He heard the fumbling of the latch, and the door was opened enough for him to see a man's eye staring at them over a chain guard.

"Who's there?" the man whispered.

"It's me, Darcy. Joseph Beecker."

The door opened a fraction wider. "What the hell are you doing here at this hour?" the man asked louder.

"Shut up and let us in, Darcy."

The door closed. Hanover heard the chain slide from its track and clank against wood, then the door opened again.

They brushed through and closed the door behind them. Hanover glanced at Dr. Beecker; he looked to have aged ten years in the last few hours, but it seemed he felt safe in this house. His friend, Darcy, stood in the dim light, a nondescript, balding middle-aged man enveloped in a garish paisley bathrobe. Not the kind of person Hanover would associate with Beecker. But then, who would have linked a person like himself with the doc?

Darcy's eyes widened when he saw the blood covering Hanover's coat. "Who's he?"

"A friend of mine," was all Beecker offered.

Hanover glanced around. The place smelled musty. Must be one hundred years old. He gravitated toward the residual warmth radiating from the stove in the corner of the tiny living room.

"Who's out there, Darcy?" a woman's querulous voice called from the back of the house.

"Nobody you know, dear. It's business. Don't fret."

"I'm not fretting." She sounded irritated. "This is a helluva time to talk about work. What do they want?"

"Shut up, dear. Go back to sleep."

Despite Darcy's no-argument tone, Hanover heard further mumbling. Silence, finally, and he released the breath he hadn't realized he was holding.

"What do you want?"

"We need something to eat," Beecker said. "A place to sleep, too."

Darcy shrugged. "I guess you can sleep in here."

"I don't think that's a good idea, Doc," Hanover said. "We need to keep moving. The FedPos could find Kant at any time."

"Who's Kant?" Darcy's eyes darted between the two men.

"He's, ah, he's—" Beecker hedged.

"He's a FedPo major," Hanover said flatly. "He was taking us to Santa Fe when we had an accident."

"What!" Darcy shrieked.

"Quiet," Beecker ordered.

"Are you out of your minds?" Darcy asked in a hushed, but no less intense voice. He moved toward the front door. "You can't stay here."

Hanover rushed to the door and blocked Darcy. "We'll leave when we're ready, and with your help."

Darcy's shoulders slumped and he sagged into a nearby chair.

Lips pursed, Beecker watched Darcy, then turned to Hanover. "What do you think will happen when they figure out we're missing?"

"From what I've seen in the past with FedPos, they'll blockade the entrances to town immediately, and start a house-to-house search at dawn. In a small town like this, that won't take long. Then, depending on who's put in charge, they'll notify Albuquerque and Santa Fe to set up roadblocks. If they're real frustrated, they'll call in helicopters to search the surrounding area."

Beecker slid into a chair opposite Darcy. "I'm getting too old for this." He shook his head.

"You have a plan, Doc?"

"I'm working on it." Beecker sat with his feet on the table and his eyes shut. "Darcy, fix us something to eat."

Darcy nodded and left the room without argument.

"What's he to you that you can order him around like that?" Hanover asked.

"Darcy was my lab assistant. I caught him stealing. He'd become quite proficient at it, too, I must say. Had a steady clientele for black-market equipment. I should have turned him in, but I let him resign. I keep the evidence in a safe place, in case I ever need it." Beecker opened his eyes and grinned. "Like now, for instance."

"I never pictured you as a blackmailer."

"These times call for us to extend the boundaries of what we consider acceptable."

"The end justifies the means?"

Beecker shrugged. "I guess you could say that."

That was the only way to describe it, Hanover thought. Changing the course of history to end GOA oppression sounded pretty drastic. Yet, here he was, caught up in this conspiracy that could have all kinds of unforeseen consequences.

But it was too late to change his mind. The FedPos were after him, and Hanover still had the S.A.D. implanted in his head.

Darcy returned, carrying a tray with two steaming bowls of bean stew and sliced bread slathered with a white spread. Hanover and Beecker took the offered bowls and ate quickly.

"Darcy, do you have a vehicle?" Beecker asked between mouthfuls.

"Yes. But it's an old electrocar, one of the early models." Darcy said the words reluctantly.

"That'll do. What about your internal passport? Is it current?"

"Yes. I renewed it last month." Again reticence.

Beecker scooted forward in his chair. "All right. Here's what we'll do. My friend and I will leave now. It's still dark, so we should be able to avoid the patrols. We'll go into the foothills outside of town and wait."

Darcy nodded. "You need to get away from here as soon as possible."

Beecker eyed the man coldly. "I'm not finished. At noon, you leave here and drive toward Albuquerque. Watch for us on the road and pick us up."

Darcy opened his mouth in protest, then snapped it shut again.

"Don't even think about not showing up," Beecker said. "It's not too late for certain information to show up on an administrator's desk at Los Alamos."

"I'll be there, okay? Just leave. Please. Before anyone comes."

Hanover and Beecker took the small bags of food Darcy had prepared for them and slipped outside. They waited a moment for their eyes to adjust, then moved out. The darkness was a curse as well as a blessing, hampering their progress while covering their movements.

They kept to the shadows to avoid being spotted by a nosey insomniac. Near the edge of town, Hanover stopped and held up his hand.

"What is it?" Beecker whispered.

"Listen."

For a moment, nothing but silence. Then they heard it. Tires crunching gravel. A roving patrol van moved stealthily around the corner, lights off.

Hanover pulled Beecker down behind a hedge. "Turn your face away and don't move."

They lay still as the electrovan approached. A light snapped on, a spotlight perched on the van's roof. The beam grazed the other side of the road, then flashed to their side.

Hanover held his breath as the light swept closer.

CHAPTER 9

Hanover peered through the branches. Two troopers leaped from the van and charged a nearby clump of bushes. There was a high pitched squeal, and the troopers hauled a couple from the shrubbery. Teenagers. The boy struggled with his pants, the girl clutched her blouse. The soldiers hustled the two adolescents into the van and drove off. Hanover swallowed the laugh of relief that welled up inside him.

Beecker eased forward to stand up, but Hanover jerked him back. "Wait," he whispered. "We have to be sure no one's watching from the house."

They hunkered down for another five minutes, then made their break across the last two blocks of town into the safety of the desert. No conversation passed between them as they struggled through the brush and rock-strewn terrain in the moonlit dark. Except for the sound of their own footsteps and an owl hooting, the night was silent.

After half an hour, Beecker slumped to the ground. "I'm not as young as I once was. And today has been an unmitigated disaster." He buried his head in his arms.

Hanover sank down to catch his breath. "It's not your fault." Their arduous climb had taken them well into the foothills. He leaned on his elbow and gazed at the darkened town below. Then he saw the flashing lights at the outskirts of town. "They've missed us. The roadblocks are up."

Beecker struggled to a sitting position. "We should move on." With a sigh, he rolled to his knees.

Hanover helped him stand and scanned the area in the moonlight. Low scrub brush and an occasional piñon pine broke the jagged rock terrain. "I see an overhang we can hide under," Hanover said. He didn't want to mention that the FedPos had helicopters to sweep the area with infra-red detectors.

They traversed the brush-covered hillside until they reached a large granite outcropping. Hanover used the knife he'd taken from the dead soldier to cut and stack branches from nearby bushes to camouflage the hiding place. Hanover eyed their primitive camp and shook his head.

He didn't really think this would fool the FedPos. They could scour the countryside at any time with thermo-sensitive detectors. But at least it bought him and the doc the illusion of safety. Beecker was near total collapse; they both needed rest before continuing their journey.

Hanover stretched out next to Beecker on the damp ground and gazed at the inky, star-filled sky. The wind whistled through the brush, sweeping around the hillside, swooping under the rocks to shake the branches that formed their perimeter. The flimsy wall parted, leaving them exposed.

He was too tired to care.

*   *   *

Early Morning
March 27, 2044

Hanover drifted from the depths of sleep, drawn by the faint tickling at his ear. He opened his eyes slowly and saw the spider skitter up its web, then drop down again on a newly-spun strand to its anchor point: Hanover's ear. He brushed the web away. The spider raced to the top of the web, then it began spinning again.

Like Major Kant, setting his trap, then starting again when it didn't work out, Hanover thought. At least the crazy major was dead. He grimaced and looked over at Beecker who was curled up in a ball, snoring softly. Hanover decided to let him sleep a few more minutes; they'd had a long grueling night, and the old man needed all his strength.

He cautiously made his way to the edge of the rock outcropping, giving him a bird's eye view. It looked like any other day; a few cars drove in and out of town, people walked down the main street, past deteriorating adobe shops with composition roofs that long ago replaced the picturesque red-tiled roofs. He could see the roadblock was still there, too, but the guards appeared relaxed, with their arms casually looped around their laser guns. He scanned the skies and saw nothing, heard nothing to indicate helicopters had taken up the search.

Relieved, he kept low as he returned to their hiding place. Beecker was awake now, sitting up and stretching. His pale, drawn face worried Hanover, but the older man looked to be in reasonably good spirits.

Beecker stood and moved about stiffly. "I find sleeping in the open so invigorating," he said with wry humor.

Hanover shook his head. "If you say so, Doc." Personally, he could do without the damp clothes, and without bugs crawling in his hair.

"Come. We'll eat while we walk. From his bag, Beecker pulled the sandwiches Darcy had prepared for them earlier. He took a bite of his own before he tossed one to Hanover. With his mouth still full, he said, "How's it look back there?"

"About what we expected, but not bad. The roadblock's checking people, but they're acting pretty casual about it. It doesn't look like they have enough troops for a ground search. I'm worried about helicopters though."

Beecker nodded as he swallowed. "They could order some, but by the time they get the proper authorizations and the helicopters arrive, we'll be long gone. We go this way to meet Darcy." He pointed in the opposite direction from the town and set off.

Hanover hoped the older man was right. Following behind Beecker, Hanover unwrapped his sandwich, but didn't eat. He had too much to think about, things he'd been too exhausted to dwell on the night before.

Now he had nothing but time to consider what Beecker and his cohorts expected him to do. So many questions, about the mission. About how time travel worked. About whether he would live to tell about it.

"Doc? I was wondering if you could explain this time travel thing again. How do you know it's okay for me to go? I mean, why do you think I won't. . .disappear?"

Beecker nodded again. "I admit, it's a sticky concept, and we're not totally certain of its validity. Let me explain it this way. Your parents, grandparents and great-grandparents all lived in Magdalena. Your great-grandparents lived there before the Occupation. We've conjectured that these same marriages would have occurred even if there had been no Occupation, especially in such a small, out-of-the-way town. There is no one in your ancestry from outside that town since before the war. And we found no one who left the town for any reason related to the Occupation. Therefore, our thinking is that you would exist as you are in either case." He seemed overly pleased with his conclusion.

"I'm glad to hear it," Hanover said, unable to keep a tinge of sarcasm from his voice. He still couldn't believe he was discussing this crazy plan as if it was a perfectly normal venture.

"You should be glad," Dr. Beecker said as if he couldn't comprehend any other attitude.

"Did you consider anyone else for this?"

"Oh, yes. We looked at a number of people. We even thought about sending Travis. In fact, we traced his ancestry back to the Alamo."

"The Alamo? Never heard of it. I take it that's pre-war history?"

"Yes, but never mind that now. We eliminated Travis as a candidate because of his unfortunate accident. Probably just as well, because he'd refuse to go without Alicia, and that's too risky."

There were elements to this that were *too* risky? Hanover shook his head. "So where are we going now?"

"Neustadt. It's—"

"Neustadt! Why in the hell're we going there?"

"That's your take-off point." Beecker looked at Hanover blandly. "It's perfect. Remote, but not too remote."

The words barely sank in. Furious, Hanover grabbed Beecker's arm and whirled him around. "You mean to tell me that all this crap I've gone through, being attacked, and arrested and escaping, and. . .and all this could have been avoided if you'd met me when I arrived in Neustadt?"

Beecker blinked and nodded, infuriatingly calm. "I know it seems odd—"

"Odd? Odd isn't the word for it, Doc. Try insane. Try. . .try life-threatening."

"I understand, Scott, but look at it from our perspective. We had no other choice. We'd chosen you because we thought you'd go along with us, but we didn't know for sure. None of us had ever met you, except for Dawes, and he didn't exactly give you a glowing recommendation. We didn't dare expose our base until we were certain you were with us."

Hanover scowled. "Did Travis know?"

"No. Travis was merely a messenger. He knew the site was a safe house, that's all. For the last ten years, we've done the research at different locations, and when we perfected a part, we'd store it at Neustadt. Power was a big concern until we found a diesel generator. It's old, but serviceable."

Hanover's anger fell from boiling to a simmer. He felt manipulated—hell, he'd been manipulated from the very beginning of this thing, kept in the dark about everything except the immediate next step. He supposed he could understand their hesitation. But still, all those unnecessary risks?

"Where are we going now?" Hanover ripped into his sandwich.

"We're approaching the road, but we'll stay out of sight by traveling parallel to it. Darcy will pick us up around noon."

They walked steadily for hours. The previous night's rain had washed away the snow, and the sun's watery rays lessened the day's chill. They reached their rendezvous point and hid in the rocks until they spotted Darcy's car.

The man slowed for them to get in, then accelerated rapidly. "They're suspicious," he said.

Beecker looked over his shoulder, then turned back, "What do you mean?" he asked sharply.

"The soldiers kept asking me all these questions. I know they didn't believe me."

Beecker exhaled slowly. "If they didn't believe you, they'd have arrested you." He glanced at Hanover and tilted his head slightly.

Hanover shifted in his seat so he could watch out the back window. Just in case Darcy was more intuitive than they were giving him credit for. So far, Hanover didn't see any vehicles behind them.

He figured they'd driven about twenty miles when they rounded a curve in the road and Beecker signaled to Darcy. "Pull over."

"Here? This is the middle of nowhere. I thought you wanted to go to Albuquerque?"

"We're getting out here," Beecker commanded. He and Hanover climbed from the car. "Go on to Albuquerque. Do some shopping, or whatever you usually do there."

"Try not to be noticed. That'd be the easiest for everyone." Hanover added. He didn't like the speculative look in Darcy's eyes.

Darcy nodded and drove off. Beecker and Hanover looked at each other. "The less he knows, the better," Beecker said.

"Isn't he part of your group?"

"No. He's been reliable in the past so long as I've had that evidence. Hope he stays that way."

Hanover hoped so, too. "Now where?"

Beecker pointed toward the mountains. "If we cut across in this direction, we'll intersect with the road to Neustadt. Shouldn't take us more than three or four hours to get there."

In silent agreement, Hanover followed Beecker as they hiked the trail toward Neustadt.

*   *   *

Mid-Day
March 27, 2044

Kant paced the waiting room of the FedPo outpost, furious at the lack of progress. The only excitement had been a couple teenagers brought in after midnight for violating curfew. The sergeant's lecture to the kids and their parents was a patronizing bore, and the paltry monetary fine was a waste of the paperwork it took to process the violation.

Suspicious that he would miss an important message, he had ordered breakfast in; now the inactivity chafed at him. Where were those damn helicopters? He'd submitted the request hours ago. How long could it take for the Albuquerque office to obtain the necessary authorization and implement it?

He stomped to the door and flung it open, only to find a lieutenant arriving for day watch. "You're here. Good. Call Albuquerque for a status report on my helicopters."

The lieutenant gave him a startled look. "Sir?"

"Didn't you see the roadblock? Haven't you paid attention to what's going on around you?" Kant waved his arms in irritation. "We're tracking an escaped prisoner and his accomplice. Find out what's delayed our search helicopters. Now."

"Yessir." The lieutenant saluted smartly and raced to the inner office.

Kant drummed his fingers on the desk top as he waited. He heard the lieutenant's voice rise and fall as he badgered the person on the other end of the telephone line. A few minutes later, Kant looked up to see the lieutenant enter the room. Kant did not like the worried expression on the man's face.

"What is it?" he snapped.

"The helicopters won't be available until late afternoon, sir."

Kant slammed his fist on the counter top. "Idiots! How the hell are we supposed to find those prisoners in this godforsaken wilderness without air support?"

"I don't know, sir," the lieutenant said in a quiet voice.

"Who did you talk to?"

"The watch commander's assistant, sir. And, ah, sir?"

"What?" Kant snarled.

"I learned that they're expecting a Lieutenant Colonel Heinz to return any time."

Kant's head jerked up. "Heinz? What do you mean, they're expecting him to return? He's supposed to be in Albuquerque. Where's he been?"

"From what they said, it sounds as if he's been to Trumanville."

Kant felt the rope tighten around his neck. He took a closer look at the lieutenant. The younger man's manner was diffident, but Kant saw intelligence in his steady gaze, an awareness that he liked. "What's your name?"

"Forrester, sir. James T."

"Lieutenant Forrester, how'd you like to be my personal assistant in this case?"

"It would be a great honor to work with the youngest major in the FedPos, sir."

Kant recognized the ambition shining through the man's eyes; he could use someone on his side right now, someone competent, someone who would work hard to make him look good. "Good. Call Santa Fe and see if you can expedite those helicopters. Call Donald Hathaway. He's Commandant Kraft's assistant. See if he can find out what's causing the delay. And find out if Heinz is assigned to this project."

Forrester raised an eyebrow. "You mean he might be interfering?"

Kant smiled grimly. "Yes, Lieutenant. Interfering in an investigation. Impeding the designated officer's progress."

"I understand, sir. I'll get right on it."

Forrester left the room and Kant frowned. What a God-awful mess. At last he had someone shrewd working with him. He pursed his lips and thought of Prinski. He'd been a good man, helpful in many ways. But perhaps at this stage of his career, Kant decided, it was better to have a junior officer as his assistant, rather than a mongrel driver.

Confident that Forrester would handle the situation, Kant left the FedPo office. He walked several blocks in the town, noted the aged buildings, the drawn faces of the people he passed, the dilapidated stores with only the most meager of offerings. If this was what living outside the city meant, he wanted no part of it. Shaking his head, he returned to the FedPo office. From the murmurs coming from the other room, Forrester was working hard.

Still the time dragged by with no results. Forrester's discussion with the commandant's office had yielded little, except the insinuation that perhaps Heinz was needed to help Kant handle this minor problem. He bristled, outraged at their response. What, in the Fuhrer's name, did they expect him to do? He had no back-up, no support. How was he supposed to canvass the desert?

Kant also didn't like the wary expression he'd seen on Forrester's face, that perhaps he'd hitched a ride on the wrong rising star. Kant's anger rose. He'd show them, he'd show them all. He had to show them. What he needed was a break.

"Sir?" Forrester stepped back into the room.

Kant straightened. "What is it?"

"A call's come in from Albuquerque. The roadblock detail is detaining a man. Would you like to talk to the watch commander directly?"

Kant sprang from his chair. "I'll take it in the office." He picked up the old fashioned receiver. "This is Major Kant."

"Major, this is Tifield. I was notified that the road block picked up a man who says he gave two men a ride. His name is Edmund J. Darcy."

"Where'd he pick them up?"

"A couple miles from you. He says he dropped them off again before they reached Albuquerque."

"When did this happen?"

"Several hours ago."

"Several—Why the hell wasn't I informed immediately?"

"I. . .I don't know, sir. Lieutenant Colonel Heinz has been here. He said he was working with you—"

Kant crushed the paper in his hand. "I was appointed by Commandant Kraft personally. Lieutenant Colonel Heinz is not assigned to this case. Do not let him question Darcy. Do you understand?"

"Yes, sir. I'll call the officer responsible for the road block and tell him."

"Have Darcy brought to county headquarters," Kant said. "*No one* else is authorized to talk to this man. Do I make myself clear?"

"Yes, sir. I understand."

"Good. I'll be there in an hour." Kant slammed the phone down and stormed out of the room, so angry he feared he would explode.

A little over an hour had passed when Lieutenant Forrester slid the electrocar into a narrow parking slot in front of the FedPo district offices in Albuquerque.

Kant hopped out of the car. "My office is on the fourth floor, but we're going to county headquarters first," he said to Forrester. They strode down the street, then hurried up the wide marble steps to the entrance of the monolithic structure.

Kant passed the duty officer sitting at the front desk, and ran his hand across the security scanner. "This is Lieutenant Forrester. He's working with me."

The duty officer lifted a clipboard. "I'll need an authorization for him to enter—"

"Not now." Kant glanced around as he strode through the lobby toward a bank of elevators. It had been a while since he had been in this building. It was old, built during the early years of the Occupation. The elevator creaked and the cables groaned as they rode to the sixth floor in silence.

Forrester opened the door to the watch commander's office and Kant stepped inside.

"Major Kant." A dark-haired man rose from his chair behind a wooden desk. "I don't think we've met. I'm Jack Tifield, watch commander. Congratulations on your promotion."

Kant nodded. "Where's Darcy?"

"I notified the roadblock supervisor to bring him here." Tifield smiled. "Lieutenant Colonel Heinz was not pleased to find Darcy had been transferred before he arrived on the scene. He apparently became quite belligerent with the supervisor."

"Did the supervisor tell him to put his complaints in writing?"

"As a matter of fact, he did, and that quieted Heinz down immediately. From what I've heard, no one's seen or heard from him since."

"Good. He knew he had no authority to be there in the first place. I'll remember your assistance in my report to General Kraft."

"Thank you, sir. Here's the supervisor's report. He wrote it up before they transported Darcy."

Tifield handed the report to Kant, who quickly scanned it. As he'd expected, it revealed little. That was good. He didn't want a long paper trail of his frustrating pursuit.

"When would you like to see Darcy?" Tifield asked.

"Now." Kant followed Tifield from the office.

As they took the elevator down to the basement, Kant breathed a sigh of relief that Heinz was off his back. At least for a little while. At least until Heinz figured out another way to interfere. Kant hoped this Darcy would give him the information he needed to find Hanover. And fast. He was running out of time; the commandant was running out of patience.

Kant still couldn't believe he'd lost Hanover to a simple accident. Of all the stupid. . .His head began to ache just thinking about the crash.

The elevator doors slid open. Tifield led the way as they approached a desk next to a set of locked doors.

"We're here to see a man brought in earlier. Darcy's his name," Tifield said to the sentry.

"Yes, sir." The sentry glanced nervously at Kant, then back to Tifield. "There. . .there's been a problem, sir."

A sinking feeling settled in the pit of Kant's stomach. "What kind of a problem." He tried to keep panic and frustration out of his voice.

"He. . .he was injured, sir."

"He was what?" Tifield exclaimed.

"Explain," Kant demanded.

"He was searched, sir, per protocol. That's when he started resisting. When we started to remove and bag his personal property before he was brought downstairs."

"What the hell—?" Kant choked. "You treated him like he was being arrested? He was coming here to give me information."

Kant struggled to control his rage. Damn it to hell. This assignment turned from one fiasco to another. "Where is he now?"

"I think they're about finished with him in the infirmary."

"Good. Have him brought to an interrogation room."

"Yes, sir." The sentry saluted and hurried down the hall.

Kant watched him leave. "Lieutenant, make sure they don't screw this up." Forrester nodded and followed.

"I'm terribly sorry, sir," Tifield said. "This is most embarrassing."

Kant only nodded, not trusting himself to speak. They waited silently, each in a different concrete corner. Kant knew Tifield cast furtive glances his way, but he wasn't interested in alleviating the watch commander's concerns about how Kant would write up the afternoon's events.

He took the time to review the roadblock supervisor's report more closely. No wonder there was confusion—it read like a damn arrest report: Darcy, Edmund J., transported for questioning. No prior arrests, no activities or affiliations of interest or concern.

The narrative was of no significance, only the usual padding to promote the supervisor's abilities. Kant grunted, then folded the report and slid it into his pocket. Forrester returned, and Kant followed him to the interrogation room.

He found Darcy sitting in a wooden chair in the center of the room, his arm in a sling and one side of his face swathed in bandages. He was a gray little man with small eyes that darted nervously around the room. Kant nodded to the two massive guards who stood with their hands resting lightly on their laser holsters. What did they expect Darcy to do that guards were needed at all?

Darcy looked up when Kant entered, and whimpered. Kant doubted the man would ever try to volunteer information again."I am Major Kant," he said briskly. "You had something to report?"

Trembling, Darcy nodded, but said nothing.

"You picked up two men on the road. Hitchhikers?" Kant prompted.

"Y—yes, sir." Darcy's words were barely audible over his blubbering.

"Ever seen them before?"

Darcy hesitated. "No, sir."

Was he lying or scared to death? "What did they look like?"

"One was young, about thirty, with blond hair. The other one was older, tall and thin."

Hanover and Beecker. "And you let them off before reaching Albuquerque?"

"Yes. That's right. I picked them up at the side of the road outside town." The words tumbled out as though Darcy wanted to purge himself of all his information. "I left them about five miles from the Neustadt turn-off."

Neustadt? Kant stopped, stunned by the news. He'd been about to ask Darcy why he'd picked up men who were obviously avoiding the road block, and thus had something to hide. But that question was now forgotten.

Neustadt. Hanover had been there two days ago. Now he was returning with the scientist. What could possibly draw them back to the site? Perhaps it was time to take that place apart. It had been ignored for so many years, there was no telling what really went on there.

"Why are you reporting this?" Kant asked.

"I just want to be on record as a good citizen. In case something ever comes up."

Kant eyed Darcy; the man had to know more than he let on, but Kant didn't have time to pursue it now. He shook his head and stepped outside the interrogation room. "Take him to a holding area," he said to Tifield. "Keep him until I get back."

"Do you think he knows more?"

"Probably, but he's said enough for now. I need some men to go to Neustadt."

"I'd be happy to send some of mine," Tifield said. "How many do you need and where?"

Kant thought for a moment. "Two squads. Have them assemble out back."

Tifield nodded. "I'll see to it."

"I'm going to my office. I'll be back in thirty minutes."

Outside, Kant caught up with Forrester and sent him to organize the troops while he went down the street to his office in the county headquarters building.

His first call was to Warden Dawes; he was going to wipe some of that smugness away. "Good afternoon, Warden. I thought you'd like a progress report on your escaped prisoner, Scott Hanover."

On the screen, Dawes looked wary. "Of course. I'd be happy to hear of any progress you've made," he said hesitantly.

Deep inside, Kant knew he should refrain from boasting until after Hanover was securely in his hands, but he couldn't resist. He wanted to see Dawes squirm, to do something that would confirm Kant's suspicions that the warden was involved.

"We've identified some of his accomplices, and have him cornered in an abandoned town near here. I anticipate arresting him within the next few hours."

"Really? I know you're pleased, Major. Let me know when you have him in custody." Dawes disconnected the call.

Kant raised an eyebrow. The warden hadn't said *he* was pleased that Hanover's arrest was imminent. Kant drummed his fingers on the desk, then took a deep breath. He had to call the commandant. If he was lucky, Kraft would be out of the office and he could leave a message. He wasn't lucky.

"I'm on my way to Neustadt, sir, and have every reason to believe I'll capture Hanover there," Kant said.

"Don't you mean *recapture*, Major? You had him once. Then you lost him."

"It was an acci—"

"Don't give me excuses, Kant. Give me results. Hanover has shown ingenuity and resourcefulness in eluding you. But then, he always had those qualities." The commandant's words sliced through Kant, opening all the old wounds.

"I'll bring him to Albuquerque tonight, sir," Kant said stiffly.

"Do your duty, Major. Do your duty." The general disconnected, but not before Kant caught the weariness in his voice.

So, the commandant still had some feelings for Hanover. Kant burned with jealousy. Once again, Hanover, who was nothing to the commandant, received the accolades, while he, the commandant's only son. . .. Kant swallowed hard and clenched his fists. He'd get Scott Hanover. He'd get him if—

"The squads and vehicles are waiting, sir."

Kant looked up to see Forrester standing in the doorway. Had the lieutenant seen Kant's distress? He hoped not. Now wasn't the time to show weakness.

"Very good, Lieutenant." Kant rose from his seat as if a ponderous weight rested on his shoulders.

What would it take for his father to give him the credit he deserved, to acknowledge his capabilities? Would capturing Hanover be enough? Bringing him back, rather than taking the easy way by detonating the S.A.D.? Probably not.

Kant told himself it wouldn't matter. What mattered was that everyone would know that he captured the escaped prisoner, that he identified the existence of a subversive group and its membership. He would be applauded for his success. No one would doubt he deserved his promotion to major. And that would be enough. It had to be.

He followed Forrester from the building, and signaled for the lieutenant to call them to attention. "We're going to Neustadt," he told the assembled troops. "An escaped convict is hiding there. We will take anyone we find prisoner, and hold them for interrogation later. These people are enemies of the state, part of a larger conspiracy. I want them all taken alive."

He climbed into the lead car and signaled Forrester to start. This time he would do whatever it took to make sure he didn't lose Hanover again.

CHAPTER 10

NEUSTADT
Late Afternoon, March 27, 2044

Hanover and Beecker picked their way through the debris-strewn streets, taking care to avoid both scavengers and random FedPo patrols. Two scavengers eyed them from a doorway, then faded like ghosts into the darkened building. Hanover glanced over his shoulder frequently, his encounter with "scarecrow" and his friends still fresh in his mind.

Hanover followed Beecker to the old administration building, which appeared even more rundown in the stark sunlight. They paused at the entrance and scanned the area. Although they saw no one, neither doubted they were watched from the shadows of other buildings.

At Beecker's knock, the door opened, and they slipped inside. The door slammed shut behind them. A man Hanover did not recognize nodded to Beecker, then turned and disappeared through a doorway.

Hanover followed Beecker down the same steps he'd descended only two days before. Two days? My God, he thought, it seemed more like two years. They entered the closed meeting room and the same odor of moldy food greeted them.

Thinking about that first night, Hanover asked, "What do you think happened to Travis and Alicia?"

"They're probably in a cell in Albuquerque," Beecker said. "The major won't do anything with them until he finds you. In the meantime, we can only hope you'll have changed the course of history and altered their circumstances. For the better, we hope."

Change the course of history. Alter their circumstances. Beecker's words hit Hanover hard. They'd made him responsible for the fate of others, of people he knew. He was now responsible for keeping Travis and Alicia alive.

He wiped his hand across his face. What in God's name was he thinking? Who did he think he was to travel through time and change all this. The GOA wouldn't exist. Neustadt wouldn't exist. People wouldn't—

But change for the better? Travis and Alicia wouldn't be sitting in jail awaiting Kant's interrogation. So where *would* they be? According to Beecker, Travis would be alive, but what about Alicia? Beecker had theorized that Hanover would be alive, too. But would he?

"Come here, Scott. I don't have much time to brief you."

The enormity of what they asked of him loomed frighteningly close. He wanted to say he'd changed his mind, that he wanted nothing to do with this craziness.

He waved Beecker away. "It's okay. I know what I need to know." Was he really ready to go? Hell, could anyone ever be ready for something like this?

Beecker sighed and looked at him sadly. "This is not the time for second thoughts, Scott."

"I told you, I know everything. Helmke and Fischer came to the U.S. and stole plans for the trigger mechanism device." He knew he sounded defensive, but he didn't care. If he didn't talk about it, he could pretend it wasn't going to happen.

"Did you know they came by U-boat and landed in Mexico? Did you know they entered the U.S. through El Paso, pretending to be Swedish businessmen? Did you know their aliases were Fegen and Holm?"

"Fine," Hanover snarled as he paced the room. "Now I know everything. I'll tell the authorities to look for them and it'll be over."

"It's not that easy," Beecker snapped. He leaned back in his chair and crossed his arms. "No one's going to believe you if you march into police headquarters and say you're from the future so they should do what you tell them to."

Hanover stopped pacing. "Why not? The FedPos believe every rumor and harass the daylights out of innocent people every day."

"It was very different than it is now. Helmke and Fischer traveled as businessmen from a neutral country. You'll have to catch them in the act of stealing the plans or after they already have the plans in their possession."

"Okay, okay. You win." Hanover rolled his eyes and sank into a chair across the table from Beecker. "Why couldn't you pick an easier way to change history?"

"Don't think we haven't tried. It's the timegate. We can send someone to another year, but only to the same date at this location. Believe me, if we had more flexibility, we would have chosen some easier way to change the war's outcome, but this is all we have to work with."

Beecker leaned forward. "We've pulled together bits and pieces of information over the years that're not included in recent history books about that time." He frowned. "We think the two agents went to Santa Fe and met a sleeper."

"A what?"

"A sleeper agent. Someone who's become part of the community. No one knows that he works for a foreign government. He may not be used for many years."

"So what does he do in the meantime?"

"He holds a regular job, maybe gets married, has a family. All the normal things."

All the normal things. Hanover shrank a little. All the normal things. The things he knew nothing about. "When does he stop being dormant?"

"When his government deems it's time. In this case, we think a sleeper brought the two agents to someone working on the atom bomb project at Los Alamos. Somehow the agents forced him to give them the plans."

"Do you know their names?"

"No, but the agents probably met the sleeper in the open, at some local gathering place."

"Why wouldn't they meet secretly?"

"This was war time. Any furtive activities by foreign businessmen, even from neutral countries, would have been suspect. No, much better to meet in the open and appear normal."

Hanover winced. There was that word again. Normal. He glanced at Beecker and saw the older man watching him intently. Better to concentrate on the future. Or was it the past? Hell, he didn't know the difference anymore.

"If I find the agents before they steal the plans, I could expose them."

"Not a good idea. They'll have an airtight cover, and you'll be dismissed as some kind of nut."

"You mean it's better to let them steal the plans, and then go after them? That's taking a big chance. What if I fail?"

"You won't fail, Scott. You can't. Too much is riding on this."

Yeah, the fate of the whole world. Hanover wished Beecker would stop reminding him.

"Whatever you decide, you'll have to involve the police," Beecker said.

"But—"

"Don't worry. It was very different back then. The city of Santa Fe had its own police force, and Santa Fe County had its own sheriff's department. Then there was the Federal Bureau of Investigation, or the FBI, as it was called. That was the national investigating agency."

Hanover groaned and slumped in his chair. "Just what I need, another FedPo gestapo group."

"They weren't anything like the FedPos. They left the local crime for the local authorities, and concentrated their efforts on big cases, like kidnapping, espionage, crimes committed across state lines, that sort of thing. You'll most likely deal with them." He caught Hanover's grim expression.

"They're nothing like the FedPos, Scott. You'll have to trust me."

"Seems like I've trusted you a lot so far."

"Then trust me on this, too."

"Yeah, fine." Hanover shook his head. "Give me the most important stuff, Doc. I'll fake the rest."

Beecker smiled wanly. "I knew you were the right one for this job, Scott. You've a quick mind and, underneath all that bravado, you've got a good heart." He patted Hanover's shoulder.

"Yeah, well, this heart and mind are going for a short meeting with the firing squad if we don't get with it."

Beecker nodded, then went to a locker and removed a bundle. He returned to the table and spread out the contents. "This is as close as we could come to simulating the clothing of that time."

He handed Hanover a pair of baggy tan trousers, cuffed at the bottom, and a matching jacket with lightly padded shoulders and deep lapels.

Hanover fingered the material. "What is this?"

"It's supposed to be linen. You better start changing. We don't have much time."

Hanover stripped to his underwear. Beecker looked at him and shook his head. "For goodness sakes, don't let anyone see you in those, or they'll know for sure you're in the wrong time."

"Don't worry. I'm not planning to stay long enough for that." He caught Beecker's odd look. "What's wrong?"

"Nothing," Beecker answered. He pulled out a striped shirt. "Put this on. And here's the belt and tie. Do you know how to tie one?"

When Hanover shook his head, Beecker said, "That's all right. I'll do it for you, then you can just loosen it and slip it over your head when you take it off."

He looked at Hanover's shoes and sighed. "If anyone asks, tell them you bought your shoes in Mexico. This little bag has a razor, toothbrush, and a comb. Also, the men at that time wore hats. We couldn't find anything close, so you'll have to buy one once you get there. Go wash up. We can't have you ignored or arrested for vagrancy just because you look like a bum."

Hanover hurried to the small bathroom. He wished he could shower, but that was a luxury time didn't permit. When he got to the other side, he'd. . .the other side. A peculiar way to think about his trip, his time trip.

Traveling through time. His mind still had trouble grasping the concept. But with the FedPos after him, it was go through the timegate, or be executed.

He shaved and cleaned up as best he could, then donned the new clothes and looked at himself in the small mirror. The trousers felt strange, wide-legged instead of the close fitting pants he was accustomed to, but not bad.

Hanover returned to the meeting room and Beecker looked up impatiently. "There you are. Now the next thing—"

Someone hammered persistently on the door. Beecker rose from his chair and opened it to admit the man who'd let them into the building. The man looked worried, and he talked in a low voice, gesturing wildly. Beecker nodded, then shut the door.

"Damn," Beecker muttered softly as he turned around. The color had drained from his face.

Hanover started from his chair. "What's wrong, Doc?"

"Warden Dawes just called. Kant's alive."

"But—he was dead. I'm sure of it."

Beecker shook his head. "Somehow he survived the crash. He told Dawes he's on his way here with another truck load of troops. This time, he won't leave until he has you."

"So now what?"

"I only have a few minutes to tell you everything you need to know. Damn it! I wanted more time to go over maps and such!" Beecker grabbed the pile of papers on the table. "Quickly, now. Here's your birth certificate. You'll have a new name. This is as close as we could get to your real one. Repeat it over and over to get used to it. The certificate's authentic, by the way, should anyone want to examine it."

"Won't the real person know?"

"No," Beecker replied. "The Germans are meticulous record keepers, even to microfilming all the old records. We went back to 1912 and 1913 to put you at the right age for 1944. We found a male infant who died about that time, then checked for his birth date. Someone checking your birth certificate won't look for a record of your death, so there shouldn't be any problem."

Hanover took the birth certificate. The name shown was William Terence Scott. The mother was listed as Louise, the father as William. Hanover blinked rapidly. Were his "parents" still alive in 1944? He shook his head and read further. "Why San Francisco?"

"We avoided the southwest because we didn't want to take a chance that someone, relatives or friends of the parents, would recognize the name and start asking questions." Beecker handed him another card. "This is a Social Security card. Memorize your number. You'll need this if you take a job."

"Is this a work permit? Why would I take a job? I'm not going to be there long."

"It's not necessary, but work may serve as a cover. This isn't a work permit, it's an identification number. If you work, the federal government deducts a small amount from your pay that goes into a fund for when you retire."

Hanover gave Beecker a sharp look and laughed nervously. "Hey, but I won't be there that long, will I, Doc?"

Beecker's expression turned grave. "I don't know. But you'll need it even if you work for only one day." He took a deep breath and shoved another card at Hanover. "Now this one's very important. It's your draft card. It states your military service status. This is war time, and every able-bodied man was expected to serve. We don't have time to create a fictitious war record for you, so we've made you 4F. That means you're unfit for military duty. If anyone asks, say you have a congenital heart problem."

"This is awfully complicated, Doc."

"I have every confidence in you, Scott. If anyone can do it you can. These are ration stamps for meat, butter, gasoline for a car, things like that. You probably won't need the gas stamps, but you can use them to trade for something you do need."

Hanover looked through the small pack. "These won't go very far for food."

"If you eat in restaurants, you won't need them. These are the agents." Beecker gave Hanover two grainy photographs. "Memorize their faces. Lastly, here's seventy-five dollars in old money. It's all we could scrape together, but it should be ample to see you through a week to ten days."

Beecker looked Hanover up and down. "I hope to God I haven't forgotten anything."

"How will I get back?"

Beecker flushed. "Of course. The timegate should remain open for two, maybe three transits. The timegate erodes; it gets smaller and weaker with each transit and with the passage of time. You need to return within ten days."

Hanover nodded grimly and they left the meeting room, with Beecker leading the way down narrow steps to the basement. Using a tunnel, they entered the basement of another building. The cavernous room was filled with an assortment of electronic equipment. A technician seated at a console of blinking lights looked up and nodded at them.

Hanover stopped and looked around. The equipment emitted a hum, a vibration that was felt rather than heard. The sharp odor of ozone permeated the air.

In the center of the room stood a pedestal with an enormous emerald green crystal perched on top. The crystal, enclosed in glass, glowed with a pulsating light that had an almost hypnotic effect. On the far side of the room, a door encased in brilliant light pulsed in rhythm with the crystal.

Hanover turned to face Beecker. Beecker nodded and said, "This is where you go through the timegate, Scott, or should I say, William. Right through that door."

"What's on the other side?"

"Right now, in our time, there's a storeroom. The building's on a slope and the storeroom is a few inches above ground level, even though this is a basement. Can't have you coming out up to your neck in solid rock, now can we?"

Beecker smiled as if attempting to add some levity to the situation, but Hanover wasn't amused. "Is there a door out of the storeroom?"

"No need. Neustadt and everything built here will disappear as you go though. It's quite amazing actually—"

Shocked, Hanover whirled to face him. "You've been through the timegate?"

"Ah. . .yes," Beecker said.

The timegate was real, it worked. Beecker's calm assertion staggered Hanover. "Then why the hell—?"

"For several reasons. I needed to know if it could be done, and the range. That's how I figured out the location and date limitations. I arrived six months before the agents, and I wasn't prepared to stay that long. Besides, Scott—I mean, William—I'm too old. We need someone smart and aggressive and in good physical condition. That's you." Beecker nodded encouragingly.

God save him from a scientist's logic. Even though he'd gone along with everything so far, a part of him had written Beecker off as a nutcase. But now, the reality hit hard, and

Hanover felt the pressure closing in around him. "What happens if the FedPos find this thing after I leave?"

"Since my test trips, I've added a self-destruct mechanism that destroys the crystal when you reach the other side. We don't want a band of FedPo troopers to follow you through and wreak havoc on the other side."

Hanover panicked. "But can I come back?"

"Oh, yes. It should be good for two, maybe even three, pass-throughs before it closes completely."

Hanover wasn't at all reassured. "But—"

"Dr. Beecker?" the technician called out. "The timegate's primed. It's set to deposit him four days before the agents arrive in Santa Fe."

"Thank you, Mark." Beecker turned to Hanover, his eyes misting. "Remember, you only have ten days to make it back."

"I hope it's worth coming back to, Doc."

"I hope so, too, Scott."

Beecker threw his arms around Hanover and hugged him. Hanover at first resisted the impulsive gesture, then returned it, feeling closer to this man than he had to anyone for as long as he could remember. An unfamiliar warmth spread through him, a connection with another human being, something he hadn't felt since he was a child.

Beecker pulled back and sniffed suspiciously. "Oh, my God! How could I have forgotten. There's one more thing you need to know—"

"Dr. Beecker! Dr. Beecker!" A man raced into the room. "The FedPos are coming."

*   *   *

NEUSTADT
Late Afternoon, March 27, 2044

Kant clenched and unclenched his fists in turmoil as the electrocar sped into Neustadt.

"Where to?" Lieutenant Forrester asked.

"Go to the old administration building." Kant pointed toward the far side of town. Whispers had circulated about the place for years, but nobody ever bothered to check out the rumors. This was the time, and he was the one to do it.

Deep inside, he knew this was a pivotal moment in his career. He couldn't afford to make another mistake. Perhaps even more importantly, he couldn't let Scott Hanover best him again. Rage flared anew, churned his stomach, pounded in his head.

Forrester pulled in front of the old administration building. Kant leaped from the vehicle and faced the troop carrier that had followed. He pointed to a squad of soldiers. "Spread out. I want everyone arrested. Everyone." He pointed to the other squad. "Half of you surround this building. The rest, come with me."

Kant ordered the door kicked in, then entered the building, laser gun in hand. The troops swooped in behind him, checking each room along the hallway. They found nothing.

Kant led them down the stairs. Again, nothing. The tight edge of fear chilled him. He couldn't fail. Not this time.

"Sir," a soldier called to Kant. "This door leads to a tunnel."

Relief rekindled his determination. Kant signaled for the troops to follow. Their footsteps echoed in the corridor, double-time to his pounding heart.

At the end of the tunnel, another door. Kant kicked it open and burst into the room, stumbling into a laboratory. He stared at an incredible green crystal pulsating in the center of the cavernous space.

Then he saw Hanover and Beecker, their eyes wide with alarm.

"Go." Beecker shoved Hanover behind him.

Hanover grabbed Beecker's arm. "I can't leave—"

"Go. Now. Change all this."

Kant saw Hanover glance at Beecker, then at the soldiers racing across the room. "Stop him," Kant ordered.

Hanover dashed through a brightly lit doorway. The lights flared, then dimmed. Beecker grabbed a metallic cylinder and threw it at the crystal. The glass case surrounding the green crystal shattered; the crystal popped and went dark, seeming to implode.

"No!" Kant roared. Hanover wasn't going to escape. Not if Willie Kant had anything to do with it.

He rushed forward. Beecker stepped in his path and grabbed his arms. Kant grappled with the older man and flung him aside. He heard his laser gun fall to the floor, but he didn't stop for it.

The light around the door dwindled. Kant saw nothing on the other side. He hesitated only a moment. He'd vowed to bring Hanover in, regardless of what it took. He had no choice but to follow.

Without another thought, Kant went through the doorway.

CHAPTER 11

PARIS, FRANCE
March 1, 1944

Sturmbannfuhrer Herman Helmke had seen enough to know that in the chaos and confusion of war lay the potential for personal profit. Paris was the best possible wartime assignment. It was more than a no-combat zone, more than excellent restaurants, gay nightlife, yielding women. Yielding women like his Annette. Paris was a city of opportunity.

In the darkened bedroom, Helmke reared back and thrust into the woman lying beneath him. She was hot, wet, and when she tightened around him, it took his breath away. He was determined to hold off this time, to make the ecstatic agony last.

The phone blared from across the room. Helmke felt himself go limp and he rolled off in disgust. Annette groaned in frustration and covered her head with a pillow. The phone rang again, and yet a third time.

He fumbled for his striped silk shorts and jerked them on. He still wore black socks, held high on his calves by garters. He reached for his undershirt, wanting to cover his sweat-slickened paunch before he turned on the light and crossed the room, but the shirt was nowhere to be found.

Furious, Helmke stumbled to the phone in the semi-dark and grabbed the receiver on the seventh ring. "What!"

"*Sturmbannfuhrer?*"

Helmke recognized his assistant's voice. "Why are you calling at this hour, LeBlanc?"

"Sealed orders arrived for you, sir."

"And?"

"The envelope is marked for your eyes only."

"So what do the orders say?" Helmke rolled his eyes at the sound of paper tearing. He'd bet last night's—no, this evening's—bottle of champagne that LeBlanc had already opened the envelope.

"It is from Berlin, sir."

Helmke wished he could reach through the telephone lines and throttle the man. Instead, he said, "I assumed that, LeBlanc. What does it say?"

"These lines are not secure, sir. Regulation number—"

"All right, all right. I will be there shortly."

"Of course. I will be waiting."

Helmke hung up the phone and without a backward glance at the woman in his bed, made his way to the living room. He glanced at the clock. Five in the morning. He slumped into the fine leather chair behind the carved teakwood desk and groaned. His head hurt, his stomach roiled.

God help him, the champagne last night. It slipped down the throat so easy.

Ach, the price he paid for escorting a beautiful woman like his Annette. A goddess, she was. He'd seen the men look at her, and then at him. They saw his short, round physique, his black hair combed across the top to cover the thinning place, and they wondered what he had that kept this woman's eyes only on him.

He shrugged, then winced with pain. She was a smart woman, his Annette. Like him, she was an opportunist. And Paris in wartime was. . .Well, a man such as he could do much for himself.

The black market thrived, and Helmke participated vigorously, buying works of art and shipping them for storage in neutral Switzerland. After Germany won the war, his acquired antiquities would finance the law offices he planned to open in Frankfurt. He'd even picked the location, a massive building near the Rathaus.

Other lawyers, they would flock to his offices, so that he might have his choice of the best, most aggressive. And they would pay to him a percentage of their fees for the honor of working under him.

His secretary must be a pretty young thing. A shame he could not take Annette home with him, but that was the way of it. No, when he returned to Germany he wanted a young, inexperienced secretary not averse to working late with her esteemed employer.

For his wife, a cottage near Baden-Baden's spas. She would much like the waters and the social station his prestige would bring her.

He poured water from a sterling silver pitcher into a goblet and sipped it slowly. His stomach rebelled, and he swallowed quickly, repeatedly, as sweat beaded on his forehead.

Maybe a little of the hair of the dog to ease the pounding in his head. He gingerly pushed himself to a standing position and hesitated until the crescendo in his temples subsided, before walking guardedly across the room to a Louis XIV cabinet. Inside, he found the leaded crystal decanters he sought.

In his present condition, he decided to forego the niceties, and sipped the brandy directly from the container. He paused a moment, waited for the alcohol to hit his stomach. The warmth, it wasn't happening quickly enough, so he drank again, deeper this time, until he felt the relief he craved.

He took a slow, steady breath, and exhaled as slowly. A smile spread across his face. Better. He topped the decanter with its stopper, then replaced it in the cabinet.

Yes, life, it was good. He returned to the bedroom. Annette was sleeping soundly. There was no point in disturbing her. He'd be back as soon as he straightened out LeBlanc.

Orders came from Berlin every day. Many times a day, in fact. He was probably being told to go to Marseille to take a deposition. LeBlanc was an idiot for making a fuss like this. Helmke shrugged into his uniform and tugged the jacket down. It had fit well when he came to Paris, but now. . ..

He slipped from the apartment and drove to headquarters. A few minutes later, he let himself into the office. The outer office was empty; where had LeBlanc gone now?

He unlocked his own office, and shut the door behind him. Sitting on the desk was a fresh pot of coffee, a peace offering. He poured some into his favorite Sevies cup and sipped. He heard a knock on his door.

"*Eintreten*," he called out. Still annoyed with his assistant, he sank into his chair and tried to appear more alert than he felt.

Pierre LeBlanc came through the door and sailed across the room. He wore all black, cut to accentuate his lithe build. His black hair was combed straight back, and his darting eyes missed nothing.

"*Heil*, Hitler." Pierre saluted the Fuhrer's portrait on the wall behind Helmke.

Why did the collaborators always shout, Helmke wondered, as he offered the perfunctory saluted response. Was it to cover any lingering of guilt for supporting the Nazi's control of France? "Where are the orders?"

"It is most exciting, sir. You are summoned to Berlin to meet with Brigadier General Shellenberg."

All the warmth drained from Helmke's body, replaced by icy cold dread. He'd been discovered. Someone had reported his entrepreneurial activities, and now he was to be shot, a disgrace to his family and to his country. He saw his dreams of a law office in Frankfurt, an eager-to-please secretary with big breasts, and a cottage in Baden-Baden disintegrate.

But, wait. If the high command suspected him of wrongdoing, they wouldn't call him to Berlin. They'd order him hauled from this office and summarily shot. Perhaps this communique was not a bad thing.

Still, he wanted to refuse. He wanted to say he couldn't possibly leave. Not with another delivery of old world masterpieces due imminently. Not with a hot-blooded woman like his Annette waiting for him every night.

Helmke had not been home for over a year, but he knew from his wife's letters that life in Germany was not good. In the beginning, she asked him to send more of his pay so she could buy herself a pretty trinket or a nicer cut of meat. Now it didn't matter how much money one had; there was nothing to buy.

He looked at the cable again. It told him nothing. Not the reason for the summons, nor how long he would be there. Which agency did General Shellenberg work for? Even that would tell him something. "Find out what the train schedule is."

Pierre beamed with the supercilious smile that always annoyed Helmke. "I have already taken the liberty of learning that information for you. A train leaves in three hours. The next one is not until tomorrow afternoon at 4:00. Shall I call your valet to deliver your bag in an hour?"

Helmke wanted to say there was no rush. What harm could come from one more day and night in Paris? One day to make alternative plans for his delivery, one night to have an exquisitely prepared dinner and to spend a few last hours with his goddess.

But someone would notice, someone would comment that he was perhaps not as loyal, not as eager as an officer should be to respond to so important an order. All it took was one raised eyebrow on the wrong face to undo his plans and preparations for the future.

With a sigh, he handed the envelope back to Pierre. "Make the necessary arrangements. I will finish some work."

Watching Pierre stride purposefully from the room, he shook his head. Maybe the train was already full, maybe it would take days to get a ticket. The thought cheered him for only a moment.

He knew his assistant well. Pierre would badger and browbeat whoever stood in his way. God help the poor ticket agent who tried to explain that all the seats were taken. Pierre would have him run through the list of passengers, challenging the right of each and every one to ride that particular train until he had a reservation. Helmke knew; Pierre often used the same persistence on him.

For now, he must concentrate on the documents locked in his files, the ones that would cause him much trouble if they were found. As long as he worked here, no one except the SS would violate his desk. But once the train pulled from the station, he had no doubt that someone eager for this plush office would empty the drawers and perhaps find something Helmke would prefer remain secret.

The next evening, the train rolled into Berlin. Helmke relaxed his grip on his bag. The trip had terrified him, and for the first time he questioned whether Germany really could win the war. As the train had streaked through the dark countryside the night before, the sky had lit up bright as midday when Allied bombs fell on the cities. All day, Helmke had stared out the window, dismayed by the devastation.

During the brief stop in Frankfurt, he'd tried to call his wife, but the harried operator could not put him through.

No matter. He would see her on his return to Paris. Unless they sent him to the eastern front. He shuddered at the thought and pulled his heavy coat tighter as the train jerked to a stop.

Once in the station, he hailed a cab to the Army's General Staff headquarters on Bendlerstrasse. The taxi stopped and he climbed out. Even the dwindling daylight could not mask the building's dinginess. The huge swastika flags and banners no longer flew proudly over the entrance.

With growing apprehension, Helmke entered the building and was directed by a guard to Shellenberg's office. He saw no smiles on the people he passed. Instead most frowned, or talked to others in quiet but urgent tones. He reached his destination and hesitated before opening the door. Overseas Intelligence? Why was he being summoned here? With growing trepidation, he stepped into the outer office.

Inside, a pert young secretary sifted through stacks of papers on a monstrous wooden desk. A young *untersturmfuhrer* sat stiffly in a wooden chair backed against the wall. Helmke approached the secretary.

She looked up and dazzled him with her smile. "Can I help you?"

"I am *Sturmbannfuhrer* Helmke. I received orders—"

"Yes, of course, *Sturmbannfuhrer*. I'll let Brigadier General Shellenberg know you're here." She pointed toward a chair next to the *untersturmfuhrer*, then returned to her papers.

The *untersturmfuhrer* stood and saluted Helmke as he approached. He nodded and sat in the designated chair.

Minutes passed; the secretary made no move to notify the general of his presence. He resisted the urge to tap his foot, wishing he'd thought to relieve himself before coming.

He stood up. "Excuse, please. The general is certainly a most busy man, but the orders implied the greatest urgency in my reporting here."

The secretary looked at him over the top of wire-rimmed half glasses. They detracted from the initial prettiness he'd seen, replacing it with an officiousness he recognized as a bureaucrat's. So that was the way of it.

She returned to her papers. "He will be with you soon."

He sat again and waited with growing impatience. The need to empty his bladder intensified, but he hesitated to leave. One did not keep a general waiting, especially when there were so many fronts requesting reinforcements.

Finally, he could stand it no longer. He rose from his seat.

The secretary stood, also. "The general will see you now."

Helmke wanted to roar in frustration. He should have known; he should have predicted it. He'd been kept waiting for an hour. Enough time to worry about the reason for the summons, to listen to nothing but a ticking clock. For this he could have stayed in Paris for another night.

He started to follow the secretary, then noticed the *untersturmfuhrer* was also coming. "There is some confusion," he said to the secretary. He nodded toward the untersturmfuhrer. "The general, which of us did he wish to see?"

"Both of you," the secretary said.

She pushed the massive wooden door open and stepped inside the next room, pulling the door after her. Helmke heard the murmur of voices, then she came out and ushered them in.

He strode into the room ahead of the *untersturmfuhrer*, and caught the spartan furnishings and supremely organized desk. As he approached the desk, a scowl crossed the face of the man seated behind it. Helmke felt the man's disdainful scrutiny, and recognized the career officer's contempt for someone like himself.

"*Heil*, Hitler," Helmke said with a firm salute. The *untersturmfuhrer* echoed his words.

Shellenberg saluted perfunctorily, then returned his attention to the papers stacked on the desk. He looked back at the two men standing before him. "*Sturmbannfuhrer. Untersturmfuhrer.* I have been reviewing your files. *Sturmbannfuhrer* Helmke, you were born in Sweden?"

Helmke felt a moment's panic that perhaps his nationality was in doubt. "Yes, sir. My father represented his company's interests in Stockholm."

"You attended the university in Goteberg."

"Yes, but I returned to Germany for law school, and then entered the Fuhrer's army."

Shellenberg sneered. "Yes, as a military lawyer. And since the war began?"

"I was assigned as an aide to General Gunther von Kluge, commander of our forces in France."

"Nice assignment. You have lived well, *Sturmbannfuhrer.*"

Sweat gathered on Helmke's brow.

Shellenberg read the paper in front of him, his finger marking his place. Without looking up, he asked, "Do you still speak fluent Swedish, *Sturmbannfuhrer?*"

It was worse than he'd thought. The north-eastern front, where it was cold and desolate. They wanted him to spy in Sweden? Did not the high command have enough problems without intruding on a neutral country? He choked on the words, so nodded instead. Shellenberg gazed steadily at him and raised an eyebrow.

"Yes. I am still fluent in Swedish," Helmke said.

His mouth a grim line, Shellenberg nodded as he exchanged Helmke's report for another folder. "*Untersturmfuhrer* Fischer. You, also, were born in Sweden."

Helmke shifted so he could take a closer look at the young man. Despite the tension that radiated from him, he stood tall and stared straight ahead. His close-cropped blond hair and pale blue eyes made him the model Aryan. Helmke wished he could move away from the untersturmfuhrer; next to him, Helmke's own portliness could only be exaggerated.

"Yes, sir," Fischer answered in a quavering voice.

Shellenberg looked sharply at the *untersturmfuhrer*, and the color drained from the young man's face. The general grunted in disgust and turned back to his report. "Your father was naval attache after the last conflict?"

Fischer nodded. He opened his mouth, then closed it again without speaking.

"You returned to Germany to attend military school, and were commissioned a *untersturmfuhrer* three years ago. You have spent your time in Norway?"

Fischer nodded again, then cleared his throat. "Yes, sir." His words were barely audible.

Shellenberg laid the report down and leaned back in his chair while he studied the two men before him. Helmke's nervousness increased. Shellenberg's gaze focused on him.

"*Sturmbannfuhrer*, get rid of that ridiculous mustache and change your hair. It is an insult to our Fuhrer to attempt to imitate him. It will also call unwarranted notice to yourself." The general shifted his attention to Fischer. "*Untersturmfuhrer*, you are to let your hair grow. You look too. . .too Prussian."

Shellenberg pointed to two chairs. "Bring those over here and be seated."

Helmke and Fisher looked warily at each other as they carried the chairs across the room and set them in front of the desk. Helmke tried to look attentive as he waited for Shellenberg to begin. But questions flowed too quickly through his mind. Shellenberg waited and watched until Helmke feared the silence would drive him insane.

"The Fuhrer has a plan," Shellenberg said at last. The words hung in the air. "It is a plan of vital interest to Germany. It requires two men who are resourceful and who will not hesitate."

Helmke saw in Shellenberg's eyes that the general did not believe he and Fischer were the two people needed. So fine, if they were not the ones, send them back to Paris and Norway and find someone else. He would not object.

"We require two men whose dedication and loyalty are above reproach. They must also speak Swedish fluently and without accent."

Ah, thought Helmke. That was why they were chosen.

"You will assume the identifies of Swedish businessmen looking for new customers for your company's ball bearing factory. From the time you leave this room, you will respond only to your new names. *Sturmbannfuhrer* Helmke, you will be known as Eric Holm. *Untersturmfuhrer* Fischer, your name will be Olaf Fegen. Papers will support these identities."

Shellenberg rose from his seat and paced behind his desk. "You will have two weeks of training. It should be more, but time is short. An Allied invasion is expected from England at any time. We must move this project along with urgency. The Fuhrer is personally interested in this mission, and is prepared to award those who complete it with great honors. Do you understand?"

"Yes, sir," Helmke answered. "What is the assignment?"

"The Americans and British are working on a new weapon that will bring great destruction to our country. Our scientists are developing a similar weapon. We must have it first, so we can bring America to her knees and save the glorious Reich with no more loss of German lives. Your mission is to steal plans for the implosion lens, the trigger mechanism for this bomb."

"But I am not a spy," Helmke blurted.

Shellenberg silenced him with an icy stare. "We all must do whatever is necessary for Germany. You have shown yourself to be quite resourceful in Paris, *Sturmbannfuhrer*.

Think of this as a new opportunity. Think of the prestige that will be yours when you return with the plans."

Helmke swallowed hard and his gaze dropped to the floor. So Shellenberg knew about his little enterprise. "Of course, General. I am honored to serve my country and the Fuhrer. You say we will act as Swedish businessmen. Where are we going?"

"I hope your English is as current as your Swedish, *Sturmbannfuhrer*. You are going to New Mexico. In America."

Blood roared in Helmke's ears and his vision turned black with pinpricks of light. The United States? They were sending him inside the enemy's country? He feared he would embarrass himself, and struggled to regain his composure.

He heard Fischer ask, "How will we get there?"

"By U-boat," Shellenberg said.

Helmke thought he heard Fischer groan. He turned toward the younger man and saw he was about to be ill. Fischer's mouth opened, but nothing came out.

"We have gone to great trouble to find two men who speak fluent Swedish and English with a Swedish accent," Shellenberg said harshly. "We do not have time to find replacements. You will go now to Hamburg for orientation. Do not fail."

*   *   *

A Dahmler-Benz sedan waited in front of the building, its motor purring. Helmke shoved Fischer into the back seat and climbed in after him. At his double rap on the window separating them from the driver, the car pulled into traffic.

He gazed out the window, and even though they drove through an urban region, the night was dark. The blackouts, he realized, and hoped no Allied bombers targeted their moving headlights. He glanced at the packets Shellenberg's secretary had given them, outlining the next two weeks of their lives. All so organized. All so rational. . .unless one thought about it for very long.

They soon reached the airport at Templehof. As they drove across the tarmac toward a Heinkel 111, Helmke stiffened. Three SS officers waited at the bottom of the ramp. The car stopped next to the plane, and one of the officers opened the car door.

Helmke slid out and saluted the officers, hoping they wouldn't see the fear he knew was in his eyes. Everyone feared the SS. Everyone. He breathed a sigh of relief when an officer escorted him and Fischer onto the plane, saluted, and departed. The plane took off a few minutes later.

So far, so good, Helmke thought. He leaned back in his seat and flipped through the two packets, which contained their falsified personal histories—down to grandmothers' maiden names. He smiled grimly. One could always count on the government's obsession for details. He turned to Fischer and frowned to see the vacant look in the man's eyes as he stared out the window. Helmke backhanded the *untersturmfuhrer*'s arm, and Fischer jerked away, his eyes wide with terror.

"What is the matter with you?" Helmke hissed. He glanced at the pilot, who ignored them. "What kind of officer are you, sitting there sniveling."

A pained expression crossed Fischer's face. "I am not sniveling," he said in a petulant voice.

Helmke settled against the seat. "What would you call it, then?"

Fischer hesitated. "I am proud to be chosen for this august assignment."

Helmke raised an eyebrow. "You hide your elation well."

"You do not understand," Fischer snapped. He turned to look out the window again.

Helmke glowered at the young man's back. Did the *untersturmfuhrer* want to return to Norway? Or be denounced for failing such an important assignment? From what he'd seen on his journey from Paris, Germany was more vulnerable than he'd ever imagined.

The high command must desperately need a miracle to win this war. But what was the Fuhrer thinking? To send one such as himself with no field experience on such a mission? He was a lawyer, for God's sakes. The whole plan, it was lunacy. He sighed heavily. Better to return to Paris, escape from the Allies under an assumed name, and live in neutral Switzerland.

Or perhaps he should have considered Sweden since he had the fluency to pass for a native. Ach, that was the way of it, always realizing too late that perhaps another path would have served better.

They landed in Hamburg, where another SS officer escorted them to another sedan that waited on the tarmac.

They did not enter the city, but drove along an empty highway.

It was approaching midnight when the silent driver turned off the main road. What pavement remained was rutted and scarred, bouncing the car from side to side. Helmke shifted his position and saw that Fischer was finally alert. The *untersturmfuhrer* had fallen into an unsettled sleep soon after their aborted discussion, and had not spoken since. Helmke wished he could have found that same oblivion. Instead, he'd spent the time lamenting the loss of his Parisian assignment.

The car jerked to a stop before a darkened building. Helmke climbed from the car and heard Fischer slide out behind him.

From the shadowy doorway, a figure approached. "*Sturmbannfuhrer* Helmke?"

"I am he." In the filtered moonlight, he saw the shiny rawhide lash of a quirt whistle through the air and strike his chest. More startled than hurt, he leapt back. "Wha—"

"You are dead, *Sturmbannfuhrer*. You just revealed your true identity to the enemy."

"What do you mean? I am still in Germany, am I not?" Bewildered, Helmke looked around. He spotted a sign on a thin patch of grass that reassured him that he was where he was supposed to be.

"You must push from your mind any memory of the man who was Herman Helmke. You are Eric Holm, from Malmo, Sweden." The man's face was still hidden in the darkness.

"Of course. I will not be making a mistake when we are on our mission."

"It is my job to make sure you and the *untersturmfuhrer* do not make a mistake again, from this moment on. Follow me." The man turned sharply on his heel and went into the building. Once inside, he led them down a long, brightly-lit corridor to a classroom.

Helmke studied the unrolled maps hanging on the walls, the chalkboards covered with writing. So many years it had been since he was in school. Perhaps he was too old to learn. As a child, he'd only feared a rap on the knuckles if he failed. These lessons, if not learned perfectly, would mean a much more serious punishment.

He stifled a yawn. He'd barely slept in two days, and his last meal was. . .a bowl of watery soup at the train station. He hoped the rest of the mission was not filled with such deprivation.

The man turned to face them. He wore civilian clothing, but stood and moved like a career military officer. Tapping the quirt against his leg, his sharp, blue-eyed gaze quickly assessed them. Helmke could not tell if he found them as lacking as Shellenberg had.

Helmke's anger grew. If he and the *untersturmfuhrer* were so important to the war effort, then they should be treated with more respect. After all, he was a *sturmbannfuhrer*. Helmke considered all his accomplishments in Paris. It was true that he made the most of his opportunities, but he always provided his commanding officer with the highest quality work. He had nothing to be ashamed of, nothing to apologize for.

"I am Helmut Schmidt. For the next two weeks, your education is my responsibility." Schmidt looked from Helmke to Fischer. "I trust General Shellenberg stressed the importance of this mission?"

"He explained it is vital to our victory," Fischer said.

Helmke looked at him with surprise. So the little boy speaks, does he? "We are prepared to make the sacrifices necessary for the Fuhrer," Helmke added.

"Good. We will start our briefings now."

Helmke took a deep breath. "Perhaps we can put off the sacrifices until tomorrow, Herr Schmidt?" Helmke smiled to soften his objection. "It has been a long journey for me from Paris. I am certain the *untersturmfuhrer* would also benefit from dinner and sleep before we begin our lessons."

Schmidt pursed his lips, clearly not pleased with the delay. "As you wish, *Sturmbannfuhrer*. Your minds will, of course, be sharper in the morning. Come. I will show you to your quarters." He led them up two flights of stairs.

From what he could see, Helmke decided the building was a former boarding school. The drab room Schmidt brought them to held two of everything in mirror image, cots, desks, chairs, and clothes closets.

"This will be your home for the next two weeks. Breakfast is at five-thirty. Our lessons begin at six o'clock. Rest well."

He shut the door behind him, leaving them alone. Fischer stripped off his uniform and tumbled into bed.

Hands on his hips, Helmke looked at the mess. He'd never before called someone on their behavior. But this young officer obviously needed strict control. Such sloppiness could only mean a lack of discipline on other levels. He would not allow it to jeopardize their mission. "What kind of officer strews his belongings like a child."

"I will pick them up in the morning."

"No. You will pick them up now. That is an order." Helmke straightened and glared at Fischer.

With an insubordinate scowl, Fischer crawled from bed and gathered his clothes. After folding and placing them in the closet, he mockingly saluted Helmke. "Is that acceptable, sir?"

Helmke approached and stood toe-to-toe with the taller man. "I may be a military lawyer and not a field officer, but I still outrank you. That means you will follow orders, and you will do so with respect. Is that understood?"

"Yes."

"Yes, what?" Helmke growled.

"Yes, sir." Fischer even saluted.

Helmke stood back. "You are dismissed. Go to bed."

He waited until Fischer had closed his eyes and the lights were off before he released a deep breath. He slid under the thin blankets and shivered, not sure if it was from the cold or from uncertainty. How he longed for the security of his assignment in Paris, for the warmth of his Annette. Would he ever see her again? He sighed; probably not.

But now he must sleep. He had a sinking feeling both food and rest would be at a premium until this was over.

The next morning, a bell reverberated in the corridor, startling Helmke from deep sleep. Fischer crawled out of bed and stumbled in the dark until he found the light switch. Wordlessly they dressed and went downstairs where they were greeted by Schmidt.

"Come. We will eat in here." Schmidt pointed toward an empty room that had been set for breakfast.

Helmke took the seat designated by Schmidt and stared at the meager bowl of porridge with bits of sausage mixed in that sat before him. Peasant food. His Annette, she could not cook, but she knew how to provide him with bountiful meals that delighted the palate. But that was another lifetime ago. Then he was a simple military lawyer with dreams of a prosperous future. Now he was destined to be a national hero—or blamed for Germany's destruction.

CHAPTER 12

Schmidt opened the folder he carried and spread sheets of paper on the table. "General Shellenberg has told you where you are going and why. We start your preparations now. By tomorrow, you will have memorized your dossiers. You will be tested."

Helmke nodded slowly. "I am concerned how we can accomplish this mission in the short time we are allocated, Herr Schmidt."

"We do not expect you to do this alone, Eric Holm. Others will assist you. We have an agent in Santa Fe, who calls himself Henry Miller. He is trailing a scientist at the research facility, a former German national we know is a communist. Before the war, as a sign of our good faith, we warned the British that this man was giving secrets to the Soviets. They chose to ignore us." Schmidt shrugged. "Now we will use that to our advantage."

"You suspect he is giving secrets still?"

Smiling, Schmidt nodded. "I am pleased you grasp the situation so quickly, Herr Holm." He looked at Fischer and frowned at the young man. "Olaf Fegen, you would do well to pay more attention to what we are saying and less to that food you bolt down."

Fischer stopped, his fork in midair, and looked at the two men. He scowled and dropped the fork with a clatter.

Helmke raised an eyebrow and glanced at Schmidt, who gave him a knowing look. "So you want us to blackmail this scientist into giving us the plans?"

Now that he seemed to have Fischer's attention, Schmidt turned back to Helmke. "Miller will assist you with this. You may also find a young waitress useful."

Fischer perked up. "Is she an agent, too?"

"No. Her brother is an American airman, confined to one of our POW stalags. She may be persuaded to help you in an emergency. Her name is Ellen Peterson. She works at Carrie's Cafe."

"How long will we have?" Helmke asked.

"You will have seven days from the time the U-boat drops you off the coast of Mexico until it picks you up again at that same location."

"That is not much time. We must be most competent." Helmke turned to Fischer for agreement and saw how pale the lieutenant had turned. "*Untersturm*—Olaf, are you ill?"

Fischer shook his head. "No."

"What is wrong, then?" Schmidt asked.

"Nothing is wrong," Fischer said harshly. "Nothing. Go on."

Schmidt hesitated, then continued. "Today, you study your dossiers, then we review your route from Mexico to Santa Fe."

"Herr Schmidt, what about my family?" Helmke asked. "I have a wife and two children living near Frankfurt. I worry not only that they may be killed in a bombing, but that what little they have will be confiscated or forced to share with refugees assigned to live in my home."

Schmidt nodded. "You need not worry about them. They will not be asked to house anyone, and your wife, she will receive extra rations."

"May I call her before I leave?" Helmke felt an unexpected yearning for her warmth and comforting ways that he hadn't felt during all his time in Paris. He tried to hide his disappointment when Schmidt shook his head.

"What about my family?" Fischer asked. "Will they receive extra rations, also?"

"You do not have a wife or children," Schmidt said.

"No, but I have parents living on the outskirts of Dresden. They have not been hurt in the recent bombings, but I worry still."

"Your father is a soldier. He will know what to do. Your mother is his responsibility."

"But—"

"The circumstances are different, Herr Fegen. That is the end of it." Schmidt pushed back his chair. "It is time to begin. We have much to do if you are to succeed. Follow me."

That night, Helmke slid exhausted beneath the covers. They'd spent hours in the classroom, learning about the many uses for ball bearings, as well as the local customs and traditions they were expected to be familiar with as frequent travelers to New Mexico. How would they ever remember the manufacturing specifications for ball bearings, the geography of their route, or the layout of the cities they were to visit? There was much to learn, too much.

They'd also spent hours in the gymnasium. Fischer had excelled in the endurance tests. Helmke sighed. The untersturmfuhrer had youth on his side, youth and a body already in prime form. While he?

Helmke groaned as he shifted his position. His cerebral duties and enjoyment of the good life had led him to ignore the high command's fitness directives. Now he must pay. It was no easier for Fischer, for he did poorly in the classroom. Hopefully, a quick mind would be far more useful on this mission than a quick body.

He sighed heavily and fell into a deep sleep.

The door crashed open, the light flashed on. "Wh—what is it?" Helmke cried out.

He tried to shield his eyes from the glaring overhead light, but strong hands grabbed his and hauled him from his bed. He could hear Fischer objecting behind him. Helmke resisted, but was no match for the uniformed men who dragged him from the room.

Terrified, he tried to resist, but it did little to slow them. "Who are you? Where are you taking me? I demand you stop."

"Shut up," one of the men snarled. "You're the one who's got questions to answer."

Helmke's eyes adjusted to the light and he recognized the men's uniforms—American. What the hell? Were they too late? Was this the invasion?

His captors flung him into a small room and slammed the door, leaving him alone. Fischer's shouting faded down the hall. Wide-eyed, Helmke looked around. The room was empty except for one wooden chair and a small table. He tested the door; as he feared, it was locked. Sweat beaded on his forehead, dampened his pajama top. Mother of God, what was going on?

He leaned against the door and listened. Footsteps approached from down the hall. He hurried across the room. The door flung open and a man dressed in uniform entered. Helmke gasped as the man slammed the door shut and turned to face him.

"I am Captain Brown." The man spoke German with a heavy American accent.

"What are you doing here?"

"We have captured this facility. Sit down."

Helmke saw the coldness in his eyes.

"Name?"

"*Sturmbannfuhrer* Herman Helmke."

"Why are you here?"

"It does not matter any more," Helmke said, sadly shaking his head.

The American backhanded him across the face. "I will tell you what matters and what does not. Answer my question."

Helmke said nothing and tried to look arrogant, the way an SS officer would respond. But the SS were a different breed; he was a lawyer, a man who lived by his intelligence, not his brawn or intimidation. He worried how long he could maintain the facade.

The American struck him again. "We know you are a spy. We know you planned to infiltrate the United States and steal top secret information."

"You have no proof," Helmke bluffed. "I do not know what you are talking about."

Waving a folder, the American said, "We have everything we need."

The folder, Schmidt's ubiquitous folder. Helmke swallowed hard. What was the point of holding back when they already knew? Perhaps he would be in a better position to negotiate if he cooperated. After all, his forte was making the most of an unfortunate situation.

"My name is Herman Helmke. I am a *sturmbannfuhrer* in the German army."

The door swung open again and Schmidt stormed in. "No, no, no! You are *not* Herman Helmke, *sturmbannfuhrer* in the German army. You are Eric Holm, Swedish businessman."

Startled, Helmke stared at him. "You. . .you mean this, it is not real?"

Schmidt pounded his fist on the table. "Of course it is real. Everything you do from now on is real. You cannot afford to think *anything* is pretend. Ever."

Helmke sagged against the chair to quiet his pounding heart. It had been a test. A test that he failed. He straightened and looked somberly at Schmidt. "This has been a most useful lesson, Herr Schmidt. I will not soon forget how it feels to be dragged from bed. I will not be tricked again."

Schmidt nodded. "See that you are not."

The next days passed quickly. Schmidt issued Helmke and Fischer clothing, all of it made in Sweden, including their underwear. They memorized their papers, their life histories, the ostensible reason for going to Santa Fe, and how to execute their mission.

Every night Helmke fell into bed, exhausted yet fearful he would again be rousted from a deep sleep for one of Schmidt's interrogation drills. One night, they returned, dragged him from bed and grilled him well past dawn. He did not break. Fischer was not as strong. Helmke shared Schmidt's unvoiced concern about Fischer's participation, but there was nothing to be done. It was too late to change the plan.

On the twelfth day, Schmidt joined them as usual for dinner. While they ate, he reviewed his ever-present file and waited patiently for Helmke and Fischer to finish eating. Helmke dabbed his mouth with a napkin as he studied Schmidt. Something was different today.

"We have done all we can in our allotted time," Schmidt said. "Tomorrow you will fly to the U-boat base in La Rochelle."

Fischer choked on his food. Schmidt stopped until Helmke had successfully pounded on Fischer's back. The untersturmfuhrer looked away from both men as if disinterested, but Helmke sensed that was far from true.

"The captain thinks you are on a temporary assignment," Schmidt continued. "The specific orders about your destination will not be opened until after you depart. That is how we maintain secrecy."

"Will you be coming with us?" Helmke asked.

Schmidt nodded. "I will accompany you to La Rochelle."

Helmke felt Fischer shiver next to him. Did the *untersturmfuhrer*'s fear have something to do with the U-boat. Every time one was mentioned, Fischer reacted violently.

They excused themselves from Schmidt and returned to their room for a last night's sleep. Helmke shut the door quietly behind them. "All right. What is it all about?"

Fischer whirled around to face him, fear haunting his gaze. "What do you mean?"

"What is it about U-boats that upsets you so?"

Fischer laughed, a harsh sound that held no humor. "You would not understand." He stripped off his clothes and climbed into bed, his back turned toward Helmke.

Helmke sat on the edge of his own cot. "I have no intention of going on a dangerous mission with a partner who looks to disintegrate when the subject comes up. You will tell me now."

Fischer did not move for many minutes, then finally, he shuddered. "You do not understand the importance of following a family tradition."

Helmke shrugged. "It would depend on the tradition."

Fischer rolled over and sat up. "The men in my family have joined the navy since Bismarck. I refused."

"You had a valid reason? You suffered from the seasickness?"

"I wish it were that noble a reason. No, I refused because I have claustrophobia. Every time someone mentions the U-boat, all I can think of is being imprisoned in a steel container with the sea pressing in on me from all sides." He closed his eyes and shuddered.

Helmke wasn't sure what to think. There was no point telling Schmidt; it was too late to change the plans. But at least he knew what the problem was. "This is ridiculous," he said, hoping a hard-nosed approach would work best. "You are a German soldier. You have no fears."

Fischer glared at him. "That's what I thought you would say. Forget I told you anything."

"I most certainly will forget this idiocy. We will never mention this flaw again." Helmke snapped off the light and found his way into bed. Such a perilous journey lay ahead of them, a mission fraught with opportunities for failure. He could only pray that his partner would not give them away.

* * *

The flight to La Rochelle was without incident. When they stopped for a brief refueling in Paris, Schmidt denied Helmke's request to deplane, and so he'd gazed longingly out the window at the city skyline.

How he missed his Annette, although he was pragmatic enough to know that by this time she would have aligned herself with another person of influence. And his masterpieces, the ones he'd already paid for. Had Jacques received the new delivery instructions? He sighed as the plane's engines revved, pressed his hand against the glass in farewell as they taxied down the runway.

That was the way of it. He was on to a new assignment, one that could bring him great honor and glory. If they succeeded. If they failed. . .Well, his art collection was still safe in Switzerland. He would think of something.

The plane touched down in La Rochelle, but not before it circled the city and its harbor, and Helmke and Fischer saw the devastation from continual Allied bombing raids. Rusted metal, broken masonry and heaps of rubble materialized out of the fog that shrouded the city. The gutted buildings and bomb craters filled with stagnant water gave the city a surrealistic appearance. Wrecked Gantry cranes mingled with twisted railroad tracks and rolling stock in the dock areas.

In the harbor, ships anchored too close to shore now lay on their sides; further out, the masts of sunken vessels rose above the surface, markers for their watery graves. Small vessels, trawlers, scows, and oil barges clustered in the harbor, floating in debris-laden water that glistened from a thick oil slick.

"*Mein Gott*," Helmke whispered against the window. The sights filled him with horror. How isolated he had been in Paris. He was, perhaps, one of the luckier ones, chosen as he was to leave before it was too late. He had not realized how desperate the high command must be to send him to America.

"Herr Schmidt, how much farther do we have to go?"

"Not far. But the bombings have done extensive damage to the road. We will have to walk after we land."

Helmke nodded and gripped his armrests for the landing. Soon he was making his way with Fischer and Schmidt across the pockmarked landing field. They strode down the road toward the harbor, and crawled through a barbed wire barricade that marked the perimeter of the U-boat pens.

An indifferent sentry called for them to halt as they approached a guard house, and extended his hand for their passes. Herr Schmidt showed his identity. The sentry glanced at Helmke and Fischer before calling the corporal of the guard to guide them across the yard.

Ahead, a bunker, looming massive and brooding, housed the U-boat pens. Helmke remembered reading that the roof was steel-reinforced concrete forty feet thick. He saw the gaping hatches that provided access to individual pens, with larger openings at water level which served as entrances to the two-boat berths.

Helmke followed the others as they picked their way along a ramp leading to an entrance inside the bunker. Concrete piers separated the berths. Two of the berths served as drydocks for U-boats requiring extensive repairs below the waterline.

He cast a furtive glance at Fischer. All the color had drained from the younger officer's face, his eyes darted wildly about, his fists clenched and unclenched. This was not a good sign, but Helmke could think of nothing to change the situation.

Two officers stood on the pier and a steady stream of seamen carried stores on board. The corporal pointed to a U-boat and said something to Schmidt, but Helmke could not hear over the din. Schmidt and approached one of the officers, a lieutenant commander, who wore a captain's white cap. Schmidt spoke to him and he glanced at Helmke and Fischer.

Helmke did not like the way the captain's jaw jutted pugnaciously as Schmidt talked, and he geared himself for confrontation. Was the captain just another field officer who had no use for civilians holding military rank? Someone who did not have the Fuhrer's great vision to see how important this mission was to Germany's destiny? Helmke nudged Fischer. "Come. We introduce ourselves."

He strode ahead, ignoring Fischer's inevitable surly objections. "*Heil*, Hitler." He saluted, looking the captain straight in the eye. "I am Eric Holm. Olaf Fegen and I thank you for assisting us."

"I am Captain Norden." The man spoke with the authority of giving orders and having them obeyed without question. He was short, with a sturdy frame and close-cropped hair. The captain looked Helmke up and down before turning back to Schmidt.

"I received a communique from the C-in-C that these two men are taking the place of regular crew members." It was clear from his tone that Captain Norden was not pleased with the exchange.

"That is correct," Herr Schmidt said. "They will need someone to show them around."

"I will arrange it." The captain saluted in their general direction, then stalked away.

"The assignment displeases him," Helmke said.

"That is not important. What is important is that he follow orders." Schmidt turned to face the submarine. "Do you know anything about submarines?"

Helmke smiled smugly. "This is a VII-C class boat. She is powered by two six-cylinder diesels, 1400 horsepower each," he recited. "She can cruise almost 8000 miles at 10 knots, more than enough for our mission. Usually, she is used in combat situations because she can dive quickly and is highly maneuverable. Underwater, she is powered by batteries, and has a range of 80 miles at four knots before the batteries need recharging."

A surprised look on his face, Schmidt pivoted to face Helmke. "I am most impressed, Herr Holm."

Helmke nodded and stared at the steel, cigar-shaped structure, their transport to America. A little over 200 feet long and 13 feet wide, the vessel normally held a crew of five officers and 45 men. For this voyage, the second watch officer and the radio man were being left behind to make room for him and Fischer.

Fischer stared in the opposite direction at the open seas. Helmke almost felt sorry for the young man. The coming trip would be a nightmare for him, and Norden was not the type to understand. As senior officer on this mission, it was up to Helmke to keep Fischer out of trouble.

A petty officer approached them and saluted. "The captain asks that you come aboard immediately."

"Of course," Helmke said. He extended his hand to Schmidt. "Thank you, Herr Schmidt. You have prepared us well."

"Do not fail. We look forward to your successful return."

The two men clasped hands, then Helmke elbowed Fischer from his preoccupation. "It is time," he said in a tone that brooked no argument.

The petty officer led them to a ladder. They descended into the body of the U-boat and found themselves surrounded by confusion. Men scurried back and forth, jumping through hatches and dodging cases of provisions littering the passageways.

Weaving his way through the maze, the petty officer maintained a steady stream of chatter. "Accommodations are tight. We have one bunk for every two men, so one sleeps while the other's on watch."

"Where is our room?" Fischer asked. Some of the color had returned to his face, but the glazed look in his eyes worried Helmke.

"You don't really have a room. You'll sleep here." The petty officer opened a door. "We call this the wardroom. Herr Holm, you can sleep on the settee. The officers sit on it for meals. Herr Fegen, there's a bunk directly under the overhead."

Helmke saw the cramped space designated for Fischer. The *untersturmfuhrer* had turned pale again, and a clammy sweat covered his face. He kept running his finger inside his collar as if to loosen it.

"I can't breathe," he whispered in a panicky voice to Helmke.

"I am not surprised. The air is stifling and reeks of diesel fuel. Come, we go outside." Helmke led the way, and they stood on the gun deck.

The submarine slipped from its berth into the harbor. The air was cooler here. A curtain of fog hid the ugliness they were leaving behind as they slowly made their way toward the open seas. Helmke left Fischer and approached Captain Norden, who anxiously peered through the fog.

Norden glanced at him, then returned to looking skyward. "The RAF will not bother us as long as the fog holds," he said. "We are most vulnerable to air attack when leaving port."

Helmke had not thought about solo aircraft stalking the harbor; he'd assumed Allied raids were organized squadrons with designated targets. He prayed for empty skies.

The fog held and Captain Norden ordered a course due west until nightfall before excusing himself to review his sealed orders. Helmke ordered Fischer into the submarine. They went to the wardroom, and Fischer turned pale again.

Helmke feared the trip would be too much for the younger man, but he was not about to let his own chances for glory be ruined. He would drag Fischer through hell and back if that was what it took. Distracting Fischer should help calm him. "Tell me about your assignment in Norway, *Untersturmfuhrer*."

Fischer turned to him, that wide-eyed panicky look in his eyes. "It was cold." He went back to staring at the windowless walls.

Helmke forced himself to chuckle. "Yes, I suppose that is the way Norway would be. Where were you stationed?"

"Vardö."

"Then you tracked convoys in and out of Murmansk."

Fischer shrugged. "It was easy. We counted the number and types of ships and reported it to the navy and airforce. They decided when to torpedo them from above or below."

Helmke saw Fischer's shoulders relax and his eyes gaze more normally around the room. That was good. "I was stationed in Paris, myself. A nice place to be during a war."

"I was doing real military work, not hiding behind some desk." Fischer turned away with a scowl.

"What you did was very important. I was merely keeping an entire country under Occupation. The French people hailed us as heros and welcomed our presence with open arms." Helmke was pleased to see a hint of chagrin in Fischer's expression.

"You are correct, sir. War is not easy, no matter what your assignment."

"At least Paris is warmer than Vardö."

"But you never saw the Norwegian women."

Helmke joined Fischer in a knowing laugh. It always came back to women.

The petty officer burst into the wardroom. "Herr Holm, Captain Norden wants to see you immediately."

It had to be the orders. From the consternation he saw on the petty officer's face, Norden was not pleased. He rose from his seat. "Should Herr Fegen come, also?"

"I—I do not know, sir. The captain did not say."

"Olaf, you—" Helmke hesitated. Fischer's new calm was fading quickly. Leaving him behind was perhaps not a wise thing. "Come with me."

They followed the petty officer through the control room to the captain's quarters. Helmke looked with dismay at the curtained off area that gave the illusion of privacy. How could he have a discussion with the captain when everyone in the control room could hear? He took a deep breath. "Wait here," he whispered to Fischer.

The petty officer pulled back the curtain and announced him. Helmke saw Norden's face, mottled with rage as he clutched the orders. Helmke stepped inside the alcove-like room, and the petty officer jerked the curtain closed again.

"Do you know what is in these orders?" Norden's voice radiated with barely suppressed anger.

"Yes. Herr Fegen and I have been preparing for this mission."

"Do you have any idea what 'this mission' will do to my vessel and my crew? We have orders to take you to Mexico and wait for your return. We are not to engage the enemy, nor are we to let the enemy know of our presence."

"Secrecy is of utmost importance to the success of our assignment."

"We are a fighting submarine, Herr Holm, not a spy ship." Norden spoke in a low voice that would not carry beyond the curtain. "My crew is the finest anywhere. They are trained and prepared to meet the enemy. Do you know what happens to men like this when they have nothing to do? They grow bored, restless. They grumble and fight amongst themselves. They lose their precision and they become sloppy in the performance of their duties. Then accidents happen. But worst of all, there will be no honors for them when they return to La Rochelle."

"Captain, we have embarked on the most critical voyage of your career. The destiny of Germany, no, of the world, rests on our shoulders. When we succeed, there will be more than enough honors for all of us. If we fail. . .."

Norden eyed Helmke critically, then nodded. "I have heard the rumors. The war is not going well. You think you will change that?"

"We are sent by the Fuhrer himself."

Norden looked skeptical; Helmke couldn't tell if the captain didn't believe what he'd said or if he doubted the feasibility of the plan. Norden nodded. "All right. We have no choice but to follow orders. I will keep the crew alert. We will do emergency dives, load and unload the torpedoes, and I will call surprise drills at all hours."

The captain smiled grimly. "Knowing this crew, they will begin betting on the time of them." He turned serious and gazed steadily at Helmke. "It is up to you, Herr Holm—or whatever your name is—to reward us by successfully doing whatever it is you must do in Mexico."

"I will." Helmke extended his hand. "There is something you should know about Herr Feg—"

The petty officer threw back the curtain and saluted. "Sir, there is a convoy up ahead."

Norden pushed past Helmke into the control room. "Clear the bridge. Dive. Dive. Periscope depth. Up periscope."

Helmke stood against the wall next to Fischer and watched, fascinated by the captain's calm efficiency and the responsiveness of his crew.

"Sir, their course points toward the Mediterranean."

"Sir, a destroyer has separated from the convoy and is headed in our direction."

"Take her down to 400 feet, and head 350 degrees, slightly west of due north," Norden ordered. "Is the destroyer on a sweep?"

"Yes, sir."

"All quiet," Norden said.

"All quiet." The order was passed quickly through the vessel.

Helmke's heart pounded, and he heard a noise. All eyes focused above, listening to the thrashing propellers as the destroyer approached. It drew nearer; the noise intensified. Tension radiated through the tomb-like silence. The sound peaked, then gradually ebbed as the destroyer completed its sweep and rejoined the convoy.

The crew exhaled as one, and nervous laughter filled the air. Smiling with relief, Helmke turned to Fischer.

Pale and breathing in short erratic breaths, the *untersturmfuhrer* stared at Captain Norden. He lunged at the captain and grabbed his arms. Fischer opened his mouth, but only guttural animal sounds emerged. Finally, he whispered, "I must leave. I must get out."

Norden shook Fischer off. "Control yourself, Herr Fegen."

Fischer stepped back and looked wildly around the control room. Suddenly he streaked across the room and scampered up the ladder to the conning tower. He twisted the handle and pushed on the hatch cover.

"Schultz!" Norden called to the officer working in the conning tower. The officer struck Fischer behind the ear with a wrench, and the lieutenant slumped to the floor.

Norden turned to Helmke. "Is there anything else I should know before we proceed?" he asked through clenched teeth.

Helmke shook his head. "I will keep Herr Fegen out of your way."

*   *   *

The time passed slowly, days and nights merging into each other. Fischer never spoke of the incident, and Helmke did not mention it, either. Instead, he spent his time drilling Fischer on their plans until they both felt confident they could pull off the deception.

It was after dinner when the petty officer approached Helmke and saluted. "Sir, Captain Norden requests you join him."

The summons caught Helmke off guard. They had done little more than nod to each other in passing since the voyage began. Norden had done what he promised, keeping the crew occupied and ever vigilant, despite their evasive route across the Atlantic.

Helmke ducked around the curtain to Norden's room, and was surprised to see a bottle of schnapps and two small glasses.

Smiling, Norden gestured for Helmke to sit down. "This is a critical time, Herr Holm. We approach the coast of Mexico. Tomorrow morning, assuming there are no patrol planes, we will take you ashore."

He poured some schnapps into the glasses and handed one to Helmke. He raised his own. "To March 28, 1944.

May it go down in history as a pivotal day for our great country."

Helmke nodded and tossed down the liquor, welcoming its burning jolt. He held his glass out for a refill. One hundred years from now, historians would still remember Herman Helmke.

CHAPTER 13

NEW MEXICO
Noon, March 27, 1944

Inside the timegate, Hanover heard an echo—Beecker's cry for luck?—and felt himself falling, over and around, inside a chamber of swirling lights that flashed and blinded him. Wind chimes tinkled in his ears, followed by the roar of wind through a tunnel. He stopped tumbling, floated as if suspended for a moment, then was flung through to the other side.

He landed on the rocky surface; a stone shifted under his weight and he slipped. He stumbled, twisting his ankle. Sharp pain shot through his foot. "Damn!"

Hanover sank to the ground and shook his head to clear it. Beecker hadn't mentioned the disorientation, the vertigo. He checked his ankle, dismayed to see it was already swelling.

As he massaged it, he looked around, then stopped and swallowed hard. Neustadt had vanished. He sat in an open area populated only by scrub brush. A hundred meters away, a ribbon of highway stretched to the horizon. Silence filled the air, pushed aside by a gusting breeze that rustled the bushes.

He wiped his hand across his face. One thing was certain. He wasn't in 2044 any more. A sinking feeling settled in the pit of his stomach, the realization that he wasn't where he had been. If this wasn't 2044, when was it? He had left the laboratory in Neustadt in late afternoon, but from the sun's current position overhead, he figured it was closer to midday. That was okay; Beecker had mentioned he might arrive a few hours off, but was this the right date?

Uncertainty blanketed him, a kind of uncertainty he'd never known before. He'd spent his life alone, but this was a different kind of aloneness. At least the world of the GOA had been familiar. He didn't know this world; all the rules had changed. He was more alone now than he'd ever been.

He staggered to his feet, still dizzy from his leap, and gingerly tested his injured ankle. Pain ricocheted up his leg. His jaw clenched, Hanover hopped around to face the timegate. All he could see was a faint trace of its shimmering outline. Beecker had told him the timegate would function for ten days at the most.

Looking around at the rocky, uneven terrain, Hanover decided time wasn't his immediate concern; it was making sure he could find the damn timegate again. No natural landmarks existed, and certainly no man-made structures, as there had been—no, make that would be—in his own time. Keeping the weight off his injured ankle as much as possible, Hanover gathered some rocks to mark the timegate's location.

He practiced his new name, William Terence Scott, tried to grow comfortable with it. He stopped and gazed at the barren wasteland, the enormity of what he was doing finally hitting him. He had a chance to make a difference under this new persona. It was frightening, really. The fate of the whole world rested on his ability to stop a pair of Nazi spies.

He hoped to hell he could do it. Hanover dropped two last stones on the mound and brushed the dirt from his hands. He had as good a chance as anyone in this situation. He knew how the mechanism plans had been stolen—were going to be stolen—and who had—would—do it. Besides, he was reasonably intelligent, gutsy, and a fast talker. Grimacing, he considered that it was his glib tongue that landed him in trouble more than anything else in his life. Well, this time he'd watch himself. He'd weigh every word before he spoke, and he'd be very careful who he talked to.

But nothing was going to change if he stood around here. He had to find a way into town. He looked for something he could use as a cane, but found nothing amidst the low-growing sagebrush. That staff of Travis' would come in handy about now.

He stopped his search. Was Travis still in jail? Or maybe he hadn't been born yet. Stop it! Hanover mentally shook himself. The incongruity of his situation would make him crazy if he let it. Better not to think about it at all.

As best he could, Hanover hobbled toward the road. The slight down-slope of the terrain aided him, but by the time he reached the highway, his ankle ached even more, and he couldn't remember ever being this exhausted. It must be the timegate that made him so tired.

Hanover glanced back and barely made out the half-meter high mound he'd assembled. He sank to the ground, yet he couldn't stop to rest. Accumulating rocks within easy reach, he built an elongated mound on the side of the road with the long axis pointing toward the other mound.

He forced himself to his feet, worried he would fall asleep if he sat any longer. Aligning himself with the long axis, the new mound was visible, but not obvious.

Satisfied, he looked down the highway to his right, then to his left. Nothing stirred. The bright sun was warm, prompting him to remove his jacket. Santa Fe was a long way, especially with his bad ankle, but that was where he needed to be. He cursed his luck for injuring himself before he'd even started, and hoped it wouldn't hamper his efforts.

He'd half-hopped his way down the road for almost an hour when he heard rumbling behind him. He looked over his shoulder and saw an ancient vehicle—what he remembered was called a pick-up truck—quickly approaching. Only it wasn't that old. The shiny black paint flashed in the sunlight. The noise was from a combustion engine that used fossil fuels, a roar so much louder than the hum and high-pitched whine of electrovehicles.

Hanover turned back and continued hobbling down the road. The truck's horn beeped and he was surprised to see the driver pull over and get out.

"Looks like you could use a lift, buddy." The man's Adam's apple bobbed as he spoke.

"A lift?"

"Yeah. I can give you a ride as far as Santa Fe." The man was thin with a long face bracketed by prominent ears, his grin friendly, genuine. He climbed back into the truck and looked expectantly at Hanover.

A lift meant a ride. In his own time, no one would have stopped, and if they had, the offer would have been viewed with suspicion. But Beecker had said these were different times, and this looked to be the fastest way to reach Santa Fe. Besides, his ankle throbbed. Hanover smiled in return. "Santa Fe's where I want to go."

"Well, hop in. Name's Putnam, Sam Putnam." He held out a strong hand with callused fingers.

"Scott—ah, William Scott." He slammed the door shut and took the proffered hand, hoping his nervousness wouldn't show. He'd almost slipped.

"You go by Bill?"

"Hmm? Oh, yeah, Bill's fine." Hanover sank against the leather seat. Getting used to his new identity was harder than he'd expected.

Putnam started the truck and shifted a lever. A cloud of black smoke belched from the rear, and the truck lurched forward. "Damnation, this thing needs a tune-up. You just out of the service?"

"The service?"

"Yeah. I figured from that limp you've just been mustered out of the army."

The service must be another name for the military, but mustard? Hanover wondered what the condiment had to do with it. "No, I turned my ankle walking off the road."

Putnam frowned, the friendliness faded from his eyes, replaced by wary alertness. Hanover thought back. Beecker had said something about the army, given him a card. What was it? Oh, yes, a draft card. "I haven't been in the service. I'm classified 4F." He tapped his chest. "Heart."

"Oh yeah? That's tough." Putnam's affable grin returned. "I'm the local veterinarian, so they classified me as essential. I know they need me here, but I'd sure like to be where the action is. Where you from?"

Hanover hesitated. "San Francisco." That was where his identity originated; probably best to stick with that. Then he was less likely to get confused, or to meet someone from that area.

"No kidding? Boy, I'd like to go there sometime. I've never been out of New Mexico. Well, except for vet's school, but that didn't count because I was so busy studying and working to pay my way that I barely left the campus."

Hanover nodded, only half hearing. He watched the passing scene, so different from his time. Road-side signs abounded, especially those advertising places to sleep and eat. No one he knew in his time smiled or had fun like the people in the signs.

They entered the outskirts of Santa Fe, and Putnam asked, "You interested in lunch?"

Hanover's mouth watered at the thought of food. Once again, he couldn't remember when he'd last eaten—that sandwich Darcy made for him a hundred years from now? He almost laughed at how ridiculous that sounded. "I'm famished."

"There's a place up ahead that's good, called Carrie's Cafe. She puts out a good meal and doesn't charge a lot for it. It's where the truckers stop."

"The who?" It was like speaking a foreign language.

"The truckers. You know, the guys who drive the big rigs. Where'd you say you're from?"

"San Francisco."

"Didn't think they talked that different from us." Putnam shrugged. "Must be wrong. That's it over there."

Relieved that the subject had changed, Hanover looked around and saw a small restaurant. Putnam turned into the dirt parking lot and jerked to a stop. The lot was full of cars and large trucks.

"Busy place," Hanover said as he followed Putnam. From the outside, he saw three or four booths on either side of the door lined up against the windows. They stepped inside and directly in front of them was a long counter with a dozen or so stools. To the right of the counter, the restaurant opened up to the back, with booths along the walls, and half a dozen tables in the middle.

A pass-through gave Hanover a view of the kitchen, where a grey-haired woman ladled steaming food onto plates. To the right of the pass-through, a swinging door suddenly pushed open. A waitress toting trays of clean silverware came through and looked at him.

Hanover stopped, his gaze locked with hers. Her wide blue eyes held a gentleness he couldn't remember seeing in the women from his time. Light brown hair framed her face and a short turned-up nose gave her a spunky air. Her lips, colored a bright red, opened in an O, revealing small white teeth.

"Hey, Ellie, how's it going?"

Putnam's words broke the spell. The waitress looked away from Hanover. "Hi, Sam. And it's Ellen, not Ellie." She dropped the trays behind the counter and glanced shyly at Hanover. "Sit anywhere. Coffee?"

"See?" Putnam nudged Hanover's arm. "Told you they was nice here." He slid into a booth and turned the cup right-side up in the saucer.

Ellen came around the counter, a pot in her hand. As she poured Sam's coffee, she nodded toward Hanover. "Is your friend going to join you, Sam?"

"Come on, Bill. Have a seat. What's the special today?" Putnam asked.

The lilting friendliness in the waitress' voice drew Hanover closer. She stood about five-four, with curves her dress accentuated nicely. When he stepped toward the booth, she turned toward him and frowned. The loss, the sense that she was disappointed or irritated by him, hit hard. He wanted this girl to smile again, only this time, to smile just for him.

"You're limping," she said.

"Wh—oh, yes. I fell on the highway."

She quickly scanned him in a detached way he found disconcerting.

"Ellie here was in nurse's training," Putnam said.

"Ah," Hanover said, relieved by the explanation.

"She had to quit and come here to help her aunt when her cousins signed up," Putnam added.

She had family, he thought; she belonged to a group of people who helped each other out.

"Your hands are all scratched up. You can wash the dirt off in back."

Hanover glanced at his hands and saw they were filthy. "That'd be great." He followed the direction she pointed, feeling clumsy and awkward as he never had before. What was wrong with him? Was it simply that he'd been too long without a woman? He shrugged; he had more important things to worry about, things like tracking down Nazi spies.

In the back, Hanover saw a sign for restrooms. He wove through the maze of mostly empty tables. His gaze stopped on a large box-like object in the back corner. Bright lights flashed on and off, and he realized it was the source of the music that filled the cafe. Intrigued, he drew closer.

Through the glass panel covering the front, he saw a disc rotate on a spindle. Below the glass was an array of buttons, and alongside each button was a printed title. Off to one side and directly above a slot, the caption "5 cents" was embossed in metal. The singer crooned something about "coming in on a wing and a prayer." The music faded to an end, the arm hovering over the disc retracted. The disc rose from the spindle and swung into a recessed space between a stack of other discs.

He waited, fascinated, for something else to happen, but the machine went quiet. Disappointed, he slipped into the restroom, then returned to find Putnam sipping on his coffee.

"Here's a menu." Putnam handed it to Hanover. "Ellie says the special's meatloaf and mashed potatoes. Hey, Ellie," he called out. "Bill's ready for his coffee."

Hanover copied Putnam, turning over his cup as he scanned the printed list of meals. He recognized most of the items, but was surprised at the amount of meat. Beecker had implied many things were scarce because of the war, but they seemed more plentiful here than in his own time. The prices seemed reasonable, too; the money Beecker gave him would be more than enough to last the ten days.

Ellen brought a pot of coffee with her and poured, glancing at Hanover with a mixture of friendliness and curiosity. "Aren't you going to introduce me to your friend, Sam?"

"Oh, yeah. This is Bill Scott. Bill, meet Ellie Peterson."

"Ellen, Sam, not Ellie," she said with a smile. "It's nice to meet you, Bill. You're new here, aren't you? I'd have remembered if you'd stopped by before."

Hanover felt a rush of exhilaration at the breathy huskiness of her voice. He stammered something about San Francisco. Putnam filled in that he was 4F, and Hanover wondered if he'd actually seen relief in Ellen's eyes.

The bell rang behind the counter. "Ellen, get these plates out before they're cold. Those two can wait."

Ellen grinned at Carrie. "I'm on it. You boys look at the menu. I'll be right back. Rest your foot on the seat next to Sam, Bill. That'll help the swelling, and it won't hurt so much."

"She sure takes charge, doesn't she? You'd think she was the doctor instead of me. Course treating a person's a little different than treating a horse." Putnam leaned closer. "She was engaged to a real nice guy, but he died at Guadalcanal."

"That's too bad." Hanover meant the words sincerely, but a part of him was pleased that there was no one in her life. Not that he had time to do anything about it. "Say, what's the date?"

"Today? It's March 27th."

The correct date. He was on schedule. Relieved, Hanover leaned against the seat.

They ordered the specials, and Hanover waited expectantly until Ellen set the plate in front of him. The smells of meat and biscuits fresh from the oven wafted toward him. He breathed deeply, closed his eyes. This wasn't 1944, this was heaven. He struggled to keep from gulping the food after his first taste. The meatloaf was moist, the gravy thick, and the mashed potatoes had lumps of real potatoes.

He hadn't realized he was this hungry, and this was the first real food he'd had since his arrest and imprisonment. The meal quickly disappeared. Ellen brought extra buttermilk biscuits and butter, real butter, to go along with cup after cup of real coffee. He ordered pie, hot apple pie with vanilla ice cream on top.

While he ate, he watched Ellen go about her work, walking with a hypnotic sway to her hips. Her warm smile crinkled her eyes, and her throaty laugh filled his spirit as the food filled his belly.

Finally satiated, he leaned back and tossed his napkin on the table. For a few moments, he'd forgotten who he was and why he was here. He couldn't believe how easily he'd shed his control, his wariness about being discovered. That didn't bode well for the rest of his time here. He'd have to concentrate, not let anything—or anyone distract him. Before this afternoon, he hadn't considered it would be much of a challenge. But after the last hour, he wasn't so sure.

With a sigh, he looked up at Putnam and saw amusement in his eyes. "What's so funny?"

"Watching you eat. It's like you haven't eaten in years, and this might be your last meal."

The man had no idea how close he'd come. "Never could turn down good cooking." Or a pretty waitress. Hanover smiled slowly, warmly, as Ellen walked toward them.

"Can I get you boys something else?"

"I don't think Bill left anything behind," Putnam said with a laugh.

"We could probably scrounge up something."

"How about you save it for next time?" Hanover suggested.

"That'd be swell," Ellen said. Hanover liked the way her gaze grew soft.

"What do we owe you?" Putnam asked. Ellen laid down their checks.

Hanover took out his money and examined it for the first time since Beecker'd given it to him. The denominations were in dollars, which he was familiar with. But the portraits on the scrip were different from those he was used to seeing. On the front of the one dollar bills, a picture of someone named Washington was shown, and on the fives, Lincoln. Hanover had no idea who these men were. From their dress and hair style, he deduced these men were famous Americans from long before the Occupation. One thing that intrigued him was the legend on top of the bills—Silver Certificate.

He had a few coins, as well, that varied from those he used in his time. Two ten-cent pieces had the profile of a woman on one side and were dated 1939 and 1942. A third coin had Hitler's profile and was dated 2014. He felt the color drain from his face and he closed his fist around the coin. Somehow this one had been mixed in with his supply.

"What's wrong?" Putnam asked. "Don't you have enough"

"No. I'm fine. I just forgot something, that's all."

"You sure? Is your foot hurting?"

"A little. But it's okay, really."

Putnam slid a coin under his plate and scooted off the bench. "I've got some appointments before going back to my ranch, so I'd better be going. Can I give you a lift anywhere?"

"No. You've helped a lot already. More than you'll ever know." Hanover shook Putnam's hand firmly. If everyone was like Putnam, this time was a good place to be.

"Well, if you're sure. You know, you shouldn't have any trouble finding a job, if you want one. With so many men gone, there are lots of opportunities for someone like you."

"I'll keep that in mind." Hanover watched Putnam leave and waved as he drove off. He turned back and saw the coin under Putnam's plate. It was a quarter. He wasn't sure what that was all about, but he put two quarters under his own.

For a few minutes, he savored the tranquility, watching the traffic, the people free to come and go as they wished, limited only by the constraints put on them by the war and by democratically-imposed laws. The heaviness he carried inside him lifted, then he remembered again why he was here.

He tested his ankle. The throbbing pain had subsided while it was elevated, but now that his foot was on the floor, the pain and swelling were returning.

"You should rest that foot."

He jerked up and saw Ellen wiping the counter across from him. She ran a damp cloth over the condiment bottles and replaced them in their racks along the back of the counter with smooth efficiency.

"It'll be okay." Hanover pushed himself from the bench. The pain intensified and he doubted his ankle would support him.

"Sit down. I'm almost finished here, and I'll fix it for you."

Grateful, Hanover nodded and sank onto the seat to wait. The restaurant had emptied out, the mid-day meal time over.

Ellen returned in a few minutes carrying a bucket of water. She knelt in front of him and removed his shoe and sock. Frowning at the swelling, she shook her head. "This isn't good."

Gently she prodded and twisted and kneaded his ankle. It hurt like hell. He wanted to jerk his foot from her hands, but despite the pain, her touch was soft and tender.

She set his foot back on the floor and pulled the bucket closer. "Put your foot in here and keep it there. The sprain's not as bad as I thought. If we soak it awhile, the swelling should go down. Then I'll wrap it. If you keep the weight off it for a few days, it should be all right. But you can't rush it."

Her diagnosis worried him. He couldn't tell her that all he had was a few days. He lifted his foot into the bucket and gasped at the icy water. "It's cold," he said with a weak smile.

Hands on her hips, she grinned. "Yeah, I know. Now don't move for a while."

The shock of the cold water faded; it felt good, in fact. Hanover leaned back and enjoyed the momentary pampering. No one had ever helped him like Ellen had. No one had ever shown him genuine friendliness like Putnam.

The need to stop the spies burned into him with an intensity he hadn't felt until now. If this was the way life was before the Occupation, he'd risk it all to keep the Germans from winning the war. He couldn't stand the thought of FedPo troops marching in here, arresting people like Putnam. . .and Ellen.

Ellen approached him with a towel. "How's the foot?"

"Numb."

"Good. Let's take a look."

He raised his foot over the bucket and she tested the ankle. Handing him a towel, she said, "The swelling's gone down. I'll find something to wrap it." In a few minutes, she returned with an ace bandage.

"Putnam told me you were in nursing school."

Frowning, she wrapped his ankle. "I wanted to do something useful. My mother thought I should be a nurse."

"Sounds like it wasn't what you wanted to do."

She grimaced and knotted the bandage. "No, I wanted to join the WASP's."

"Wasps?"

"Not many people know about it. It's a division of the Air Force for women. They fly the planes from the factories to the carriers that take them overseas."

Somehow he could see her doing something like that. "So why didn't you?"

"According to my mother, ladies don't do things like that." She sighed. "Then. . .some things happened. . .and my cousins enlisted, and that left Aunt Carrie alone, so I decided to come here and help her."

The "things that happened" must have been her fiance. Hanover looked down at the neat bandage encasing his foot. Gingerly, he tested it and felt reassured by the extra support. "Great job. How much do I owe you, doc?"

Ellen grinned up at him. "It's on the house." She stood and picked up the bucket. "Say, Bill, um, Aunt Carrie was wondering if you were looking for a job?"

"A job?"

"We're kinds short-handed here, and she was wondering if you needed something to tide you over. I told her you probably already had plans. . .."

"I do have something I have to do the next few days."

"I understand. It's just that you're new in town, and I—Aunt Carrie figured you probably didn't have a place to stay or anything. There's a room behind the kitchen, it's a storeroom now, but it has a cot, if you want it."

The offer stunned him. "Why are you doing this?"

Ellen's face flushed and she shrugged nonchalantly. "I—we thought you might need some help, that's all."

"Maybe when I'm finished—" The door opened and they both looked up.

A tall man in uniform stepped inside. Hanover stiffened. The man's iron-gray hair was combed back and he had a large mustache, twirled to a point on each side and swept upward. A star was pinned to his chest, and a pair of aviator glasses covered his eyes. He quickly glanced around. His gaze reached Hanover and stopped.

CHAPTER 14

Hanover glanced at Ellen and saw the worried look in her eyes.

"Are you in trouble with the law?" she asked in a low voice.

He winced at the anxiety he heard in her words. "No. I swear. In fact, I may need help."

The sheriff whipped off his glasses and checked Hanover over; his well-trained gaze would miss nothing. Hanover stood firm, refusing to show fear or nervousness. He'd been through it before with the FedPos, and he'd learned to mask his true feelings. He must have passed inspection because the sheriff changed direction, ducked behind the counter and poured himself a cup of coffee.

"Hey, Carrie, you back there?" The sheriff's baritone voice reverberated in the restaurant.

"Of course, I'm here. Where else would I be?" Carrie's gravelly voice came from the back.

"Come on out and dance with me. I'll put a polka on the juke box and push back some chairs. We'll have the whole place to ourselves." He winked at Ellen and grinned broadly; it changed his whole persona.

"Go on with you," Carrie said. She shoved a plate through the pass-through. "Here's your pie. Ellen'll get your coffee. Ellie, you out there?"

"She's here, and I poured my own coffee." He straddled a stool at the counter, and turned toward Ellen and Hanover. "Hey, Ellen, who's your friend?"

Ellen blushed. "This is Bill Scott."

"Nice to meet you Bill. I'm Deputy Sheriff Charlie O'Rourke." He extended his hand.

Hanover hesitated a moment before reaching out. This was the first time in his life he had shaken hands with a lawman. But then, he'd done a lot of things for the first time today.

O'Rourke shoved a generous bite of pie into his mouth and grunted with satisfaction. "Ellie, I sure am sweet on your aunt. She makes the best damn pie in the county. Think she'll marry me?"

"You'll have to ask her, but I hope it's for more than her pies."

O'Rourke cupped his hands and called out, "Hey, Carrie will you marry me?"

Hanover heard a muffled response from the kitchen, something that sounded vaguely like "kiss my ass", but he wouldn't swear to it.

"She loves me." O'Rourke winked at Hanover and finished the last of his dessert. He held his cup for Ellen to refill it. "Where you from, boy?"

"San Francisco." The response rolled out more easily now. The sheriff didn't intimidate him, and Hanover felt his confidence returning. Still, for some inexplicable reason, he wished Ellen had stayed with him rather than leaving to set up the tables for dinner.

"You're a long way from home." O'Rourke sipped his coffee. "Been in the service?"

"No. I'm 4F." The lie bothered Hanover. He knew he appeared fit, and people acted as if there was a stigma to not being in the military.

"You here on a visit?"

"In a manner of speaking. I've got business in Santa Fe." Hanover wasn't fooled by O'Rourke's nonchalance; he was being interrogated by a pro.

"You got friends or relatives here?"

He hesitated, not wanting to be too explicit, yet reluctant to appear he was dissembling. So far, everyone had been friendly and helpful, but he couldn't brush off a lifetime of suspicion of the police. "No. I'm here on my own."

O'Rourke straightened on the stool, the easy manner shifting to a more official air. "What kind of business you here on?"

Hanover took a deep breath. Beecker had told him the police were different in this time, that he would probably need their help in stopping the spies. "Actually, I'm looking for someone, someone who'll be here in a couple days. They have business in Los Alamos."

"Los Alamos, hmmm?" A funny look crossed O'Rourke's face.

From O'Rourke's reaction, Hanover realized he'd misspoken, but he wasn't certain what he'd said wrong. "I need to talk to some people about a project there."

"Must be important people. Perhaps I can help." O'Rourke glanced at his watch, then slid off the stool. "Time to check in with headquarters. Wait here, and we'll have dinner."

The atmosphere around the sheriff had shifted from calm to electric so quickly, Hanover wasn't sure what to make of it, but then everything was different and unexpected. He brushed off the warning prickles on the back of his neck.

At least he'd taken the first step. Hell, who would've believed he'd be eating with a law man. He followed O'Rourke's example and helped himself to another cup of coffee and watched the sheriff enter a telephone booth outside the restaurant.

*   *   *

WASHINGTON, D.C.
Evening, March 27, 1944

Many men wandered aimlessly through life, drifting into careers or jobs by happenstance. Thomas Francis Butler, however, knew exactly what he was doing and where he was going. For the last fifteen years, he'd steadily worked his way up the organization. Now there was only one thing standing between him and his destiny as Director of the FBI: J. Edgar Hoover.

Butler sat in his Deputy Director's office. He had finished reviewing reports on two current cases, but inertia kept him from going home to his two martinis and solitary dinner. It was more than inertia, he thought. He was restless, and today his ambitions seemed farther away than ever.

He had to find a way to get Hoover out of the way. Yawning broadly, he stood up and stretched. He was tall, well over six feet, and his two hundred plus weight wasn't all muscle any more. A slight cleft in his chin and his carefully combed hair made him a Hollywood casting office's ideal for a matinee idol.

In college, he played fullback on the varsity football team. Thinking about those glory days brought a smile to his face. The girls, the adulation. The smile faded as he remembered that disastrous situation with the homecoming queen. He'd escaped the nightmare only because he found two acquaintances to testify that they, too, had taken her to a motel.

His father had been a successful corporate attorney, so Butler followed in his footsteps. After law school, he practiced for a few years with his father's firm, but quickly grew restless. He wanted more action, more glory, neither of which he would find in a windowless office pouring over briefs and legal precedents.

He applied for a position with the FBI, and was appointed as a special agent. J. Edgar Hoover had reorganized the Bureau into a first class investigative agency, and Butler knew this was where he belonged. Hoover was impressed with his aggressiveness and resourcefulness, and Butler rapidly moved up the ranks to his present position.

He was as far as he could go in the FBI, unless the director stepped down. And it didn't appear Hoover planned to do that any time soon.

Butler thought of the rumors and whispers about the director, his drinking habits and other aspects of his private life. Nothing concrete, yet Butler was certain something solid would turn up. But then what? Hoover would never be convinced it was in his and the nation's best interest to retire and name Butler as his successor. And if Hoover refused, Butler couldn't think of a single reporter who would take on the director—or a newspaper publisher who would print it. Hoover was simply too popular, and impugning his reputation was too great a risk to Butler's own ambitions.

So how to force Hoover to step down? How?

He jumped as the phone rang, grabbed it on the second ring. "Butler, here."

"Sir, there's a call from Agent-in-Charge, Jonathan Robbins in Santa Fe, New Mexico," said the on-duty operator. "He asked for the Director, but he's out of town and unavailable. Will you take the call?"

"Sure." He heard the series of clicks as the call was put through.

"Hello? Anyone there?"

"This is Deputy Director Thomas Butler."

"Jonathan Robbins here, sir. Sorry to bother you so late, but we may have a problem."

Butler had dealt with these rural agents before. It was amazing what they sometimes considered serious enough to call for guidance. "What's up?"

"I have Deputy Sheriff O'Rourke on another phone. He's at a local cafe and says he's got a vagrant who's talking about the atomic bomb work at Los Alamos. I thought the Director should know. How do you suggest we handle it?"

Robbins had Butler's full attention now. What the hell was a vagrant doing with top secret information? No one was supposed to know about that work, no one except those with the highest level of security clearance.

The FBI knew a few scientists were smuggling secrets to the Russians, but the Bureau had that covered, and were learning more about the Soviet's codes than the Soviets were learning about the bomb. But nobody walked around in public talking to just anyone about the project.

"Where is the man now?"

"O'Rourke says he's inside the cafe."

"Does he have a name?"

"Bill Scott. He's from San Francisco. Thirtyish."

Butler stared at the blackout-shaded window as he considered his options. "Okay, Robbins, have the sheriff pick him up and hold him. Send a wire to the San Francisco office and get some background on Scott. Family, friends, known associates, has he done time. . .you know the drill. I'll catch the next plane out. We'll let you know when to pick me up."

"Yes, sir. I'm glad you're coming." Robbins sounded noticeably relieved. "I'll handle it until you arrive."

Butler listened to the click, then set the phone in its cradle. He drummed his fingers on the desk. Robbins' story didn't jibe. Spies didn't walk around talking to local cops about top secret projects. They didn't telegraph their intentions.

Was this a trick? Did Hoover suspect his ambitions, and cook up this scheme to get him out of D.C.? To humiliate him by leading him to a phony spy ring?

But what if Robbins was telling the truth? If he played it right, this could be his big break. Maybe this was a big espionage case, and this vagrant was just the tip of the iceberg. Solving this would make Butler a national hero—and perhaps earn him the director's seat. After all, where was Hoover when a national emergency arose?

He picked up the phone again and asked for Travel. "This is Deputy Director Butler. Get me on the quickest flight to Santa Fe. I can be at the airport in—" He glanced at his watch. "In three hours."

He hung up, but his hand stayed on the receiver. He looked at it thoughtfully before picking it up again. "Give me the director's office." Better to act as if everything was normal.

"Director Hoover's office. Edwards, here."

"This is Butler. When do you expect him?"

"I'm not certain, sir. I think he'll be gone another three or four days."

"The Santa Fe office needs assistance. It's probably nothing, but they asked me to come out, so I'm leaving on the next available flight. Travel will know how to reach me; otherwise, I'll talk to him when I get back."

"I'll tell him you called."

Butler hung up and smiled as he headed home to pack.

* * *

As he waited for the sheriff to complete his phone call, Hanover couldn't ignore the uneasy tightening in his stomach. For a quick check-in with his office, the call was taking a long time. He glanced at the clock hanging over the door. Way too long.

He slid off the stool when the sheriff's back was turned toward him, and slipped through the swinging door into the kitchen. He turned quickly and stumbled on his weak ankle, colliding into Ellen carrying a tray of silverware. Knives and forks and spoons crashed to the floor and slithered across the room.

"Hey, I'm sorry," he said. He scooped up a few handfuls as he hurried toward the back door.

"That's okay. Accidents happen." Ellen smiled. "If you come to work here, we'll have to rig up a warning system so we don't crash into each other all the time."

Something in her eyes told him she wouldn't mind crashing into him. But he didn't have time for that. He straightened and tossed a handful of silverware onto the counter. "I have to go—"

"You Bill Scott?" An older woman stepped from the pantry. "Ellen says you need a job."

"Maybe." He reached for the door and twisted the knob. "In a few days."

"I guess that's okay. You ever worked in a restaurant?"

"No, I—can we talk about this later? I have to—"

The kitchen door swung open and Sheriff O'Rourke stepped into the room. Hanover didn't like the way the deputy's mouth formed a grim line, and he didn't like the way O'Rourke's hand rested on his holster. The sinking feeling deep in Hanover's stomach told him the change in O'Rourke had nothing to do with a casual telephone call to headquarters.

"Going somewhere, boy?"

"And if I am?"

"It'll have to wait." O'Rourke approached. "I'm taking you in."

"What for?" Hanover demanded.

"There's no charge against you. The FBI just wants to talk to you. I'm not going to put cuffs on if you promise to come quietly."

Hanover looked over O'Rourke's shoulder and saw Ellen staring at him in dismay. Her hands covered her mouth, the color faded from her cheeks. Carrie stormed toward the sheriff. "What the hell's going on here, O'Rourke?"

The bell above the door tinkled as a group of customers came in. Their laughter and chatter floated into the kitchen. So different, Hanover thought, from grim scene they'd interrupted. Ellen pushed the swinging door open to greet them, her movements rapid and jerky. She grabbed some menus and led the customers toward the back, glancing over her shoulder as she went.

Hanover slowly approached the sheriff. He still wasn't sure how he'd blundered, but something he'd said had triggered the deputy into action. The jocularity had disappeared from O'Rourke; he was all business, a no-nonsense officer of the law.

Hanover only hoped he could straighten this out before it was too late. Beecker had told him the police needed something called probable cause to arrest someone. So why was

O'Rourke arresting him? He thought about his last words before O'Rourke looked at him oddly and left to call the station. He'd mentioned Los Alamos.

It dawned on him that Los Alamos might be top secret, unknown to the general population. And by mentioning it, he'd touched on the unmentionable.

But O'Rourke had said the FBI wanted to talk to him. That could be a good sign; Beecker had suggested he try to work with them to stop the spies.

"Let's go." O'Rourke held out his hand.

Hanover tested his ankle. It didn't crumple under his weight, but he tried to favor it anyway.

Ellen hurried into the kitchen. "Here. Somebody left this and never came back for it." She shoved a cane at him.

He caught the disappointment in her eyes before she returned to the front. Carrie watched her go, then turned back to Hanover, shaking her head.

Still puzzled by how quickly O'Rourke had reacted, Hanover limped to the deputy's car. They drove through the sprawling city, the streets busy with evening traffic. Despite his apprehension, Hanover saw the people smiling and talking, the store windows full of items for sale, the general sense of prosperity and well-being. The contrast to his own Santa Fe was astonishing. It saddened him that they'd lost so much. In a few minutes, they reached the County Detention Center.

"Here you go, Sarge. William Terence Scott. Book him for. . .vagrancy."

Hanover whirled to face the sheriff. "Vagrancy? But, but, you said—"

"Sorry, boy. I didn't want you making a scene at Carrie's." A troubled look in his eyes, O'Rourke nodded once to Hanover and left.

Stricken, Hanover watched him leave. He didn't resist as he went through the booking process and was placed in a cell. What was the point? It would accomplish nothing, maybe even make things worse. Ignoring the two men who eyed him as the door clanged shut behind him, he crossed the shared space and leaned against the concrete cinder block wall.

Damn. For this he could have stayed in 2044.

*   *   *

NEW MEXICO DESERT
Dusk, March 27, 1944

Willie Kant covered his eyes and stepped past the light, expecting to be in another underground room. Instead, he was outside, staring at the sun descending behind the Ortez Mountains.

"What the hell?" he said. Dizzy, he slowly turned. His mouth fell open. The foothills looked vaguely familiar, but the old administration building was gone. Shit, all of Neustadt was gone. Desert shrub and rocky sand covered the barren place. There was no sign of buildings, his soldiers, or the vehicles they'd driven.

And there was no sign of Scott Hanover. Kant shivered, both from the cold evening wind whistling across the undulating landscape, and the shock of finding himself alone who-knew-where. What had happened? Where was he? He looked around for some clue.

A few feet away, he spotted a pile of stone that seemed too precise to occur naturally, but he didn't know what it meant. A vehicle, lights blazing and raucous music blaring, passed by a few hundred meters from where he stood. It was headed toward Santa Fe—if Santa Fe still existed—and made a growling, rumbling sound rather than the high-pitched whine he was accustomed to. In the dwindling light, it didn't look like any car he was familiar with.

He followed the car's path, and saw the faint glow of ground light reflected from the clouds in the eastern sky. It must be Santa Fe. If this was a rational world, it had to be Santa Fe, although at this moment, he wouldn't wager on anything.

Another cold gust from the north reminded him he couldn't stay where he was. Following the vehicle made the most sense. Walking unsteadily, he reached the paved highway in a few minutes. The sun had dropped lower, with only the moon and the stars providing light.

He headed east, wondering how far it was to the nearest habitation. Neustadt was a little more than thirty kilometers from Santa Fe, which meant it would take him six or seven hours to reach the city.

If it was still there.

He looked back over his shoulder. Where in the hell was Neustadt? And what happened to Hanover? He had to have come to the same place, and since he went through the door only a moment earlier, he should be in sight. Yet, Kant was alone.

He started down the road, fighting fatigue and nausea. He knew he was probably in a state of shock. The dizziness had not left him, and he stumbled. He hit the ground hard, scraping his hands, jarring his knees. He staggered to a standing position.

In the moonlight, he spotted a large rock. He took a step toward it, but had trouble setting his foot on the undulating ground. He sank to his knees and crawled.

Hanover would not escape again. Hanover would not—

*   *   *

The sun shining in his eyes woke Kant. The early morning was bright and clear, the air crisp. He shivered from the cold and struggled to his feet, stiff from spending a night in the open. He shook his head to clear it, and once again attempted to understand where he was and what had happened.

The last thing he vividly remembered was racing across the laboratory in pursuit of Scott Hanover, chasing him through a brightly lit doorway and ending up. . .here.

Whatever had happened, it had altered his world. He scanned the barren wasteland around him. Neustadt was gone. He brushed sand from his uniform and scowled at the rumbling in his stomach. He continued on the highway toward what he hoped was Santa Fe.

A few kilometers down the road, he reached the top of a ridge. In the valley below, he spotted an isolated two-story house about a kilometer from the highway. He followed the ridge until he was directly above the buildings, then crouched down. He couldn't remember anyone living out here. Unless they had a special permit, the GOA required people to live in the cities or towns where they could be monitored.

As he watched, a man crossed from the barn to the house. Was the man alone or were others inside? Were they armed? Normally, only the GOA and FedPos had weapons. But nothing was normal now. Kant reached for his laser pistol. His holster was empty. He fingered the holster and remembered the laser dropping as he'd chased Hanover.

He frowned, wondering how to proceed, when the man left the house, this time followed by a woman and a teenage boy. They climbed into an obsolete vehicle and drove down a hard-packed dirt side road, leaving a cloud of dust in their wake as they turned onto the highway.

Kant sat back on his haunches. That car looked to be an old gas combustion motor, yet it had started right up. He'd seen similar models in a museum. Where would they find parts, let alone fuel for something that antiquated?

He continued his surveillance of the buildings, reluctant to show himself. No one else appeared. Without a weapon to protect himself, Kant approached the house with caution, alert for any sign of life.

He stepped onto the porch. The thunderous bark of a large dog inside the house jolted him back. He waited next to the corner of the house for someone to respond to the warning, but nothing happened. The dog was between him and food, weapons, and whatever else he needed to continue his pursuit of Hanover. He had no way of judging the dog's size, although the deep bark indicated it was large. He could take no chances that the dog would hurt him. So, the problem was to get the dog out and let himself in.

Kant went to the barn and found an old rake handle and some straw which he quickly fashioned into a large oblong parcel. He carried it back to the house and set it on the bottom step, then shoved the handle through the upper part of the straw bundle.

Reluctantly, he draped his uniform jacket over the form. He patted the silver epaulets, and brushed the fine fabric. He hated to part with the jacket, tailored specifically for him, but unusual circumstances required unusual measures. Stepping back, he surveyed his work and hoped it would do.

Returning to the porch, he found a shovel leaning against the side of the house. He picked it up, just in case his plan didn't work, and hefted it. He stood to one side of the door and tested the doorknob. It turned easily. Kant smiled. The ignorant farmer thought a dog would be sufficient deterrent. He hadn't taken into account someone as resourceful as Major Kant.

Inside, the dog barked frantically, jumping against the door, its claws scratching at the window. Kant turned the knob and shoved the door open, pulling back from the dog's view. The dog leaped across the porch and knocked the straw man to the ground. Kant swung inside the house and slammed the door shut.

He leaned against the wall and breathed a sigh of relief, while on the outside, the dog barked its frustration. Kant found himself in a tidy, old-fashioned kitchen. The smell of cooked bacon still hung in the air. Ravenous, he tore bread from a fresh loaf sitting on the counter. His gaze rested on an ancient icebox standing in the corner. He stopped, swallowed hard and took a slow look around. Something was not right.

Partially hidden behind the door, he saw something hanging on the wall, the top half a quaint picture, the lower half a grid of boxes, most of which had been x'd out. He crossed the room and yanked the door away to reveal an old-fashioned calendar. He glanced at the mediocre landscape, then at the date. An icy hot wave flushed through him. It was impossible. It could not be. The calendar said it was March, March of 1944.

The residents had marked off the days as they passed, and the current day was the 28th. He shook his head, confused by what he saw, and growing angrier. Someone was playing a joke on him, a very bad joke. And yet, that was ridiculous. No one could arrange for the disappearance of Neustadt. No one could set up a one hundred year old farm in the middle of nowhere.

And even if they could, who would want to? He may not have engendered much loyalty or good will in his drive to reach his rank, but no one already in power hated him. He was what the GOA and FedPos wanted in an officer.

He walked around the kitchen, touching the appliances. He picked up the old coffee pot, still warm with—he sniffed it—real coffee. The existence of cars powered by internal combustion engines. Everything on this farm indicated he was in the mid-twentieth century.

That would explain the disappearance of Neustadt and his troops. It seemed impossible, but all that equipment in the laboratory, the pulsing green crystal had to serve some purpose.

He leaned against the wall and plucked at his lower lip. Could that laboratory have been set up to create a time warp? He'd heard of the concepts, but had also heard it was impossible to travel through time. The Beecker Time Displacement theory was just that, a theory. Beecker. . .perhaps the scientist's theory was more than speculation. Kant shook his head at the unbelievable suspicion, but could not rid himself of the idea that it was the only explanation for this farm house, for Neustadt, and for Hanover's disappearance.

Dazed, he went to the window, looking for the telltale dust of a returning car. The air was clear; he wished his head were as unclouded. So if the preposterous were true, then why had Hanover come here? At this particular time?

Kant returned to the calendar and stared at it. The date, March 28, 1944, must be significant. It was during the war between Germany and the United States. They'd been at war for several years.

Finally, a memory was triggered, something he learned in military intelligence and history classes.

In four days, Herman Helmke and Erwin Fischer would secure plans for the trigger mechanism Germany needed to complete its atomic bomb.

The whole scenario dawned on him, slowly at first, then with building certainty. Could Scott Hanover have been sent to stop the two German agents from carrying out their mission?

The daring of such an incredible plot stopped Kant cold. It was impossible. . .yet what else so neatly explained all the facts before him?

Kant returned to the kitchen table and sank into his chair. No one in the GOA or FedPos had ever suspected a conspiracy of this caliber. If what he surmised was true, could he stop Hanover? Kant tried to recall details of the two spies from the biography he'd once read, but it had been so long ago. He vaguely remembered that they stopped at a restaurant in Santa Fe when they first arrived in town. What was its name? A restaurant, a. . .a. . .a cafe. A cafe, that was it. It was named after the owner. Campbell's. . .Catherine's. . .Carolyn's. That was closer. Carrie's. That was it. Carrie's Cafe.

All he had to do was help the German agents succeed and thwart Hanover. Kant did not want to even begin considering the consequences if Hanover stopped the Germans. Hanover could be setting a trap for them at that moment.

Kant started toward the door, then stopped. He couldn't go out wearing a FedPo uniform. He needed other clothes. He quickly went to the bedroom and sifted through the closet until he pulled out a pair of trousers and a jacket in a non-descript brown that would blend well with the landscape. The fabric was coarser than he would have chosen, the workmanship obviously mass produced, but it could not be helped. At least it fit tolerably well. Tossing the contents of a cedar trunk, he found a flannel shirt for warmth, and grabbed an extra pair of socks to stuff into the pants pocket.

In the top drawer, he discovered some paper money. He jammed all of it into his pocket. He tugged the next drawer open; it felt odd, weighted. He jerked it from the dresser and found a gun taped to the back. He frowned as he examined it. He recognized the type as common to the mid-twentieth century, but it was clean, freshly oiled, and loaded. An extra box of bullets was tucked into the next drawer.

The kitchen larder was well stocked, and he gathered the items he could readily carry in the checkered tablecloth. The coffee was still warm, and he gulped it down. The icebox contained a brick of cheese and a small ham, which he added to his supplies.

The dog barked suddenly. Kant rushed to the window and saw a dust cloud coming toward the house. He had to leave. Now. But the dog—. He could not afford to leave a witness that could track him. Kant grabbed the shovel and flung open the door. The dog charged in and Kant hit him hard. The dog slumped to the floor, blood flowing from its ears and mouth.

Kant snatched his tablecloth-wrapped bundle and ran from the house. He crossed the yard and ducked behind the barn. From there, he stayed low and clutched the food bundle to his chest as he raced toward the ridge.

* * *

COUNTY DETENTION CENTER, SANTA FE
Early Morning, March 28, 1944

Hanover sat on the edge of his bunk and glowered at the clock hanging outside the cell. Time was passing, wasted hours that should have been spent preparing for the Germans. How much longer before the FBI deigned to meet with him? When it was too late?

He glared at his cellmates. They'd coughed and groaned all night, keeping him awake, and now they slept like babies. He slumped against the wall and wondered if he could really blame them. He'd spent the last two years sleeping under similar conditions and never had a problem.

He snorted. But then he hadn't been responsible for saving the world. Damn Beecker for putting him in this position. He'd hated the injustice of the GOA, was destined to be executed at any time because of a judge's whim, but at least he'd only had to think about himself.

Beecker changed all that by sending him to this place. This place where he'd met some decent people: Sam Putnam, trusting and friendly enough to pick up a total stranger on a deserted highway. And Carrie who had a warm heart beneath a blustery facade, offering him a job without knowing anything about him except that he might need one. And Ellen Peterson who gazed at him with those soft blue eyes and pretty smile.

He remembered how devastated she'd looked when O'Rourke arrested him. No one had cared enough to worry about him before, and he wasn't sure he liked the feeling.

Caring made one vulnerable; not caring left one empty. Hell of a choice.

Frustrated, he rolled off the bunk and crossed to the bars that confined him, hitting them with his fist. He had to be released, and soon; otherwise the Nazi spies would steal the plans and Germany would win the war. Yet he couldn't stop them without help. He wasn't sure who to turn to. Deputy Sheriff O'Rourke was only a local officer. He probably didn't have the authority to help with something this important.

The F.B.I. had the authority, but would they believe him? Would *he* believe a story this incredible? He groaned, knowing he would write off someone who talked about time travel and spies as a nutcase.

He eyed the half-full cells up and down the hall, holding a mix of those serving regular prison sentences and others, like himself, who were simply waiting. With the short supply of able-bodied men to serve as guards, the state and county had combined their staff to operate one facility for the duration of the war.

"Okay, boys. Time to get up." A guard entered their wing of the jail and paced the long hallway, running his nightstick across the bars of each cell. The other prisoners roused from sleep.

Hanover sluiced his face in a basin of cold water and shook the excess from his hair. Some things, like the early morning routine in a prison cell, hadn't changed that much over time. He joined the lengthening line of men marching to the already crowded dining hall. Picking up a tray, he loaded it with a bowl of lumpy oatmeal and slices of cold toast. That also hadn't changed much.

But at the least the coffee substitute tasted a whole lot better than what they served at Southwestern Regional prison. He went back for a second, then a third cup, ignoring the elbowing of the others at his table and the undercurrent of amusement that he liked the Center's "rotgut" brew. If they only knew how bad it could be, they'd never complain.

At the guard's whistle, he followed the other prisoners outside to the exercise yard, stood off to the side while they chose up teams, and when he wasn't picked, told himself he wasn't in the mood to join their ball games anyway. Instead, he found a sunny spot against the wall and hunkered down to watch. He felt safe with his backside covered. No one approached him, although a few glanced at him with speculative looks.

Another whistle summoned them to return to their cells. Once inside the building, a guard tapped Hanover's arm. "You. Step over here."

Hanover stiffened. "Why? What's wrong?"

With a shrug, the guard said, "Nothing. Just your turn to earn your keep." At the guard's signal, Hanover preceded him down a hallway to a janitor's closet. "Take this dustpan and broom out front and clean up."

Hanover took the supplies to the booking area. He'd been too upset the night before to pay much attention to it, but now he saw that the back of the room where he swept was separated from the front by a six-foot high wire fence and locked gate.

On the other side of the gate was a long counter staffed by two officers. Signs over their heads said "citizen complaints" and "booking." Some of the equipment he saw on the desks looked primitive, and there wasn't a computer in sight. He caught himself; what was he thinking? Of course there were no computers.

He quickly swept his area, amazed that an officer let him through the gate to clean the front without interrupting his conversation with the other officer. Hanover couldn't believe they didn't have their guns drawn, or weren't silently watching for him to make a wrong move. Instead, the atmosphere was relaxed and friendly, everyone cheerfully going about their jobs. Hanover shook his head, unable to believe these people. So different from his time. So very different.

"Hey, you."

Hanover jerked upright, his heart pounding. He'd been considering how to escape out the front door, but hadn't taken a step in that direction. Had the officer guessed?

The officer under the "booking" sign waved to him. "Get a mop and bucket out here. I want this floor so clean I can eat off it."

"You'd eat off anything that had food on it," a deputy said. The other officers laughed.

Amazed that they'd laugh at such a stupid joke, Hanover went to the janitor's closet and returned with the mop and a bucket of soapy water. He had covered most of the area when a man stormed in, his muddy boots leaving tracks of dirt and manure in his wake.

Hanover groaned. "Damn it, mis—." The odd bundle in the man's hands stopped him.

"I've been robbed," the man hollered. "And they killed my dog."

"Step right over here, sir. When did this happen?"

"This morning. Took the missus and the boy to the neighbors. When I got back, the door's wide open, my dog's lying on the floor with his head bashed in. God damn, if I catch the bastard who did it, I'll kill him."

"Where do you live?"

"About ten miles out of town, a mile off the highway. I can't understand it. I wasn't gone more'n an hour. If they'd wanted the stuff, all they had to do was ask. I'd have helped them out. But they murdered my dog!"

"What'd they take?"

"Near as I can tell, some clothes, about a hundred dollars, and some food."

"See any strangers around?"

"No one, but they left this behind." The farmer unrolled his bundle. "From what I could tell, they used the jacket to distract my dog so's to get inside, 'cause it looks like he chewed the hell out of it. But the pants, they were in the bedroom, like he dropped them to put on the ones he stole. These look to be some sort of uniform, but it's nothing I've ever seen before."

Riveted by the fabric unfolding on the counter, Hanover inched closer, unable to believe what he was seeing. A cold chill swept through him. It was a FedPo uniform. An officer's uniform. A major's to be exact. There could be only one explanation.

Willie Kant had followed him through the timegate and was in Santa Fe.

CHAPTER 15

F.B.I. OFFICE, SANTA FE
Early Morning, March 29, 1944

Snarling, Butler stomped toward Jonathan Robbins' office in the Federal Courthouse. This was the last time he took one of those puddle-jumping airplane trips. The up and down was enough to turn a grown man green—from Eastern Air to Transcontinental to Western Air, going north when you wanted to go south, flying farther west than you wanted. The only thing that made the trip tolerable was the pretty stewardesses. He shook his head in disgust. Flying would never catch on, he decided. Give him the trains instead.

When he walked in, Robbins was on the phone. Butler dropped his bag next to a chair and paused to study the man behind the desk. Robbins had been with the Bureau since before Hoover became the Director in 1923. His short hair was almost snow white, and he was within two months of retirement. Despite his sixty-some years, his gestures were fluid and his speech precise. According to his personnel file, his tenure had been dedicated but colorless. Hardly the alarmist type, and, except for occasionally losing his temper, not given to easily excitable emotions.

At Robbins' wave, Butler sank into a chair and looked around. The office was furnished in war-time austerity. In addition to Robbins' drab metal desk and chair, the room held three filing cabinets, each with the drawers shut tight, a bookcase filled with law tomes, and two wooden guest chairs.

Butler shifted for a more comfortable position on the hard wooden chair. The only personal items on the desk were three small pictures: an older woman with Robbins, a smiling young man in uniform with a woman and two children, and a young woman on horseback—she didn't look half-bad, but Butler didn't plan to stick around Santa Fe long enough to meet her.

"Have Drake stand by." Robbins slammed down the receiver and extended his hand across the desk. "Glad you're here, sir. This is getting messier by the moment. I'm due to retire in two months, and I don't want any trouble before then. You'll never believe what we've learned about this Scott fellow." He tossed a folder across the desk toward Butler. "Or whatever his name is."

"What do you mean?" Butler picked up the folder, but didn't open it.

"Our agent in San Francisco went to the Hall of Records to run a check on Scott." Robbins leaned back in his chair as if he were settling in.

"And?" Butler snapped. He wasn't in the mood for a long, drawn-out story.

"As luck would have it, the woman in charge of records has been there since before World War I and remembered the name."

"Really? How on earth. . .after all this time?"

"William Terence Scott was born on May 17, 1913, to a very prominent family. Now here's the clincher. William Terence Scott died on November 27, 1913 of pneumonia. The woman in records remembered because of all the publicity."

"How do we know the woman's telling the truth?"

"Our agent double checked. He went to the newspaper morgue and it was all there, just like she'd said. From the news coverage, you'd've thought this baby was next in line for the throne."

Stunned, Butler sank back in his chair. "So what we have is a vagrant with false ID who has information about what's going on at Los Alamos. A man we never would have detected except for the chance questioning of a gossipy old woman."

"That about sums it up, sir."

"So who the hell is the man the sheriff's holding?" Butler scowled again; his mood was worsening by the minute. "Where did he get his information? Who else has he shared it with?"

"We haven't questioned him yet. We were waiting for you."

"Hell, let's get on it."

Robbins snapped the intercom on. "Send Agent Drake in here."

The door opened and a dark-haired man about Butler's age came into the office. "Yes, sir?"

"Go to County and bring William Terence Scott here for questioning." Robbins glanced at his watch. "It's almost seven, so let's make that nine o'clock." He clapped Butler on the shoulder and guided him out the door before he could object. "You'll feel better after you've had a good breakfast. I know just the place."

*   *   *

F.B.I. OFFICE, SANTA FE
Mid-Morning, March 29, 1944

Hanover wasn't sure what to make of the man who sprang him from the detention center and brought him to the Federal Courthouse. He was polite, yet distant; he answered no questions, volunteered no information. The only encouragement Hanover felt was when they stopped in front of a door painted with gold lettering: Federal Bureau of Investigation.

Once inside the office, the man who had brought him removed Hanover's handcuffs, and left the room. Hanover rubbed his wrists to restore feeling, and faced the two men who eyed him with undisguised interest. They wore dark suits in the style of the time, white shirts and ties, and looked like they knew what they were doing. He hoped to God Beecker had been right about working with these guys. One looked to be a few years older than himself, while the other was about Beecker's age.

The younger of the two men had been leaning against the window sill, his arms crossed. He gestured for Hanover to sit in one of the two wooden chairs. "What's your name?" he asked.

"William Terence Scott."

"And you're from where?"

"San Francisco."

"And you're here on business?"

Hanover hesitated. "That's right."

With a humorless smile, the man rose to his feet, his arms still crossed. "Okay. That was good enough for the local law. Tell us who you really are."

Hanover blanched. "I told you. I'm William Terence Sco—"

"William Terence Scott died at the age of six months, on November 27, 1913 of pneumonia." The man let the words hang in the air before he continued. "That means your birth certificate, draft card, and other papers are phonies. Well done, but still counterfeit. So let's start over. And we want the truth this time. Who are you?"

The FBI's speed in uncovering his deception unnerved Hanover. These guys were good, much better, in fact, than the FedPo's, who had technology to help them.

So, how much should he tell them? If he told them he was from the future, it could jeopardize the credibility of the rest of his story.

But if he didn't tell them he was from the future, how could he explain knowing so much about things that hadn't happened yet? Oh, God, why had Beecker chosen him for this?

He took a deep breath. "Who are you?"

The two agents looked at each other, apparently taken aback by his directness.

"Listen, you." Robbins rose from his seat behind the desk. "We don't need some punk coming in here—" He stopped at the pressure of Butler's hand on his arm.

Butler watched Hanover, his gaze speculative. "I'm Thomas Butler, Deputy Director of the FBI. This is Jonathan Robbins. He's in charge of the Santa Fe office."

These were the men who could help him. If he trusted them. But he didn't have much choice. It was tell his story, or go back to jail and stare at four walls while the Germans repeated history. He reminded himself that Beecker had told him to trust the local officials. He tamped down his deep-seated suspicion of the government, determined to be convincing.

He gazed steadily at Butler. "Good. You're just the men I need." Hanover saw their eyes widen; he had piqued their curiosity. "What I'm about to tell you will be difficult to believe, but it is true. There are two German agents coming from Mexico to Santa Fe who intend to steal plans for the atom bomb trigger mechanism." The two men stared at him in disbelief.

"Wait a minute," Butler said. "Don't say any more. Robbins, get a secretary in here. I want all this written down."

"No! No recording," Hanover insisted. "You two are the only ones who can hear this. No other record." He was supposed to do his job and return home, not leave a trail documenting his presence in this time period.

"Where do you get off making demands like that?" Robbins asked in anger. "Since when does a prisoner—particularly a prisoner who's hiding his own identify—stipulate what we will and won't do?"

"Do you want this information or don't you?" Hanover had expected skepticism, but not belligerence.

"Hold it, both of you." Butler glared at them. "We're not going to accomplish anything if you start a dog fight. If you have information, give it to us. And stop fooling around."

He turned to Robbins. In a low voice, he said, "Look, he obviously knows something. We've got twenty-two agents stationed in Santa Fe specifically to prevent this sort of thing, and here it's happening without them knowing a thing about it. What are your men doing out there? Picking their noses?"

Robbins' face turned vermillion with rage, but he clenched his jaw shut and glared at Hanover. Butler signaled for Hanover to continue.

Hanover took a deep breath. This was his big chance; he hoped to hell he didn't blow it. "Bill—William Scott is not my real name."

Robbins snorted. "Yeah, tell us something we don't know."

"Be quiet," Butler growled.

At Butler's nod, Hanover continued. "My real name is Scott Hanover. I was born in Magdalena, New Mexico." He saw Robbins reach for the intercom, most likely to request confirmation. When his birth couldn't be verified, Hanover knew they wouldn't believe anything more he said. There was no way around telling them the truth, at least most of it. And even then they probably wouldn't believe him.

"There won't be any record of my birth because. . .." He took a deep breath. He had no choice. "Because I won't be born until the year 2013. I've been sent here from the future, from the year 2044, to be exact."

For a moment, his words hung in the tomb-like silence. Then Robbins erupted from his chair. "Oh-my-God, a lunatic! We've been taken in by a damned crackpot. Of all the—to come here with a story like that." He turned to Butler. "And you came all the way from Washington for this. Oh, God, I'll never hear the end of this. I'll *never* live this down." He slumped into his chair and buried his head in his hands.

"Shut up," Butler said distractedly. He came around the front of Robbins' desk, staring hard at Hanover, as if he could see inside him and read the truth. There was something about the scrutiny that made Hanover uncomfortable, but he couldn't put his finger on it.

"He's too rational to be mentally deranged." Butler's voice was quiet, as if he were talking to himself. "How many nuts tell you in advance that their story is unbelievable?" He turned to Robbins. "And if he is crazy, how did he get information about the atom bomb project? We need to know that."

Hanover watched the two men reach a silent agreement. Butler faced him again, leaning against the desk as he had the window sill, his arms crossed. "Okay, Scott Hanover, I want some answers, and I want them now. No games. Understand?"

Hanover nodded.

"You say you came from the future. How?"

Hanover briefly explained Beecker's Time Displacement Theory and the development of the timegate.

Butler pursed his lips, his chin resting on his hand, and he glanced at Robbins who rolled his eyes and shook his head. "Do you have any proof?" Butler asked.

Hanover thought for a moment, then reached into his pockets. He stopped. "When I was booked into the jail, they'd emptied my pockets. I, ah, I had a coin that was minted in 2014. It's at the County Detention Center, along with all my other things."

Robbins groaned with dismay. Butler barely angled his head toward Robbins. "Check it out." He turned back to Hanover, his gaze intensifying. "Why are you here?"

Butler's question filled Hanover with hope that maybe, just maybe, the FBI man believed him. He was less reluctant now to tell his story to someone who would listen, and who could help. He quickly told of the theft that resulted in a German victory and occupation of the United States. He described what it was like to live under the GOA, and his role in the conspiracy to alter the course of history.

Butler listened in silence. Even Robbins seemed drawn into the tale, only occasionally glancing at his superior in disbelief.

"So," Hanover concluded, "my job is to prevent, by any means possible, the two agents from completing their mission. Then maybe the United States will win because they'll hav—-"

"How do you know the Allies win?" Robbins interrupted. "We haven't even landed in northern Europe yet."

"You will," Hanover answered. "You'll land in France on June 6, and the landing is successful."

"Shit!" Robbins roared. "That's so secret, Ike hasn't even decided yet. How the hell do *you* know?"

Hanover shrugged. "It's history to me. It's not talked about in my time, but it is history. By fall, the Allies will be pushing into Germany. That's when the Germans detonate the two bombs, one off Los Angeles in San Pedro Harbor, and one in Boston. The Allies surrender, and that ends it. Hitler wins." Hanover looked seriously at the two men. "It's up to us to stop the spies and prevent this from happening."

Butler eyed Hanover in silence. "Take him back," he said to Robbins.

Hanover jumped from his chair. "No! You've got to believe me," he cried. "Look, get the coin. The coin will prove I'm telling the truth."

"We'll check on that." Robbins hit the intercom. "Send Drake back in."

"But we don't have time. The spies will be here in the next two days. You can't ignore what I've told you."

"Don't get excited." Butler's voice was calm. "We have time to check out your story. After all, look how quickly we discovered you weren't who you said you were."

"Come with me." Drake approached Hanover and slipped the handcuffs over his wrists.

Hanover jerked away. Thoughts of escaping flitted through his mind, but where would he go and how far would he get with his hands cuffed? Drake grabbed his arm and hauled him from Robbins' office.

This was too much like being caught by Kant. Maybe things weren't that different from his time, after all. He held onto the hope that they would do as they said and check his belongings for the coin.

*   *   *

In Robbins' office, Deputy Director Butler looked at Robbins. "What do you think?"

"I think we should contact the Director and get some guidance from him. Even if the guy's crazy, he knew more than he should about Los Alamos."

Contacting Hoover was the last thing Butler wanted to do. If this was a big case, he wanted to break it on his own. If it was a set-up, he didn't want the director thinking he'd fallen for it. "No. Think a minute. Remember what you said when this Hanover told us he was from the future? You apologized for dragging me out here from Washington."

"That's true, but—"

"If we notify Hoover too early, and it is a hoax, then we'll spend the rest of our careers in Nome, Alaska. If we're not forced out." Robbins blanched, the result Butler had counted on. He'd use Robbins' retirement plans to help maneuver the situation to his own benefit.

Butler paused a moment as he collected his thoughts. "As I see it, we have three options. One, we write this Hanover off as a nut, I go back to Washington, and we forget the whole thing."

"That sounds like a good idea."

Butler raised his hand. "Hear me out. Two, we release him from the County Detention Center and keep a tight tail on him to see what happens."

"What if he slips through?"

"Doesn't sound like you have much confidence in your own men, Robbins. The third choice is to join forces with him as he suggested." Butler frowned. "This guy's no dummy. He had high quality forged papers, which indicates he probably isn't working alone. And he is good. He almost had me believing his story. You have to ask yourself why would someone go to all this trouble?"

"He has some nerve," Robbins muttered. "I think he's a phony. We can keep him locked up for false ID."

Butler was silent. Ignore it or follow-up. . .? Which way should he go? If he erred, it would be a ruinous reflection on his record, destroying everything he'd worked so hard to build. Not attaining the Director's post would be the least of his worries.

"You're probably right. If he has a coin minted in two thousand-something, it's probably as bogus as the rest of his things. As for his tale about coming from the future. . .." Butler shook his head. "We'll keep him in jail so he doesn't stir up any trouble. But you might want to mention to your men to keep an eye out for any foreign businessmen. Especially Swedish businessmen. Just in case."

∗   ∗   ∗

OFF THE COAST OF MEXICO
Early Morning, March 29, 1944

The surfaced U-boat glided silently toward shore, a black shadow in the predawn darkness. A faint breeze rippled the water and it lapped at the sides of the submarine. The rendezvous was set for 0400 hours. On the bridge, Helmke and Fischer watched as Captain Norden peered through binoculars at the shore, searching for the signal of three rapid flashes repeated every minute.

"There, Captain, to port," the lookout called.

Norden shifted his binoculars to the indicated direction. Helmke saw three blinks of light in the darkness. He waited a minute; the pattern was repeated.

"Bring the passengers' gear on deck," the captain called to the control room. "Helmsman, steer 180 degrees. Return the signal."

Helmke was ready, and from the relief on Fischer's face, he was ready to swim the rest of the way, if necessary. Seamen dropped their bags into a small inflatable boat bumping against the side of the submarine, then climbed aboard and prepared to bring the two men ashore.

Helmke shook hands with Captain Norden. "Thank you for a safe voyage," he said.

Norden looked away. "I will be at this location at 0400 hours on the seventh through the tenth day. If you do not appear on those four days, I am ordered to depart and resume operations in the Gulf of Mexico."

Helmke nodded and urged Fischer into the inflatable. The captain probably hoped they would not appear so he could return to "real" war activities; if he only knew how vital—albeit preposterous—was this mission.

Forty-five minutes later, the rubber boat scuffed against the sandy beach. Helmke and Fischer scrambled ashore. The seamen tossed out their luggage, then pushed off and rowed toward the submarine. Helmke searched the darkness for their contact.

"Over here," a voice called out. A light blinked off to the left.

"Come," Helmke said to Fischer. "We must follow." They headed toward the light, picking their way over beached debris, occasionally stumbling, until they came to two men standing on a berm.

"Here." The taller of the two men reached out a hand to help them up. When Helmke and Fischer stood next to them, he saluted. "I am Colon—Herr Kessler. Welcome."

"I am relieved to be here," Helmke said. "I am Eric Holm, and this is Olaf Fegen."

"Of course. We have a car. Miguel," he said, pointing to the short, dark-skinned man, "will drive. Come this way."

Helmke followed Kessler as he led them over rows of dunes to a waiting sedan. Helmke slid into the backseat, not quite believing they were here. What in God's name was he doing in Mexico? This assignment, it was insanity. He'd repeated that refrain throughout the long voyage. He peered out the window as Miguel drove the car over ruts that barely marked their path as a road.

Kessler leaned over the back of his seat. "We must traverse these roads for the next ten miles. Then we travel on paved roads, and the ride, it is much smoother."

"What is the plan?" Helmke asked.

"We will travel far between now and tomorrow evening when you meet your contact in Santa Fe. Miguel will stop only for petrol. Tonight we stay in Chihuahua. Here is five hundred American dollars for expenses." Kessler handed Helmke a thick envelope bulging with small denomination bills. "It is real, not some that is printed in Germany."

Helmke fingered several of the bills. "That is good. We do not want to jeopardize the operation by something as stupid as using counterfeit money."

Kessler nodded and grinned. "Besides, you are wealthy Swedish businessmen. You do not resort to such crude methods to defraud your potential customers." He turned around to face the front. "We have a long drive. I will answer any questions."

"Has Mueller been told to expect us?" Helmke asked.

"He is known as Henry Miller. To use his German name is to expose him. Yes, he has been informed. He is to meet you at a restaurant, the Santa Fe Inn, in Santa Fe. It is near the hotel where you will stay, so you should have no trouble finding it. He will go to the restaurant every evening between 1800 and 2000 hours. At 1830 hours, he will order dinner so as not to be conspicuous. It is a popular place, No one will think anything about you meeting there."

"Then what?"

"He will arrange for you to meet a scientist from Los Alamos who can give you what we want."

Helmke fell silent. He thought about Kessler's comments. If everything happened the way it was planned, it would be a success. Still he worried. "What about crossing the border?"

"It is not a problem. You have passports as businessmen from a neutral country. People pass back and forth all the time. No, that will not be a problem."

Reassured, Helmke settled back in his seat. Fischer stared out the window, appearing oblivious to all that went on around him. Helmke sighed and wondered how it was that the lieutenant was assigned to this mission. Could not the high command find someone more worthy?

With only a few brief stops, they arrived in Chihuahua late that night. Bone weary, Helmke climbed from the car and bid Colonel Kessler goodby.

Tomorrow, he and Fischer would take the car and be on their own. All he could hope was that everything happened as planned.

*   *   *

COUNTY DETENTION CENTER, SANTA FE
Late Morning, March 29, 1944

Disheartened, Hanover leaned against the cinder block wall of his cell. They hadn't believed him. The Nazi spies were scheduled to arrive in Santa Fe tomorrow, and the FBI didn't believe him. He reviewed his meeting with Butler and wondered where he'd slipped up.

His story of coming from the future, of course, sounded preposterous, but he'd told them about the coin, which they could easily check. How else could they explain his knowledge of the Los Alamos project?

Ah, hell. Maybe he should have lied, made up some reasonable explanation for how he knew about the espionage.

He couldn't let it go, though. He had to try something else. "Guard! Guard!" He strafed the bars with his cup.

"Stop that racket!" A burly guard hurtled down the corridor. "What'd you want?"

"I want the officer who brought me here, Deputy Sheriff O'Rourke."

"Now why should I call him?"

"Because I want to talk to him."

"I'll see." The guard stomped from the cell block and slammed the door.

Hanover wasn't sure if the guard would respond to his request, or ignore it. Time passed even more slowly. From the shadows angled through the high barred windows, Hanover guessed it was close to noon.

The door opened and a guard stopped in front of Hanover's cell. "Step lively, now. Sheriff's here to see you."

Now he was getting somewhere. Hanover preceded the guard to an interrogation cell. O'Rourke was waiting for him, a dubious frown on his face.

"What's this all about, Scott?" He gestured for Hanover to sit, and he took the opposite chair.

Knowing he'd already blown his chances with the FBI, Hanover eyed the sheriff with misgivings. The sheriff was obviously dedicated to his job, and probably very good at it. But his jocular behavior at Carrie's Cafe showed he was a decent person, too. The kind of person the GOA would bring down first when they invaded next year. Which meant Hanover had to trust him with the truth and hope O'Rourke did the right thing.

He took a deep breath. "My real name is Scott Hanover, not Bill Scott. But that's not important. What is important is why I'm here." He related the same story to O'Rourke that he had told Butler and Robbins, but this time he omitted the part about coming from the future.

"You say these alleged Nazi spies are coming to Santa Fe as Swedish businessmen?" O'Rourke's voice was heavy with skepticism.

"Yes! I know who they are. I've seen their pictures. Why won't anyone believe me?" He pounded his fist on the table.

"Hold on." O'Rourke rose from his seat. "You better cool down, son. When you're feeling better, talk to the prison chaplain." He knocked on the door and slipped out without another word.

The guard returned and led Hanover back to his cell.

CHAPTER 16

COUNTY DETENTION CENTER, SANTA FE
Early Afternoon, March 30, 1944

Hanover slammed his fist against the wall, but the pain did little to diminish his frustration. He continued pacing. Why the hell wouldn't anyone believe him? It wasn't that preposterous to think that the Germans would try to steal the plans. And while he was stuck in here, where the hell was Major Kant? Helping the Germans? He hoped not.

The guard came to lead the prisoners outside for a brief exercise period after lunch. Hanover eased to a place where he could keep his back to the wall and remain apart from the others. He had nothing in common with them, even less than he had with the prisoners at Southwestern Regional. At least then, everyone had shared a common injustice, but he had nothing to say to these men who eagerly joined into the ballgames.

"Hey, buddy, you got a match?"

Hanover stiffened at the voice. A short, wizened-faced man sidled next to him, rolling tobacco in a piece of paper. Hanover shook his head.

The man patted his own pockets and discovered matches. Grinning, he lit his cigarette, then flicked the still-burning match away. He took a long pull on the cigarette and blew a series of rings before releasing the rest of the smoke in a steady stream. "Wadayu in for?"

Hanover watched the man; he was casual, too casual in his motions, but little things gave him away. Little things like his hand shaking ever so slightly as he brought the cigarette to his mouth. Like the way his eyes darted nervously toward a group of prisoners standing on the other side of the yard pretending they weren't watching. Finally, Hanover said, "What are *you* in for?"

"They got me for robbery. It's a bum rap. They claim I was trying to hustle this old dame outta her relief check in front'a the bank. I was framed. All I was doing was asking directions to the bus station."

Hanover did not respond. He continued leaning against the wall, watching the other prisoners.

"Did they nab you for something stupid, like vagrancy?" The prisoner seemed intent on continuing the conversation. "That's an easy rap. You'll get thirty to ninety days, depending on how the judge's old lady treated him the night before." The man guffawed at his own joke and elbowed Hanover, who simply moved out of range.

"When you get out, they give you a free ride to the edge of town and tell you to keep moving." The man glanced around, his nervousness readily apparent now. "It's bigger'n that, isn't it?" he asked in a low voice. "The grapevine has it you're bein' held for the FBI, that some bigshot came all the way out here from Washington to see you."

Hanover pushed away from the wall. "Where the hell did you hear that?"

The other prisoner shrugged. "A 'trustee' heard someone tell the booking sergeant." He inched closer to Hanover, his eyes wide with speculation. "What's it all about? You some kind of big man in the rackets? If you are, the boys wanna show you the proper respect. They picked me to ask you."

Hanover snorted at the thought. Now he understood the man's nervousness. Being chosen the messenger, the one to approach a "big shot" as he'd put it, must be traumatic.

But just maybe he could use this guy to his advantage. Playing it straight hadn't gotten him anywhere. So what the hell? He looked the man up and down with a cold stare.

"You tell the boys I'm here because the Feds didn't like what I told them."

The man inched closer. "What was that?"

"I told them a pair of German spies were headed here to steal top secrets that will let Germany win the war."

The man gasped. "What did the Feds say?"

"I'm here, aren't I? They didn't believe me, and figured if they locked me up, no one would know. Makes you wonder whose side they're really on, doesn't it?" Hanover gave the man a knowing look, then backed against the wall and stared straight ahead. "Think what this place will be like when the SS takes over."

"Yes, sir. That sure is something to think about. It surely is." Casting furtive glances over his shoulder, the little man scurried away, taking the long way to rejoin his group.

*   *   *

In the FBI office, Butler leaned across the desk to accept the phone from Robbins. He settled back in his chair. "Deputy Director Butler."

"This is Deputy Sheriff O'Rourke. Remember me? I brought in the guy who knew about the project at Los Alamos."

Butler straightened. "I remember you, sheriff. What's up?"

"This Scott fellow, or Hanover, or whoever he is, asked to see me this afternoon. He told me some cock-and-bull story about German spies."

"He told us the same story."

"Oh." O'Rourke was quiet for a moment. "What do you think?"

"We're checking it out," Butler replied cautiously.

"Do you think it has any validity?"

Butler didn't like a deputy sheriff pushing him. "I said we're on it," he snapped.

"That's great, *sir*. I just thought you'd want to know that he's talking to other prisoners. Maybe he thinks he'll get more of a response if he spreads the word. Maybe it'll leak to the newspapers."

Newspaper reporters. Butler inhaled sharply. That was something to avoid at all cost. At least until *he* was ready to release the story. Hanover was a loose cannon that had to be corralled. Quickly.

"Okay, sheriff. Put him in isolation. Keep him incommunicado. Nobody talks to him. And I mean *nobody*!"

*   *   *

Hanover sprang from the bunk when the guard motioned for him to leave the cell. "What's going on?"

The guard shrugged, but said nothing. He nudged Hanover with a nightstick, and Hanover preceded him from the cell block to the interrogation room. Maybe the FBI was finally ready to believe him.

To his surprise, O'Rourke was waiting for him. But Hanover didn't like the way the sheriff avoided looking directly at him. "What's wrong? What's going on?"

"You're being moved. Follow me." O'Rourke moved toward the door.

Hanover started after him. "Where're you taking me?"

"The FBI wants you. . .protected. Just in case. . .."

Hanover stopped. "Just in case what?"

"Don't make this hard on yourself." O'Rourke turned to face him. "Just go along with it and everything will be fine."

"What do you mean 'don't make this hard on myself'?"

O'Rourke let out a long slow breath. "They want you away from the others. What you know is top secret, and they don't want it leaking to the press or the public. Before you know it, everyone'll think the Germans're launching a major invasion and it'll start a panic."

"So where are you putting me?" Hanover stepped back.

"In a separate cell."

"You mean solitary!" Hanover reached out and grabbed O'Rourke's arm. "You can't do that. You can't ignore me. I've told others. The story's going to spread."

O'Rourke broke free from Hanover's grip. "I don't want to have to hog tie and gag you—"

"Listen to me," Hanover insisted. "I didn't tell you the whole story. You didn't ask how I knew about the spies. Look, there's proof that I'm telling you the truth. It's in my things."

O'Rourke looked at him like he was crazy. "What are you talking about, boy?"

"There's a coin there."

"So, what?"

"A coin that proves I'm from the future and—"

"A. . .Get out of here." O'Rourke grabbed Hanover and flung him toward the door. "I don't have time to listen to this crap." He hustled Hanover down the hall to another room and shoved him inside.

"It's not nonsense. There's a coin with my stuff that was minted in 2014. Check it out. It's got Hitler's profile on it, because unless we stop the two spies from stealing those plans, Germany's going to win the war."

O'Rourke gripped the doorknob and started to close the door.

"Wait." Desperate, Hanover wasn't above pleading. "Please, wait. You know that strange uniform that farmer brought in? Said it was left behind after a burglary? I know whose it is. It belongs to Major Willie Kant, FedPos. He's followed me through the timegate. If he meets up with the German spies, we might never stop them."

O'Rourke stared at him, his eyes wide with amazement. Slowly, he shook his head. "Oh man, you are crazy," he said softly. "They ought to put you in the loony bin and throw away the key." He slammed the door shut.

Hanover stared after him. All the trouble Beecker had gone through to send him back in time, their last chance to change his world, and he'd failed. The FBI had brushed him off with promises. O'Rourke had been his last hope, and the sheriff didn't believe him, either.

He looked around at the barren room. He was back in a cage with no way to stop the spies, no way to change the future. Before, he hadn't known what a difference winning the war could have made to his country; he only knew what it was like after.

Now he knew what they'd all lost, the open friendliness of the Sam Putnams, the honest decency of the Sheriff O'Rourkes. The warm smile of the Ellen Petersons. The freedom, the carefree happiness. In despair, he sank to his knees.

He'd failed.

*   *   *

SANTA FE, NEW MEXICO
Mid-Afternoon, March 30, 1944

Willie Kant stood in front of Carrie's Cafe and eyed the sign. It was here that he would meet Helmke and Fischer and warn them of Hanover's plan to expose them. He glanced around the empty parking lot before pushing the door open and stepping inside.

He sniffed at the leftover fragrances from lunch that still filled the air: meatballs, warm bread, coffee. His stomach rumbled in response, reminding him he was hungry. The bundle of food he'd collected at the farmhouse had been adequate the night before, but that had been a long time ago.

He chose a table where he could watch the parking lot and the door, but not be seen from the outside. If Helmke and Fischer arrived, he wanted plenty of time to observe them so he could plan his approach.

The waitress walked to his table and smiled. She waited expectantly. He slowly looked her up and down, the way he did the waitresses at home. He knew from experience they were all looking for ways to supplement their incomes. This one had a nice ass, but her tits were smaller than he usually liked. What the hell, he thought. If he had time later, he'd come back. He did need a place to sleep, and he had no intention of spending another night in the open.

"What's your name?" he asked.

"Ellen." She took a step back, her eyes filled with wariness. Good; he liked it when they resisted.

"Well, Ellen, where does a guy go to have fun in this town?"

She bristled with indignation. "I wouldn't know. What do you want to order?"

He took her hand and rubbed his thumb gently around her palm. She jerked her hand away. "Look, mister. I have a lot of work to do. Either order something, or leave."

This wasn't the way waitresses responded to his advances at home. Who did this girl think she was to reject him?

"Hey. No need to get angry. I'm just trying to be friendly." If he had time, he vowed, she would pay for this. He would come back and show her that no woman refused Willie Kant. But right now, he couldn't afford a scene.

"I don't have time to 'be friendly'," Ellen snapped. "Do you want something, or not?"

"I'll have a sandwich. What kind do you have?" He was sullen now. No reason to pretend to be nice if she wasn't going to play by the rules.

Ellen pointed to the sign. "We don't serve meals between 2:00 and 4:00. Only pies, sweet rolls and lemon cake."

"Coffee and a piece of cake." Damn bitch, wouldn't put out, wouldn't feed him. He was tempted to say more, but didn't want to take the chance that she'd try to throw him out. He needed to wait for the Germans.

Two customers came into the cafe. Kant watched surreptitiously as they sat at a nearby table and spread out papers for what appeared to be some kind of negotiation. Disappointed, Kant swore under his breath. The bitch served his cake, and he ate slowly to make it last. Whenever she looked in his direction, he raised his cup for a refill, if only to annoy her.

He finished his coffee and looked around for that girl. He scowled. She must have returned to the kitchen. Sunlight flashed off a car pulling to a stop in front of the cafe. A car with Mexican license plates. The waitress forgotten, Kant focused his attention on the two men who left the car and hesitated at the door.

The older man looked around as if searching for something but not sure what. He turned to speak to the younger man. It was them, Kant was sure of it. They didn't look exactly like their pictures in the academy texts, but then the photos had been old and grainy. Kant remembered the older man was Major Herman Helmke, aka Eric Holm, and the younger man was Lieutenant Erwin Fischer, aka Olaf Fegen. Yes, that was it. Their real names and their cover names.

They had successfully completed their mission and returned to Germany. But this time there was a complication—Scott Hanover. Kant clutched his cup. He would be the one to explain it to them. He would be the one who helped them carry out their plans as history had recorded. He might even have time to share in the glory of their triumph before taking Hanover back to justice in their own time.

*   *   *

Helmke hesitated outside the cafe. They had been driving for hours, leaving Chihuahua before dawn and crossing the border at Ciudad Juarez before continuing on to Santa Fe. He was still nervous, but so far, everything had been as described by Herr Schmidt. Even the sign advertising this little restaurant.

"Why are we stopping here? We are supposed to go to our hotel," Fischer said in German.

"Speak English, *Olaf*. From now on, speak only English." Helmke shook his head. How many times did he have to repeat himself? He had noticed the *untersturmfuhrer's* distracted agitation throughout the day. "Remember where we are."

"So why are we stopping here?" Fischer repeated, this time in English.

"Think back. Herr Schmidt, he told us that the sister of a prisoner at one of our stalags is a waitress here. Perhaps she can help us."

"I do not see how," Fischer said. "This is not on the plan. We are to go to the hotel first."

"Stop complaining! Always you whine about something. We will do what I say." Helmke glanced around. He was not sure what he was looking for, but found nothing that alarmed him.

It was as it should be. They were merely two travelers, Swedish businessmen on a trip to find new customers for their company's ball bearings. Still, he felt an uneasiness, a nagging concern that he could not explain, as though some danger was imminent, a threat to him and his mission.

He tried to shake off the feeling. "Let us go in and have coffee, *Olaf*." Perhaps if he continued to repeat the name, the lieutenant would at last respond to it. Still, he despaired; even a dog learned its name with only a few repetitions.

Plagued by foreboding, he led the way into the cafe and looked around. Two men were seated in a corner booth, deeply engrossed in conversation as they poured over the papers scattered in front of them. They posed no threat.

At another table, one that looked out on the parking lot, Helmke noted a man in ill-fitting clothes watching them intently. He could not remember seeing the man before. In his late twenty's or early thirties, he was far too young to be their contact, Henry Miller. Besides, this was not where they were to meet him. As Helmke gazed steadily at him, the man looked away. Helmke shrugged; perhaps it was only his imagination.

A pretty waitress came from the kitchen and greeted them with a smile. "Take a seat anywhere. I'll be right with you."

Helmke smiled in return, even though she no longer looked in their direction. A lovely *fraulein*, the first pretty thing he'd seen since leaving Paris. Sparkling blue eyes and trim ankles. But, he digressed.

He pointed to a table away from the other two men. Unfortunately, it lay within view of the disturbing younger man. Fischer slouched wearily into a chair.

"Sit up. You are not a small child who is to be coddled."

Scowling, Fischer straightened and stared at the jukebox with an intensity that Helmke wished the untersturmfuhrer had applied to their studies.

The waitress brought them glasses of water. "Hi."

"Good afternoon, Miss."

She smiled and said, "Just traveling through or are you new around here?"

"Just traveling through," Helmke said cautiously. "We are here on business."

"From Sweden," Fischer added.

"Really? You sure are a long way from home. What would you like?"

"We will have coffee and a pastry, please."

The waitress frowned. "Pastry? Like a bear claw? Or do you mean a piece of pie?"

"Yes," Helmke said, hoping he had not made a blunder. "Pie would be very nice."

"We have apple, coconut cream, and banana cream."

"Apple would be fine." He watched as she scribbled the order on her pad. As she turned to leave, Helmke said, "Miss, you have a bro—"

The cafe door swung open and a uniformed man strode in. The patch on his shoulder identified him as a deputy with the Santa Fe County sheriff's department. "I'm running late, Ellen. No time for your aunt's pie today."

"Pour yourself a cup of coffee, sheriff. I'll be right there." She turned back to Helmke. "You started to say something, sir?"

"Wh—? No. No, it is nothing." He would delay his conversation with the waitress until the police officer left.

Helmke glanced at Fischer, who had become agitated again with the sheriff's arrival. The waitress delivered their pie and coffee, and Fischer gulped his down. Helmke understood the untersturmfuhrer's nervousness, but struggled to keep his own from being observable. He felt as if everyone watched them, especially that man sitting alone.

"Calm down, *Olaf*. We are in no danger," he said in a low voice, more to reassure himself than Fischer. "Unless you call undue attention to us."

"I cannot help it. I am not suited to be a spy."

"You should have told that to Shellenberg when he gave us this assignment," Helmke snarled back. Fischer not only endangered the mission, his fear, it was contagious. Helmke was battling his own demons, and did not need Fischer's, too.

He drained the last of his coffee and set his cup on the table. When he looked up, expecting to see the waitress coming to refill his cup, he was dismayed to see the lone man approaching instead. He had an unpleasant half-smile on his face, and recognition in his eyes.

Mein Gott, Helmke thought. Are we betrayed?

*   *   *

Kant forced himself to wait. It angered him to see the spies act so casually, as if their mission was no more important than a routine practice drill. His annoyance increased as he watched the waitress smile nicely and chat with them after spurning him.

The Germans had blanched at the sheriff's arrival, although the waitress seemed to be very friendly with him. The deputy looked around the cafe, missing nothing before seating himself at the counter. Kant observed the younger spy—Fischer? that was it—grow visibly agitated, and he smiled to himself. These were the cool, daring super agents depicted by historians in the official accounts?

The Germans had finished eating and Helmke was trying to catch the waitress' attention. Kant had to make contact with them now, before they left, despite the presence of the officer. He had to warn them about Hanover and the danger he posed to their mission.

Kant made his way toward their table. The man's already pale face filled with consternation as Kant approached. He seated himself and wordlessly looked from one to the other.

"What do you want?" Helmke said, his hushed words full of suspicion. Fischer had stiffened at Kant's arrival, as if he had been turned to stone.

"It is not what *I* want, Eric Holm." Kant was rewarded with Helmke's sharp intake of breath. "It is what I can do for you."

"Olaf, put some coins in the jukebox." Helmke's face was now a chalky white and a sweaty sheen was visible on his skin. His eyes never left Kant's. When the cafe filled with music, he said, "Wh. . .how. . .how do you know my name?"

"Allow me to introduce myself. I am Major Willie Kant of the Federal Police."

"Police! We have done nothing wrong," Helmke hissed, his eyes bulging with terror.

"You have nothing to fear from me. I am here to help you with your mission."

"What mission? We are Swedish businessmen," Helmke said. He sounded blustery now, full of indignation.

Kant chuckled mirthlessly. "*Real* businessmen, legitimate businessmen, go to Washington, D.C. They do not come here to the backside of the country. No, gentlemen, let us be honest with each other. You are here to steal plans for the atom bomb trigger mechanism."

For a moment, Kant feared he had gone too far. Helmke had turned apoplectic red, sputtering for words that would not come.

"How. . .why would you think something so preposterous?"

Kant leaned back in his chair, certain he was in control of the spies, and enjoying the feeling. "For me, this is all history." Then he launched into an explanation of past events as he knew them from 2044.

"You come from the future? That is insane," Helmke said. "You cannot expect me to believe that."

Kant leaned forward. "Nevertheless, it is true. Eric Holm. . .or should I call you, Major Helmke?" He was rewarded by the instant evaporation of Helmke's newfound bluster.

"My name is Eric Holm," Helmke insisted. "But if what you say is true, how did you get here?"

"That's a long story, which I'll attempt to shorten. I was pursuing an escaped convict who leaped through what I thought was an ordinary doorway. It turned out to be an entry to the past, to 1944, to be exact. I believe certain people arranged for him to escape so he could be sent here to stop you from carrying out your mission."

Helmke glared at him, still clearly suspicious. "Why would you want to help us?"

"If he succeeds, Germany may not win the war. That would mean my world won't be the same, and I rather like it the way it is. I also need to bring the bastard back to my time for punishment."

"Who is this. . .this person who would make so much trouble for us?"

"His name is Scott Hanover."

The music stopped, and the waitress approached. The three men fell silent. She laid two slips face down on the table. "Can I get you anything else?" She avoided looking at Kant, a feat he found amusing. They shook their heads and she left.

"What do you want of us?" Helmke asked.

"Carry on as you were instructed. As I remember, you are to check into your hotel, and try to meet Henry Miller at the Santa Fe Inn this evening. Then you arrange to meet with Hans Kuster, who will give you the plans."

Helmke nodded and glanced at Fischer, who had remained silent throughout the discussion. "Who are you really? Gestapo sent to check up on us?"

"Think what you will. It doesn't matter to me as long as we get those plans to Germany," Kant said. He pushed back his chair. "We should not be seen together again. You may not see me, but I'll be near you."

"Why would you do that if we are not to be seen together?"

"I'll be watching for Hanover to show up. Then I will stop him."

"How will you do that?" Helmke asked slowly.

"I will. . .be discreet. Don't worry."

The three men paid their bills and left the cafe. Kant looked back and saw the waitress point at him as she talked to the sheriff. Kant continued walking, not the least concerned about an officer who shirked his responsibility for pie and coffee while he was on duty.

CHAPTER 17

F.B.I. OFFICE, SANTA FE
Mid-Afternoon, March 30, 1944

"It's that deputy again." Robbins passed the phone over the desk.

"Now what?" Butler growled as he grabbed the receiver. "Yes, Sheriff. What can I do for you?" He rolled his eyes, and Robbins chuckled and shook his head as he leaned back in his seat.

"I did what you said," O'Rourke said from the other end of the line. "I put that fellow in isolation."

"That's fine. Thank you for your assistance. And I'll mention your contribution in my report to Mr. Hoover. Good-bye, now."

"Mr. Butler?"

Butler sighed heavily. "You had something else?"

"You know that story he was telling about those spies?" O'Rourke's words came slowly, hesitantly.

"Yes, I know about that."

"He told me he was from the future."

"He told us the same story."

"He also said you were checking it out."

Butler didn't like the accusation that lurked behind the deputy's words. "We discussed his claim of proof."

"Well, sir, I wouldn't want you to think I'm telling you how to do your job—"

"But?"

"I don't want to believe what he's saying is true, it's just that there's no other way to explain some things."

Butler hesitated. "What have you found?"

"Well, I checked his belongings. He'd said there was a coin that would prove he was telling the truth."

"And was there?"

"Yes, sir. It has Hitler's profile instead of the Liberty head, like our dime, the date is 2027, and the word 'Lebensraum' is where 'Liberty' is on ours. And there's no 'In God We Trust.' On the back, it's got a swastika, with the words 'United States of America, One Dime' around it. The 'E Pluribus Unum' is missing, too. It looks like it's made of a base metal, not silver."

"We've heard reports that the Nazis are counterfeiting our paper money. It wouldn't be that hard to make a fake coin," Butler said.

"I don't know about that, sir. But there's another thing. We had a reported burglary outside the city, and the thief left behind a jacket and a pair of pants like nothing we've ever seen before. Looks like a military uniform, with epaulets and all. But the fabric isn't cotton or wool. One of our men checked with the army and they can't place it with any country's armed forces."

"So what does this have to do with our man?"

"He claims the uniform belongs to a major from an organization he calls 'Fedpos.' From the future. Says this major followed him through time."

"Sheriff. . ." Butler struggled to be diplomatic. "We have arrested a man who is obviously crazy, but extremely clever. People like him are dangerous because they make absurd statements that make normally reasonable citizens go off the deep end. Our job, as protectors of the people, is to isolate those who threaten their security. And not fall prey to these madmen ourselves."

"I agree. It's just that there's one more thing."

Closing his eyes, Butler shook his head. Why he had ever answered Robbins' late call two days before? He could be in D.C., spending a pleasant evening with an accommodating woman. Instead he was in Santa Fe talking to a country sheriff about a crazy vagrant. "What is it, Deputy?" he asked.

"I made my usual stop for coffee at this little cafe on the outskirts of town. Called Carrie's Cafe. There were three strangers sitting at one of the tables. I've never seen them before. After they left, the waitress told me two of them told her they were businessmen. From Sweden."

"Ah, shit." Butler bounced out of his chair. "Tell me this is a joke, O'Rourke."

"Sorry, sir. It's the plain and simple truth."

O'Rourke's words stopped Butler cold. There was too much supporting Hanover's claim. And yet. . .If he were Hoover, he would make certain the story was irresistible to an ambitious young deputy director. Butler knew he had to do something, but he would remain cautious, not include any more people than was absolutely necessary.

Butler covered the mouthpiece. "He says he saw two Swedes at a local cafe," he said to Robbins.

"I don't need this," Robbins moaned. "I only have two months until retirement. Is he sure?"

Butler nodded. "I don't think we can ignore this Hanover any longer. As much as I don't believe his wild story about time travel, we need to check it out."

"What do you want to do?"

"Bring him here for another interview."

Robbins pushed himself up. "I'll have Drake bring him. I don't need this. Only two months to go." He left the office shaking his head.

Butler uncovered the receiver. "You still there, O'Rourke?"

"Yeah, I'm here."

"Good. We're sending Agent Drake to bring Hanover back here. Can you keep him in isolation until Drake gets there?"

"No problem."

"One more thing," Butler said. "Who else have you told about this?"

"I haven't said anything to anyone." The deputy sounded offended that Butler would even suggest he'd blabbed it around.

"Good. Let's keep this under wraps until we figure out what the hell's going on."

Butler hung up and walked to the window. Hands on his hips, he stared outside. What the hell was going on? Was there something to this Hanover fellow's story? Maybe this *was* the big case he needed. Maybe this was his chance to prove he was qualified to take over the Bureau from Hoover.

*   *   *

Hanover stood in Robbins' office. Wary and suspicious, he studied the two FBI men as they stood against the opposite wall and observed him. He searched their shuttered faces for any clue as to why they had summoned him.

The agent who brought him had revealed nothing when Hanover was released into his custody, only that he was needed for further questioning. He would wait for them to take the first step.

Butler pushed away from the windowsill, his gaze still on Hanover. "We're going to risk our reputations, and our careers, that you're telling the truth. At least about the spies."

Hanover bit back a contemptuous remark. "Is that so," he said.

Robbins glowered at him. "This better pan out, because your ass is on the line. I'm not taking the blame for some sucker-plot."

Hanover clenched his fists and took a step forward. "Your ass will be on the line if those spies succeed."

"Why you little—"

"Gentlemen, gentlemen." Butler raised his hands. "We have work to do. Hanover, sit down."

Butler gestured to one of the wooden chairs and nodded at Robbins to sit behind the desk. "You say the Germans have sent two spies, parading as Swedish businessmen, and they'll arrive in town tonight?"

"The information I have is that they meet their contact tonight at a restaurant called the Santa Fe Inn. I assume they'll arrive sometime today."

Butler jotted some notes on a pad of paper. "Do you know who the contact is?"

"No. We couldn't find any information about him. But he's a local person, what's called a sleeper agent?" Hanover said. When they didn't correct him, he continued. "He puts them together with someone at Los Alamos. His name is Hans Kuster."

Robbins gasped. "Kuster! Did you say Kuster?"

"Yes," Hanover said. "That's what I was told."

"Do you know him?" Butler asked Robbins.

"He's, ah, part of the contingent England sent to work on the project."

"Really? Is there a file on him?" Butler asked.

Hanover watched Robbins raise his eyebrows and nod once. So they knew Hans Kuster, and were already watching him. Hanover hoped that added credibility to his story.

Butler turned back to Hanover with renewed intensity. "What do the spies look like?"

"One is short and round with thinning dark hair, and the other one is tall, thin and blond."

"Okay, a dark and light Mutt-and-Jeff team." Butler stared at the ceiling for a moment, then glanced at Robbins and Hanover.

"There's something else I think you should know," Hanover said. "I think another man came through the timegate after me."

"Oh, shit." Robbins leaned back in his chair so fast he almost tipped over. "I don't need this."

"Shut up, Robbins," Butler snapped, his eyes never leaving Hanover. "Sheriff O'Rourke said you mentioned that. Let's hear it. Who is this other guy?"

"His name is Willie Kant. He's a FedPo—a Federal Police—major who was chasing me when I reached the timegate," Hanover said. "I was mopping floors at the jail when a man came in to report a burglar, and he had Kant's uniform."

"You're sure it was this Kant fellow's?"

"Positive."

"You say he was right behind you? Did you see him after you came through the timegate?"

"No. I was told there's a big loss of energy when someone goes through, so Kant probably landed several hours, or maybe even a day later than me." Hanover watched as Butler silently mulled over his story.

After a few moments, Butler asked, "Do you think he knows about the German spies?"

"If he's any good at history, he'll figure it out. In our time, there's a bronze statue of them in front of the GOA headquarters."

"GOA?"

"German Occupation Authority." Hanover was gratified to see both men blanch at his words.

"What do you think Kant will do?"

Hanover shrugged. "He probably knows more about the Germans than I do. My guess is he'll try to contact them and warn them about me."

"From what you say, we don't have a lot of time to run around looking for him. We'll go to the Santa Fe Inn and see who shows," Butler said. "Robbins, better call your wife and tell her not to expect you until late."

Robbins glanced at his watch. "It's only 3:30. What'll we do with him in the meantime?" He hooked a thumb toward Hanover.

"You don't have to do anything with me," Hanover said, bristling at Robbins' disdainful attitude. "I'll get myself a hotel room and get cleaned up."

"Why don't we just toss you back in the can and you can shower there?" Robbins said.

"I've about had it with you," Hanover retorted. "I came here to save your butt, and all I get in return is a lot of crap. Maybe I should just go back through the timegate and let your world fall apart."

"Robbins, stop it."

Butler looked at Hanover thoughtfully. "Why was a Federal Police major following you to begin with?"

"The people who sent me through the timegate helped me escape from prison."

"You were in prison?"

"Yes, for political crimes." Hanover told them the story.

Butler leaned back and shook his head. "You're either telling an incredible truth, or you're the most innovative confidence man I've ever heard. The thing is, a con man expects to gain from his little game, and I don't see any profit in this for you."

Hanover shrugged. "If I win, we win. There'll be no bombs dropped on Los Angeles or Boston. No German Occupation Authority." *My family won't be destroyed.*

"Hanover, I think I'm beginning to believe you. We'll go to the Santa Fe Inn tonight, and you'll identify the spies for us. We'll also find out who their local contact is." Butler stood up and stretched. "Just out of curiosity, what's it like to go through the timegate?"

Hanover hesitated. "I don't really know how to answer that. You're in one time and the next instant, you're in another time, but you haven't moved more than a few feet." He shrugged. "That's about the only way I can describe it."

"Sounds like a lot of bullshit to me," Robbins mumbled.

Butler cast an irritated glance at his subordinate. "Okay, Hanover. We'll let you go on your own recognizance. Meet us in front of the Santa Fe Inn at 6:30."

Hanover didn't like the too-friendly tone of Butler's voice, especially when the agent avoided looking at him. After the way they'd kept him locked up, away from anyone else, Hanover was suspicious of Butler's new attitude. "What about my money? It's at the county jail."

"No, Agent Drake brought your belongings," Butler said. "Sheriff O'Rourke opened the envelope, but everything is still there."

"Everything?"

"Yes. Including that coin."

Robbins leaned over to Butler. "How do we know we can trust him?" The whispered words carried across the room.

"We don't, but we're going to," Butler said brusquely. "The Santa Fe Inn at 6:30, Hanover."

"I'll be there." Hanover left the office.

* * *

As the door shut quietly behind Hanover, Robbins turned to Butler "I can't believe you're letting him go like that."

Butler shook his head. "Do you really think I'm that big a fool?" He crossed the room and grabbed his hat. "Think about it, Robbins. The best way to find out what's really going on is to set him free—and follow him. Grab your hat and come on. We don't want to lose him."

* * *

Hanover exited the Federal Courthouse and looked up one side of the street, then down the other. He doubted he was really free. Butler must have a plan, probably already had someone tailing him. It didn't matter; he had nothing to hide.

He searched the faces of the people walking by, scanned the shadowed nooks and doorways for Willie Kant. The major was here somewhere—had he connected with the spies or was he intent on catching Hanover? No one looked suspicious or out of place. He took a deep breath and smiled to himself. Maybe, just maybe he was going to pull this off.

Right now, he needed a place to clean up. On the way over from the county jail, he'd spotted a hotel only a couple of blocks away. He started down the street, wanting a better look at this world he was trying to save. If only for a few minutes, he would be one of the people laughing and talking as they walked along.

He passed a store window and stopped to look. "Haberdashery" the sign said; from the items on display, he could tell it was a men's clothing store. He gave in to the urge to step inside, and quickly found a new shirt, underwear and socks. The clerk suggested a tie and helped him choose one, then offered to give the jacket a good brushing to freshen it up.

A half hour later, Hanover left, amazed at how inexpensive everything was. He'd only made it to the corner when he spotted a shoe store. He glanced at the ones he wore, remembering the odd looks they'd received from the clothing store clerk and people at the jail. He wanted to fit in here, to look like he belonged.

He entered the shoe store and saw a hunched-over older man helping two matronly women, boxes of shoes scattered on the floor around them.

"I'll be right with you, sir," the man called to him.

"No hurry." He strolled around the store, examining the shoes that claimed to be made from real leather.

"I'm sorry you had to wait, sir. How can I help you?"

"I need a new pair of shoes."

"Certainly. Do you have your coupons?"

"My what?"

"Your shoe coupons, sir." The man looked perplexed. "You need your ration coupons to buy shoes."

Hanover suddenly remembered. Quickly, he ran his hands through his pockets as though searching for something. "No, I don't. I guess I forgot them."

"I'm sorry, sir. I can't sell you shoes without the coupons."

Hanover pulled his gasoline ration stamps from his pocket and held them out. The man shifted nervously from one foot to another and licked his lips. He looked furtively at the two women still seated and discussing shoes, then at the curtained doorway to the back room, as if he expected someone to come through it at any minute. "We, ah, we might be able to arrange something for, say, ten gallons worth of stamps?"

"Done." Hanover handed him the stamps, which quickly disappeared into the man's pocket. Smiling, Hanover followed him to a table of men's shoes. So corruption existed even in this time.

From the shoe store, he went to a drugstore, then to a pawn shop where he found a small leather bag and a soft leather wallet. At both stores he found the number and variety of merchandise overwhelming. If he stayed more than a few more days, he would run out of money for sure.

Whistling, he headed for the hotel. He passed an old Indian woman seated on the sidewalk. Spread on the blanket beside her lay an array of trinkets and jewelry. Calling to him, she held up a bracelet and mumbled something.

Hanover stopped. It had been a long time since he'd bought a gift for someone. He ignored the bracelet and knelt down to examine the display. A necklace had caught his eye, a cabochon-cut turquoise pendant encased in silver on a short silver chain.

Turquoise, the color of Ellen's eyes.

"How much?" he asked.

"Twenty dollars."

He shook his head and rose.

"Fifteen," she countered.

He shook his head again. He only had forty dollars left, and still had to get a hotel room and pay for meals.

"Ten."

He hesitated, imagining Ellen's eyes lighting up with pleasure.

"Five."

That convinced him. He pulled the bill from his new wallet; the woman snatched it and shoved the necklace into his hand. Grinning, he dropped it into his tote bag and ambled down the street toward the hotel.

How easy it had all been. No long lines, no insulting sales people. Despite supposed shortages because of the war, everything he could possibly want was readily available. It was hard to believe the extreme difference one hundred years—and losing a war—could make on a society.

And he had a chance to affect the future.

On Don Gaspar Avenue, he found the DiVargas Hotel, only three blocks from the Federal Courthouse. He pushed through the double doors and approached the reception desk.

To his right, down a corridor, he saw a dining room. On his left was an informal lounge dominated by a huge fireplace. Several people were seated, enjoying an animated conversation. One man sat reading a newspaper in the corner. None of them looked suspicious; none appeared to be trailing him, or in any way interested in him.

He registered, giving his home address as San Francisco. The desk clerk eyed his small tote bag and insisted he pay in advance. Hanover climbed the stairs to his room, pleasantly surprised by how light and airy it seemed. But then, he thought, anything would seem light and airy after an isolation cell and some of the other places he'd stayed lately.

He tested the bed. It was soft, inviting, unlike the cots and hard ground he'd been sleeping on. It beckoned to him, but he dared not fall asleep. Instead, he went down the hall to the bathroom to bathe and shave, then put on his new clothes. It felt good to be clean again, energizing and relaxing at the same time.

His ankle ached from all the walking he'd done. He sat on the bed, and the throbbing immediately subsided. Maybe he'd stretch out—only for a minute, he told himself as he closed his eyes.

Only for a minute.

* * *

Helmke drove slowly as he searched for the DiVargas Hotel. Neither he nor Fischer had spoken a word since leaving the cafe, and he had to break the silence. "What do you think about that man who says he is from the future? Do you believe him?"

Fischer continued to stare out the window. "I do not know what to believe anymore. This mission, it has been a disaster from the beginning."

"It has not. We made a successful voyage across the Atlantic Ocean, we crossed the border with no problem. This is the only trouble we have had."

Fischer turned to him. "The man says he is from one hundred years in the future. That is more than a small problem."

Helmke shook his head in disgust. This man was supposed to be an officer in the Wehrmacht; instead, he was a sniveling weakling who should never have been chosen for such an important mission for the Fuhrer.

Helmke finally found the hotel and parked, then sat for a moment and scanned the surrounding area. He could see nothing to cause alarm. Very little vehicle traffic, and only two men walked down the street. He led Fischer into the hotel where they registered. The bellhop carried their bags to the room, and once they were alone, Helmke held his finger to his lips. Silently, he searched the room, checking behind pictures, under chairs and tables, around lamps. Satisfied there were no listening devices, he nodded.

Fischer flopped on the bed. "Thank goodness we do not meet our contact until tomorrow."

"Do not be ridiculous. He will be at the meeting place, the Santa Fe Inn, at 1800 hours. That is three hours from now. Herr Schmidt said we are to minimize our exposure. Every extra minute we stay in the enemy's country increases the danger that we will be captured."

"Fine. We will stay here until then." Fischer closed his eyes.

"No. We do not wait. We find Herr Miller's shop this afternoon. Perhaps he can arrange the transfer sooner."

"Why? Why can we not go tomorrow? It is late, and I am tired. One more day will not matter," Fischer whined.

"Because now we have an added complication, if what that man at the cafe says is true."

"I do not believe him," Fischer said, lapsing into German.

"I agree his story sounded incredible, but he knows too much about us. We must hurry. And *Olaf*, remember to speak English. Only English!"

*   *   *

Butler and Robbins had tailed Hanover from a safe distance. They stood on the corner across the street from the DiVargas Hotel.

"This was a waste of time." Robbins moved as if his feet hurt from the walking.

Butler scanned the street and sidewalk for anything out of the ordinary. "Well, well, well. Would you look at that," Butler said, his words soft and slow.

A car with Mexican license plates pulled to a stop in front of the hotel. Two men climbed out and went inside.

"Look like anyone we know?" Butler asked.

"I can't believe it," Robbins said. "They match Hanover's descriptions."

"Yep. And right on time, too."

"The DiVargas must be a magnet for time travelers and spies," Robbins commented.

Butler rolled his eyes at Robbins continued suspicions. "We'll give them a few minutes to check in."

"Why don't we rush them now, and put a stop to all this?"

"On what grounds do we arrest them? We have nothing, only Hanover's story." The light changed and Butler started across the street. "No, we'll let this play itself out and round up the whole bunch when we have enough to make the charges stick. Besides, I don't want to create an international incident."

Butler approached the hotel entrance. The Mutt-and-Jeff pair stood at the front desk. He stepped away from view and lit a cigarette to give the impression he was casually waiting for someone.

"Wish I'd brought my pipe," Robbins grumbled.

"We won't have that much time." Butler took a couple more long drags on the cigarette before flicking it into the bushes.

"Careful, sir. It's real dry here, and that could cause a fire."

Butler turned to Robbins. "If you don't shut up, I will personally sign the orders sending you to the farthest solitary outpost we have. And no one will ever process your retirement papers."

Robbins stepped back. "Yes, sir. I understand, sir."

"Thank God. Now come on." Butler approached the front desk. He smiled pleasantly at the clerk. "Is Scott Hanover registered here?"

The clerk eyed him cynically. "What's it worth to you?"

Butler flashed his ID. "Be a good boy and tell us what room he's in."

"Yes, sir." The clerk's hands shook as he flipped through the registration forms. "Mr. Hanover is in Room 207. I, ah, hope there's no trouble. We don't need the manager, do we?"

"No, no trouble. He's a friend of ours. Butler leaned against the counter in a friendly way. "By the way, what can you tell me about those two men who just registered?"

"The Swedes? Mr. Holm and Mr. Fegen are salesmen. They're in Room 214. Are they in trouble?"

"No, no. Professional habit, you know. Always asking questions. Is Mr. Hanover in his room now?"

The clerk glanced at the rows of boxes behind him. "He must be. His key's not here."

"Great." Butler smacked the counter. He stepped away, then turned back. "By the way, call me if there are any calls between 214 and 207? Here's the number." He scribbled Robbins' office phone number on a piece of paper.

The clerk picked up the paper and nodded. "You're sure there'll be no trouble?"

"I guarantee it," Butler said as he led Robbins toward the entrance.

CHAPTER 18

SANTA FE, NEW MEXICO
Late Afternoon, March 30, 1944

Herman Helmke cautiously eyed the police car approaching from a side street. He braked at the stoplight and glanced at the map spread out next to him. It was difficult, reading the strange street names, driving in this foreign city, without losing one's way.

The mission was becoming so complicated, like those old silent movies he had seen as a young man, with the cobblestone police—no, no, the keystone kops—running around half-witted after the thieves. It had been so funny in the movies, but he did not feel so funny when he was the one pursuing and being pursued up and down these roads.

He found the street he searched for and slowly pulled to the curb and parked. "Olaf?" The *untersturmfuhrer* continued gazing out the opposite window. "Olaf!" Helmke poked Fischer's arm.

"What?" Fischer sounded annoyed, which only increased Helmke's frustration.

"Come. Let us find Herr Miller's shop."

Fischer shrugged and turned to look out the window again. "You go. I will stay here."

"I was not giving you a choice." Helmke tamped down his annoyance as Fischer sighed heavily and climbed from the car.

As they walked along the empty sidewalk, Helmke compared the numbers with the address he had taken from the hotel's telephone book. Some of the stores were empty, displaying "For Rent" signs in the windows. Accumulated litter in the corners gave the neighborhood a rundown appearance.

Helmke stopped in front of a store with the words "Miller's Small Appliance Repair" in faded red and chipped gilt paint on the door. "Here it is," he said.

They entered the shop, setting a small bell above the door tinkling. Inside, shelves scaled the walls, cluttered with small radios, mixers, toasters and irons jammed together, each with a hanging tag.

A man emerged from the rear of the shop through a doorway covered by a frayed and soiled drape. "May I help you?"

"We are looking for Mr. Miller."

"I am he."

Helmke was surprised by how small and nondescript the fiftyish man appeared. Miller's gray hair was combed straight back, and behind his glasses, his eyes were crossed, forcing him to cock his head to look directly at an object. Helmke thought fleetingly that it must be exceedingly difficult to repair items if they could not be looked at directly.

"I am Eric Holm." Helmke nodded toward Fischer. "This is Olaf Fegen."

Miller paled. He hurried to the window and searched the street before scurrying back behind the counter. He looked nervously from Helmke to Fischer and back to Helmke. "Come into my office."

Helmke signaled for Fischer to follow Miller around the counter to the back room. They stepped into a combination office and workshop. A workbench on the left was piled high with tools, parts, wiring, and appliance casings.

Toward the back, a metal-topped table held a hot plate with a pot of coffee that smelled stale and bitter, as if it had been brewing for a long time. To the right, a desk was buried under catalogues and correspondence. Helmke spotted a padlocked closet in the far corner. He sniffed, finally identifying the pungent smell of axle grease that permeated the room.

"What are you doing here? We are supposed to meet at the restaurant tonight, not here." Miller said.

Helmke glanced at Fischer. "We decided it would be best to obtain the plans as quickly as possible."

"You shouldn't have come here. It's too dangerous." Miller brushed stacks of catalogues from several chairs to the floor. "Sit down."

"We will not take much time," Helmke said.

Miller nodded. "Tell me, please. How is it at home? How is it really?"

"Not good," Helmke replied. "Do you not read the news?"

"Yes, but it's all American propaganda. I don't know what to believe."

Helmke had a few questions of his own he wanted answered before they proceeded any further with this impossible situation. "How did you know when to expect us?"

"I have a radio in my bedroom." Miller pointed toward a door in the rear of the workshop.

Incredulous, Helmke asked, "In the open, you use a radio?"

"Yes and no. To look at it, it's an ordinary radio to receive local broadcasts. Inside is a powerful short wave receiver. I listen two times a week at 0400 hours for a message. That's how I learned of your arrival from a U-boat in the Gulf."

Helmke panicked. "But who else is listening? How can you be sure you have not been identified? Someone could be watching us now."

"You don't need to worry about that. There's no way anyone can trace me, because I don't transmit." Miller smiled obeisantly. "I'm not a courageous man, Herr Holm. But I want to serve the Fuhrer."

"Are you certain no one suspects you?"

"I don't see why they should. I've lived in Santa Fe for two years. Before that, I lived in New York for more than ten years. It was at the time the Fuhrer was coming into power and the networks were being established. I was sent to Santa Fe because I was raised in America and spoke without an accent."

"What other operations have you been a part of?" Helmke asked.

Miller shrugged. "Nothing. My assignment was to become part of the community until I was needed."

From the main part of the shop, the doorbell tinkled. Helmke glanced worriedly at Miller.

"It is nothing," Miller said. "I have a shop. Customers come for service."

"Of course," Helmke said stiffly, embarrassed that his nervousness had shown. He wanted to finish here and be gone before they were discovered. He glanced at Fischer, who had picked up a catalog.

Miller returned, carrying a toaster. "One minute, please." He set it on the workbench, opened the bottom and peered inside. A frown creased his brow.

Alarmed, Helmke asked, "What is it? What is wrong?"

"I'm not sure," Miller said. "A well-dressed man brought this in. We don't get the carriage trade here, so I ask myself what's an uptown gentleman doing in this part of town claiming his new toaster is broken? Now I find it has a part missing. A part that has obviously been removed deliberately."

"You understand now why we must not delay." Helmke said.

"Yes, I agree. I'll call Kuster and tell him to bring the plans tomorrow morning. He thinks he is helping the Russians again."

"Do you know Dr. Kuster personally?" Helmke asked.

"When I was ordered here from New York, I was instructed to cultivate a friendship. I found the places he frequented and arranged to be there when he was. We were introduced and became. . .friends," Miller said. He smiled smugly. "I also have photographs of Kuster passing information to our enemy to the east."

"Good," Helmke said. "We will use them to encourage his participation."

Miller nodded. "Now, go. Please," he said. "I only hope you haven't aroused unnecessary suspicions by coming to my shop."

"There is no time to worry or place blame," Helmke said. He started toward the door, then turned back to Miller. "Just do what is necessary."

* * *

Butler led Robbins into the Santa Fe Inn restaurant shortly after 6:30. The aroma of sizzling steaks greeted them. Butler looked around for Hanover before approaching the dark-haired hostess. She was a pretty thing. At home he would enjoy flirting with her, maybe even going home with her later. But that was impossible with nooney-nannie Robbins hovering around.

"We're meeting a man here," Butler said to her. "Tall, blond, thirtyish."

"No one's come in like that, at least not alone," the hostess said. "Do you want to sit down to wait for him?"

"That son of a bitch stood us up," Robbins snarled in Butler's ear.

Butler glared at his subordinate. "Calm down," he said quietly before turning back to the hostess. "We'll come back later. Probably got the time wrong." He flashed her a dazzling smile simply to stay in practice, then nudged Robbins back outside.

"See? He skipped out, just like I told you."

"What would he have to gain? We'll go to the hotel and see if something held him up."

When they reached the hotel, Butler approached the front desk. The same clerk was on duty. "Is Mr. Hanover still in his room?"

The clerk looked around nervously and pushed his glasses higher on his nose. "Yes, sir. At least, I haven't seen him leave."

"Good." Butler looked at the rows of boxes on the wall behind the clerk. The box for 207 was empty; the key for 214 was in its box. So the Swedes were still out. "Have there been any calls to or from either 207 and 214?"

"No, sir.

"That's fine. You're doing a good job, young man."

Butler and Robbins took the stairs to the second floor and quickly found Room 207. Butler knocked on the door. When there was no response, he knocked again, louder and more urgently this time. He heard a scrambling noise inside, and the door opened a crack.

*   *   *

Still drowsy and disoriented, Hanover cautiously opened the door. Robbins crashed against the door, slamming Hanover against the wall.

"Where the hell've you been?" Robbins demanded.

Butler closed the door softly. "Robbins—"

"What does it look like?" Hanover snapped back. He groaned and wiped his hand across his face. Here we go again, he thought. "I fell asleep. So throw me back in jail."

"Go wash your face," Butler said with a sharp look at Robbins.

"Give me a minute." Hanover flung the door open and stalked down the hall to the bathroom. After splashing cold water on his face, he combed his hair. A glance in the mirror told him he didn't look as bad as he felt. But he needed a solid night's sleep so badly he was ready to kill for it.

Still scowling, he returned to his room and glared at Robbins. "Do you mind?"

Pushing the agent aside, he retrieved his new clothes from the chest of drawers. He slipped into a white shirt, then picked up the tie. He hadn't a clue how to tie it, so he tossed it to Butler.

The Deputy Director smirked. "Windsor or square knot?"

"What?"

"What kind of knot to you want? Oh, never mind." Butler looped the tie around his own neck and deftly knotted it. He slipped the tie off and handed it to Hanover. "We saw some friends of yours in the lobby a while ago."

"Who? Kant?"

"No, your Nazi friends checked in."

"To this hotel? I didn't know they were staying here," Hanover said. "Did you arrest them?"

Butler shook his head. "We don't have anything to arrest them for."

"What about bringing them in for questioning?" Hanover jerked the tie over his head.

"We can't do that either. If their cover story is as good as I suspect it is, we have no grounds for approaching them. They're supposed to be from a neutral country on legitimate business."

"Their story's good enough that they passed through Customs and Immigration," Robbins said.

"That's not saying much," Butler threw out.

"There must be something we can do," Hanover said. "You didn't have any problem hauling me in."

"That was different. You opened your mouth about something civilians aren't supposed to know about," Butler said. "We're going by the book on this. Aside from your word, we have nothing. Besides, I want the whole bunch, not just these two. I will say this, Hanover, their arrival raises your credibility by a hell of a lot."

"So you believe me now."

Butler smiled dryly. "I won't go so far as to say I believe your time travel fantasy, but the rest of your story is playing out just like you said it would."

"Thanks. I think," Hanover said. He shrugged into his jacket. "I guess I'm ready. Let's see what happens at the restaurant." He ushered the two FBI agents from his room.

After he turned in his room key to the desk clerk, they walked several blocks to the Santa Fe Inn. In a few minutes, they entered the restaurant.

The hostess led them past a long bar resplendent in brass and highly polished, heavy-grained wood. At the end of the lounge, they stepped into a large dining room.

Hanover found it difficult to see clearly in the ornate room. Candles in brass candelabra served as the centerpieces for each table. The tables were arranged around a postage-stamp sized dance floor.

A placard next to a small stage advertised 'Audrey Summers accompanied by Cal's Swing Combo, Friday and Saturday Nights, 9 pm to 1 am.' Hanover wondered if today was Friday or Saturday, and realized he didn't have a clue what day of the week it was, only the date.

The hostess directed them to a table and passed out large menus. "Would you like something to drink?"

"I'll have a beer," Robbins said, ignoring Butler's objection.

"Coffee," Butler said pointedly.

"The same," Hanover said.

"I'll send your waitress over right away." The hostess smiled, her eyes lingering on Hanover.

Hanover tried to appear casual as he scanned the room. Several men were sitting alone at tables large enough to accommodate four to six people. One man occupied a booth against the wall.

"See anyone who might be the contact?" Butler asked.

"I have no idea who he is," Hanover said. "We'll have to wait for the Germans to arrive." He didn't even try to make small talk. What could he tell them that they hadn't already heard and either accepted or rejected?

The knot in his stomach had returned. For a while, at least, the fear was gone. He still worried about failure, but for now he wasn't working alone.

The thought buzzed through his mind that he wasn't just working with people, he was working with the government.

If someone had told him that a week ago, he would have laughed in their face. But then he hadn't known about a world like this one, about people like the ones he'd met. This world was so different from his own.

And he was different. He could feel himself changing. In his old life, he'd been angry at the world, disenfranchised from everyone around him. The unjustified brutality of his death sentence turned him bitter at Southwestern Regional Prison. But that bitterness was fading, along with his anger and disillusionment. This world had no place for it.

"Look over there." Butler nudged Hanover's arm. "Those your two friends?"

Hanover studied them, one short and dark, the other tall and blond. "It sure looks like them. Of course, the picture I saw was one hundred years old—"

"Are you going to start that crap again?" Robbins said in hushed tones.

"Quiet," Butler said.

Hanover watched as the hostess led the Germans across the room to join the man in a booth. The waitress quickly followed and scribbled on her pad.

"My information is that they meet the person from Los Alamos here tomorrow night," Hanover said.

"Good. We'll see what we can find out now, then return tomorrow. Drink up," Butler ordered. He finished his coffee and raised his cup to attract the waitress' attention.

She returned to their table holding a pot of coffee. "Refills?"

"Please." Butler flashed his best matinee idol smile at her and held up his cup. While she poured the coffee, he placed his FBI badge flat on the table where it was not visible to anyone else.

"Two men just joined that man in the booth—don't turn around," he cautioned as she started to look in that direction. "Do you know the man who was first sitting in the booth?"

"Ye—yes, sir," the waitress said. Her chin quivered and she set the shaking pot on the table. "It's Mr. Miller."

"Does Mr. Miller have a first name?"

"It's Henry."

"You know him pretty well," Butler said.

"Yes—I mean, no, sir. He eats here occasionally. He's always very nice and he tips well. And he never makes any trouble," she added hastily.

"Do you know what business he's in?"

"No, sir. He's been coming in for the last year or so. Usually he's alone, but sometimes he comes in with another man I don't know."

"That's fine. You've been a big help. Now, not a word of this to anyone. Do you understand?"

"Yes, sir. Would. . .would you like to order now?"

"No, just bring us our bill," Butler said.

After the waitress left, Hanover said, "I'm impressed. Quite different from the interrogation tactics in my time."

With a conceited smile, Butler shrugged. "All it takes is a badge, a little charm, and they'll tell you their deepest secrets."

The man identified by the waitress as Henry Miller slid from the booth and left the restaurant. Butler turned to

Robbins. "That's the man they visited this afternoon at that repair shop. How is he tied in with the Los Alamos group?"

"I have no idea. But I'll go back to the office and get right on it," Robbins said.

"Good." Butler looked at Hanover. "You're sure they don't meet Kuster until tomorrow night?"

"That's the time line I was given."

"Okay, then. No point hanging around here any longer." Butler slid a healthy tip under his saucer, and led the way outside. He stopped on the sidewalk. "I want to catch the whole network tomorrow night, including the Los Alamos leak, not just the errand boys here now. Have Agent Drake continue to keep an eye on our two German friends anyway."

"Shouldn't I alert the other agents and set up rotation watches?" Robbins asked.

Butler hesitated. He still wasn't completely convinced that this wasn't a trap set by Hoover. "No. The fewer people know about it, the less chance they'll suspect we're on to them."

"If you say so." Robbins didn't sound convinced of Butler's logic.

"We'll meet you here at 6:30 tomorrow night, Hanover," Butler said. "Stay out of sight. If that major is running around, I don't want him spotting you and scaring everyone underground."

✶   ✶   ✶

Willie Kant leaned against the building, watching the entry of the Santa Fe Inn across the street. It was dark, cold, and he shivered as he lurked unseen in the shadows. The street was busy; a steady stream of people entered the Inn.

He saw three men approach the restaurant. One of them was Hanover. Kant smiled and fingered the gun he held in his belt.

Kant had fired the gun several times to get the feel of it and found it had considerably more recoil than the laser gun he was used to. Despite that disadvantage, he was confident he would be successful at close range.

Still, he decided this was not the time to eliminate Hanover. The street was too crowded, and the risk of being caught was too great. Hanover would have to wait.

He saw Helmke and Fischer go in, and for a moment he panicked. What if Hanover saw them and had them arrested? How would Germany get the plans? But Kant hesitated to enter the restaurant with Hanover inside with two men.

He waited a few more minutes, thinking of different strategies to monitor the Germans and Hanover. To his surprise, Hanover and the two men came out of the restaurant and spoke for a moment before separating.

Kant breathed a sigh of relief. Perhaps it had been a coincidence that Hanover came here at the same time as the Germans. Or perhaps, he didn't recognize them.

Kant wondered about the two men with Hanover. The entire operation was growing increasingly complex, with many more players than should be involved. Kant stepped further into shadows as the two men crossed the street and walked in front of him.

Yes, he would have to be very careful.

CHAPTER 19

SANTA FE, NEW MEXICO
Evening, March 30, 1944

Outside the Santa Fe Inn, Hanover left Butler and Robbins and returned to his hotel room. He sank onto the bed, but despite his exhaustion, he couldn't sleep. Instead, he stared at the ceiling, his fingers laced behind his head. All they had to do was catch the German spies with Hans Kuster at the Santa Fe Inn tomorrow night. They would stop the conspiracy; then he could go home.

Dr. Beecker had said he would find 1944 attractive, but Hanover knew the twenty-first century was his time. If—or when—he succeeded in stopping the Germans, things could only improve in 2044. But some people he had known either no longer existed, or lived a totally different life. His father wouldn't have died in the endless war against the Russians.

He could meet his father.

The thought hit him hard, made him hot and cold at the same time. What would he say to him? In the changed future, Hanover would have grown up with his father, yet when he saw him, what would he say? Good Lord, would he return only to find himself already in existence? He wished Beecker had taken more time to explain it all.

He shifted his position and worried about something easier: the timegate. Beecker had said it was good for two, maybe three passages. He and Kant had both come through. Was there enough energy for him to pass through again? What if Major Kant beat him back to the timegate and went through first? Then Hanover would be trapped in this time.

His stomach turned queasy at the thought, and he groaned. Maybe thinking about the timegate wasn't easier. Maybe he'd think about. . .Ellen.

* * *

SANTA FE, NEW MEXICO
Early Morning, March 31, 1944

Helmke woke to a gentle rap on his hotel door. He glanced at Fischer and heard a light snore emanating from the lump of covers. That was the way of it with these young people, they could sleep through anything.

The knock repeated, urgently but without authority.

Helmke stumbled from his bed and pulled on a silk robe as he crossed the room. At the door, he hesitated. "Who is it?"

"Miller. Let me in."

Helmke unlocked the door and opened it wide enough for Miller to slither into the room. Helmke glanced up and down the empty hall to be sure no one was watching, then shut and relocked the door.

He turned to chastise Miller but stopped when he saw the other man head straight for the window and pull the shade back slightly to peer outside to the street below.

"Wh—what's going on?" Fischer's voice sounded shrill as he sat up, clutching the covers to his chest.

"Yes." Helmke strode across the room. "What is going on? You are crazy to come here."

Miller continued his inspection out the window. "There's a man in a black sedan, fourth car from the corner. Can you see him?" Stepping aside, Miller held the shade for Helmke. "He's following you."

Helmke glanced at him sharply, then looked back at the sedan. "What makes you think that?"

"He's the same man who was sitting outside the restaurant last night when I left."

"You do not think it is a coincidence?"

"Mr. Holm, we can't afford any coincidences."

"We are ruined," Fischer wailed.

"Be quiet." Helmke frowned and moved away from the window. "Let me think."

Who would know about them? Only a few people knew about the mission: the three of them in this room. And that madman who claimed he was from the future. The man who had more information than even those assigned to the mission, including how it was to end.

Helmke dared another look at the sedan, wishing he could understand why the man had followed them to the restaurant. Ach, it was too much.

"Has he seen you?" Helmke asked Miller.

"I'm certain he hasn't. I saw him when I came around the corner, but he was busy reading his newspaper. I entered the hotel from the back and took the stairs." Miller shook his head in disgust. "Stupid Americans. I don't understand how it can be so difficult to win this war against them."

"We must leave soon. When can we pick up the plans?"

Miller brightened. "That's what I was coming to tell you. I called Dr. Kuster last night and told him I was ready to fix his radio—"

"We don't have time for that," Fischer interrupted.

Miller looked at Fischer, then at Helmke. "I'm beginning to understand why we're having difficulties winning this war."

"We all have our burdens." Helmke turned to Fischer. "Dr. Kuster and Herr Miller were using a code message."

"Oh, of course." Fischer climbed from his bed and stretched. "I will be back in a minute."

Incredulous, Helmke stared at him. "You will not move from this room until I say you may." He glared at Fischer to stifle any objections. "Mr. Miller, please continue."

"Where was I? Oh, yes. I told him to bring the radio to my shop this morning between nine-thirty and ten o'clock. We should leave now. It'll be safer to have you away from this stake-out, as the Americans call it."

"Fischer, you may go now. But be quick about it. We must leave." Helmke stripped off his robe and pajamas.

"This will be good. We can leave for Mexico as soon as Dr. Kuster delivers the plans."

Miller checked out the window again. "He's still there."

Helmke and Fischer dressed and packed swiftly. Helmke paid the bill and checked out, then he and Fischer followed Miller through the rear exit. Taking the long way around, they reached Helmke's rental car without being spotted by the man in the sedan.

Helmke started the car. "Are you sure no one else is watching for us?"

"I'm sure. I checked very carefully both when I came in and when we left."

"Still, it would be best if we made certain. Olaf. . .*Olaf*!"

"What?"

"Watch behind us. I will take a circuitous route to the shop. You tell me if anyone follows us."

After they had driven several blocks, Helmke began to relax. From his rearview mirror, he detected no suspicious cars, no one watched them with interest.

"We should stop for gas," Miller said. "I have plenty of ration stamps. We'll fill up your tank now, and I'll give you more stamps to use in Socorro."

"That is a good plan," Helmke said.

"Yes, the plan is simple and that is best," Fischer commented from the back seat.

Helmke rolled his eyes and caught Miller stifling a smirk. Soon he would be rid of this incompetent young man. Perhaps Fischer would panic when the time came to reboard the U-boat. Then it would be up to Helmke to take the plans back to Germany.

And it would be Helmke who received all the honor and glory for this great service to the Fatherland. Perhaps he should encourage Fischer to stay in Mexico, offer to help him contact other loyal Nazis who were busily transferring assets to South America. . .to diversify, of course, not as protection in case Germany lost.

The more he thought about it, the more he liked that plan. It would take little to convince Fischer to miss the return trip. Helmke smiled as he considered exactly how he would do it.

* * *

Hanover tossed and turned before he finally fell into a fitful sleep in the early morning hours. He dreamed of Ellen. She smiled, her blue eyes dancing in welcome as she approached. Then Major Kant stepped between them. He grabbed Ellen and flung her to the ground. He picked up a rock and threw it at Hanover. It missed him, landing nearby with a loud crash.

He woke with a start and sat upright. The blankets were thrashed and half on the floor. Another crash sounded outside. He jumped from his bed. He saw a garbage truck parked beneath his window. In the early dawn, two men loaded the hotel's trash into the truck and dropped the empty containers on the pavement.

He sagged against the walls. "Assholes," he muttered. Butler wanted him out of the way all day, to stay out of trouble, avoid Kant, and wait until this evening when he helped them follow the German spies and their contacts.

But he'd spent too many years cooped up in a jail cell to stay in this room and hide. Besides, he had other things he needed to do. This was his last chance to give Ellen the necklace he'd bought for her.

An hour later, he stood outside Carrie's Cafe. From the parking lot, it looked like the place was busy with the breakfast crowd. He struggled to subdue the combined excitement and uncertainty churning inside him, annoyed that he lacked his usual detachment. He couldn't explain what drew him here, or what had possessed him to buy the necklace in the first place. He didn't care about other people, he told himself; they didn't care about him.

Yet he quickly scanned the cafe through the glass door, uncertain how Ellen would greet him. The welcome in his dream was more than he could hope for. They had barely started to talk three days ago when O'Rourke had taken him into custody.

He saw her. She stood behind the counter, drawing coffee from the large urn into a smaller pot. He opened the door and as he stepped inside, the little bell tinkled.

"Be right with you. Take a seat anywhere." She turned and glanced in his direction. Gasping, she flushed, then quickly looked away, concentrating on refilling a counter customer's cup.

Hanover watched her for a moment, noting that her hand trembled, that when she smiled at the other customer, her mouth quavered. She seemed shaken by his sudden arrival. He went to the far end of the counter and slid onto an empty stool.

Without looking at him, she set a cup and saucer in front of him and poured the coffee.

"I need to talk to you," Hanover said.

She glanced at him, and then away, and he was surprised to see her eyes were wet. "There's a couple leaving that table in the corner. Sit there and I'll be right over to clean it up."

Hanover took his cup to the vacated table. Did she want him here so she could talk to him privately? Or so she wouldn't have to look at him every time she picked up an order? He saw her grab a tray and come toward him.

"You're still limping," she said as she loaded the dirty dishes onto the tray.

He wished she would look at him. "It's doing better. I've tried to keep it wrapped, but I can't do it as well as you did." He was rewarded with a hint of a smile. Her expression was both wary and hopeful.

"It wasn't as bad as it looked the other day."

Wiping the table with a damp cloth, she nodded, but still did not look at him. "Sheriff O'Rourke wouldn't tell us anything."

He clenched the mug in his hands. "That's because. . .I can't explain the whole story, but I will tell you that I'm working with the F.B.I. It'll all be over in a couple more days."

He felt he was babbling like an awkward schoolboy. From Ellen's closed expression, he couldn't tell if she believed him or not. He hadn't really told her anything that explained his disappearance.

Ellen picked up the tray and balanced it on her hip as she gazed steadily at him. "I'll bring you some more coffee, Bill. Do you want the breakfast special?"

He nodded, discouraged that she hadn't said anything more. "There's something else you should know. My name's not Bill Scott. I've been using that as an alias. My real name is Scott Hanover."

"Really." Her mouth curved into a skeptical half smile as she turned away. "You're just full of surprises, aren't you?"

Hanover sipped on his coffee. At least she hadn't totally rejected him. But with her reserved manner, he couldn't tell how she felt about him.

No woman from his time had interested him as Ellen did; no one else had made him care about what they thought of him. He wondered if it was because he was in a different time and place. Or was it he who was changing? And if it was, did he want to?

Ellen delivered his breakfast, then moved quickly on to another large party. He watched the easy way she laughed and joked with the family, and felt a tightening in his gut. He'd wait until she wasn't so busy to give her the necklace.

And to say goodbye.

*　　　　*　　　　*

Helmke paced the floor of Miller's back room. He scowled at how easily Fischer lost himself in the catalogs piled everywhere. The *untersturmfuhrer* did not have the intelligence to know they were in serious trouble; he had contributed nothing to this glorious assignment. Helmke had already shed any hesitancy about leaving Fischer behind. The door bell in the front tinkled, and Helmke whirled around, his stomach churning with nerves and acid.

Miller glanced at a clock and shook his head. "Too early." He slipped past the curtain, and Helmke approached the doorway. He drew the curtain back slightly and saw a woman explaining the problem she was having with her mixer. As she spoke, the door opened again, and a man entered.

Helmke's breath caught. It was Kuster, carrying a radio. He heard Miller say, "I'll be right with you, sir," and Helmke wanted to scream at him to get rid of the woman.

Miller finally finished with the customer, and he signaled Kuster to follow him into the back.

Kuster entered the back room and stood quietly, clutching the large radio. His eyes held a nervous excitement, anticipation at sharing more information with the Soviets.

Helmke reached for the radio. "I will take that, Herr Kuster."

Dr. Kuster blanched and hugged the radio to him. "You—you're German. But I thought. . .." He turned to Miller. "What's going on here?"

"We are taking the plans you are so eager to give to the Soviets," Helmke said.

"What? Are you crazy?" Kuster started to back from the room, but Miller blocked his path. "I'll call the authorities and turn you in."

"That would be ill-advised," Helmke said. "You would have to tell them what you are doing with the plans you have hidden inside that radio cabinet. And we would have to tell them of your ties to the Soviets. We know that before the war, when you left Germany for England, German Intelligence reported your communist activities to the British, but they chose to ignore the report." Helmke shrugged. "The Americans, they may not be so lenient, especially now."

"You can't prove anything," Kuster said.

"We have photographs," Helmke said.

"Ph—photographs?" Kuster stammered.

"Yes. Ones such as this." Helmke held up a picture clearly showing Kuster in the company of another man. "Of meetings the Americans will find very interesting,"

Kuster grabbed the photo from Helmke's hand. "There's nothing incriminating in that photo," Kuster exclaimed. "It appears I'm talking to someone. Yes, I remember, he was a stranger asking for directions. That is not a crime."

"And did you give the directions in a package?" Helmke held up another photo, this one of Kuster handing the same man a large envelope. "We know the other man. He is a Soviet agent. The Americans, I am sure, would be most interested in your friends."

Kuster seemed to shrink inside himself. "This can't be happening," he whispered. His eyes clouded. He turned and took a step, stumbling. "I am ruined."

Miller plucked the radio from Kuster's arms and quickly pulled the back off. The usual tubes and wires were missing from inside the cabinet. Miller withdrew a packet.

"That is what you're looking for," Kuster said. "You have used me shamefully."

"I do not understand, Dr. Kuster," Helmke said, taking the packet from Miller. He turned it over and looked at it. "Why would you not do for your own country what you do for the Soviets?"

"Men like you would never understand," Kuster snapped. He grabbed the empty radio and hurried out.

"Should we let him leave like that?" Fischer asked.

Helmke shrugged. "He is nothing to us now. Come, we must go."

"We don't have time to microfilm the plans before you leave," Miller said.

"It will be all right. We have only to drive across the border."

The door bell tinkled again. Miller shrugged apologetically. "Wait, please. I forgot to put up the closed sign. I'll be quick with this customer."

*   *   *

Willie Kant stood in the small repair shop and looked around. How fortunate he had remembered the name of Helmke's contact. Tonight was when they would meet Dr. Kuster at the Santa Fe Inn to arrange tomorrow's transfer of the plans.

He'd been shocked to see the scientist enter the store, one day ahead of schedule. History had already been altered, but why? Was it because of his presence, or Hanover's? He didn't know, nor did it matter. What was important now was that he was here in time to connect with the Germans before they left for Mexico.

A small man appeared from behind a draped doorway. "Can I help you?"

"Are you Henry Miller?" The uneasiness in Miller's eyes pleased Kant.

"Yes. Do you have something you want repaired?"

"I am looking for. . .Eric Holm."

Helmke stepped into the room, followed by Fischer. "What are you doing here? What do you want?"

Miller looked nervously from one to the other. "Who is this man?" he asked Helmke.

"He says his name is Willie Kant. He also claims he is from the future."

"The what? The future?" blurted Miller, more disbelieving.

"Not so impossible, *Herr* Mueller."

Miller gasped. "How. . .?"

Helmke stepped further into the room, his gaze steady on Kant. "He seems to know everything about our mission. He knows your real name, and ours. I still do not know what it is he wants."

Kant clasped his hands behind his back and smiled smugly. "It's very simple. I know you have the plans. Kuster just left here. Now you'll make your run for the border. I'm going with you. We can't let anything stop those plans from reaching Germany."

"Out of the question," Helmke exclaimed. "Absolutely out of the question."

Kant pulled out the gun tucked in the back of his pants. "Shall we leave? We don't want to waste time arguing. The local authorities might catch up with you."

Fischer moved closer to Helmke and plucked at his sleeve. "He is right. We cannot wait any longer."

"You must go. Now," Miller said. "We are all at risk if you delay."

"Where are the plans?" Kant asked. No one moved. He wouldn't be satisfied the plans were safe until he was holding them. Kant leveled his gun at Helmke. "I suggest you set them on the counter, and all of you step back."

When Helmke hesitated, Kant cocked the hammer. "As *Herr* Mueller said, we have little time to waste." Helmke dropped the packet and Kant scooped it up and shoved it inside his shirt.

Then he waved the gun at the two Germans, signalling them to leave. "We can discuss my coming with you while we drive."

*   *   *

Uneasy about leaving Hanover alone all day, Deputy Director Butler entered the DiVargas Hotel. What if Hanover talked, and word of their activities leaked? Butler wanted no one outside Robbins, Drake and himself to have any knowledge of the spies until he had them arrested and the plans safely retrieved.

He crossed the lobby and spotted the local agent, Drake, at the front desk. The agent slammed his hand on the counter and the clerk turned away from him. Drake reached out, grabbed the clerk, spun him around, jerked on the clerk's tie so that his chin hit the counter.

"Now, do I have your undivided attention?" Drake said.

Butler hurried over. "What's the problem here?"

"You're choking me," the clerk gasped.

Butler took in Drake's angry red face. "Let him up," he ordered.

Drake eased his grip, but did not release the tie. "Where are the occupants in Room 214?"

"They checked out over an hour ago." The clerk grabbed his tie and yanked it from Drake's grasp.

"What do you mean they checked out?" Butler asked. "I thought you were watching."

"I was," Drake said defensively. "I was watching out front. They must've slipped out the back way."

Butler faced the clerk. "Is that true?"

"I wouldn't know. I left the desk to tell housekeeping to get the room cleaned."

"Yeah, right," Drake snarled.

"What about the man in Room 207, Scott Hanover?" Butler asked.

"He's gone out."

"What do you mean?" Butler felt a flush of panic. "Did he check out, too?"

"No, no. He just went out."

Butler frowned. "When did he leave? Did he say where he was going?"

"Yes. When he turned in his key—about half an hour ago—he said he was going to breakfast at a place called Carrie's Cafe."

Butler's eyebrow went up along with his curiosity. That was where Hanover had been picked up by the deputy. And it was where the Germans were first spotted. But since then, they had made contact with Miller, and that was the priority now. "Call Robbins," Butler told Drake. "Tell him to meet me at Miller's store."

"What about Hanover?"

"We'll catch up with him later," Butler said as he hurried from the hotel.

Fifteen minutes later, Butler waited impatiently for Robbins and Drake to arrive outside Miller's shop.

"There's an alley in back of Miller's shop," Drake offered.

Butler nodded. "Good. We'll try to surprise him, then. Drake, you go around back and come in that way. I don't want anyone else slipping away because we're in front." He gave the humiliated agent a minute to circle around the block to the alley.

"Want to tell me what that was about?" Robbins asked.

"While your man was sitting on his ass in front of the hotel, the Germans escaped unnoticed out the back." Butler tapped his foot impatiently. "Let's go. I have a bad feeling about this," he said.

They entered the shop and waited for Miller to come from the back room. Miller frowned when he saw them. "May I help you?"

Butler flashed his ID. "Yesterday, you were seen with two men who are believed to be German agents. Where are they now?"

Miller paled and clutched the counter. "German spies? I know nothing about German spies."

"You had dinner with them last night."

Miller's brow furrowed as he tried to mask his fear with wide-eyed innocence. "I know nothing about any German agents," he repeated. "I had dinner with two Swedish businessmen. They have done business here before."

Butler felt a cold chill. Miller spoke with a calm smugness, as if he wasn't worried about tonight's meeting. Butler spotted Drake coming through the doorway. Drake shook his head, indicating there was no one else in the shop. "We can wait. Drake, take him in and hold him. I want to question him further."

After Drake left with Miller, Robbins asked, "Do you think you'll get any more out of him?"

"I hope so. He looked familiar to me last night, and I've finally placed him. About ten years ago, I worked out of the New York office. We monitored the activities of a German Bund. Nothing came of it, but Miller was in that group. Now he turns up here. Makes you wonder what happened to the others."

Butler followed Robbins from the shop. "What do you think we should do now?"

Shoving his hands in his pockets, Robbins frowned. "If the Germans have already checked out of the hotel, and this guy's not the least bit concerned about getting rid of us. . .It plays like the show's over."

Robbins' observation surprised Butler. Perhaps there was more to this small town agent than met the eye. He nodded. "It does sound like Kuster has been here already."

"Which means they have the plans?"

"Hanover said they weren't supposed to meet Kuster until tonight, and the exchange made tomorrow. But if they met Kuster this morning—Come on, let's go."

Robbins hurried after Butler. "Where are we going?"

"To Carrie's Cafe, to get Hanover."

"Why do we need him?"

"Because he's the only one who knows where the spies are headed next."

CHAPTER 20

Hanover waited impatiently as the breakfast crowd thinned out, leaving only a couple of people lingering over their coffee and newspapers. He needed to give Ellen the necklace and say goodbye.

When he'd reined in his impatience for long as he could stand, he left the booth. He pushed through the swinging door to the kitchen. "Hello, Carrie. Where's Ellen?"

"Humph. What're you doing here? I thought you was in jail." Carrie brandished a large wooden spoon at him.

"I was, but it was a mistake."

"That's what they all say," she grumbled. She waved the spoon toward the exit. "Ellen's out back emptying the garbage. Maybe she needs some help."

"Thanks, Carrie. I—." The bell tinkled out front.

"Hanover! You in here?"

Butler's voice caught Hanover by surprise. From the pass-through, he saw Butler fuming, and Robbins eyeing the dome-covered plate of donuts. "Yeah, I'm here," he called back. "What's the matter? Can't a guy go to breakfast?"

"Don't move." Butler ducked around the counter and into the kitchen. His eyes narrowed when he saw Carrie. "Is there someplace we can talk? Privately."

Carrie pointed to the exit. "The alley's the only private place around."

Butler grabbed Hanover's arm and hauled him outside.

"What the—"

"We don't have time," Butler snarled. "The Germans already have the plans."

"But, how? They aren't supposed to meet Kuster until tonight."

"They didn't read the same schedule you did. They must have met Kuster this morning and they checked out of the hotel."

Butler's words stopped Hanover cold. They'd have to scramble now to stop the Germans from taking the plans across the border. "What about their contact? Miller?"

"We're holding him, but all he has to do is stall a couple of hours. We have nothing to charge him with, no concrete evidence against him—just what you've told us—and no judge is going to be impressed when we say you know because you're from the future. So where're they going?"

"If they have the trigger mechanism plans, they'll head for the border," Hanover said. "They're supposed to cross at El Paso."

"Okay. We'll handle it from here."

Butler turned to leave, but Hanover caught his arm. "Wait a minute. I'm going with you."

"This doesn't concern you," Butler said.

"It sure as hell does. You wouldn't have known anything until they dropped a bomb on your head if it hadn't been for me. Think about it. My being here has already affected history— they're a day ahead of schedule."

Butler eyed him thoughtfully, then grimaced. "Okay. Maybe you'll be useful. But civilians aren't allowed on Bureau activities. I'm taking no responsibility if you get hurt, understand?"

"Understood."

"Good. Now where's a phone?"

"There's one out front," Hanover said.

"I'll call the border guard and warn them. Be outside in five minutes."

Butler stormed back through the cafe. He quickly spotted the telephone booth located outside the front of the cafe and picked up the receiver, punching the plunger several times until the operator answered. "Operator, this is an emergency, an A-1 priority call to the El Paso border crossing supervisor."

"I'm sorry, sir," a woman said with the nasal tonality common to telephone operators. "The lines are all busy. There will be at least an hour's delay."

Butler didn't have time for this. "Listen, honey, my name is Thomas Butler. I'm the deputy director for the F.B.I. We're dealing with a national emergency here. I need to talk to the supervisor at the border station and I need to talk to him now."

"Everyone's call is important, sir. I'm sorry, but you will have to wait your turn."

He couldn't believe what he was hearing. "Listen, you incompetent twit, get me your manager," Butler shouted.

"He's on another line."

"Then you pull his goddamn plug and connect me."

"You can't talk to me like that." The operator's voice quavered. "Hold on. Mr. Mason is free now. I'll try to put you through."

Butler heard a click, and hoped—for the operator's sake—she hadn't disconnected him.

"Mason here. What seems to be the trouble?"

Butler took a deep breath, attempting to regain control of his temper. "My name is Thomas Butler," he said, using the same tone and speed one used with small children. "I am the deputy director of the F.B.I. and I'm dealing with a critical national emergency. I urgently need to talk to the border crossing station in El Paso. Now."

"Well, sir, the calls are backed up. What with the war, and all—"

Butler struggled to keep his temper. "You've got ten seconds to put me through, or so help me, I'll have the FCC, the IRS, the Justice Department, and whoever else I can think of all over you. Do I make myself clear?"

Without closing the key, the manager called the operator. "Erma, put this *gentleman* through. It's a crying shame how these government people bully us civilians."

Thirty seconds later, Butler reached Ben Davies at the El Paso border crossing. Finally. He rubbed the pounding headache building behind his eyes. And to think his biggest case, his chance for recognition—and the director's seat—had almost been destroyed by an incompetent operator.

When Davies answered the phone, Butler identified himself and said, "Two men are headed your way in a blue sedan with Mexican license plates. We believe they're German agents using forged or stolen Swedish passports. Hold them until I get there."

"Well, now," Davies drawled. "I don't know if I can do that."

Butler turned cold at the words. "What do you mean, you don't know if you can do that?" After his go-round with the phone company, he was in no mood to wrestle with a government bureaucrat who couldn't see beyond interdepartmental rivalry.

"I mean, if they have valid passports and there're no irregularities, I can't legally hold them, now, can I?"

"All right," Butler snapped. He glared at Robbins, who stepped from the cafe and started toward him. "All right, you want to play hard ball? Here's how she plays, Davies. We have two German spies with classified material stolen from Los Alamos. We ask your cooperation in apprehending these people. You don't have to arrest them, you don't have to question them. You don't even have to search them. You don't have to do a goddamn thing except hold them until we arrive," he said, his volume escalating as he spoke.

He paused and swallowed hard before continuing in a more normal tone. "Now listen closely. If these two men are not waiting for us when we arrive, you are in shit so deep you'll never climb out. Do I make myself clear?"

"Yeah, yeah." Davies still sounded unimpressed. "I read you loud and clear. No reason to get your dander up."

"Just so we understand each other. I don't care how you do it, just make sure they don't get through." Butler slammed down the phone.

*   *   *

Hanover started to follow Butler back into the cafe when he heard a muffled sob. Ellen. He rounded the corner and found her huddled against the wall next to the trash cans, her face buried in her apron. "Ellen?" He felt awkward, uncertain if he should approach her.

She looked up, her eyes damp. "Why do you have to go?" she whispered, her voice filled with anguish. "That man says it's dangerous. Stay here, let the authorities do the job."

He wished she hadn't overheard Butler, and hoped it wouldn't create problems for her later. "I can't stay. It's something I have to do."

"That's what you all say," she said bitterly. "And where does it get you? My brother's in a German P.O.W. camp. My fiance was killed at Guadalcanal. Now you. . .."

Ellen stepped into Hanover's arms. He held her, amazed at how right it felt. When she tipped her head to gaze at him, he couldn't help himself. He bent down and kissed her, tenderly at first, then with greater urgency. She responded hesitantly, then pressed into him. His hands roamed her back, sliding lower, holding her against the length of him.

She eased away, her lips puffy. "Slow down, soldier boy." A smile softened her words.

"What the hell is going on here?"

Hanover turned to see Carrie standing in the doorway, a deep frown on her face, the large wooden spoon still gripped in her hand.

"Nothing's going on, Aunt Carrie."

"Must think I'm blind or something. Get on in here. These men are in a tizzy, and one of them wants to take food with them." The screen door slammed shut behind her.

Ellen reached up and kissed Hanover again, hard. "When this is all over, please come back." She ran into the cafe.

Shaken by her kiss, by the intensity of her words, Hanover followed her inside. Robbins was rattling off a list of the food he wanted packed for them.

"She says you're coming, too?" Robbins asked.

"Yeah," Hanover responded, surprised the usual hostile edge was missing from the agent's voice. "Where's Butler?"

"On the phone hollering at some poor clod." Robbins looked at Carrie. "Okay, ma'am, make that six of everything."

"You got it," Carrie said. "Now out of my kitchen so I can work."

"Hey, Carrie, where's my pie?"

"O, Lordy, there's another one. You'll have to wait, O'Rourke," she hollered as she shooed Hanover and Robbins through the swinging door. "I've got paying customers to feed first. Get yourself a cup of coffee and sit."

O'Rourke's eyebrow raised when he saw Robbins and Hanover exit the kitchen.

"I better see what Butler's doing." Robbins said to Hanover. "Bring the food when it's ready. He'll be in a snit to get out of here."

O'Rourke watched the agent leave, then he poured another cup of coffee and handed it to Hanover. "Looks like you're coming up in the world, boy."

Hanover hesitated. Outside, he saw Butler shake a clenched fist at the telephone as he shouted into it. What the hell, Hanover thought, as he watched Butler's livid expression. No point in running head-on into that rage. He smiled wryly at Sheriff O'Rourke. "At least they believe me. I guess I have you to thank."

"It weren't nothing." O'Rourke shook his head, then stabbed the air in front of him with a fork. "Boy, that was some whopper of a story you told. Ain't never heard nothing like it before. Problem was, it all fit into place, and I don't like to ignore the facts just because they don't fit my idea of what's normal, you know what I mean?"

"Yeah, I know. I wouldn't believe me, either, if I'd been you."

"Well, you let me know how this all turns out."

Hanover hesitated; he wouldn't be coming back. "Won't Butler or Robbins fill you in?"

"Nah. The Feds never like to let us locals know what's going on in our own backyard." O'Rourke stared thoughtfully at his half-empty cup. "We could use a good man like you. Law enforcement's nice work. Good pay. You can raise a family on it," he added with a quick nod toward the kitchen.

O'Rourke's offer startled Hanover. Law enforcement? Scott Hanover part of the government? He almost laughed, but then he glanced at the pass through and saw Ellen working with Carrie.

"When you come back," O'Rourke continued, "think about joining up with me."

When he came back? Not likely. He belonged in his own time. Hanover saw Butler outside, his arms flailing as he shouted at someone on the other end of the telephone line.

"I better go," he said.

When he swung off the stool, his gaze fell on the bowl of matches sitting next to the cash register. 'Carrie's Cafe' was stylistically emblazoned on the small white books. He grabbed one, the only memento he would take back with him. He clutched it in his fist, then shoved it deep into his pants pocket.

Hanover stepped outside as Butler slammed the phone down.

"Where the hell's Hanover?" Butler yelled at Robbins.

"I'm right here," Hanover said, coming up behind him.

"Good. Get your ass in the car. I don't trust those border guards not to screw this up." Butler strode to the car, then glanced over his shoulder. "Now where the hell'd Robbins go?"

"Probably to get the food."

"Sonnavabitch," Butler snarled. "Get in." He started the car and swung it around to the front door, laying on the horn.

Hanover slid into the passenger seat and opened the back door for Robbins.

"Coming, coming." Robbins scurried up, loaded with bags. He hadn't even closed the door when Butler stepped on the accelerator, the tires spitting gravel as they roared from the parking lot.

* * *

Kant's excitement grew as he watched the countryside rapidly glide by. A smile crept across his face as he considered how well things were going.

They had evaded Hanover and the authorities from this time, stolen the plans out from under their noses. Now he considered staying rather than returning to 2044. He could return to Germany with Helmke and Fischer. His phenomenal "understanding" of coming events and Hitler's belief in astrology would help Kant easily manipulate the Fuhrer and establish himself as a principal adviser. Yes, coming to this century might have been the best possible thing to happen.

"We have done it!" exclaimed Fischer as they drove toward Socorro. "No one has followed us."

"We aren't assured of victory yet, although history from my time says that you're successful," Kant said from the back seat. "Of course, that history didn't mention you were assisted by a man from the future, or that your mission was threatened by another such man."

"No one will believe such rubbish," Helmke snapped.

"But it is not rubbish, is it, Major?" Kant leaned forward. "Think about it. We have already altered history. You are returning one day earlier than history documented, so you see, I helped reduce your risk of discovery."

"You have no proof that we are a day early. It is only your word that we are. No one knew anything about this mission. No one would have discovered us if you had not interfered."

"It wasn't me who interfered. It was the man who came through the timegate in front of me. He's to blame for all your worries." Kant fumed at their idiocy. How could the

Fuhrer have gambled the future of the whole world with these two?

And where was Hanover? If he was working with the authorities, he could ruin Kant's new plans. Kant kept the gun within easy reach.

*   *   *

From the driver's seat, Helmke allowed his mind to wander, fantasizing the ceremony held in his honor, the thousands of spectators watching as he approached the Fuhrer in the coliseum, Hitler smiling broadly as he pinned the Iron Cross on Helmke's tunic, embracing Helmke, shaking his hand and telling him what a hero he was to the Fatherland. The German people would be forever in his debt.

His mind snapped back to reality. He must rid himself of this unwelcome meddler, this man called Kant who claimed he came from the future—and claimed someone came with him.

Perhaps it was a hoax perpetrated by this crazy man to infiltrate and ingratiate himself with the Fuhrer. But how did this Kant know about their mission and their real identities? Was he sent by Shellenberg to spy on *them*? To ensure they succeeded? Or to see they did not defect and disappear into the American hinterlands?

For a moment he considered the possibilities; what he had seen on this brief foray into the country was impressive. But he rejected the idea of defection. He was loyal to his country. Besides, despite the intelligence and shrewdness that served him so well in Paris, he doubted he'd survive the strain of pretending he was someone else for the rest of his life.

Which brought him back to disentangling himself from this lunatic in the back seat. "Where would you like for me to stop?" Helmke asked.

"Stop? I have no need to stop," Kant responded.

"But you cannot come with us," Helmke said. "The U-boat captain will not allow an unauthorized passenger. And space is extremely limited. For you to come, someone else must stay behind."

"I will sta—"

Helmke cut Fischer off with a frigid glance and a twist of the unterstrumfuhrer's wrist.

"I'm confident the captain will see it is in his best interest to take me along," Kant said.

So, that was the way of it. It would not be so easy to shed themselves of this man. Drastic measures were required. The rearview mirror told him no one was behind. Slowly, deliberately, he increased the speed until he reached a place in the road where the shoulders were wide and flat. Then he swerved hard to the left, to the right, then slammed on the brakes.

Kant was thrown forward. Helmke grabbed his neck and pulled him across the seatback. He pummeled Kant's head and face with his free fist.

"The gun!" Helmke cried. "Get his gun."

Fischer scrambled from the car and yanked the back door open. He fumbled on the floor, avoiding Kant's flailing legs. "I have it!"

Helmke flinched under Kant's thrashing arms. He struck Kant twice more in the face. Blood spurted from Kant's nose. "You have lost," Helmke said. Kant's struggling stopped. "I will release my hold on you, then you will climb slowly from the car. Fischer!"

"Ye—yes, sir?"

"Stand back. Keep the gun on him, but do not let him get too close."

Helmke eased his grip around Kant's neck. "Get out. Slowly. With your hands up." He pushed Kant off the backrest.

Kant fell into his seat. He wiped at his nose, seeming oblivious to the blood flowing freely. "I will not get out. I'm going to Germany with you."

Helmke climbed from the car and jerked the back door open. "Get out," he repeated. "Or I will have Olaf shoot you."

Kant snickered. "You don't have the balls to do that."

"I will not allow you to jeopardize our mission. What are you thinking, man from the future?" Helmke sneered. "You have no passport, no papers to cross the border. No. To take you only is trouble."

Kant hesitated, then looked from Helmke to Fischer. Helmke used the moment to seize Kant's arm and yank him from the car. Kant hit the pavement. "Olaf, bring me the gun. Quickly."

When he was holding the gun on Kant, Helmke said, "Take the packet from him, then return to the car. Lock all of the doors except for mine."

Fischer hauled Kant to his feet and had him lean spread-eagle against the car. Watching Kant's every move, Fischer plucked the packet from Kant's jacket pocket. He stepped back and grabbed Kant's collar, flinging him to the ground before climbing into the car.

The gun still aimed at Kant, Helmke eased into the driver's seat. "You will find your way back to your own time. This is my moment for glory." He slammed the door shut and shifted into gear.

*　　　　*　　　　*

Hanover rode in silent concentration. They'd driven half a mile when he realized he'd forgotten to give Ellen the necklace. Its weight rested heavily in his pocket. But there was no turning back. Catching up with the Germans—and saving Ellen's way of life—was more important.

Butler and Robbins seemed lost in their own thoughts. Hanover glanced over his shoulder and saw Robbins sitting back, relaxed as he watched the country-side, after sifting through the bags of food Carrie had packed for them. If there was one thing Hanover found amusing about Robbins it was that he made a point of never missing a meal.

Hanover saw Butler's hands clench the wheel with a white-knuckled grip, while his jaw gnashed from side to side. Despite the anxiety he shared with Butler, images of Ellen's tear-stained face flashed in his mind, the touch of her lips soft and yielding against his, the sheriff's suggestion, all jumbled together. They wanted the impossible; they wanted him to stay. No, they expected him to.

He couldn't let what-might-have-beens distract him. What would he and Butler do when they caught up with the Germans? Would the border guards hold them as Butler had asked?

After stopping in Socorro for gas, Butler seemed calmer. Still intense, but not as obsessed. When they were driving again, he said, "Tell me more about this timegate thing of yours, Hanover."

"There's not much to tell."

"You said it was as if one minute you're in one time, then you're in the same spot, but the time is different. What happens in between?"

"It's like you're falling through a brightly lit tunnel."

Robbins snorted, but Butler ignored him. "That must've been quite an experience."

"Hmmm," Hanover responded noncommittally.

"How do you know what date you'll return? I mean, is the date preset?"

Hanover's uneasiness increased. Something about Butler's manner was too blasé. "I really don't know how all that works. I'm assuming I'll return to the same time I left."

"I bet that'll be interesting, to see what it's all like after you've changed the world." Butler chuckled, but it sounded phony to Hanover. "What do you think? Could someone go through the timegate, look around for awhile, then come back to this time?"

So that was it. Hanover had sensed Butler was an ambitious man. Knowing the future would give someone like him tremendous power to manipulate that future in his favor, change it even more than they were already doing. "While it was being tested, that might have been possible."

"Why not now?"

"Because the timegate loses power each time it's used. And I think the crystal was broken at the time I came through."

"Why would you think that?"

"The FedPos and Major Kant were right behind me. He made it through, but no one else did."

"So, you're stuck here?"

"I don't know," Hanover said honestly, not sure how he felt about that possibility. Beecker had said he had ten days to return, and if they caught the spies today, it would only be four. But he wasn't about to tell Butler. Maybe Kant had come through so close behind him they hadn't used the full power of two pass-throughs. Maybe there was still enough power for him to return.

But what about Kant? Where was he—with the Germans, or on his way back to 2044, or still chasing Hanover? It was enough to make Hanover check out the back window. And have mixed feelings that no one was behind him. Where *was* Kant?

"Well, we'll make sure you get a proper send-off and aren't stranded somewhere in the desert," Butler said cheerfully.

Somehow, even though the agent was an ally, Butler's words didn't make Hanover feel any better.

* * *

Helmke guided the dark blue sedan into the queue waiting to cross the border. He glanced at Fischer; the untersturmfuhrer stared straight ahead with stone-like rigidity. Helmke drummed his fingers against the steering wheel, impatient at the delay. So close they were, so close. Only a hundred meters to freedom.

But why the delay? It was the country one was entering that was supposed to ask the questions at the border, not the country one was leaving.

A sheen of sweat formed on his brow. Did they know? Had they somehow learned who he and Fischer really were?

The madman they left on the road, he would not report them; if they failed, he failed, and Helmke sensed this man who said he was from the future preferred victory to revenge. It must be some other reason.

"We must be very careful," he said in a quiet voice to Fischer. "We must not do anything to call attention to ourselves."

The car behind them blasted its horn. Helmke started, then realized the car ahead had moved up a space. "Impatient fools," he muttered, but quickly brought his car forward. "Do nothing to attract attention," he said to Fischer, more for his own benefit.

At last it was their turn. The border guard approached. "Good day, officer," Helmke said with a smile he hoped to be sincere but not too obsequious.

"Where are you from?"

"Sweden. We are here on business."

"May I see your passports, please." The guard held out his hand.

Helmke flushed with nervousness. Of course, he should have anticipated this. "Olaf, your passport," he snapped at Fischer. As he fumbled for his own, he chastised himself for letting the incident with Kant rattle him. He should have had the passports ready. But then, only in Germany did they care who left the country.

When he had both passports, he handed them to the guard. "Is there a problem?" Helmke asked.

The guard looked slowly at the pictures, then at Helmke and Fischer. Helmke thought the study much more acute than when they had entered the country.

"Is there a problem?" he asked again. "You can see they are in order."

"Un-huh," the guard said. He stepped into his booth and picked up the phone.

"This, it is not good," Fischer said. "We should run for it."

"We must not panic," Helmke snarled.

"But why are we stopping? He should have waved us on. They know about us. They will throw us in prison and execute us for treason," Fischer wailed.

Helmke feared Fischer spoke the truth. He glanced at the barrier in front of him, at the long straight stretch to the border after the three lanes funneled into one.

Could they do it? Could they make their escape into Mexico? He shifted the gear from neutral to first, the adrenaline pounding through his body.

CHAPTER 21

Helmke watched in horror as a car from the next lane rolled forward, then stopped, obstructing the single lane that led across the border.

"No," he whispered. This could not be happening, not now, not when they were this close.

"Please pull into the parking area next to that building," said a voice next to his window.

Helmke had not seen the guard approach. His foot slipped off the clutch; the car lurched and stalled. Agitated, he pumped the gas pedal, flipped the key in the ignition to restart the engine. "Is there a problem, officer? Our passports, they are in order?"

He glanced at the crowd clustered around the car blocking the way in front of him. He could not overcome the obstacles mounting before him. Had Miller been correct? Had they been discovered in Santa Fe? He rapidly reconsidered the hours since their arrival in Santa Fe, but he could think of no mistakes, nothing except that madman who claimed he was from the future.

"It's just routine, sir. What with the war and all. . . .You know how it is." The guard shrugged.

Helmke scowled; he had no choice but to drive the sedan out of line and park next to the building. A glimpse over his shoulder told him the stalled car still blocked the border crossing. He turned to Fischer. "Oh, *Gott*," he murmured. Fischer had grown rigid again, his upper lip damp with nervous perspiration.

Helmke had so much to lose if they failed, so much more than just his hard-earned plans for the future. He wanted now to grow old with his beloved wife, surrounded by fat little grandbabies. He wanted his freedom. His life. He did not want to be executed for treason in this foreign land.

Yet he had so much to gain if they did succeed, the glory and rewards of victory. All he could hope to do was bluff his way through. Another glance at Fischer threatened to undermine what little remained of Helmke's confidence.

If Miller was correct, their pursuers could arrive at any time. A last glance at the border. So much hinged on traversing those few meters.

"Stay here. I will handle," he said to Fischer, who nodded woodenly. Helmke looked at Kant's blood drying on the dark upholstery and scowled. The last thing he needed was for some official to question them about that, too. As long as no one came too close. . ..

Helmke climbed from the car as a man exited the building and approached. Helmke read the badge. As calmly, as pleasantly as he could, he said, "Mr. Davies, I am Eric Holm. This delay, it will not be long? We have connections we must make to return to Sweden."

Davies barely nodded in acknowledgement. With the eyes of a professional, his gaze scanned Helmke, then the car. This official was not easily read. That worried Helmke. What had made him a successful negotiator in Paris, and even before the war, was his astuteness at understanding people, reading the deeper, hidden meanings to their words, their gestures, their eyes. Yet this man eluded him.

Helmke noticed that the stalled car had been removed; traffic again flowed smoothly. And here he stood.

"Your passports, please," Davies said.

Helmke handed them over. "Our passports, they are a problem?"

Davies flipped them open and gave them a cursory look. "No, there's no problem with your passport. Do you have your driver's license?

"A driver's license?" Helmke repeated the words, his voice cracking as he felt sweat pop out on his forehead. "I am afraid that was forgotten. So many things to pack to show our clients." Helmke shrugged and held up his hands. "Surely we can make this right?"

"I'm sure we can," Davies said smoothly. "It's illegal to drive in the United States without a valid license. Your Swedish license would've been acceptable." Davies gestured toward the door. "I'll have to ask you to come inside. Bring your friend, too."

Sheissdreck! Those idiots in Berlin had not provided them with a driver's license. To be tripped up by something as trivial as a driver's license, what a colossal blunder.

Helmke took another look at the border crossing, took a step in that direction, then stopped. He would never make it. Besides, he could not bring himself to die for his country, not shot in the back like a common thief fleeing from his crime. No, better to try something else. The time had passed for subtle bargaining. "The penalty for such a violation, is it harsh?"

"It's not too bad, usually a fine and a warning for the first offense."

"Perhaps we could reach an accommodation. My associate and I, we are on a tight schedule." Helmke said. "I leave some funds in your possession to meet the fine. . .and something extra for your trouble?"

Davies stopped, his expression neutral. "Are you offering me a bribe?"

Again, Helmke felt the frustration of not reading past the surface of this man. "A bribe?"

"Un-huh. That'll land you in prison."

Alarmed, Helmke backed away. "Oh, no, no. I was. . .I simply recognize that in these cases there are often expenses."

Davies started walking again. "You know, for a Swede, you speak English very well. Where did you learn it?"

"We have an excellent program in our schools," Helmke said. Did he detect a softening in Davies' attitude? That was a good sign. Perhaps they were not in as much trouble as he had first thought. A glimmer of hope returned. Helmke signaled Fischer to join him.

When they entered the building, Davies directed them to a small waiting area, then excused himself to make some telephone calls. Helmke guided a catatonic Fischer to a row of hard wooden chairs. He had to think of another way to escape without endangering himself.

"Sit, *Olaf*. You can relax. We will pay a fine and soon be on our way."

Fischer looked at Helmke with glassy eyes. He nodded, then faced forward again and stared straight ahead at a blank wall.

*   *   *

"We're almost there."

Butler's words repeated what road signs had told Hanover for the last mile. "Do you have a plan?" Hanover asked. During the silent ride, he'd considered how the FedPos would handle the situation; the rules were different here.

"I'm working on it," Butler snapped. "We've got nothing but a hatful of wind. Everything depends on finding incriminating evidence."

"Where I come from, they haul you in, then make the case fit," Hanover said. "If they want you out of circulation, it doesn't matter if you're guilty or not."

"We sometimes stretch the rules, too," Butler admitted. "But this is different. We have to be careful with these two men, or the whole thing'll explode into a major international incident. I don't have to tell you that's something I want to avoid at all costs."

"You're not the only one," Robbins said. "I'm too close to retirement to have my career ruined."

"Stuff it, Robbins. If we screw up, they'll let you slide; it's my carcass that'll be hung out to dry by Hoover, the State Department, the press, and God knows who all else."

"Bad press is your big concern?" Hanover said. "I'm more interested in keeping those plans from leaving the country."

"If the border guards haven't screwed up, the Germans will be waiting for us. I told the supervisor to just hold them, and we'd take care of everything when we got there. If the plans are on them, then we'll have them dead bang," Butler said. His brow furrowed as he turned the corner. "If not, it'll be more complicated."

Hanover frowned. Butler's words summation didn't inspire a lot of confidence in their success.

Butler drove around the line of waiting cars and pulled into the parking lot next to a blue sedan with Mexican plates. They climbed from their car and glanced inside the sedan. To Hanover's disappointment, nothing was visibly obvious.

Hanover scanned the cars in line, the people walking across the border, and searched for any resemblance to the German spies.

Or to Willie Kant. Where the hell was he? With as much to lose as the major had, Hanover couldn't escape the feeling that Kant had to be close by.

Hanover glanced at Butler and Robbins. Now that they'd reached the border, they didn't look like they were in a hurry. It was up to him to find those plans. They didn't have time to fool around with procedure. "You two go in and see what's going on. I'll stay here and, ah. . .get some air," Hanover said.

Butler nodded distractedly as he disappeared into the building, Robbins dogging his heels.

Hanover strolled around the sedan, considering the most likely hiding place. He suspected the chance of a secret compartment in a rental car was slim. But did the Germans still have the plans, or had they made other arrangements to transport them across the border? Given them to Kant? If they kept them, how much time had the Germans had to hide the plans? Hell, he didn't even know how big they were, or in what form.

A uniformed man approached. Hanover stiffened, jammed his hands in his pockets and leaned casually against the car. The man nodded; Hanover responded in kind. He started breathing again when the man entered the building. No more hesitating, he told himself. He had to search the car and be done with it. Quickly.

He grasped the trunk handle, twisted and lifted, surprised to find it unlocked. Two leather bags and a spare tire were visible, plus a few tools. He reached for the luggage, then paused. That was too obvious; only a fool would hide the plans there. He quickly lifted the mat, moved the spare, poked into the recesses behind the back seat. Nothing.

He shifted to the front of the car. That prickly warning crawled up the back of his neck. He glanced over his shoulder to see if anyone was watching, then he opened the driver's door.

As soon as he leaned inside, he saw the blood on the seat back. What the hell? He touched it, and his fingers came away a damp red. Who's was it? He hesitated only a moment before resuming his search.

He ran his hand under the driver's seat, groped under the dash board. He pressed a lever to slide the front seat forward; nothing but an outdated Mexican newspaper and assorted candy wrappers came into view. Lifting the carpet on both the driver's and passenger's sides revealed nothing except dirt.

Hanover's search grew more intense. What if he couldn't find the plans? What if the Germans were involved with someone else— someone like Kant? Hanover shoved the front seat back until it locked into place, and slammed the door. Time was running out. He had to find those plans!

He opened the door to the back seat. The carpet gave with a slight tug. In his haste, Hanover flipped it up and back down so quickly that he almost missed the dark brown color against the black metal. His heart pounding, he lifted the carpet again, higher this time, until a large envelope came into view. He pulled the packet from its hiding place and slid the contents out. Blue prints, marked "Top Secret—Los Alamos" lay in his hand.

"We did it, Doc," he whispered in awed tribute to Dr. Beecker. "We did it."

He stared at the envelope. This was why he was here. It was now in his power to thwart the Nazis, to change the course of history. He looked around. He was still alone by the car, no one nearby paid him any attention. No one knew how close they'd come to having their world destroyed.

Hanover shoved the plans inside the envelope. Clutching the packet, he started toward the building. All that was left was to return the plans to Los Alamos.

Then he could go home.

* * *

Across the highway from the border, Willie Kant stepped from the curb, brushing aside the swirling dust. The illiterate old man who'd picked him up on the highway had been gullible enough to give Kant a ride in a decrepit vegetable truck all the way to the border crossing.

Kant's mood had not improved as they approached the border. His fury at Helmke's preemptive action still raged. How dare the man deny him his right to glory and recognition. Without him, the incompetent German agents surely would fail, especially with Hanover working against them.

Kant stared across the road at the station. Somehow he must cross the border, difficult to do without the proper papers. He searched the lines for a blue sedan with two men. Nowhere. They could not possibly have crossed yet; he'd been picked up only a few minutes after they'd thrown him out of the car.

A car moved forward, and for an instant, Kant glimpsed a blue sedan parked next to the building. Another car moved, and Kant saw the sedan was empty. Where the hell were Helmke and Fischer? Why were they out of line?

But more to the point, where were the blueprints? Still in the car, or had they been moved? Kant hurried across the street, blending with the other pedestrians. Not that he expected to be recognized, but who knew where Hanover was.

The car stood unattended. All he had to do was approach the car, steal the plans, then slip away before anyone caught him. He'd find an isolated spot to cross the border, then make his way to the rendezvous point with the submarine. Once he traveled to Germany with the plans, he would be hailed a hero, and assured his rightful entry into the upper echelons of German power.

He stepped up to the curb, the sedan still in view. Another car pulled in next to it; three men got out. Kant recognized one of them immediately: Hanover.

Seething, Kant backed across the street as the three men spoke. Then two went inside, leaving Hanover outside. Standing behind a lamppost, Kant watched Hanover circle the car, then open the trunk. He rifled through contents, slammed the lid, and started on the front of the car. From the frustration on Hanover's face when he shut the car door, he clearly had not found the plans. He climbed into the back seat, emerging moments later with a flat packet. Even from a distance Kant could see the elation on Hanover's face.

A wave of nausea, vertigo, engulfed Kant. He grabbed the near-by lamppost for support. This was no time for weakness. Hanover had found the plans.

Struggling to control the increasing feebleness, Kant crossed the road and hid in the shadows of a building. From his new vantage point, he watched Hanover standing alone, still holding the envelope. The vague weakness returned, leaving Kant struggling to stand.

If the plans were taken from Helmke, then they would not reach Germany. Then Germany might not win the war, the GOA would not take control of the country.

And seventy years from now, a young German officer would not be sent to the United States and be seduced by an American woman. She would not have a child named Willie. . ..

The plans. It must be Hanover taking the plans from the car that made Kant feel this way. The realization staggered him more than the vertigo he'd experienced moments before.

*   *   *

Hanover slipped into the waiting area. Butler and Robbins were standing near two men who had to be Helmke and Fischer. Butler glanced at Hanover, clearly annoyed at the interruption, then approached.

"I found them," Hanover said quietly. He held the envelope up for Butler to see.

From across the room, Fischer rose from his chair. "Nein, nein," he screamed, then vomited violently.

"Oh, shit," Davies jumped back, but not far enough. "All over—get that man out of here! Son-of-a-bitch!" A uniformed guard hauled Fischer from the room; Davies left to clean himself up.

"Robbins, follow them." Butler nodded in the direction taken by Fischer and the guard. "I don't want them out of our sight for a minute.

"I do not understand," Helmke said from the opposite side of the room. "My friend, you make him sick from your questions and suspicions. We are businessmen. From Sweden."

"Yeah, yeah, so I've been told." Butler turned to Hanover. "Where the hell'd you find that?" he whispered fiercely.

"In the car. Under the floor mat in the back seat."

Butler glanced at Helmke. "Did anyone see you find it?"

"No. I was alone," Hanover said in a low voice.

"Shit. That blows a hole through our case. Now I'll have to bluff. You," Butler said, pointing at Helmke. "Outside. No trouble."

Still clutching the envelope, Hanover followed Butler and Helmke outside. Butler reached for the packet. Hanover hesitated, reluctant to let it out of his grasp. Butler's eyes narrowed, his gaze intensifying, but instead of insisting, he pointed at it.

"Where did you get this?" Butler asked Helmke.

"I know nothing about it."

Hanover opened one end of the envelope and partially slid out the contents. "Blueprints," he said. "Marked top secret."

"I'll ask you again," Butler said. "Where did you get this material?"

"I have told you," Helmke responded. "I know nothing about it. I want that you should call my embassy."

Hanover begrudgingly admired the older man's bluff. He had to know the Swedish embassy would disavow any knowledge of an Eric Holm traveling in the United States on business. But what other choice did the spy have but to carry through with his charade?

"I found the envelope in your car," Hanover said.

"I rented the car in Mexico. It must have been there when I rented it." Helmke glared defiantly at Hanover. "Or you placed it there."

Butler beckoned for Hanover to move to one side with him. "He's a cool one," he said in a low voice. "This espionage charge is going to be real hard to stick."

Hanover took a deep breath. "It doesn't matter. We've stopped them." He allowed himself a faint smile.

Butler gave him an odd look, but Hanover didn't care. "I'll have Robbins take them to the local jail and hold them for interrogation. In the meantime, I'll take the plans to Santa Fe."

Hanover glanced at Butler's outstretched hands. "You can do whatever you want with the envelope, but I'm not letting those plans out of my sight until they get back to Los Alamos."

Butler raised an eyebrow and smirked. "Fine. You," he said pointing to Helmke. "Back inside."

Butler's reaction bothered Hanover. The agent was acting strangely. Hanover waited outside for Butler to return. He didn't want to be confined inside a building, and he didn't want to release the plans.

Butler returned in a few minutes. "Robbins'll take them to the jail and I'll send a car to bring him back to Santa Fe. Come on. We have a long drive ahead of us." He headed for the car.

Hanover followed and climbed in on the passenger side. It was over, and he couldn't keep from feeling deflated. They had prevented a disaster, probably changed the course of history. He'd done what he'd been sent to do. And yet. . .no one knew. Would anyone know when he returned home? Would the history books even note this now minor incident? Probably not.

It didn't matter. Fame or notoriety didn't interest him. What was important was home. He could go home.

Home. He clutched the plans and wondered about the world he had left behind.

Only one problem remained. Kant. He had no idea where Kant was. It was too late for the major to change history back. But there was only enough energy for one of them to return to their time. Hanover prayed he wasn't too late.

*   *   *

From across the street, Kant stared hard at Hanover, then watched as Helmke and Fischer were escorted from a side door to a police car by uniformed guards and one of the men who had arrived with Hanover. From the front of the building, he saw Hanover follow the third man to their car and drive away.

He must stop them. He must retrieve the plans and take them to Germany himself. The alternative was unthinkable. Returning Hanover to their own time paled in importance. Kant forced himself to stand straight, to walk, not stagger, across the street.

Wary, he sidled over to the sedan and peeked inside. The keys sat in the ignition. Kant didn't hesitate. He climbed in and started the car. After watching Helmke drive, Kant figured he knew enough about operating the vehicle. The gears screeched when he released the clutch too quickly, but no one challenged him.

He eased the car into traffic. The car was not that different than some of the farm equipment he'd driven as a teenager at the GOA youth camp. Night was approaching; Kant saw a knob on the dashboard marked 'lights'. He turned, pushed, then pulled it until the headlights came on.

Kant drove as quickly as he could, slowing at every cross street to look for Hanover's car. He stayed on the main road until finally he saw the car in the distance ahead of him.

Kant wished he had his gun. With his eyes on the road, Kant groped under the driver's seat. He glanced at the floor on the passenger side, thinking that Hanover would have taken the gun if he'd found it. Kant remembered seeing only the envelope in Hanover's hand.

On the faint chance the gun was still in the car, Kant leaned over and opened the glove compartment. His gun lay on top. Kant smiled grimly. Hanover wasn't as clever as he thought he was; he should have searched the car more thoroughly. Now his oversight would be his downfall.

As he approached Socorro, Kant glanced at the energy gauge. The needle rested perilously close to the red 'E'. No wonder they had exhausted fossil fuels; these cars guzzled gasoline. Angered that he had to stop, Kant searched for an open gas station.

The attendant stepped outside the bay. "Fill 'er up?" he called.

Kant nodded and climbed from the car. He stumbled, almost fell, but caught himself.

The attendant rushed to him. "Hey, are you okay?"

"I'm fine. Just fill the tank." Kant leaned against the car. The weakness was worse now, much worse. At this rate, he didn't have much time left to stop Hanover. Somehow he sensed that all he had to do was take the plans away from Hanover, and then his strength would return. He slid back into the car and closed the door.

"Gotcher stamps?" the attendant asked.

"Stamps?" Helmke had gone through some sort of exchange when they bought gas on the way to El Paso, but Kant hadn't paid much attention. "What stamps?"

"Your ration stamps." The attendant sounded annoyed. "Look, don't play games, just give me the stamps or I'll have to call the authorities."

Kant's hand settled on the gun. His hand tightened over the handle. . ..

Wasting no thoughts on the attendant lying on the ground with blood seeping from his gut, Kant raced through the night. He concentrated on keeping the car ahead of him within sight. On the empty straight-aways, he fell back as much as half a kilometer; where the road curved, he closed in.

Except for running their car off the road, he could think of no way to stop Hanover and the other man before they returned the plans to Los Alamos. In his weakened condition, Kant doubted he could subdue two men if they were not at least knocked unconscious by an accident.

The weakness intensified the further Hanover took the plans from the border, and it required all Kant's concentration, all his strength, to stay on the road.

Still, he could not give up.

*   *   *

Hanover guessed it was close to dawn when they drove silently through Albuquerque. The envelope lay on his lap, his hands framing the edges. Touching it reassured him. After Butler took him to Los Alamos, Hanover figured he'd catch a ride back to Neustadt—or at least to the markers where Neustadt had been.

He looked at Butler. The Deputy Director stared straight ahead, his jaw shifting as if he were grinding his teeth.

Butler must have sensed Hanover's gaze, because he glanced over at him. "What's wrong?"

"Nothing. I'm just glad this is almost over."

"I bet you're in a hurry to go back where you came from."

Hanover hesitated. He fingered the necklace in his pocket. Was he really in a hurry? Well, yes. In a way. The implication of what he'd done still awed him. He wanted to see how the future had changed.

Yet another part of him wanted to stay here. He liked what he'd seen in this time. In his old world, he'd been alone, separate from others. Here he'd been welcomed from the beginning by total strangers, made to care about something more than just his own survival. He'd met some decent people. He'd met a girl with fire in her eyes and the promise of passion in her kiss.

"I'll be ready after we return these plans to Los Alamos," he said finally.

"Where is this timegate?" Butler asked.

"A few kilometers from here," Hanover said without thinking.

"I can drop you off now," Butler offered.

The prickle returned to the back of Hanover's neck. "Thanks, but I'll wait. I want to be sure these plans reach Los Alamos." He touched the edges of the envelope, reassuring himself again that the plans were safe.

"Can you see the timegate at night?" Butler asked.

"Not really."

"But you marked it so you can find it again."

"I think so."

After a few minutes, Butler asked, "Why can't you see the timegate at night?"

Hanover grew increasingly uneasy. "It's like a force field that slightly distorts the space surrounding it. You can only see it in the light."

"In that case, we'll have to wait until it's light enough." With his left hand, Butler whipped out a .38 Special and aimed it at Hanover. "Tell me where to stop."

Incredulous, Hanover stared at the gun. "This is crazy. What're you doing?"

"I'm taking care of a national security problem. We can't have people jumping in and out of our time, upsetting the balance of things." Butler slowed the car.

"I don't understand. I told you I was going back and that should close the timegate. No one else will come through."

Butler laughed derisively. "Not you. Me. I'm going through the timegate," he said. "If I'm ever going to be Director, I need to know the future. This case was my big chance. You couldn't wait to let me find the plans, you had to go looking yourself, and now we have no evidence. You ruined it for me. Now, where's that marker?"

Hanover realized Butler had gone over the edge. Dealing with him would be as unpredictable as dealing with Kant in his own time. But Hanover had come too far, gone through too much.

He gauged his chances of jumping from the car before Butler fired the gun. It was too great a risk. His only hope was to get Butler in the open and catch him off guard. "It's a pile of rock by the road."

Butler eased the car to the side of the road and flicked the headlights on high beam. They'd gone about two kilometers when the lights swept a mound of rocks.

"Is that it?" Butler demanded.

Hanover looked at the pile that was similar to the one he'd left behind, but he wasn't sure. It was too dark, and he'd been disoriented that day. He needed a chance to disarm Butler, but he couldn't do it in the car. He didn't want Butler too close to the timegate. "Yeah. That's it," he said, hoping he was wrong.

Butler brought the car to a stop. Still holding the gun on Hanover, he said, "Wait here." He climbed from the car and walked around to the passenger side. "Get out. Don't try anything funny."

Hanover slid from the car. Butler wouldn't be easy to take down; he was a trained professional, but maybe he'd grown a little soft from straight administrative duties. Hanover eyed the gun warily.

"Where's the other marker?" Butler asked impatiently.

"I don't know. It's too dark."

Butler took a step closer and cocked the hammer.

* * *

The car ahead rounded a curve, and Kant accelerated to close the gap. Then he saw the brake lights flash as the car slowed and pulled over to the side. Kant killed his headlights and stopped, waited, then followed as Hanover's car crept down the road. Without his lights to give him away, Kant narrowed the distance between them.

The car in front stopped again, the taillights went off, and the inside overhead light flashed on as the other man climbed from the car. Kant rolled closer, then cut his engine. He looked up and saw his car also had an overhead light. Looking away, he smashed it with his gun so the light would not give him away.

Kant saw Hanover exit the car and stand warily, still holding the envelope in his hands. Kant eased from his car, then stiffened. The man with Hanover held his arm at an odd angle, as if he were aiming at Hanover. Kant drew closer; he had to retrieve those plans.

* * *

The sun crept over the horizon, its watery light dispelling the darkness. Hanover glanced around, alarmed when his gaze rested on the second marker. In the dark he hadn't realized they were so close. His eyes hesitated for only a moment on the second marker, but it was a moment too long.

Butler strode to the pile of rocks. "So, this is it. Ah, yes, I see what you mean. It's all shimmery here." He used his free hand to trace the outline.

The entrance had dwindled, reduced to the point that Hanover questioned if he could fit through it again.

"Looks like a tight fit," Butler said, his words mirroring Hanover's thoughts. "How does it work?"

"It doesn't matter. Don't you understand? You can't go through. You'll never return. The timegate's set for only three pass-throughs at the most. Kant and I have already come through. That leaves one more trip." Maybe.

"Shut up, Hanover. You're lying," Butler said. "I'm going through, and you're staying behind. Now give me the plans."

Hanover stared at the gun. He couldn't believe Butler would shoot him in cold blood. "Why? What're you going to do with them?"

"I can't leave you with the plans. How do I know you won't take them to Germany yourself. I can't take that risk." Butler glanced again at the shimmering timegate.

"Come on. Give me the plans." Butler took a half step forward and snatched them from Hanover. He raised his arm, deliberately aimed the gun at Hanover's head. "Adios, amigo."

A shot rang out, then another. Hanover threw himself to the ground, then rolled away. Pain seared through him. He touched his shoulder; his hand came away wet and sticky. He tried to move his arm, but couldn't. Holding his injured arm close to his body, he looked up and saw Butler's shocked expression as the FBI deputy director stumbled, then crashed to the ground; a circle of red spread across his back.

"What the—" Hanover looked around wildly. Where had the shot come from? He heard a scuffling noise. He inched his way to Butler and grabbed the plans from the dead man's grasp, then lay flat, listening. His hand tightened around the envelope hidden beneath him. No way was he letting these plans fall into the wrong hands again.

He fumbled for the pack of matches he'd picked up at Carrier's Cafe and jerked some out. Blocking the wind with his back, he braced the matchbook on the ground with his knee and struck the matches. They only sparked on his first two tries, then they ignited, and he held them to the envelope until it caught. He yanked out more matches, ignited them from the existing flames and lit the other corners of the envelope. In seconds, the plans burned brightly.

Ignoring the outline he made, a perfect target for whoever shot them, Hanover hovered over the papers until the flames diminished, leaving charred remains.

As he watched, he heard a groan. Satisfied the plans were destroyed, he turned to the sound.

"Help me." The whispered words drew Hanover toward the source. He saw a figure slumped forward on hands and knees. The person looked up, the face recognizable in the growing light.

"Kant." Suspicious of a trick, Hanover eased toward him. The gun lay on the ground next to Kant, but he made no effort to retrieve it. Hanover hurried to him, grasped the major's hand with his good one. There was no strength left in Kant's grip. The hand was cold, icy, like the hand of death.

"Where are the plans? Bring them to me," Kant said.

"They're gone. I burned them."

"You've destroyed the future," Kant whispered.

The truth in Kant's words hit Hanover hard. He had stopped the Germans from stealing the plans, changing the future.

Kant's hand tightened on Hanover's. "Listen to me. You were always the bane of my life."

"What are you talking about?" Hanover asked.

"My father used you as an example. I've always hated you. You took what should have been mine."

Bewildered, Hanover shook his head. "But I don't know your father. I never met you."

"My father is Commandant Kraft. When you were small, your mother seduced him."

"My mo—"

"Listen. He couldn't bear the humiliation of marrying a mongrel American, so he took me away at birth. You've murdered your own brother."

Kant gasped for air, choked, then collapsed. As Hanover held him, Kant's body seemed to disappear, disintegrating into a pile of dust. In moments, all that remained was a rumpled heap of clothing. Hanover knelt there, paralyzed with shock. His brother?

Doctor Beecker had said Hanover would probably survive the mission because his birth would not be affected by that change. But not everyone from his time would survive.

He heard a car door slam, the sound of footsteps hurrying across the hard sand.

"What the hell's going on here?"

Hanover looked up. "Robbins." He tucked his injured arm inside his buttoned jacket, then staggered to his feet and looked around. He wiped his sleeve across his face. "You wouldn't believe it if I told you," he said wearily.

Robbins pushed back his jacket and rested his hand on the butt of a gun holstered at his waist.

"Try me."

Hanover waved toward Butler's body. "Butler forced me to take him to the timegate. He said I'd ruined his chances for being Director. He planned to shoot me and go through the timegate, see what the future was like, then return. I told him there was only energy left for one passage, but he didn't believe me. He aimed his gun at me, then someone else shot him."

Robbins eyed Hanover's shoulder. "Looks like someone clipped you."

"It must have been Butler. His gun went off when he was hit."

"Where'd the other person go?"

Hanover pointed at the pile of clothes.

Robbins stared at them. "What the hell is that?"

"It's all that's left of Willie Kant, the FedPo major who followed me through the timegate. Since the spies didn't take the plans to Germany, history was changed. He won't be born." Suddenly exhausted, Hanover shrugged; it sounded preposterous, but it was the truth.

"How do I know you didn't shoot Butler, dump a pile of clothes, and come up with this story?"

"You don't," snapped Hanover. "You'll just have to take my word for it. I have no reason to kill Butler, or Kant."

Robbins gave Hanover a hard stare. He walked to Butler and knelt beside the body.

"Aren't you supposed to be in El Paso with the Germans?" Hanover asked.

"Yep. But since you messed up the only evidence we had tying them to the plans, I figured it was a waste of time to hold them. Davies deported them. Walked them across the border and told them to either find their way home empty-handed or stay in Mexico for the duration.

Robbins rolled Butler's body over. He shook his head. "Something kept nagging at me. It didn't feel right for Butler and you to go off alone with those plans. By the way, where are the plans?"

"When Kant shot Butler, I burned them."

Robbins stood and rejoined Hanover. "Okay, buddy-boy. I don't want a big investigation that's going to interfere with my retirement. Any suggestions?"

Hanover's thoughts drifted to Kant's last words. Brothers. Half-brothers, really. Hanover had a vague childish recollection of playing with a tall man who visited Hanover's widowed mother when he was about three years old. Had that been Commandant Kraft? Had his mother wanted the affair with a German officer, or was she forced?

Hanover had always wondered about his mother's depression, had assumed it was because of his father's death. But maybe it was the loss of her child, the baby Kant who Kraft had taken away from her.

Kant had said that Kraft talked about Hanover. Had the general continued an interest in him as Hanover grew up? Was that why he wasn't as severely punished as he should have been for his schoolboy antics? Had Kraft arranged the soccer scholarship? The government job? Commuting a death sentence for being in the wrong courtroom was probably beyond his authority, although he may have been behind the delayed execution.

"Hanover? What are you going to do?"

Robbins' question pulled Hanover to his present dilemma. He crossed the short distance to the timegate, watched the faint shimmer. Was it even smaller now than it had been only a short time before?

Robbins approached him. "Is that it?" he asked.

Hanover nodded.

"But it's so small."

"It was as large as a doorway when I came through." He should go now, before it was too late. Still he hesitated. What was he going back to? O'Rourke had offered him a job here. Ellen had asked him to come back. Could he choose to not go back? "Can you write a report that leaves Kant and me out of it?"

Robbins shrugged. "With all the paperwork I have before I retire, I'm going to be hard-pressed to finish it all. I'll make a note that we followed up on a rumor, but nothing could be substantiated."

"Can you do that? What about Butler?"

"I never saw him after we checked out the Swedish businessmen. No one at the border saw the plans. Don't worry. I'll cover when someone calls about him. Maybe he decided to follow those Swedes to Mexico and see who met them?"

Hanover nodded in agreement. He piled Kant's clothes and gun on top of Butler's body and dragged it to the timegate. "He wanted to go to the future."

With Robbins watching his every move, Hanover shoved Butler's body, Kant's clothes and the gun through the timegate. He watched the shimmering outline flare for a brief moment, then disappear.

"That's it?" Robbins asked.

"That's it. It's over." He stared at the spot where the timegate had been. He could never go back, never see how the future turned out. It no longer mattered.

"Can I give you a lift?"

Hanover turned to Robbins and smiled, a slow lazy smile. The long night was over, his new life dawning. "Yeah. Can you take me to Carrie's Cafe?"

AUTHOR'S NOTE

Although this story is fiction, it is based on historic fact.

The United States and Germany both had active nuclear research programs during World War II. U.S. scientists working on the atom bomb project assumed the Germans' progress was equal to their own. Specific information was difficult to obtain. To be effective, an agent needed training in isotope separation techniques and nuclear fission research. There was fear that any agent who was captured by the Germans, or who turned, might give away American nuclear secrets. An intelligence unit to infiltrate the German program was not authorized until late 1943, and did not enter Europe until after the Normandy invasion in 1944.

The German nuclear bomb program came to a halt after the heavy water plant in Vemork, Norway, was damaged, and heavy water supplies were lost as a result of sabotage in early 1944.

Klaus Fuchs, a German, was sent to the United States with a British contingent of nuclear scientists. He was later detected passing nuclear secrets to the Soviets from 1942 to 1949. The British convicted Fuchs of espionage after he gave Moscow an outline for the first atomic bomb in 1945.

He died in East Germany in 1988. The National Security Agency has since revealed it cracked Moscow's code in the mid-1940's, and decoded fragments of cables from over 100 Soviet agents during the war years.

The Japanese also had a nuclear program, but it was not nearly as advanced as either the United States or the German efforts. The Imperial Navy's program concluded in early 1943 that, while an atom bomb was possible, it would require ten years to build. They also doubted the United States' and Germany's abilities to produce a bomb in time to be used in the war.

An interesting footnote to the atom bomb's development involves the capture of the Nazi submarine U-234 by U.S. forces in May 1945. It had a diverse cargo bound for Japan that included 1200 pounds of uranium oxide. An unanswered question is: was the uranium developed by the Germans and destined for Japan's atom bomb program actually used by the Americans in the atom bombs dropped on Japan?

ABOUT THE AUTHOR

W.L.Hesse is a pseudonym for writing team, Walter H. Hesse and Liz Hesse Osborne. A retired university professor, Dr. Hesse authored numerous science textbooks. Ms. Osborne worked in healthcare for many years and has published several healthcare management books and one novel. This is their first collaboration.

0-595-21264-6